PENGUIN BOOKS

A FINE FAMILY

Gurcharan Das is a professional manager and an author. He has a degree in Philosophy and Politics from Harvard University, and is the author of three plays. His prize-winning play, *Larins Sahib*, was first produced in Bombay in 1970 and was published by Oxford University Press, UK. *Mira*, and another play, premiered off-Broadway in New York and were later produced in many cities in India and abroad.

He is presently President and Managing Director of Procter & Gamble India Ltd. He lives in Bombay with his wife and two sons.

A FINE FAMILY

Gurcharan Das

PENGUIN BOOKS

Penguin Books (India) Limited, 72-B Himalaya House, 23 Kasturba Gandhi Marg,
New Delhi-110 001, India
Penguin Books Ltd., Harmondsworth, Middlesex, England
Viking Penguin Inc., 40 West 23rd Street, New York, N.Y. 10010, U.S.A.
Penguin Books Australia Ltd., Ringwood, Victoria, Australia
Penguin Books Canada Ltd., 2801 John Street, Markham, Ontario, Canada L3R 1 B4
Penguin Books (N.Z.) Ltd., 182-190 Wairau Road, Auckland 10, New Zealand

First published by Penguin Books India Limited, 1990
Copyright © Gurcharan Das, 1990

Typeset in Palatino by Tulika Print Communication Services Pvt. Ltd., New Delhi
Made and printed in India by Ananda Offset Private Ltd., Calcutta

For
Vimla and Barkat Ram

PART ONE
Lyallpur

1

Unlike other country towns on the Indo-Gangetic plain, Lyallpur was not merely a white, dusty, anarchic jumble of flat-roofed brick houses. Thanks to the canal, it was greener than most, and many of its roads were lined with trees. First came the canal in the last quarter of the 19th century; then an orderly town was planned and built; and they named it after the ruling British Lieutenant Governor of the Punjab, Sir James Lyall, BA. My grandfather, an ambitious young lawyer, proudly moved to Lyallpur in the early twenties of this century to start his practice. I was born there a generation later when the sheesham trees soared to the sky.

In the middle of the town was a brick clock tower, from where eight roads emanated, and the town spread out in concentric circles. Our house was off one of these roads, called Kacheri Bazaar, because the district courts were located there. Our road led to the Company Bagh, which sprawled sumptuously over forty acres, and was named after the East India Company. We were not far from the clock tower and our street was lively in the mornings and evenings, but quiet in the hot afternoons when most people slept. The days were drenched with sunshine and the nights were so clear that the stars seemed to hang like lamps as the fireflies glittered around the mango tree.

Since it was hot in the summer and cold in the winter, our daily life varied considerably with the seasons. We spent most of our time in the two open courtyards of our house. The main courtyard was on the ground floor, towards the north end of the house; the women's courtyard was smaller and upstairs, towards the south side. In the middle of the main courtyard grew a tall shady mango tree, under which was conducted the chief business of the household. In the summer we even slept in the courtyard. As the sun became warm, we moved to the covered veranda which surrounded the courtyard. By midday we went deeper into the cooler rooms inside, as the chick blinds made of finely-split bamboo were lowered on the veranda to cut the glare of the burning sun. The servant sprinkled water over the matted screens, made of the roots of the fragrant khus-khus, which covered the important rooms, and the house prepared for sleep. Later in the afternoon we returned to the veranda around tea time, then back to the courtyard to enjoy the evening breeze and the brilliant stars at night.

In the winters, the process was reversed. The household slept inside in the cold nights and gradually came out with the sun. We spent most of the day in the luxurious warmth of the North Indian winter sun, moving our jute charpais according to the sun's path, and returned inside at sunset.

Around four o'clock in the afternoon, Grandfather, whose name was Dewan Chand but whom everyone called Bauji, used to come home from the courts. We would eagerly await his arrival since he always brought home fresh sweets from the Bengali hunchback. He would bring spongy rasgullas of fresh cream, lustrous gulab jamans which floated in a thick syrup, and occasionally pistachio barfi for the sophisticated, but which attracted us kids because it had shiny silver paper on top. As soon as he reached the massive wooden gate of the house, Bauji would loudly clear his throat, which was a signal to everyone in the house. Bhabi, his daughter-in-law, would quickly cover her head and face with an airy dupatta so as not to be directly seen by her father-in-law; Bhabo, his wife and my grandmother, would say her last goodbyes to the Khanna ladies who would quietly slip out of the back gate after an hour of tea and gossip; Tara, his eldest daughter, would go to the kitchen and put on water for tea; Big Uncle, his stylish son, would go to his room and change for tennis; the grandchildren knew that it was the last round of the dice before scores would be tallied in the afternoon game of Parcheesi.

Bauji had other uses for his harsh, grating cry. When he cleared his throat in his office it was a signal to his client that the interview was over, much as in a government office the bureaucrat signals the end of an interview by noisily pulling back his chair. Occasionally in the middle of an interrogation he would suddenly strike terror in the witness's heart with the same piercing, strident sound as he deliberately cleared his throat.

'Bauji' was a Punjabi corruption of the Bengali 'Babuji'. It meant a man of western learning, specifically someone who had learned the English language. The word had not yet acquired its pejorative connotation of 'a petty clerk', and Grandfather was happy with it since it had a sense of honour attached to it.

As we sat drinking tea on cane chairs in the veranda, Bauji would talk of his latest case in court. Big Uncle would sometimes interrupt with an appreciative remark on the quality of the hunchback's sweets. 'Today the hunchback has used just the right amount of sugar and milk,' he would say. Everyone would agree and Bauji would continue, not noticing the interruption. The children were not allowed to drink tea. Instead we got flavoured sweet milk diluted with ice and water. Once in a while as a treat we were allowed to drink coloured soda water from bottles which had a marble on top.

One day, much to our horror, Bauji did not bring sweets. Instead he brought fruit. Immediately the whole house rose in revolt. Bauji eventually won the day as he brought out all his legal tricks and by the end of the evening persuaded us that sweets were bad for health. And so the house reluctantly switched to eating fruit in the afternoons. He would bring mangoes, leechies and chickoos in the summer, apples in the autumn, and oranges and maltas in the winter. Slowly the air began to smell differently. But for months on end we talked nostalgically about the hunchback's sweets.

Conversation was the great pastime in Bauji's house. If two people were together at home, they would not read or work or go to the club and play sports; they would sit down with a cup of tea and talk. If there were three, so much the better. And they talked endlessly about people—who was doing what, where, to whom. They could talk for hours about people they had never met.

Around five in the afternoon Bauji's friends came to play bridge. Bauji would go downstairs to a secluded part of the main court-yard, separated by a brick screen and filled with flower pots and surrounded by jasmine shrubs. There the men played and smoked the hookah. Soon after came the family barber, and he gave each bridge player a shave; he even obliged with a haircut if anyone was willing. He worked skilfully and the bridge game was never disturbed while he performed.

One hot July evening in 1942, this peaceful routine was suddenly interrupted as Chachi, my grandmother's aunt, burst into the house. She was tall, erect and seventy, and she wore her white hair in a bun at the back.

'Hari Om! Hari Om!' said Chachi, invoking the gods as she entered the house.

'It's Chachi!' exclaimed Bhabo from above.

'Of course, it's Chachi,' replied Chachi sharply. 'Who did you expect at this hour? The Collector's wife?'

Having put her niece in her place, she directly went to the 'men's courtyard' and sat down beside Bauji and his friends, who were in the midst of a bridge rubber. She took out her knitting and made herself comfortable. (She was forever knitting socks for herself.)

'Well, well, you old fox, Dewan Chand,' she addressed Bauji, ignoring the game in progress, 'What mischief have you been up to?'

Bauji, a perceptive man of the world, quickly realized the futility of continuing the game. He put down his cards and the others followed suit.

'Will you have a glass of fresh lime, Chachi?' asked Bauji.

Chachi was the widow of a civil surgeon. Everyone was afraid of her because she was rich and she was honest. Although people laughed behind her back and told stories about her, they respected and feared her as well. They said that she had fought in the courts to deprive her drunken, good-for-nothing son of his inheritance in order to provide for her grandson and daughter-in-law. Bhabo used to relate how Chachi combined religion and management: 'She wakes up before dawn, bathes and goes to her puja room; she picks up her beads, closes her eyes, and begins her mantra. Suddenly she interrupts herself. She has remembered that she must wake up the servants. So she screams at them to get up. In the next breath she resumes "Ram, Ram, Ram". After a while she again shouts at the servant to go and milk the buffalo. A little later she is reminded of last night's dinner and she intersperses her chant with curses at the cook for spoiling the pullao. And so it goes on.'

'Well, are you going to the Collector's "At Home" on Friday?' Chachi asked the bridge foursome.

Bauji nodded.

'Chah!' spat out Chachi. 'To be seen in a white man's house during these days—I would rather die.'

'He is the Collector, Chachi. It is a question of courtesy,' said the bridge player who was playing the north hand.

'Hitler is teaching them enough courtesy in Europe,' she retorted.

'The English are saintly compared to the Germans, Chachi,' said Bauji.

The Collector's party on Friday was the most talked about subject around town. The bazaars hummed with gossip about who was and who was not going. It was an attempt by the young new English District head to introduce himself and to create goodwill with Lyallpur's gentry.

In the past an invitation to the Burra Sahib's would have been regarded as a great honour, and the town's elite would have scrambled for invitations. But now, in 1942, when everyone was politicized by Gandhi, there was much ambivalence, and Lyallpur's society was divided into two well-defined camps. Originally it was thought that the Hindus would boycott the party and the Muslims might attend. Surprisingly the grouping was not taking place along communal lines—despite the growing alienation among the two communities—but between moderates and extremists in their political attitude to the British Raj.

'Tell me, Dewan Chand, do you think the English will ever go away? Will I see India free in my lifetime?' asked Chachi, suddenly becoming thoughtful.

Bauji sighed. 'Once this war is over, perhaps,' he said after a long pause. 'But Chachi, do you think *we* are ready for freedom?' He asked the question gently, as if talking to himself.

'What kind of a damn fool question is that!' exploded Chachi. 'If I didn't know you better, Dewan Chand, I'd say that is a very unpatriotic sentiment.'

There was a pause.

At this point Chachi noticed Bauji's three youthful unmarried daughters peering down with curiosity from the first floor.

'Look at those roofs you have raised!' she said, pointing to the young girls above, who quickly turned away. 'Remember, you have to marry them soon. You've done well with your older boy, Dewan Chand. You have found him a good wife with a good dowry. But don't get complacent. When a man has daughters to marry, he cannot sit around playing cards.'

Bauji hands strayed to the cards he had put away, then withdrew.

'Good boys don't come easily' she continued. 'You should have thought of it when you were enjoying yourself with my niece.'

Bauji blushed. Bhabo shooed her daughters away from the railing upstairs. The bridge companions made murmuring sounds.

'I have found a boy for your older girl, Bau,' she announced sternly.

Bauji's face lit up. Ears perked up upstairs.

'Who is the boy?' he asked.

'Do you want the whole world to hear about it?' she said staring at the bridge players, who sheepishly started to get up.

'Now call my niece downstairs,' she said as soon as the bridge players had left. Bhabo came down instantly. Big Uncle followed her downstairs looking sporty in his tennis whites. He bowed down as if to touch Chachi's feet in the traditional gesture of greeting of the young to the old.

'And what have you been doing, you young sinner?' asked Chachi of Big Uncle.

'Nothing, Chachi,' said Big Uncle, looking confident and very much the elegant young man about town.

'Boy, I don't want you spoiling our family name with scandals.'

'Scandals exist in the feeble minds of your town gossips,' said Big Uncle boldly.

'I like this boy,' said Chachi appreciatively, 'even though he spends too much time in his wife's room.'

Chachi was referring to an incident a few weeks ago when Big Uncle had taken his fifteen-year-old bride for a drive in a horse-driven tonga, and had immediately created a sensation. In conservative Lyallpur young men and women were still not seen together in public. Men went out with men and women with women. Young brides and grooms were especially not exempt.

'All by themselves, they shamelessly went out for all eyes to see!' the town gossips had whispered.

Her friends had been pouring in streams to 'commiserate' with poor Bhabo, who had not been able to show her face in society for days.

Bauji too was constantly having his ups and down with Big Uncle. To begin with, Big Uncle preferred to play rather than work. And he preferred to play with women. To save the family embarrassment, Bauji had him married off young, while he was still a student. No one imagined, though, that Big Uncle would fall so completely in love with his fifteen-year-old bride, whom he saw for the first time on his marriage night. The result was that he was constantly with his beautiful bride and failed his law exams.

'Get out of your wife's room, you good-for-nothing fool!' Bauji would shout every morning just as he was leaving for the law courts. 'I curse the day I arranged your marriage.' He did not mean that, of course, because secretly he was pleased with the shrewd match that he had made: the bride, whom everyone called Bhabi, had brought in a big dowry and was expecting a fat inheritance, which would become part of Bauji's joint family property.

Big Uncle did finally get his law degree, and before he could get into further trouble, Bauji quickly took him on as his legal understudy. They both worked in the same office and Bauji passed him his easier cases. But Big Uncle did not mean to exert himself, and he was out on the tennis courts every afternoon. In the evenings he liked to play cards or give lively dinners where chicken was served. Bhabo would not allow meat to be cooked in her kitchen. So Bhabi used to cook the chicken outside. The pot in which the chicken was cooked had to be cleaned the next day with red hot charcoal.

'Well, who is the boy you have brought for Tara?' asked Bauji.

'It is a difficult match,' replied Chachi softly, 'because the boy is in the hands of a guru.'

Bauji looked puzzled.

The boy's name is Seva Ram and he is an up-and-coming engineer. He is a class one, gazetted officer with the government in the Irrigation Department, and he earns two hundred rupees a month. But he is a bit of a rebel.'

'Why?' asked Bauji.

'Because he has renounced the religion of his father. He has left his family in Pindi and spends all his time with his guru.'

'Guru?'

'His guru is a wise old man named Sant Singh. His ashram is on the banks of the river Sutlej, near Nangal.'

Chachi gave a dozen other particulars, which Bauji calmly took in, and gave her a look which satisfied her that he knew what to do. Although they had received a number of offers for Tara, Bauji had found them all unsuitable. He was determined to find her a well-educated professional for a husband, this was why he had eagerly listened to what Chachi had to say. Chachi abruptly got up with a 'Hari-Om'. Big Uncle echoed an irreverent 'Hari-Om' in mock solemnity.

'Don't you Hari-Om me, you rascal,' said Chachi affectionately. 'Come walk me home on your way to the tennis club.'

As they were walking out Big Uncle asked Chachi if she had missed any trains recently. 'You devil!' she said, 'I am never going to the station with you again.'

A month earlier Chachi had missed the five o'clock train for Lahore, but no one was supposed to know. Big Uncle had gone to leave her at the railway station in the afternoon. Since she had a real fear of missing trains, they had arrived two hours before the train's departure. Big Uncle thought this ridiculous, but who was going to argue with Chachi?

During the first hour they paced the platform. Thrice they went to the Assistant Station Master's office to check if the train was on time. Thrice they synchronized their watches with the railway clock. Whenever they heard an engine whistle or a goods train being shunted, they looked up wondering if it wasn't time. Around four o'clock Chachi told him to run off to the tennis courts, saying that she would manage on her own. But before he left, they ascertained the exact place where the ladies compartment would stop on the platform and they moved her luggage to that spot.

As chance would have it, Chachi met an old friend on the platform who was waiting for the same train. They decided to have a cup of tea in the Retiring Room where they got into a bitter quarrel over something that had happened forty years ago. As a result both of them missed their trains.

Quietly Chachi returned home and equally quietly she left for Lahore the next day. But the truth somehow came out, and everyone had a laugh.

2

As soon as Chachi left, Bhabo and the girls went upstairs, and Mashkiya arrived to water the courtyards. He was a dark, thin man, of the untouchable caste, with shining hair and a handsome moustache. He carried a round goatskin bag full of water, which he skilfully and proudly sprinkled over the three courtyards in the house. Bauji smelled the fragrance of the wet earth from the Mashkiya's cool water, and he mused over this strange routine, which was as old as his house. He recalled the Mashkiya's humble father, who did not dare raise his eyes as he brought refreshing coolness to the evening. Once he had touched Bhabo by mistake with his elbow, and she had taken countless baths 'to wash away the pollution from the outcaste's touch'. Today, here was his proud son, who Bauji instinctively knew, would not do this menial work for long. The problem was his dark wife, whom Bauji had once taken to bed in a moment of lust. She had looked at him with her opaque peasant's eyes, had refused him nothing, and been compliant in every way. In the final moment of intense pleasure she had exclaimed 'My Bauji!' He smiled with satisfaction at the memory, and pictured her head deep in his pillow.

The fragrance of the wet earth took Bauji back twenty years when he had built this house. It was one of the first big houses on Kacheri Bazaar and he had been proud of it. He tried to recapture the confidence of a young ambitious man on the way up. Like many of his friends, he was filled with hopes. He had actually believed that the English had done some good in India. Their railways had bridged the country and the first cotton mills were transforming the economy. Bauji's own hero had been Gopal Gokhale, a lawyer like himself, who had combined Indian tradition with English moderation and orderliness. He had believed with Gokhale in the gradual evolution to self-rule for India. About Gandhi, who had recently arrived on the political stage, Bauji had felt distaste, particularly for his 'bazaar politics'. Deep down he was convinced that Britain was fair, decent and just, and would not stand in the way of the natural aspirations of Indians for self-rule.

Now, a generation later, Bauji was disillusioned with English motives, cynical about Indian leaders, and disappointed with the inability of Hindus and Muslims to live together. The British had, of course, taken advantage of this division and vigorously pursued a divide-and-rule policy. And despite his moderate views, Bauji had grown tired of English promises of self-government for India when her actions continually belied them. He admired the British because they had brought peace, law and order and they had built canals and irrigated the land of the five rivers. They had introduced modern education which had liberated the young people from the grip of the brahmins and the mullahs. Bauji had been amongst the first in his village to benefit; he had regarded his law degree as a passport to break away from his superstitious village and its hereditary occupations. In the past the only jobs open to his caste would have been soldiering or farming; if a boy had been particularly ambitious he might have tried his luck at the court of one of the Sikh princes, and with influence he might have become a minor revenue official. With education not only came new occupations, but a young professional like Bauji also came under the sway of the Arya Samaj, which sought a return to ancient Vedic tradition, and was palatable because it bypassed avaricious brahmins with their endless rituals.

As the sun set, Bauji watched Bhabo lead the women and children up to the roof to perform the *sandhya*. They lit an earthern oil lamp and chanted Sanskrit verses in praise of the evening and the setting sun. As he heard these beautiful sounds from above, Bauji was amused by the thought that not a single one of them understood the meaning of the Sanskrit words they repeated every evening. Once the *sandhya* was over, the lights were gradually turned on in the house.

Bauji valued routine, and every evening after playing a few rubbers he would ask for his cane and leave with his bridge friends for the Company Bagh. As they walked, Bauji and his friends discussed the politics of Lyallpur and India. He liked an audience and he was always trying out new ideas on his companions.

Although he lived his life predictably, he did not plan very far ahead for he liked the flexibility to make changes. He was a successful man of the world who instinctively knew when to make a move and take advantage of a situation. He would have probably become a more famous lawyer had he not devoted so much time to making money. He had found that by closely managing his properties he could multiply their value, and in recent years he had begun to limit his professional activities even though he excelled in them.

He was accustomed to let circumstances and social relations govern his actions. He had quickly perceived the opportunity presented by Chachi and had determined to go to the guru's ashram. He had also made a mental note that he must return Chachi's favour one day.

Now sitting in his cane chair and smoking the hookah, he watched the summer light fade while he half-listened to the evening sound of Lyallpur. The peacock's cry occasionally interrupted the chirping parrots and also his musings about his elder daughter. He reasoned that his evening walk was dead anyway since Chachi had unceremoniously bundled out his friends. He consoled himself with the self-righteous thought that he had been compensated by listening to the *sandhya* after many months. For a man accustomed to balancing profit and loss and risks with opportunities, he could justify giving up two dozen walks in order to fix up a husband for his favourite daughter. And as the first jasmine smells of Lyallpur's summer night filled the air, he decided to act.

He had heard of the guru, and since he made it his business to know who was influential to achieve what end, he quickly decided that Rai Bahadur Shankar Singh, who lived in Civil Lines, was the man to give him an introduction to the guru. He called out to Suresh, his syce, to hitch up the tonga. Then he changed into a freshly-starched turban, trousers and shirt, all in white, and he was soon on his way. While he rode in the tonga he savoured the rich evening smells from the gardenias and the bela, overlaid with an abundance of jasmine, which lined the road to Civil Lines. A touch of irritation briefly clouded his brow as his eyes fell on a tiny mango stain, which the washerman had not succeeded in removing from the otherwise immaculate shirt.

As he rode past Company Bagh, he let himself be carried away by a different odour from the exotic plants minutely cared for by the Company gardeners. Flowers sprouted in all directions but they seemed muted by the languor which enveloped much of Lyallpur's daily life. The garden was exhaling scents which were fleshy and mildly erotic, especially the oily emanations of the magnolias, but these were again drowned by the heavy scent of jasmine. Suddenly from somewhere below he caught a faint fragrance of fresh mint, which disappeared just as quickly. He tried longingly to recapture it, but gloomy thoughts overtook him instead.

He remembered the nausea that had come over him a month ago during his Sunday evening walk with the family in this same garden when he discovered the corpse of a young Hindu boy, who had been stabbed by a Muslim youth and had come up here in the gardens to die all alone under the leechi tree. He had found him face downward in the carnation beds, his face covered in blood and vomit, his nails clinging to the soil. He had turned him over and covered his face with his white handkerchief. The dead boy continued to be the talk of the house. As the image of that innocent boy recurred Bauji wondered what had he died for, poor boy.

'Of course, he died for his community,' Chachi had replied emphatically. This same opinion was echoed by his friends. But the explanation did not satisfy him. What he saw was the madness of Hindus and Muslims killing each other. It had increasingly become part of everyday life as Jinnah brought the possibility of a homeland for the Punjabi Muslims ever closer to reality. Who would have thought that this would be a consequence of India's struggle for freedom from the English, he wondered. When was the lunacy going to stop? Why didn't the British take a firmer position on 'one India'? Perhaps Chachi was right: the British had after all promoted Hindu-Muslim rivalry through their policies. Why should they stop now when this enmity could actually prolong their stay in India just a bit longer? But did they not realize that the madness was getting out of hand and could envelop them as well?

Some of his friends argued that Hindus and Muslims had lived together in peace for hundreds of years. They would continue to do so for hundreds more. This was a temporary insanity created by Jinnah, they said. After all, most Indian Muslims had been Hindus earlier, who had been converted to Islam. So why shouldn't they live together in peace?

He was not so sure. Indian Muslims being recent converts were likely to be more fanatical. And was it really true that the two had lived peacefully together? Ever since he could remember, there had been tension and clashes between the two communities. He sighed as he realized organized religion's enormous capacity for mischief; it exaggerated differences between human beings rather than narrowing them.

These dark ruminations were interrupted as the tonga entered

Civil Lines, where the small British community and the western-ized Indians lived. The avenues became broader, the bungalows more spacious. He passed the imposing Government House, the residence of the District Collector, where he would be going on Friday. It was a dazzling white building, surrounded by a colo-nnaded veranda set amidst acres of green lawn and enclosed by a high, grilled boundary wall. Against the white walls there was an occasional splash of pink and purple bougainvillaea. The overall effect befitted the dignity of the seniormost official of the British Raj in the district. Next to it was the equally spacious two-storied Government College in brick, surrounded by vast green playing fields. As the tonga went along the geometrically laid out straight and wide roads, shaded by sheesham and kikar trees, past curving gravel driveways of the lesser officials of the Raj, Bauji began to feel uneasy.

Civil Lines had an unmistakably different atmosphere from the town. It was not English. The sun was too strong, the land was too flat, the buildings were too imposing, the drainage too perfect, the ceilings were too high and the grounds too spacious. Although the conquerors from the small and distant island may have attempted to create a little bit of their own green country, the attempt had not been successful. What they had achieved instead was an antiseptic and incongruous imposition which was alien to both races. The ordered smells of Civil Lines were in contrast to the chaotic odours of the town. They made him uncomfortable because they seemed to proclaim the superiority of the alien ruling class.

Bauji felt ambivalent because he admired the order and the civil sense which the island rulers had displayed here, but he could not forgive them for their aloofness. Otherwise why should a confident man like himself feel uneasy? Perhaps, he wondered, it was not their fault; it was in the nature of the imperial relationship. The rulers were not expected to make the ruled feel comfortable in their presence. Every time he entered Civil Lines, every time he set foot on one of the avenues, which intersected at right angles, and which had foreign sounding names of successive British Viceroys, he felt a shiver.

Thoughts about the English came to an abrupt end as the tonga stopped at Rai Bahadur's gate. He was one of Bauji's more Western-ized friends. Bauji was quickly led by a servant to a manicured lawn surrounded by a riot of gulmohar. Shankar Singh was sitting in a corner relaxing with his family. As soon as Bauji arrived, his wife got up, modestly covered her head with the end of her sari, and greeted him with folded hands. He returned the greeting and accepted the fresh lime drink which she offered him.

Bauji's business was over quickly. Shankar Singh knew the boy and he gave his whole-hearted support to the match. He was more than happy to give him a letter to the guru and Bauji was pleased that his mission had been so easily accomplished. He realized the value of this introduction, for Shankar Singh was reputed to be a great devotee and a favourite of the guru. Shankar Singh also gave him careful instructions on how to get there, including train timings. He would have to take a train to Lahore, the provincial capital, from where he would get onto the mainline to Delhi and get off at Jullunder; from there he would take a local for Nangal. The ashram was a two mile tonga ride after that.

On his way back home, Bauji was filled with admiration for the way Shankar Singh had synthesized his orderly western ways with devotion to a guru and a deeply eastern spiritual life. It was tempting, thought Bauji, to live like this among stately avenues and shady trees, in houses surrounded by green lawns and orchards of maltas and grapefruits in the back. But it was also lonely here, he felt, and it was too late in life to change his ways. He liked living in the bustle of the town. Besides there were too many English here and they mixed only with their own. And the Indians who lived here were either snobs or too Anglicized for his taste. Shankar Singh probably felt comfortable here because he was 'England returned'. Besides Bauji did not think he could get used to living in one of these 'inside-out' houses. The only sensible way to live he felt was in a high-walled house with a courtyard in the middle. He felt naked in these high-ceilinged PWD style bungalows which had verandas and gardens on the outside, exposed to the whole world.

As he was turning into Kacheri Bazaar, he caught a glimpse of a veiled Muslim woman. She was entirely covered by a burkha, which had slits through which her eyes could see the world. This by itself was not unusual. What caught his attention was the unmistakable and expensive scent that lingered behind her. He recognized the subtle fragrance. But the identity of the lady eluded him. The rich quality of the burkha confirmed that she was a woman of the upper class. He had a curious feeling that he knew her, but he wondered what she was doing alone at this time of the night in a non-Muslim part of the town. Had she come to pawn a gold ring to a Hindu *bania* in order to pay a gambling debt? Or was she seeking the services of a Hindu lawyer in a poisoning case? He surprised himself when suddenly he ordered the tongawalla to turn in order to follow her. Not that he meant to accost her. It was merely to give himself time to identify her. He had a strong feeling that she was in trouble. And his instinct was to help her. But his gallant gesture was in vain, for she quickly turned into a narrow lane and disappeared in the dark night.

He turned around to go home. He watched the ground below and the narrow tarred, metalled road slowly opened up the soft, light earth on either side at the cantering speed of the horse. He kept thinking of the tempting lady, and the titillation he must suffer on her account. As he recalled the peculiar scent he tried to eliminate one Muslim friend after another, but the exercise was fruitless. She remained a mystery and he unfaithful in his heart.

3

The next morning Bauji took a train to the guru's ashram.

At the railway station Bauji did what he had done for years: he bought a first class ticket and went and sat in a second class carriage. As the train pulled away he looked out at his beloved city from a distance. They crossed the bridge over the canal and the familiar white temple on the banks and the bathing steps which went all the way down to the canal. Although he had donated for the building of the temple, he had never thought much of its architecture. The mosque in the distance, however, was a much more impressive structure. Its design was pre-Mughal, inspired by the domes of the Sultan period. Further along the canal they passed the burning ghat, where he had gone over the years to cremate many relatives and friends' relatives. Soon they were on the dusty plain, with eroded ground on both sides. They crossed the Old Nallah, which was a dry river bed that filled up during the monsoons, got flooded and wrought havoc to the surrounding villages, washing away their cattle and their goats. Lyallpur was now a white speck in the distance, and he remembered how this landscape glowed at twilight during the rainy season. Everything became a golden yellow, especially the white walls of the town on the horizon.

As the train picked up speed, an officious Ticket Collector entered his carriage. Bauji frowned. More than the interruption it was the embarrassment. The TC wanted to know why he was travelling second with a first class ticket. Bauji muttered something about being comfortable where he was. But the TC persisted, reassuring him that the first class carriage was empty. He had immediately understood the real reason for Bauji's strange behaviour—which was that Bauji was afraid of a chance meeting with an Englishman in the first class coach. Before the TC left, he reminded Bauji to get a refund for the difference. Bauji thanked him, but he was upset by the intrusion, and of having been reminded of his humiliation of many years ago.

In early 1931 Bauji had been travelling by first class on this same train, when an English Army officer had come in before Lahore and told him to leave the compartment. Where another Indian might have complied, Bauji had protested and stuck to his right to travel in the same carriage. It had soon become ugly since neither the Indian station master nor the railway police would support him. In the end, the English officer had physically pushed him out.

It was not the end of the affair for Bauji complained officially and the matter went up higher. At first the English officials tried to cover up, but Bauji persisted, until it eventually reached the Governor. An official enquiry was held, and Bauji had the satisfaction of seeing the officer reprimanded, the station master censured and the policeman transferred. During the enquiry, the press took it up as well. The Anglo-Indian paper of Lahore, the *Civil and Military Gazette*, sided with the English officer, asking the authorities to call off 'a frivolous enquiry'. The English population of the Punjab closed ranks and openly sided with their own officer. But the Indian press and opinion heavily supported Bauji. In Lyallpur, the local Superintendent of Police tried to harass him in small ways, but he quickly gave up when he realized that Bauji was not about to be cowed down easily.

In the end Bauji felt that his faith in the British rule of law had been vindicated. From a private hurt, which would have scarred him forever, it had become a public affair and in his eyes the British system went on trial. And in the end the system was found to be sound. Thus a personal injustice, which might have radicalized him and pushed him into the nationalist camp, in fact reinforced his faith in the impartiality of the British Raj. In the meantime his law practice did suffer on account of this. It scared away many of his clients. They did not share his faith in the neutrality of the British judicial system. A couple of times, Bauji too had reason to doubt this faith. Once an English Magistrate was unduly sarcastic and rough with him in court. But all in all, not a single verdict went deliberately against him because of his involvement in this matter. Slowly, after about six months his practice picked up again, and the affair was soon forgotten.

It was an unfortunate experience for one who was basically a private man. The personal humiliation that day at the Lahore station forever took away much of his earlier romance and appetite for railway travel. It also accounted for his odd behaviour today in insisting on buying a first class ticket for there was always a hope, even when he was sure that at the last minute he would not have the courage to enter a first class compartment.

It was late afternoon when he arrived at the tiny village platform. A porter in a red turban scrambled to lift his luggage. 'Hot tea,' cried the tea boy as he scurried past. Bauji stared at the proud yellow sign which proclaimed to the world the existence of this sleepy village. The porter loaded his bag onto a waiting tonga and he rode towards the river. The tonga took him for two miles through wheat fields and here and there they passed flat houses of unbaked mud. They came along a line of buffaloes, moving down towards the river, flicking flies with their tails from their gleaming skins.

'The guru be blessed!' shouted a passerby. 'The guru is merciful!' responded the tonga driver. Bauji smiled at these old courtesies of the road. Suddenly the tonga turned and they were at the river Sutlej. The sun was coming down and the ashram was in full view. Bauji's face filled with pleasure at the sight. The ashram was on the banks of the river. From the front, it looked like a jumble of simple brick huts surrounding an imposing building in the Muslim style with domes and minarets, where the devotees assembled twice a day to listen to the guru's discourse. As expected, Shankar Singh's letter opened all doors at the ashram and he was treated with respect and courtesy. Since he had been travelling the whole day, he was pleased with the chance of a bath in the river. He luxuriated in the cool stream, and allowed his mind to wander aimlessly over the memory of the burkha lady.

Bauji was not religious by nature, but he was impressed by the tranquil atmosphere of the riverbank. Silence seemed to fill the evening. Around six he was invited to tea on the terrace of the guru's apartment. The guru, he noted, was six feet tall. He had a flowing white beard and wore a white turban. He kept smiling at everyone. Bauji was taken up by his awesome bearing. He thanked the guru for his courtesy and briefly stated his marriage proposal. The guru smiled and gently called in the boy, Seva Ram, to meet Bauji. Although Bauji found his potential son-in-law quiet and aloof, he was impressed with the young man's intelligence and simple manners. The only thing that bothered Bauji was his short stature because he would have liked a tall grandson.

One of the disciples struck up a conversation with the guru. Seva Ram listened attentively, but he had a distant look and Bauji could not tell what he was thinking. He was sitting on the opposite side of the room and every now and then Bauji glanced at him. He looked to be in his mid-twenties. He had a pleasant face, thought Bauji, neither handsome nor plain, rather shy and in no way remarkable. His looks were certainly not capable of winning Tara's heart.

Bauji was struck by the fact that though he had not said more than half-a-dozen words since entering the room, he seemed to be perfectly at ease and in a curious way he appeared to take part in the guru's conversation without opening his mouth. Bauji noticed his hands. They were not long, but they were nicely shaped, even though they were large for his size. He was slightly built but not delicate in appearance; on the contrary he was wiry and resistant. His face was tanned, a minor disadvantage thought Bauji, because fairness was preferred. But he was not naturally dark, Bauji realized, and he felt reassured; it was probably because he spent a lot of time in the sun. His features, though regular enough, were undistinguished. He had normal cheekbones and his temples were hollow. He had wavy black hair which he combed to the back. His eyes looked larger than they really were because they were deep set and his lashes were thick and long. His eyes had a peculiar intensity.

A few notables of the ashram now entered the room. Among them were a princess of a small state in central India and a professor of philosophy. The conversation suddenly became livelier. As people were chatting and enjoying the breeze from the river, Bauji leaned over the edge of the terrace and looked out at the river. In the setting sun, the river glowed along its quarter-mile width, framed by ravines and reeds on the flat plain. He was struck by the beauty of the moment. When he turned back to the company, he heard the professor of philosophy ask, 'Guruji, if there is a God why does he permit such suffering and pain in the world? Why isn't the world a better place to live in? Why aren't people happy?'

The guru laughed as he always did, not at the questioner or the question, but to convey that it was a difficult one and hence a good question. 'God did not intend this world to be a perfect place for human happiness or to be our permanent home,' he replied. 'It is a school, where you come to learn.'

'Learn what?' asked the princess.

'Learn, my child, the way to your real home, which is the place for true human happiness.'

'And how do I learn that?' she asked.

'You learn through meditation. By emptying your mind of all

distracting thoughts and concentrating your attention between the eyes. During meditation you will forget your body and you will be guided either by an inner light or the sound of inner music. The light will sometimes appear in the form of your guru, who will guide your spiritual journey towards God with the help of the light and the music.'

'Guruji, if this world is not my true home, then why do I get involved here? I mean get attached to my family?'

'Child, you must teach your heart. What a waste these attachments are! One day you will die, and that too without warning. Suddenly you will leave your family and friends. You see, the world is not a permanent place. Nothing is forever.'

'Look upon this world as a passenger on a train looks at a wayside stop. On the train journey the traveller makes acquaintance with fellow passengers. Some passengers get off earlier, some later; some have a short journey, some have a longer one. But no one makes deep friendships, because they all know that each one has to get off. That is how you must learn to live in the world. Do not imagine for even a moment that your parents, children, friends, are going with you. They are all passengers.'

Bauji was alternately moved and disturbed by this analogy. Even though he felt sceptical about the possibility of a true home or a perfect world, he was drawn to the perspective of the train passenger. He wondered what the world would be like if all relationships were as casual as those of passengers. Slowly a vision of that world appeared. And it was a bleak vision. Surely this world, he thought, with all its failures and sorrows, is better for the emotion that we invest in it, especially in human relationships. He began to be repelled by the vision. In the meantime the guru had changed the analogy.

'Look at how the wise bee sits on the jar of honey!' continued the guru. 'The bee sits on the jar and licks honey from its edge, and flies away when it is content. That is how you must live in this world. Enjoy the world, but do not get involved. Be ready to fly away at any time. Most of us, however, live like the stupid bee who sees the honey with hungry eyes and plunges in—with the result that it gets stuck in the honey as we get stuck in our involvements.'

This was more than a lesson in moderation, Bauji felt. Despite the fact that the analogy was more convincing, he still felt uneasy. He thought to himself that he liked getting involved and attached. Although he did not think of himself as the greedy bee stuck in the jar, he liked to plunge in and form attachments. His world was the richer for these entanglements. If he hadn't felt as he did for Tara, why would he trouble himself with these arrangements for her happiness?

As the evening wore on, the professor of philosophy kept interrupting the guru with countless questions. 'Who created the universe? If God created the universe why did he create it? Etc., etc.'

Finally the tired guru sighed and said, 'Listen, professorji, I shall tell you a story. Once there was a blind man who fell into a deep well. Fortunately a shepherd happened to pass by; he heard the blind man's cries, and took pity and offered to pull him out.

'Instead of taking hold of the rope lowered by the shepherd, the blind man started to argue. He questioned the shepherd about his motive in helping him. "Where was the guarantee," he asked, "that he wouldn't fall again in a well? Why didn't they make safer wells for blind people? Why did they make wells at all, in fact?"

'The patience of the shepherd was taxed by these questions, but he gently replied that it would be in the blind man's interest to take advantage of the rope. After coming out he could study the situation for himself at leisure and form his conclusions.

'The blind man, however, persisted and asked the shepherd why he had not also fallen into the well. The kind shepherd said that he was in a hurry to get home where he had a number of tasks awaiting him.

'"All right," said the blind man, "but first answer only two questions: when was this well built and how deep is it?"'

'"It is deep enough to be the grave of some people," said the shepherd and left in disgust.'

Everyone laughed heartily at this tale, including the professor.

As the evening came to an end, the guru turned to Bauji. 'You have been quiet all evening. I perceive disquiet in your heart. What is it?'

'Guruji,' said Bauji. 'I have always believed that a man should lead a virtuous life, do good to others, avoid causing pain or harm to fellow human beings, and earn an honest living. I never thought anything more was necessary.'

'Bauji, I applaud your beliefs. You are in fact far better prepared to undertake the spiritual journey because your mind is pure. A pure mind is like a beautifully arranged table before dinner, with clean plates and silverware. Now you must place in them food. Your hunger will not be satisfied merely with plates and spoons, just as the soul's hunger for the Infinite cannot be satisfied purely by virtuous living.'

Bauji thought about what the guru had said. He was struck by the logical strength of the guru's arguments; however, his heart shied from commitment. Religious faith was too far away from his worldly temper.

'Why don't the two of you go for a walk in the morning?' suggested the guru to Seva Ram and Bauji. 'Shall we say at 5.30. The day breaks early nowadays.'

The next morning Bauji was woken up at four when a gong went off. It was the start of the day at the ashram, beginning with a bath and followed by meditation. The two men, so unlike in physique, met as planned. The boy, shorter and slimmer, wore the working dress of a Punjabi peasant—a thin long shirt and baggy pants held up by a drawstring. Bauji again noticed the boy's large hands and curly hair. His eyes were innocent and sincere, thought Bauji, but they were also remote.

There was an awkward shyness between the two. Bashfully Seva Ram led Bauji up the river.

'I suppose you sleep late in Lyallpur.'

'No, as a matter of fact, I'm usually in my office by eight.'

The boy smiled, and with a laugh Bauji added, 'Yes, I suppose that is late by your standards.'

Bauji saw a hazy mist rising from the water. The air was not yet warm, and the sun was ascending behind the main dome in the east. The boy led the way and they walked on, making small talk, until they reached a clearing, from which they could see the railway bridge in the distance.

Bauji wanted to ask Seva Ram about his job, his career prospects, and other things appropriate of a future son-in-law. Instead they talked about the guru and the spiritual life.

'What does the guru teach?' asked Bauji.

'To seek the truth,' replied the boy.

'And how do you find the truth?'

'Through meditation.'

'How do you know when you have found it?', asked Bauji.

'When I have become free from the demands of my ego and from the control of selfish longings which bind me to my body and other daily concerns.'

The boy had a natural grace, decided Bauji. It seemed that he had also thought about what he was saying.

After the walk Bauji went to listen to the guru's discourse. He sat cross-legged on the ground in the impressive hall, which had minarets at each corner. The guru was dressed in a loose and comfortable white *kurta*. He sat slightly higher on a platform, so that he could be seen by everyone. At his side sat another bearded old man, who chanted verses of the medieval saint, Nanak, which the guru elaborated and commented upon. Everyone's eyes were adoringly fixed on the guru and they listened in rapt attention.

In a low and clear voice the guru explained that the purpose of human life was to merge with the Infinite. He likened Infinite to an ocean and the human soul to a drop of water, which has a natural urge to merge with the ocean. 'Fortunately,' he added, 'the Infinite is within each of us, and by emptying our mind of all thought and concentrating attention at the eye centre, one can journey inwards towards the Infinite. The journey begins with meditation, when the five senses and the mind are stilled and the intellect is silent. Meditation helps the mind to become free from the awareness of subject and object and attain one-pointedness.' To help quiet the mind, the guru offered a mantra. The mantra, he explained, was merely a set of words, whose meaning was not relevant, but it had to be repeated quietly in order to divert one's mind from the restless chain of thoughts. The practice of meditation, he added, was helped by living simply, eating only when hungry, drinking only when thirsty, and reducing living to essentials. The guru concluded by saying, that if they didn't believe him, why didn't they experiment and find out for themselves.

Bauji was impressed with this logic, and moved by the possibilities of meditation. Sceptical by nature and shy of religion, he was amused to see himself being swept by the guru and the ashram's atmosphere.

From the mystic calm of the ashram, the guru and the river, Bauji was brutally thrown into the mundane world. On his way home, as he was getting into the train at Jullunder, he found himself trapped in the middle of what the next day's newspapers called 'a minor communal disturbance'. The papers went on to praise 'the speed and firmness with which the police put down the disorder', but Bauji remembered only his humiliation.

Suddenly, as if out of nowhere, two handsome Muslim boys, scarcely twenty years old, emerged. They confidently walked into his compartment, and with extreme courtesy asked Bauji his name. Bauji gave it to them. When they heard it they spat in his face and turned to run away, but their way was blocked by a gentleman with a suitcase who had entered at that precise moment. The gentleman had seen what had happened. He slapped the boy closest to him squarely across the cheek. The blow was struck with such force that the sound was heard all over the noisy platform. The boys were taken aback and managed to beat a quick retreat. Bauji smiled gratefully at his benefactor, though he felt ashamed. The ironic discovery that his benefactor was a Muslim momentarily diverted him from his own humiliation.

A third passenger entered shortly, and informed them that there had been a communal riot that morning in the area around the railway station. The trouble had apparently started because a Hindu procession had played music outside the Muslim mosque. The Muslims had regarded this as a provocation and had retaliated. The next morning's papers placed the casualties at 'four dead, twenty wounded, two shops burned, two cases of rape'. By the time the police arrived on the platform Bauji's train had started to move. Just as well, he thought, that he was spared the ordeal of publicly recounting his humiliation. Neither he nor the Muslim gentleman mentioned the incident again during the journey.

As the train gathered speed, Bauji's feelings of shock and humiliation were gradually replaced by calm reflection of what had happened. He was surprised by the clarity of his mind so soon after this unpleasantness. He did not feel hatred for the two boys: they were part of a tide which was carrying the Punjab towards an unthinkable doom. The mischief had been unleashed not by Jinnah alone (as everyone believed) but also by Gandhi.

Bauji felt comfortable with the Congress movement so long as it was led by men like Gokhale, who spoke the familiar language of liberalism and the law. But the entry of Gandhi at the end of World War I had set it on a path of 'direct action' and given it a more Hindu complexion. Bauji distrusted Gandhi's methods of civil disobedience and mass agitation. They caused division everywhere—the biggest one being between Hindus and Muslims. And Gandhi seemed oblivious of it. For Gandhi—with all his fads and fasts, his mud baths, goat's milk, days of silence, non-violence—was fundamentally a Hindu. Although he claimed to be a 'Muslim, Parsee, Christian, and Hindu', who else but a Hindu could expect people to take such a quixotic idea seriously?

Like a true Hindu, who prefers dreams to facts and ideals to reality, Gandhi did not seem to realize that he was playing with fire. The more he succeeded with the masses the more he alienated the Muslims. Where was all this leading to? Today's incident at the railway station was merely a sign of what was to become of the Punjab. His own life had not been in danger today, but no one had been able to save that poor innocent boy in the Company Bagh last month. In their quest for independence the politicians had ended by inflaming latent communal passions. He could not believe that they would sacrifice the Punjab as a price for gaining India's independence. He was convinced that dreamers were dangerous and should not be allowed into the realm of public affairs.

The next day was a holiday and the sun shone on a refreshed Bauji. He had just finished a glass of cold, frothy buttermilk, and he sat in the courtyard, feeling pleased with himself, waiting to be shaved. The barber had been especially summoned, not only because Bauji needed a shave but because Bhabo had insisted that his advice be taken on the marriage proposal. After all, her own marriage and that of her mother and grandmother had rested on the counsel of the family barber who had also acted as a go-between. She was finding this manner of deciding her daughter's future exceedingly irregular, especially since the groom's parents were not even in the picture.

Bauji looked in the barber's mirror and saw the razor cleanly wipe the lather from his face in the luminous stillness of the morning—a calm which was periodically broken by the cry of a peacock in the distance. As he watched the sun's rays fall at different angles on the gleaming razor, he could not bring himself to share his proposal with the barber; instead he let his mind wander pleasantly over recollections of his favourite daughter, Tara.

He remembered the day she was born. He had wanted a son, and at first he would not pick her up. Bhabo had called him a stubborn fool: it was God's will that they should have a daughter and they should rejoice in His will. Gradually he got used to her. Even as a child, she had a restless will to succeed which was similar to his. She thought for herself and she acted quickly, but always with a clear sense of purpose.

When she was seven, he recalled that her teacher had asked Tara to bring her buttermilk at midday. Since they lived close by Tara was initially happy to bring a jugful of Bhabo's creamiest. It pleased her that her teacher really enjoyed it. Soon she realized, however, that something was wrong. The teacher began to take the buttermilk for granted, and even scolded her if it wasn't sufficiently creamy or cold. Tara also felt guilty, even though the other girls didn't say anything. Abruptly one day she stopped bringing the buttermilk. When questioned by the teacher, Tara replied that she wasn't going to bring it anymore. Initially she suffered for this, but eventually the teacher understood that Tara had a mind of her own.

Bauji smiled at the picture of his seven-year-old Tara standing up to her primary school teacher. His agreeable meandering came to a sudden end as he looked up in the barber's mirror and noticed a handsome, confident and triangular face. It belonged to his nephew, Karan. He did not turn around but pretended to concentrate on the razor's movement in the sensitive area between the chin and the lips. He knew that his solitary communion with the lather was over as Karan's arrival was always an event, especially amongst the women in the house.

'Shh. . . .', said Karan putting his finger on his lips, 'an eminent barrister of Lyallpur was seen turning his tonga around at the corner of Kacheri Bazaar two days ago in pursuit of a dubious objective.'

Bauji noticed the sparkling brown eyes reflected in his mirror and the naughty smile, and he realized why this young man was so attractive to women. But he was clearly taking liberties with his uncle today.

'Really, I wonder who it was,' said Bauji innocently.

'That shouldn't be difficult to find out. I should say that he was tall and well built, with greying hair; he sported a smart moustache, and. . . .'

'Enough, you insolent wretch! Don't you have anything better to do?' This was too much. Bauji felt that he should be offended, but he could not bring himself to be angry at this elegant and confident youth, who was a favourite of the entire household.

Karan became serious. 'Didn't you hear, Bauji?' he said in his slightly nasal voice, 'Gandhi announced the "Quit India" resolution last night in Bombay !' The seriousness of this historic news was in complete contrast to the ironic tone of its messenger.

'How do you know, boy?'

'It was on the radio this morning,' replied Karan as he placed his long, self-possessed hands on the back of Bauji's chair. 'We are not expected to cooperate with the British government—not until they give a commitment for the independence of India.'

'No one is going to give Gandhi that kind of commitment—not in the middle of a war,' burst out Bauji.

There was a pause. Bauji looked into the mirror and saw the mysterious eyes smiling again with subdued irony. Meanwhile, the unmistakable nasal twang was a powerful signal to the rest of the house. Everyone came rushing downstairs.

'But what does it *really* mean?' asked Tara, who was the first to arrive. 'What is going to happen?' She looked up adoringly at Karan.

'You are not mixed up in all this, are you my boy?' interrupted Bhabo anxiously.

Karan gave Bhabo a shy look, and turned his thin frame towards Tara. His light-hearted eyes became serious.

'It means that we are not to cooperate with the police, the civil administration, and in fact the entire machinery of the British Raj.'

'Oh, Gandhi's usual stuff!' remarked Tara cynically.

'No Tara, this is different,' said Karan and he smiled.

At the mention of her name, Tara reddened visibly.

The barber had finished shaving Bauji and was now massaging his face. Bauji sensed a subdued sensuality in the sultry air. He seemed to see his daughter with a fresh eye. She appeared to be visibly affected by the voluptuousness of the moment. Although no beauty, she was attractive enough. She had an arresting face, with a square jaw and a pointed chin. Her dark, spirited eyes were crowned by thick black eyelashes, and surrounded by jet black hair. The colour of her skin was what Bhabo's match-making friends called 'wheatish'.

Her upper lip curved prettily on her fine oval face. Standing in a white and blue cotton sari under the shade of the mango tree beside her family, Tara presented an attractive picture. A closer look, however, revealed that the same dark brown eyes could be turbulent and resolute. She was tall and generously proportioned, he thought, glancing at her youthful rising bosom. Her smooth skin was framed by a mass of raven hair which fell down to her rounded hips. The immoderate atmosphere reminded him of the stranger in the burkha and it seemed to seduce him too. He felt envious of Karan's youth and sorry for himself and his missed opportunities. His thoughts began to wander along a decidedly erotic direction, although without a specific object. He continued to watch the two excited people without fully taking in what was being said. The massage stopped and he was suddenly jolted back to reality.

'The man is mad,' said Bauji lunging forward and almost knocking down the barber. 'To launch civil disobedience when the Japanese are at our doorstep!'

'Bauji, can you blame him?' said Karan. 'Gandhi asks for so little: give us a promise of freedom after this war, and we shall help you in your war against fascism.'

'But Churchill won't even do that,' added Tara, in support of Karan. She blushed again as she looked squarely at the handsome face of her cousin. There was no mistaking it, thought Bauji. He had an animal intuition of the current of desire flowing from his daughter to his nephew. He suddenly felt old and worried. He looked at the charming intruder, who went towards his daughter. He was relieved when he saw on Karan's face only a grateful acknowledgement for her supportive remark.

'Don't you get mixed up in this stuff, boy!' admonished Bhabo. The narrow, brown eyes smiled again as the nephew looked at his aunt with affectionate irony. He impulsively went up and grabbed Bhabo by the waist and gave her a hug. She too was dominated by his charm.

'Stop this nonsense,' she said laughingly. 'And promise me.'

Karan did not say anything; everyone knew that he was heavily involved in the nationalist movement of Gandhi.

'Bhabo, I am tired of always getting ready to live, but never living,' he said.

'You've got a big future before you, boy. Don't lose it over this silly business,' warned Bauji.

'What makes you think I would do anything so patriotic? It's certainly not part of the family tradition,' said Karan with a mischievous smile.

'Don't you insult us, boy!' said Bauji pretending to be angry.

'What does one say to someone who insists on going to the DC's party?' said Karan.

'One does not say anything.'

'Will someone still go, even after Gandhiji's resolution?'

'All the more. Someone has to tell the English, after all.' Bauji smiled.

'Are you taking Bhabo with you?' asked Karan.

Before he could answer, Bhabo interrupted, 'Karan, he never

takes me with him.'

'Oh Bauji, take her with you!' pleaded Tara.

'The invitation clearly says "Mr & Mrs",' added Big Uncle.

'Out of the question. She doesn't know enough English and she will be quite lost,' said Bauji.

'See that, Karan. And he believes he is a modern sahib,' said Bhabo.

'What do you plan to wear to the party, Bauji?' asked Karan.

'Come and see for yourself.'

Although Bauji sometimes wore Western clothes, he used to say to Karan that when an Indian abandoned his own dress for the shirt and trouser of the West, he gave away a little bit of himself. He entered an unknown path, where he had few to guide him. The Englishman certainly did not accept an Indian more for that. On the contrary, the English had contempt for the Indian who was educated in Western learning. And Indians too were suspicious of their countrymen who gave up their traditional ways. Thus a Westernized Indian risked losing entry in his own world, without gaining admission into the Englishman's. He had to be unusually brave and make his own rules, since the rules of the white man did not yet apply and the brown man's rules had ceased to apply.

'Bauji, must you go to the DC's party?' asked Karan.

'Karan, the new DC is an inexperienced man, but he is sincere. He is trying. He is not a *pukka* sahib as yet. And before he gets that way, isn't it worth our while to set him on the right way? There is no point in boycotting his party.'

'But he is also a white skin and a ruler. Why should he listen to a brown skin of a subject race? Even the friendliest white cannot forget that. Deep down he scorns and despises us. This party is a gesture, a condescension. And Bauji, you want to go there and alleviate his guilty imperial conscience.' Bauji reddened and Karan looked at his watch to hide his own embarrassment. 'Oh, I must go, I'm late,' he said after a pause.

'Oh Karan, don't go away so soon!' said Tara. 'Where are you going?'

'Boy, you be careful,' said Bhabo as Karan was leaving.

'Won't you at least stay for a cup of tea?' implored Tara.

He turned around at the gate, smiled, picked up his bicycle which was leaning against the gate, and was gone.

'See, you have driven him away,' said Tara accusingly to Bauji. After a pause she asked, 'Why doesn't he come here like he used to?'

4

As usual the house was left in a daze after Karan's departure. Bauji's family had still not got used to his contradictory moods which oscillated between light-hearted bantering and sudden moments of extreme seriousness. Karan was the son of a spendthrift father who had married Bauji's sister, squandered his whole fortune and then died. The family's ruin had been total and included the linen Bauji had given his sister as part of the dowry. Since that day Bauji had taken on the responsibility of educating his nephew. And the boy had proved equal to his uncle's hopes. The nephew had slowly become very dear to Bauji.

Karan was a success. And Bauji admired success. Karan had stood first in school and had an outstanding academic record in college; he had captained his college cricket team; and women wilted when he played the sitar. In comparison to his own son, Karan stood out like a dancing star. Bauji had resigned himself to Big Uncle's mediocrity, and concentrated whole-heartedly on his nephew's future. He had seen to it that Karan went to the best school and college in Lahore and did not suffer financially. After completing college, Karan was now preparing for the competitive examination to join the prestigious Indian Civil Service (ICS) which now admitted more and more Indians. No one doubted that Karan would get in. Recently, however, Bauji had become worried about a change in Karan's life. He had heard rumours. Instead of playing cricket, or enchanting females with his sitar, Karan had been attending political meetings. At first Bauji dismissed it as healthy nationalist sentiment, but now he was concerned by the seriousness of his pursuit. He was also shocked by some of Karan's views which he thought to be dangerously close to the Communists'. He had the boy followed for a few days, but he was relieved to learn that Karan had only gone to a meeting of the socialist wing of the Congress. Nevertheless, a nagging fear persisted because Bauji distrusted all political activity.

After Karan's departure the family dispersed quickly, including the barber. Bauji was left alone with uneasy feelings. They were a strange mixture of hurt because of Karan's abrupt departure, but also of envy for Karan's youth and threatening sensuality, and distress at having been a witness to Tara's blatant infatuation. He felt a fatherly urge to protect his daughter from inevitable pain, but he also felt remorse at succumbing to the voluptuous sensuality of the moment with unbecoming thoughts, which in the end had left him feeling disagreeable. He attributed the sensuality to the humid torpor in the air, magnified by the laziness of the morning. He was troubled by Karan's restless nature. Karan was at an age when he was bored by the mundane and needed a cause. If his affectionate irony attracted him, his political activities offended. He was afraid that the 'Quit India' call given by Gandhi might pull his nephew into deeper waters, from which he could not be rescued.

Bauji did not look forward to the DC's party. He was always embarrassed at the gatherings of the English and the Indians. The Indian guests invariably arrived too early because they did not want to be late, and thus put their hosts in an awkward position. Then they kept together in a group without speaking, and there were long uncomfortable silences. They tried to copy English dress, but no matter how hard they tried they never looked right but because they were uncomfortable. Even the lowliest Englishman at these gatherings put on superior airs while talking to the most distinguished Indian. Deep down, the educated Indian was a threat to the Englishman, not only because the latter was often less educated, but also because the Indian was filled with liberal and seditious ideas of equality and freedom.

Bauji blamed Englishwomen for having created these rigid barriers between the men of the two races because they were narrow-minded by and large. Also because they could not easily mix with Indian women, who were often in purdah and did not speak English, they prevented their men from socializing with Indian men. They made constant demands on their men to have social teas, to walk the dogs, to play mixed doubles at the club, and so on. He really found this influence on the men by the women very odd.

Nevertheless, he admired the English. Even though they did not mix with the Indians, they were honest and they were just. They worked hard to keep law and order and they tried their best to be fair. They tried to protect the weak from the strong and the honest from the dishonest. He could speak from personal experience in the courts about the lengths to which the lowest English judge would go to discover a fair solution.

So what if they did not extend a hand of friendship as well? So what if they wanted to be *burra* sahibs! He would rather have their justice than their friendship. They were after all the rulers. He would rather be slighted socially than have to live with injustice. Perhaps it was a virtue for the rulers and the ruled to keep apart.

Early in his career Bauji had learnt a lesson. An Englishman named Coates, who was the new City Magistrate, had befriended him and invited him to tea. He was a bachelor, new to the country, and not accustomed to the social barriers between the English and the Indians. Bauji was proud of the invitation, but made the mistake of telling his friends about it. Some of his friends, being full of envy, spread the news quickly, and it reached the Collector's ears in a distorted form: that the Magistrate was taking bribes from the Pleader. As a result both Bauji and Coates got into trouble. But in the end a scandal was averted because the facts were otherwise. It taught them both a lesson, however. Curiously it also had the unintended effect of increasing Bauji's practice. His new clients brought pockets full of cash in order to bribe the Magistrate. But Mr Coates, like most English officials, was an honest and a fair man.

Bauji suddenly got up and went inside to change. When he reached the top of the steps above the courtyard, he paused a moment. He could see the minarets of the mosque beyond the Clock Tower, and the dusky horizon which merged with the trees of the Company Bagh. He felt a weightless quality in the air and was overcome by a majestic calm produced by the brilliant dazzle of the noon sun. He thought that the rains came and the rains went but the sun reigned supreme in this land. As soon as he was inside, a servant came to help him with his clothes and shoes. As he put on a starched loose muslin kurta, depressing political thoughts overtook him.

'Would the British really leave India?' he asked himself, echoing Chachi's concern. 'And if they did, what would happen after they left?' Especially after Karan's visit, he felt discomfort at the thought that his own sentiments might not be very nationalistic. 'Are we ready to govern ourselves?' he wondered. As a legal man his views tended to be moderate and he believed in evolutionary change. All forms of direct action were unpleasant to him. Would Indians be able to maintain the magnificent British institutions of law and order? For the past hundred years, people had got used to the peace brought by the British Raj. And peace was one of those things that people only noticed when it was absent. Could the Indians hold it together? We have competent people, but they are forever fighting with one another: Hindu against Muslim; Jat against Bhangi, the landed against the landless. The spectre of India breaking up haunted Bauji. Would the subcontinent, left to its own devices, he wondered, degenerate into narrow parochialisms? Again he was assailed by the guilt that many Indian conservatives felt. He wanted the English to leave, but he wanted their institutions to stay. He wanted a gradual transfer of power.

The servant brought in his polished shoes and helped him put them on. Then he assisted him with his waistcoat. It was time to put on the turban, an important moment, so all political thoughts were suspended. He wore his turban in a particular fashion which he had acquired as a youth from a stylish judge whom he admired when he first set up his practice in Lyallpur. He made one, two and then three turns around his head with the starched white cloth. And it was done. The servant offered him a silk handkerchief and his gold watch. He glanced at the mirror as he was leaving and was pleased with what he saw, especially by the trim moustache. He felt that he looked like a man of substance, which reflected his own view of himself. He smiled at this thought and marched off briskly to his office rooms on the ground floor.

His chambers were normally airy and bright. The white-washed walls shone as the brilliant sunshine streamed in through the open window, which the servant opened daily when he came to dust in the morning. In the summers, especially before the monsoon, they became too bright; so a straw mat of khus-khus grass was thrown across the window which cut the glare; periodically, cold water poured over the mat kept the room cool. The white fan on the ceiling circulated the cool air.

To Bauji's relief, his Munshi was not present, and so there wasn't any bad news to start the day. The energetic Munshi delighted in showing him the ledgers first, and insisted on depressing him with a detailed account of all the debts which had not been paid. He never volunteered information on the other side—the income which had been received from numerous urban and rural properties.

On an impulse, he pushed aside the straw curtain and looked out of the window. The brightness hurt his eyes at first. As they got accustomed to it he felt the same luminous quiet in the air caused by the blazing midday sun.

He turned around, and for an instant luxuriated in the contrasting sensation produced by the cool and dark room. He walked over to his desk. Before sitting down, he gently felt the minute carving on the dark Burma teak chair. It had a woven cane bottom, which had been periodically restrung. He had got the chair twenty years ago when he had been a 'promising young lawyer', much talked about in the courts and in the club, because of two sensational murder cases that he had won in quick succession. The chair had been ordered from the fees of the first case. Every evening he had begun to visit the club to play tennis and bridge, and to talk. He used to enjoy being made much of, and felt he was one of the fortunate people alive.

While he was no longer a 'promising young man', he was aware of his considerable achievements and public successes. He continued to be highly respected in the town and in his profession. He felt that he was much freer from the vanity, animosity and envy of his younger days. His bodily and mental powers, though, were somewhat diminished. His instincts especially were not as sharp as they used to be. But he certainly was not lacking in manly drives—in lustful passion, in moral indignation, in ambition and assertiveness. However, he suffered less and less from the tyranny of these drives. There were exceptions, of course, such as during Karan's visit.

The first awareness of his loss in youthful vitality had been accompanied by a hurt to his narcissistic pride—especially when he compared himself to Karan. But that feeling was mostly behind him, although it could flare up on occasion when Karan came to visit. He had begun to deal with his age and his mortality. With the recognition of his own vulnerability had emerged a new empathy and compassion. The suffering of others had started to have a new meaning.

He sat down to read the daily papers that were meticulously folded on his desk. After three-quarters-of-an-hour his reading was interrupted by the smell of onions and garlic frying in the kitchen upstairs. Soon the aroma of a dozen spices joined in, and he knew that the cook was putting the finishing touches to the roasted aubergine that Bhabo had ordered last night. He felt hungry.

He liked to eat and feed his family well. That is why he personally selected fresh vegetables on the way back from his morning
walk to the Company Bagh. Unfortunately, the cooking left much
to be desired. Perhaps because there were too many in the house—
at any time there were twenty to thirty mouths to feed, including
servants, relatives and friends. Any visitor to Lyallpur from his
village felt it his right to stop at his house for a meal before returning
to the village. Sometimes he felt that Bhabo had extra food cooked
in order to serve leftovers to the poor. He didn't mind feeding the
poor, but why must they eat the same food as the rest of the family?

To the earlier smells was now added the aroma of baked rotis,
fresh out of the tandoor. And he knew lunch was ready. Fortunately, when it came to bread, there was no compromise because it
was made by Bhua. Twenty years ago an impoverished widow
from a 'decent family' in his village had arrived at his doorstep. He
had given her shelter temporarily; but she had shown such skill in
making rotis that she had stayed on. She had built a magnificent
four-feet-tall tandoor out of baked clay. And she personally went to
the bazaar to select the charcoal which was burned inside, and the
whole wheat flour which she kneaded into dough. She began to
address Bauji as 'younger brother' and she had become a member
of the family.

He got up and walked towards the dining room. At Big Uncle's
insistence a few years ago, they had converted one of the east rooms
into a dining room, but he hadn't liked the idea. The food always
got cold by the time it reached them from the kitchen. It was a new
fashionable idea amongst their class, which they had learned from
the English. Since most of Big Uncle's college friends ate in a dining
room, they too had to eat in one. He much preferred eating in or
near the kitchen. In the winters, they still ate in the kitchen, where
it was nice and warm.

About twenty famished people were already assembled eagerly
waiting for their brass thalis to be filled with food when he reached
the dining room. Apart from the immediate family, there were
nephews, grandsons, aunts, friends of nephews, friends of friends,
and a few others whose faces he did not recognize. But he hoped
someone did. It became quiet as soon as he entered. The older people
from the village had not joined in, as they felt uncomfortable sitting
at a table; they ate near the kitchen on a straw mat. The meal started
quietly and proceeded uneventfully. Just as he was about to remark
on the delicate quality of the lentils, Bhabo suddenly burst out, 'I am

getting tired of your clients knocking down the door in the middle of the night when all godly people are fast asleep. The night before last we had a dozen from Akalgarh. We had to cook for them at midnight and prepare their beds. Is this some kind of inn? And would you believe it, one of them even complained about the salt in the food!'

Since Bauji was in no mood to spoil his lunch over a subject they had discussed for the past twenty years, he merely smiled and concentrated on the aubergine. As the silence was uncomfortable, the others also smiled. But he felt contrite; he sympathized with poor Bhabo's problem. It had become customary for a successful lawyer to feed and house his out-of-town clients. The lawyer more than made up for his trouble through his fees. It had probably started because there were no inns or hotels in Lyallpur. Even if there had been, rural clients were unwilling to stay at impersonal places. But this situation was getting out of hand because a client didn't come alone; he sometimes brought half the village along, and they often stayed for weeks. The villagers were quite happy to enjoy the sights of the city free of cost, and were more than willing to offer false testimony in return. Bauji wanted to end this practice at his house, but he did not know how to do it. He was willing to lose the business, but he didn't want his actions to reflect a lack of hospitality in the eyes of the world. Big Uncle, who sometimes returned late at night, would tell everyone the next morning how many beds he had found outside each lawyer's house in the neighbourhood. It had become a status symbol and the number of charpais reflected a lawyer's prosperity and standing.

Bauji's eyes fell on his fat and bald nephew, Megh Nath, who was sitting diagonally across to his left, and who happened to belch at that moment. Bauji scowled. But the thick-skinned Megh Nath did not take notice and continued eating. Belching was traditionally a mark of appreciation of the food, and no one thought anything of it, except the younger children who glanced at each other and tittered. When they saw Bauji's disapproving look, their smiles quickly faded. Bauji intensely disliked his greedy nephew.

'I hear you are becoming a rich man, Megh Nath,' said Bauji. There was a rumour that his nephew had recently multiplied his land holdings by driving out peasant proprietors, and replacing them with tenants. The rumour had gained credence because he had invested his ill-gotten gains in a grain shop in the Lyallpur wholesale market.

'It is God's will, heh... heh... heh. I merely fulfil my dharma. I give all I earn back to God.' Megh Nath was also famous for his donations to temples.

'Was it God's wish that you should bribe the Sessions Judge last week?' asked Bauji.

'What bribe?' asked Megh Nath looking sweetly innocent.

'I was told that the Sessions Judge received a hundred oranges last Thursday.'

'Oh, it was merely a small goodwill gesture from my orchards in Rampur,' said Megh Nath unctuously.

'Ah... I see. It was merely coincidental that your case was to be heard the next day.'

Megh Nath smiled sanctimoniously.

'But your orchard does not grow oranges, Megh Nath. Those oranges were bought in the wholesale market.'

'Heh... heh... heh. How can a judge tell where an orange comes from? It is all God's creation.'

'This judge apparently can tell the difference. And it seems he does not approve of bribes either. So you do have a problem, nephew,' said Bauji, smiling sardonically at his nephew. He was trying hard to control his temper. He saw a hint of worry on his crooked nephew's imperturbable brow, and he was pleased.

'By the way, what is your case all about?'

'Oh the usual tenancy troubles, Bauji. As a matter of fact I wanted to take your advice.' Megh Nath was relieved that the subject had changed from oranges. Everyone knew that he only visited Bauji's house when he was looking for free legal advice.

'Does it by any chance concern a certain widow named Bibi Pritam Kaur, dear nephew?'

For the first time Megh Nath's face changed colour. After a short pause, he asked, 'How did you know, Bauji?'

'She happens to be my client, nephew.' Bauji smiled.

'Disgraceful!' interrupted Bhabo. 'Bauji, how can you side against your own flesh and blood? And against such a god-fearing, religious man like Megh Nath, who does puja daily, who visits all the temples, who bathes in the Ganges every year. It's not right.'

'It so happens that our pious nephew has fabricated evidence and collected false witnesses for the purpose of depriving this widow of her sole means of livelihood.'

'I still think it is wrong to go against your own in public, whatever the case,' said Bhabo. 'Now enough of these matters.

Enjoy your food, and let the others do the same.' From Bauji her eyes turned to Megh Nath. 'You are not eating properly, nephew. What can I pass you? We seem to be forgetting how to treat a guest in this house. And tell us about your last pilgrimage.'

As his nephew launched on a pious and long-winded account of his latest religious pilgrimage, Bauji realized that neither his sarcasm nor the exposure of his evil ways was likely to have any effect on his two-faced relative. Megh Nath had a powerful following among the conservative members of the family, and especially those who still lived in the village. In their eyes, Megh Nath was like a god who could do no wrong. They talked incessantly about him: how he woke up before dawn, bathed with cold water both in the summer and the winter, and sat down to puja for two hours; how he was a strict vegetarian, and ate only one meal a day; how he spent months on pilgrimages; how he was constantly donating money to temples. He was held up to be a model and admired by many, including Bhabo.

For this reason Bauji knew that he had a delicate problem on his hands. The conservative side of the family would certainly condemn him, if he publicly defended the widow in court against his own nephew. They would regard it as a betrayal. Yet Bauji was determined not to let this insincere man get away. He would have to be careful with his family. And the opinion and the esteem of his family mattered to Bauji. As he was a successful man, Bauji too could count on the support of many family members whom he had fed and looked after all these years. As a man of the world he had also learned to manipulate opinion in his favour. Bauji knew that he had a formidable adversary, and he never underestimated an opponent.

Bauji felt disgusted with a religion that could not only condone but praise evil men like Megh Nath, who brought incalculable suffering to poor vulnerable widows. What kind of religion was it, he questioned, that not only accepted the wicked gains of such men, but held them up as models of social behaviour? It was people like Megh Nath and their supporters, who gave a bad name to all Indians in the eyes of the English. It was no wonder that English magistrates distrusted the testimony of all Indian witnesses. When every second witness was willing to give false testimony without any moral compunction, the English were not wrong in believing that Indians were liars. Honesty was probably a less important virtue to a Hindu than loyalty and piety, he concluded.

After lunch Bauji returned to his study for a nap. He lay down on the white diwan and his mind wandered again to Tara. Despite Megh Nath, the meal had revived his spirits and he felt generous and kindly towards the world. He had by now forgiven Tara her display with Karan in the morning. He felt it was a passing fancy which Karan aroused in all women, who would always fall for him like ripe mangoes. Yes, he liked his daughter. She had zest. He enjoyed her company more than any of his children. She was the only one he could talk to, and he would be sad to lose her.

He recalled the hot June day two years ago, when Tara had returned home from Lahore and had calmly announced that she was going to work. While sipping a glass of cold fresh lime, she had matter-of-factly recounted how she had got the job of a school teacher in Lyallpur.

After Tara had finished school, he had agreed to let her go to Lahore to attend college. After completing her BA, she had trained to be a teacher; then one day she had quietly gone to the Department of Education in Lahore and applied for a job. They had offered her one in a distant village. Tara had known that it would be a battle to persuade her family to be permitted to work. Women teachers were still a novelty: the few that were there tended to come from lower caste converts to Christianity 'who needed the money'. Thus to work outside her home town was out of the question. With great difficulty she had persuaded the Department to let her have a post in Lyallpur instead. The Department at first was reluctant to agree, since she had a mediocre academic record, but she seemed to have a strong will which counted in her favour. Thus she had arrived in Lyallpur with a job and had immediately created a sensation.

'Tara is going to work, Tara is going to work,' the whole town had whispered. Even Bauji, who was more progressive than the others, had found this hard to stomach. He had regarded the education of his daughters as a respectable and leisurely way for them to kill time before they got married. That education also increased their prospects in the marriage market was not lost on him.

In any case, Tara's demand was the subject of heated discussion in the family for weeks. Chachi disapproved. Big Uncle sided with Tara and put up a spirited defence on her behalf, but his vote did not count for much. Bhabo, as expected, had put up the biggest fight. She had vehemently protested, 'Can't we feed her? My friends keep asking. Why does she have to work?'

'You obviously have the wrong kind of friends,' he had replied.

'Not just my friends. Your side of the family keeps needling me too,' moaned Bhabo.

'They are all living in the Dark Ages, woman. They are trapped in the old ideas of the village. We are now living in a modern town and it is 1942,' he had retorted.

Chachi had supported Bhabo, but Karan had come out strongly in favour of Tara, and he counted for a great deal with Bauji. Bhabo had finally given in, and his favourite daughter had gone to work. A few months later, Tara wanted her own room, and to her surprise she got it easily. Tara furnished her room with much care. She always kept flowers in a vase, and often invited her friends there for tea. He used to enjoy the sight of her pretty friends around the house.

With that recollection, he calmly slid off to sleep.

5

The British government reacted quickly. A few hours after Gandhi called for the English to 'Quit India', all the members of the Congress Working Committee were arrested in Bombay. They were bundled into a special train at five a.m. the next day for the journey to prison. The arrest of the Congress leaders set off a political reaction in towns and cities across the sub-continent. And Lyallpur was one such town. As the news arrived of Gandhi's arrest, the students of the Government College burned the Income Tax office, much to the delight of the tax payers, including Bauji. From their terrace, Bauji's family could see the smoke coming out of the Lal Kothi, the railway accounts office. For a brief period they saw flames in the clock tower, but the fire brigade came quickly and put it out. The family stood on the roof counting the columns of smoke. There was much excitement throughout the day. Big Uncle returned home on his bicycle in the afternoon and reported that the mill workers were on strike, lamp posts had been uprooted in Kacheri Bazaar, and there were hundreds of police in the other bazaars. He had seen Karan leading a procession towards the Company Bagh; this news upset everyone, especially Tara.

Rumours flew about the house, many of them untrue: for example, that the railway bridge, which was the crucial link to the city, had been blown up. In the evening Big Uncle went out again, and he was arrested for breaking curfew. But fortunately he was released immediately through Bauji's intercession. The entire family were enthused by the demonstrations of patriotic fervour; Bauji was shocked by the destruction of property. He warned of harsh British repression, which came the very next day. Police fired on unarmed crowds, there were mass arrests, and lathi charges broke up demonstrations. Official reports in Lyallpur said that eleven people died, forty were severely wounded. According to the people the count was at least three times bigger. Four Sikh students were killed while trying to raise the national flag over their college building. Karan miraculously escaped arrest, but the family dhobi was shot with his son, as they were passing the railway crossing on a bullock cart. The police sentry asked them to halt, but the washerman did not understand and he got scared; both he and his son ran and they were gunned down; the bullocks also died. At this news the entire family was thrown into a depression.

There were long discussions at home in which Bauji often found himself isolated. He argued that the government reaction was to be expected since this rebellion was a grave threat to the Raj. It was wrong timing on Gandhi's part to embarrass the British when the Japanese were poised to strike against eastern India. He knew that civil disobedience could play havoc with the defence of India and loathed the thought of a Japanese conquest. He felt deeply the misery of those who had come under Nazi, Fascist or Japanese domination.

'For pity's sake, Dewan Chand,' said Chachi one evening, 'the Quit India Movement is the outcome of British stubbornness. We were all frustrated and we needed this symbolic act of defiance.'

'Hardly symbolic, Chachi?' said Bauji.

'Gandhi made it clear from the beginning that the Quit India Movement would be non-violent,' said Karan.

'How could it be, Karan?' said Bauji.

'It is the fault of English,' said Tara. 'It is they who put Gandhi in jail and there was no one to control the crowds afterwards.'

The disturbances lasted for several weeks. At the end about a thousand people lost their lives throughout the country; over sixty thousand were arrested. However, calm was restored quickly in Lyallpur. Bauji had been deeply distressed by the violence but he was secretly pleased that at least the DC's party had been cancelled because of the trouble. He wouldn't have to tiresomely defend himself before Chachi, Karan and the others. Bhabo was also happy. Because of the curfew there was peace in the house from unwelcome callers and Bauji's clients.

After it was all over, Bauji matter-of-factly asked Big Uncle one day, 'Tell me son, why did you have to go out in the middle of the curfew? Remember that evening when you were arrested?'

'I went to the bazaar to get a haircut,' replied Big Uncle.

'Haircut?' Bauji could not believe his ears.

'I needed a haircut.'

Bauji tried to control his temper. 'In the middle of a curfew, he needed a .aircut.'

Big Uncle nodded. Tara giggled.

'What is wrong with our family barber? He comes every day. Why do *you* have to go to the bazaar?' asked Bauji.

'He cuts hair too closely, and he doesn't know how to make a puff. It's the fashion these days,' said Big Uncle.

There was an uneasy pause. Bauji tried to hold himself but he did not succeed. 'Bhabo!' he roared, 'This is not my son. He must have got exchanged in the hospital.'

A week later, while the family was having lunch, a telegram came from the ashram saying that Tara's marriage proposal had been accepted. There was immediate excitement, and everyone started to talk of Tara's forthcoming marriage. Bauji felt relieved but Bhabo was not.

'We shall finally have spirituality in this house,' Bauji said jovially. 'Now I shall get someone to tell me about this meditation business.'

'You don't need a son-in-law for that. Go and get initiated by the guru,' said Bhaboji.

The conversation was suddenly interrupted by a chorus of school boys at the gate. They were reading aloud the inscription on the newly installed letterbox outside: 'Varma Billa, Dewan Chand Barma, BA, LL B, Advocate, Punjab High Court, Lahore, Punjab.' Everyone smiled, except Bauji, who was visibly angry at his name being abused by every street urchin who wanted to test his command of the English language.

The letterbox had been Big Uncle's brainchild. Thinking it the fashionable thing to do, Big Uncle had got a letterbox made by the carpenter and inscribed by a sign painter. Unfortunately the sign painter had written 'Billa' instead of 'Villa', and 'Barma' instead of 'Varma'. Big Uncle had not bothered to have the mistake corrected, and hung it up on the main gate. Thus Bauji's home had joined the small fashionable group of Lyallpur houses that had a letterbox with an English name. There were many admiring 'oohs' and 'aahs' from the younger set, in whose eyes Big Uncle was a big hero. Everyone was encouraged to write letters to each other to 'try out' the letterbox. A number of 'trial letters' were written in fact. But the mailman had to be repeatedly instructed to put the letters in the mail box, rather then delivering them personally. He was not too happy about the box, since he stood to lose a glass of buttermilk which he received when he delivered the mail personally.

No one, however, anticipated the nuisance that this harmless idea of Big Uncle's would create, as every school boy who passed by felt compelled to practice his newly learned skill loud enough to warm the heart of any fourth class school master. Bauji contained his anger, and calmly told Big Uncle that if he did not remove the letterbox in the next hour, he would receive a sharply diminished monthly allowance. He again reminded his son that he was more than convinced that the nurse must have accidentally switched him at the hospital when he was born.

Bauji eventually won over Bhabo's agreement to the marriage. He consoled her, 'You should be happy Bhabo, Tara won't have to work any more.' He knew this would make an impression, because Tara's working continued to be a liability in the eyes of Bhabo's social set. Bhabo's friends never failed to chide her about it.

A couple of days later Bauji sent a confirmation in the traditional form to the bridegroom's family. It consisted of trays of fruit and dry fruit—almonds, cashew nuts, raisins, dates, sweet lime, apples, bananas and pomegranate.

To everyone's surprise Bauji received a letter from Seva Ram informing him that he would be stopping in Lyallpur for a day on an inspection tour of the canal. He wrote that he would be accompanied by his English boss and an overseer, and he would stay at the Canal Rest House of the Irrigation Department. The news created a sensation in the house not only because it was somewhat irregular for a future son-in-law to visit like this, but also because everyone wanted to meet Seva Ram and see what he was like. Chachi insisted that she be invited 'to meet the boy'. There was also the possibility that Seva Ram might bring the English boss, and they wondered how they were to treat him. Big Uncle said that they should leave the Englishman to him and he had already planned the English clothes he would wear for the occasion and what he would talk about. Karan thought it unpatriotic to play host to an Englishman in the midst of the Quit India Movement. Bauji put these speculations to rest, saying that it was highly unlikely that an Englishman would visit the Indian section of town during these troubled times. He promptly replied to Seva Ram inviting him to stay at Kacheri Bazaar and bring his colleagues to tea.

In all the excitement no one bothered about Tara. She was nervous and afraid at the prospect of seeing her future husband. Bhabo made it clear to her that it would be inappropriate for her to meet him, let alone talk to him. She would have to be content with seeing him from the upstairs terrace. Bhabo was already upset by the strange way the marriage was being arranged and she did not want a scandal if it got known that her daughter had been seen with the boy before marriage. She could not understand why the boy's parents were not in the picture.

On the day Seva Ram was expected, Big Uncle brought advance information to Kacheri Bazaar that the Irrigation Department party had been seen going towards the canal headworks. Big Uncle made it his business to know what was happening in town. He had been loafing around the Clock Tower on his bicycle and one of the shop-keepers had casually mentioned that the Englishman's car was noticed speeding in the direction of the canal. Thus everyone was ready when the Irrigation party arrived. Tea had been elaborately laid out and Bauji, Chachi, Bhabo were dressed and waiting. Even though it was the hot season, Bhabo and Chachi had worn silk. Big Uncle had stationed himself at the gate and he let the visitors in.

A six-foot Englishman entered, followed by a very short Seva Ram and the Overseer. All three men wore sola topees which they took off as soon as they came in.

'Well, well! Come in, come in,' said Chachi.

'Welcome!' said Bauji, getting up and going towards them. 'Do sit down.'

As they sat down they were offered tea. But they were hot and thirsty and preferred cold drinks instead. Seva Ram in his easy going way tried to put everyone at ease. He asked Bauji about Lyallpur. He made small talk with Big Uncle. But everyone (except Seva Ram) was clearly uneasy. The Englishman was not stiff but he was unused to such a social situation. He thought everyone was staring at him. Bauji's family wanted to please him but this only added to his discomfort.

'Did you have a strenuous day?' asked Chachi.

'Not at all,' replied Seva Ram with an engaging smile. 'As a matter of fact it was one of our easier days.' He looked warmly at the Englishman and then at the Overseer, as he tried to include them in the conversation.

'Don't trust a word he says. He works like a horse,' said the Englishman.

Seva Ram again smiled and Bauji noticed that it was a smile of great sweetness. It was not a flashing or brilliant smile, but a smile he remembered from the ashram which lit his face with an inner light. Seva Ram seemed about to speak but he did not say anything for a long time and the others soon began to find the silence awkward. He looked vacantly in the air, his face grave and intent. They kept waiting, curious to know what it was all about. When he began to speak it was as though he were continuing the conversation without being aware of the long silence.

'Guruji sends his regards to you. He was touched that you came all the way to the ashram.'

'Yes, I too was moved by the atmosphere of the ashram and his message. You will of course stay here with us, won't you?'

'No, I think I shall stay at the Canal Rest House. It's quite comfortable and I am here on work after all.' Seva Ram turned his head and looked at his two colleagues without embarrassment, but with an expression in his eyes that was at once scrutinizing and amused.

By now Big Uncle was busy telling jokes to the Englishman, who roared with laughter. The atmosphere thawed. Seva Ram, realizing that Bhabo did not speak English, addressed her in Punjabi. He also brought the Overseer into the conversation. Bhabo asked the Overseer about his family, and she looked up occasionally to see if Tara was watching from above. Seva Ram did not expect to meet Tara. He was also too shy to ask for her. Everyone seemed to slowly relax.

Chachi was struck by the fact that Seva Ram treated his superior and his junior in exactly the same way. He was not excessively deferential to his boss nor haughty or off-hand with his subordinate. He looked them both in the eye in the same sincere way and tried to make them feel equally comfortable. Later, when the visitors had gone Chachi mentioned this to the family. Bauji and the others agreed with her that this was a most remarkable quality. Most Indians, they felt, were very conscious of position and power and did not behave normally either with people above or below them. Seva Ram was indeed exceptional.

Bauji turned to Seva Ram and asked him about a dilemma that he had been grappling with ever since his meeting with the guru.

'If it turns out that what the guru says is true—that there is a life of the spirit,' said Bauji, 'then not to participate in it is clearly wrong. But if it turns out not to be true, then I certainly wouldn't want to live in this world like a passenger. You see, an old man like me doesn't have much time left in the world. Whatever little bit I have, I want to savour it. I like being involved. I like this world with all its imperfections. I don't want to give it up.'

'Bauji,' replied Seva Ram with a smile, 'it is a matter of choice. If there is a world of spirit and you do not participate in it, you will have truly lost something. If, on the other hand, there is none, and you remain ignorant of it, then you haven't lost anything. The third possibility is that if you work hard, meditate and try to attain the Infinite and there turns out to be none, then too you haven't lost anything except your effort. Finally, if there is a spiritual world and you attain it through meditation, then you have obviously won.

'I believe you have no choice,' concluded Seva Ram, 'but to try. You have nothing to lose and everything to gain.'

Seva Ram had spoken all this lightly, almost gaily, as if to suggest to the others that this was small talk, of little consequence. Chachi became conscious of the melodiousness of his voice as he spoke.

Bauji thought that his argument was very persuasive. But later on reflection he couldn't bring himself to agree. He felt strongly that he had everything to lose by making the spiritual effort. He loved this life too dearly to risk losing it—even to a more perfect world. If opting for the spiritual world meant giving up this one, or living in it like a passenger, then he might as well choose the imperfect one.

After the visitors had gone, Tara came rushing down with her sisters.

'But he is so short,' moaned Tara.

'In front of the Englishman he looked like a pygmy,' said Big Uncle with a laugh.

'He eats so little, no wonder,' said Bhabo. 'He hardly touched anything.'

'What do you think of him, Chachi?'

'Of course, he's attractive. There's something modest and friendly and gentle in him that is very appealing. He's got a lot of self-possession for so young a man. He isn't quite like any of the other boys I've met.'

'Well, you can marry him then. I don't like him,' said Tara and she ran upstairs with tears in her eyes.

6

Bhabo's day started early. She woke up at dawn, bathed and churned butter from milk. As she churned, she sang devotional songs by the Rajput princess, Mira. These poems passionately recounted Mira's love affair with her god and lover, Krishna. After she finished churning butter, she got dressed in a white cotton sari and went off to the temple.

Like most Hindus, Bhabo believed that God was present in all temples. So she alternated between the gurdwara of the Sikhs, which was situated in Kacheri Bazaar, diagonally opposite their house, the Shiva temple of the orthodox Hindus, and the prayer hall of the reformist Arya Samaj. Big Uncle once asked Bhabo not to go to all the temples but to choose one and visit it regularly. She innocently replied that she wanted to make sure that at least one god would listen to her.

Bhabo's choice of temple on a particular day often depended on whom she expected to meet, for her social life frequently started at the temple. She would often meet a friend and go off with her. Her social life consisted of consoling her friends when there was a death in the family or congratulating them on engagements, marriages and births. Since she did not discriminate between the rich and the poor or the powerful and the humble, she was welcome everywhere. Virtually every day there was either a birth, a death, an engagement or a marriage in her wide circle of friends, and so she always had somewhere to go. In the case of a death, the mourning lasted for thirteen days, and loyal friends were expected to visit daily. Thus her problem was to choose where to go.

Today, however, her mind was troubled. She was uneasy about her daughter's forthcoming marriage. She was concerned that the boy's side had not come to see Tara. Nor had her family barber gone to find out about the boy's family background. Everything was most irregular, and she wanted to avoid her friends and their uncomfortable questions relating to the marriage. She decided to go to the Sikh gurdwara near the house, thinking that she would be least likely to meet her friends there. But she miscalculated. All her friends, in their starched white cotton saris, were there this morning, almost as if they had read her mind.

'Bhabo, your daughter is going to be married and you don't even know the family? Is your family barber asleep?' Her friends voiced her worries.

Bhabo told them about the guru, Bauji's journey to the ashram, and Seva Ram's visit to Lyallpur.

Bhabo patiently explained that the guru meant a great deal to the boy, even more than his own family.

'If it was *my* daughter, I would have personally gone to see the family.'

'I don't understand where your Bauji finds these boys. As for us, my dear, we have always gone in for landowning families when it comes to finding matches for our daughters,' said another with a superior air.

'What can you expect, sister: who will marry a girl who has been working? We warned you two years ago when your daughter started going out.'

'Your family may be professionals, Bhabo, but you shouldn't throw away our good traditions.'

Bhabo returned home thoroughly humiliated. The family discovered her distress when she did not come down from her room at noon. For years Bhabo had faithfully adhered to a routine: between noon and one she would serve buttermilk and thick wheat rotis to anyone who came by the house. Consequently, a stream of poor people regularly came to receive her charity.

Some were holy men, others performed some service in the house, a few were just beggars, and there were others who did not want to pass up the free food. Since Bhabo had never missed this ritual, and had always made it a point to return home by noon, everyone was concerned when the poor started arriving and there was no Bhabo. To the servant who knocked on her door, she gruffly replied that she did not want to be disturbed and asked him to take over her noontime duties.

When she did not come down for lunch either, the situation became alarming. An air of crisis permeated the house. Bauji, in a rare gesture, went up to talk to her. Soon both of them came down, Bhabo walking behind him, drying the tears from her reddened eyes. She had relented because Bauji had promised to send the family barber to the boy's parents' home to formally request the hand of their son for her daughter. She smiled as she ate a mango cut by Bauji's hands.

Bhabo was in good humour by the time the two Khanna sisters dropped in for their daily visit. The two sisters were married to the Khanna brothers, both accomplished lawyers from Lahore. The ladies always looked fresh and smart, dressed in white saris of Manchester Muslin No. 26. They came punctually at three every-day, had tea with Bhabo, gossiped and left promptly at four before the menfolk returned from the Courts.

The Khanna ladies enthusiastically supported Bauji's efforts to find a professional husband for Tara, and Bhabo felt relieved. Since they had grown up in Lahore, the Khanna ladies brought modern and enlightened ideas to the provincial mind of Lyallpur. Among Bhabo's friends, they were the first to install a sink for washing hands. This was a novel and clever idea which was the talk of the house for days. They also heated their water in an electric heater, which impressed Bauji because it was clean. Bhabo's children admired them because they were modern and systematic: they budgeted their expenses, observed regular hours, ate at a dining table, and lived in separate houses and not in a joint family as Bauji's family did.

'Sister,' said the elder one to Bhabo, 'What is Bauji's secret in finding such a good match for his daughter? Imagine, an irrigation engineer for Tara! Tell us, sister, for we too have daughters to marry off.'

Bhabo smiled and replied honestly that she did not know. She then naively recounted her humiliating experience with her friends in the morning.

After the Khanna ladies left, Bhabo invited Tara to visit her 'treasure room'. It was an unexpected honour since no one was allowed to enter this tiny room on the first floor, which was situated next to the 'cotton carpet room'. In the narrow, dark, cool room Tara saw neatly stacked rows of silk saris, embroidered linen, silver utensils and velvet covered boxes filled with gold jewellery.

'This is part of your dowry, my child. I have been collecting it for years,' Bhabo whispered conspiratorially.

Tara was left breathless. She had tears in her eyes. But she was diverted by the sight of a hundred rupee note which was torn in shreds on the floor. Bhabo picked it up and laughed.

'The mouse must have eaten it,' she said. Tara smiled uneasily for she knew that it was a lot of money.

'Don't tell anyone,' she said. 'Your Bauji will be angry if he finds out.'

Tara nodded.

Tara kept her promise, but Bhabo could not contain herself and related the fate of the hundred rupees that same night to everyone's discomfort. At that time it was indeed a great deal of money to lose to a mouse. Bauji did not say anything, but the atmosphere became tense.

'Imagine, that is more than the cook's wages for a whole year!' groaned daughter number two.

'How could you let it happen?' said daughter number three incredulously.

Big Uncle came to Bhabo's rescue and diverted everyone with a hysterical account of Megh Nath's wife's brother's marriage, from where he had just returned. Big Uncle had attended the wedding as the representative of Bauji's family. At the mention of his contemptible nephew's name, Bauji suddenly became attentive. It turned out that Megh Nath had selected a temple for the *sehrabandhi* ceremony rather than his house. 'Probably to save money,' interjected Bauji. While the crown of flowers and gold thread was being solemnly tied onto the groom's forehead, the priest of the temple suddenly let out a shriek when he noticed that the groom was wearing sandals. In the confusion of the ceremony the poor groom had apparently forgotten to take off his sandals. He had thus defiled the temple according to the enraged priest. Any amount of apologies would not quiet him. The indignant brahmin insisted on an outrageous fine of two thousand rupees in order to purify the temple. After prolonged negotiations the matter was finally settled. But Megh Nath's pocket was lighter by five hundred and one rupees, they were late by two-and-a-half hours, and Bauji's entire family, including Bhabo, had a big laugh.

A few days later the family barber set out on his delicate mission after being thoroughly but contrarily briefed by both Bauji and Bhabo. Before entering the boy's home, the barber went to the bazaar in Pindi, and he met members of his caste to circumspectly enquire about the boy's family and also to alert the boy's family to his mission. Later that evening, after he had prepared the ground for his visit, he went to Seva Ram's father's modest house, where he was received with cold courtesy. The groom's family were naturally cut up because they had been denied any part in the engagement by their rebellious son. It was politely suggested that the barber should go to the guru. But the barber was clever, and he slowly won over the parents-to-be with tact and praise. They were simple-hearted people, and they generously offered their hospitality to the barber. He ate heartily and slept comfortably in the future groom's uncle's room, which was especially prepared for him. The next morning, they served him a rich breakfast of fried puris, curried vegetables, yogurt, halwah and buttermilk and fruits. He reciprocated by delicately singing the praises of the bride-to-be before the future mother-in-law. He showed her the bride's photograph and invited her to visit Lyallpur to see the bride. The boy's parents were flattered by the proposal, and gave their unreserved consent. They also thanked the barber and praised him profusely.

When he returned to Lyallpur, the barber related the result of his mission with much self-importance. Not receiving his due attention from Bauji, he went to talk to Bhabo and tried to change her mind against the match. His arguments related to the economic and social status of the boy's family. He claimed they were virtually impoverished landowners compared to Bauji.

'Look at you,' he told Bhabo, 'here you are in a big house, with horses and servants. Look at them, so poor they couldn't even feed me in the manner appropriate to such an occasion.'

Bhabo was naturally up in arms. But Bauji quickly attacked the source of this mischief. He called in the barber and vigorously cross-examined him in Bhabo's presence. Using his legal skills he got the barber to finally admit that it was a good match, because Tara would be marrying a boy with excellent prospects in life, which was more important than the number of servants and horses his family owned. The barber volunteered that the boy's family were good people even though they were not rich. Bhabo was finally appeased.

Although Bhabo was reconciled, Tara was not. After the barber left and the others went upstairs, she said to Bauji, 'I won't marry him.' She tried to appear calm and decisive, but the boldness of the statement surprised her as well. Her dark eyes were stormy, wilful and anxious.

Bauji could tackle Bhabo and the barber, but Tara, he knew, would be a different matter. He feigned interest in the hookah's smoke in the dark space in front of his nose. The shadowed shrubs in the courtyard lay awake in the warm lifeless air. From outside the gate came the hoot of an owl. The summer sky was clear and the stars looked inert in the sultry atmosphere. He was vexed at having to conduct negotiations with his own daughter.

'What is the matter?' he asked gently.

'I won't marry him,' she repeated.

'Why?' he asked.

'He is short, he isn't good looking, and I don't like him.'

'First impressions are often wrong. Besides you haven't talked to him.'

'No, first impressions are always right,' she said.

He had the uncomfortable sensation of finding himself in a conversation not to his liking. He did not want to employ the verbal dexterity and guile, which he used in dealing with outsiders. He had always been open and affectionate with his favourite daughter. But tonight he found it tiresome to try to persuade her as well. There was a time, he thought with regret, when he could say anything that came into his mind. And everyone accepted his words and behaviour unquestioningly. Children were expected to be obedient and respectful, and did not oppose their parents blatantly. It was a matter of good breeding. But Tara had always been independent and ever since she went to college the problem had become more serious. Bhabo had of course warned him. She had constantly been opposed too much schooling for the girls. It was he who had stubbornly persisted in educating his daughters, especially in the English language. He now looked at Tara's face, and he remembered that he liked her precisely because she did not submit easily. Her sisters, in contrast, were quick to compromise and to comply. Bhabo had felt that he over-valued this characteristic in Tara. Ironically, at this moment he sought precisely the opposite virtue—obedience and submission.

'There is much more to marriage, young lady,' he said. 'He is a good boy, and he will take good care of you.'

'Why can't I marry someone I know?'

'Child, we usually have to marry someone we do not know. Look at Bhabo and me: we did not know each other; look at your older brother; look at all our relatives and friends. It has always been that way.'

'All those marriages haven't been so wonderful, have they? None of you are good companions. You hardly ever speak to Bhabo.'

The girl was going too far, thought Bauji. No one else would have dared to speak to him like this. What position was she in to judge the marriages of those older than her? But he did not want to get into that.

'Young lady, don't you worry about our marriage. We have had four children who are healthy, and we are prosperous. Thank you.'

'But how much better would it have been if you and Bhabo had grown up together, known each other and been friends before marriage,' argued Tara.

'Who were you thinking of marrying?' asked Bauji suddenly.

'No one especially,' replied Tara reticently.

'Come, come, you must have someone in mind,' persisted Bauji.

'Why can't I marry someone I know?' she said more hesitantly.

'Like whom?' asked Bauji.

'Like Karan,' she whispered.

Bauji raised his head and looked steadily into his daughter's eyes.

'Don't look at me in that way, Bauji. Don't look at me. I shall cry if you do.'

'But he is your brother,' said Bauji.

'My cousin,' she corrected him. Her voice broke; tears started in her eyes, and she turned away to hide them.

'Still, it is not done. Not amongst Hindus. How can you even think of it? It's sinful.'

'Well I meant someone *like* him. Not him necessarily.'

'Who else?'

'Someone I like,' she said.

'You will learn to like your husband. One learns to like one another *after* one is married. It happens. Liking is created by habit, common interests, and children.'

'No, some one I like *before* marriage,' she persisted.

He was aware that the conversation was taking a dangerous turn. He wanted to change its direction. These romantic fancies were clearly the product of too much Western education. The English novels which these girls read were full of subversive ideas.

'That sort of liking, my child, grows weak in time. But friendship is strengthened by time. The liking after marriage is like friendship. It lasts. Your kind of liking doesn't last.'

'I don't care.'

'Does Karan want to marry you?'

She was silent.

'Well, he does not. He doesn't even know that you exist.'

'Bauji, I don't want to marry a stranger!' she said in tears.

Bauji understood her fear of the unknown. A different and affectionate layer of his nature came to the fore, and he felt his heart wrenched. He was equally distressed at the prospect of losing his daughter to a stranger. Apart from sympathizing with her fears, he also thought of his own loneliness: who would he talk to after she left the house? As he was trying to hide his heart under the mask of patrician authority, he became suddenly aware of the presence of a third person.

'Karan!' exclaimed Tara, and she let out a cry of joy.

He had not heard his nephew come in. The boy was positively like a cat. He had on his usual amused smile. Neither Karan's approach nor his eyes were those of a person wanted by the police.

'Bauji, I am leaving. I have come for your blessings,' said the young man, bowing to touch his uncle's feet.

Although he had expected it to happen any day, this confident statement upset Bauji. But he did not show his feelings and continued to puff gently on his hookah.

'And where are you going, may one ask?' asked Bauji, after a long pause.

Karan threw his head back with youthful zest—a gesture which Bauji secretly envied, as it emphasized the difference in years between them—and he flippantly answered, 'I am leaving Lyallpur. It's not safe here, and I have work to do.'

Despite the manner in which it was announced, Bauji took the news seriously. The idea of his talented nephew going away to pursue the Quit India Movement was distressing. Even if he did not become a corpse like the one he had found in the Company Bagh, he would most likely rot in jail for the rest of his brilliant youth. This boy, whom he had seen grow from a child to a handsome young man of twenty; this boy, in whom he had placed high hopes and ambitions; this boy was now calmly asking for his blessings to ruin that brilliant future which he had clearly charted for him. There he stood with a confident twinkle in his eyes, just as he used to when he was sixteen after winning a cricket match.

Like most successful people, Bauji valued his peace of mind and tended to avoid anything that upset his calm. But there was no escaping from this situation, and he found himself getting irritated. It was difficult enough dealing with his daughter's tiresome infatuation. He was conscious of Tara's agitated state, which was not helped by Karan's presence. But these worries were swept away by his prescient concern for Karan. With his sensitivity for public events, Bauji had developed an uncanny ability to read symbols and to presage what was to come. And what he saw overwhelmed him with regret.

'Give me a list of books, boy, that you want sent to jail. You will have lots of time on your hands there. You are too young to write your memoirs.'

Karan smiled.

'You're mad, my boy, to go off with those people. You have such a future before you! Your mother has told you that we plan to send you to England. You could even clear the ICS exam there and then India will be yours to rule.'

Karan nodded and then touched Bauji's feet, which at first the latter thought was from gratitude. But he quickly realized that it was a gesture of farewell.

'Don't you realize what you are giving up?' Bauji persisted.

'I'd rather be an ordinary citizen of a free country.'

Karan's eyes smiled again as he turned to leave. Even though Bauji didn't agree with this defiant youth, he felt strongly that this was his true son. He got up suddenly, pushing the hookah aside, and asked the departing youth to wait. He went inside with a quickened step and quickly returned with a wallet, which he thrust into the embarrassed boy's pocket.

The bold youth mischievously said, 'Bauji, don't tell me that you are financing our side! I better not tell that to the police when I am caught.' After a pause the boy added, 'It doesn't harm to buy a little insurance, does it, in case we come to power.'

'Stop being insolent! Go and pay your respects to Bhabo before you go.'

As Karan went upstairs, followed by Tara, Bauji was left to his own thoughts. Fortunately, it was a dark night and he could hide his troubled face in the cloak of darkness. If only Gandhi had accepted in March the sensible offer of Cripps, he thought, we wouldn't be having this terrible business. Once the offer was rejected the country's mood naturally became bitter and frustrated. The future again looked gloomy. The British, on their side, had also stiffened their attitude. Gandhi, through his strange logic, believed that the British in India were a provocation to the Japanese. Thus they must quit India so that a free India could mobilize its full strength against the Japanese menace. What could be more imprac-

tical at this stage, thought Bauji. Now with the Congress leaders in
jail, what would happen in the future? The Muslim League would
again be in the center of the stage, and Jinnah would go all out to
exploit the religious fears and emotions of the Muslim masses.
Gandhi and Nehru at least tried to bring the communities together.
But Jinnah only spread his poison to keep them apart. With Gandhi
out of the way, Jinnah would surely hold sway, felt Bauji.

He wondered if this thought had crossed Karan's mind. Probably not since he was too obsessed with getting rid of the British.
Everyone seemed to think only about the British and no one seemed
bothered about what would happen to India after the British left.
Slowly Jinnah's poison was bound to affect the body politic.

As the wedding approached, the house began to fill up.

Countless aunts, uncles, cousins and nephews began to arrive from the village. To many of them it was a great opportunity to visit the city, make merry, enjoy Bauji's hospitality, and ventilate old grudges.

A family of Muslim craftsmen was engaged from Kashmir to embroider the bride's trousseau with gold thread. They worked in Bauji's house and were a source of fascination to everyone. The entire east wing of the house had been turned into a kitchen to feed scores of people daily. The hunchback was hired and located in the east wing in order to produce massive quantities of sweets for distribution to what appeared to be half the city. Lists were made endlessly of those who were to receive sweets. An army of tailors also moved into the only room spared from the cooking brigade. All day long there was a bustle of blouses being altered, petticoats being hemmed, salwars being stitched.

Bauji's house had the festive atmosphere characteristic of Punjabi homes where there are eligible young girls and where a marriage is to take place. Tara's sisters and their friends were continuously in and out of the house, chatting interminably, laughing incessantly. Their excitement and happiness was infectious and fed the match-making and gossip of the older women. The house was filled with the delicious breath of feminine anticipation, like the sensuous air before a thunderstorm. Although it was Tara who was getting married, it was the younger girls who found themselves immersed in the currents of desire which traversed the house, reverberated around them, and grazed their untouched maidenly bodies.

Every night for three weeks before the marriage, all the women in the family and Tara's girl friends collected in the upstairs courtyard and sang folk songs late into the night, to the accompaniment of the round two-sided dholak. The courtyard smelled of jasmine as each lady was offered a string of jasmine for her hair. Big

Uncle, much to Bauji's annoyance and everyone's amusement, took great interest in these songs, especially those relating to marriage and sex. He had a good voice and goaded on by the women, he sang night after night.

As the music and festivity went on upstairs, Bauji would smoke his hookah in the secluded part of the courtyard downstairs. He would sit in his usual cane chair, coax the tobacco bowl, and slowly the smoke would enter his lungs and the familiar sweet smell of burning cow dung would fill the courtyard. It was a delicious feeling and he would settle down in a comfortable, sensuous reverie through which came filtered the smells and sounds of the autumn night. Occasionally he would be rewarded by a gust of cool breeze, which left lingering behind the smell of jasmine.

Tara sometimes stole downstairs to sit beside him for short intervals. She did not say much, but seemed happy to be near him for the few weeks that were left before she went away to her new home. Their thoughts often wandered in the same direction: what would her new life be like? Would her husband be kind? What about her mother-in-law? Both of them were glad that the boy did not live with his family. But what kind of home would he provide her?

Bauji's thoughts moved from the emotions he felt for Tara to the ironies of nature. Did he give her all his love and care for the past twenty years so that she should go away from him just like that? It did not seem right. Yet it was the way of nature. Birds did it. Animals too. So why not people? Perhaps it *did* make sense to live like a passenger on a train.

One evening, about ten days before the marriage, Bauji made a discovery. He smelled the same unmistakable fragrance right in his own house. He was certain that it was she. It occurred to him that anyone among the many women who had come to sing could be wearing the expensive scent. But somehow he had an intuition that it was the tantalizing veiled lady he had glimpsed on the corner of Kacheri Bazaar. His pulse quickened.

The burkha lady was in his house—he could not believe it.

He went to his rooms with an excited step to bathe and to change and to contemplate on the possibilities which fortune had brought his way. As the cold water fell on his tall brown body, he rehearsed what he would say to her. He wondered what she looked like. Would she be young or old, pretty or ugly? Like a little boy he felt nervous with anticipation. He dressed in a cool flowing muslin kurta and sprinkled some scent on his handkerchief. Feeling clean and refreshed he walked out with a swinging gait.

Snatches of a vigorous folk song could be heard upstairs. He went and sat down in the private part of the courtyard on his usual wicker chair, away from the bustle of the house. The immediate problem which presented itself was how to meet her. He did not generally go up to the ladies courtyard, he contented himself with greeting Tara's friends and the other womenfolk downstairs when they entered or left the house. He would have to think up a reasonable pretext to go up this evening. Once he was upstairs, he would have no trouble identifying her, he was sure.

But fortune was on his side. As he was thinking over the problem, Tara came rushing downstairs followed by the mysterious lady, whose distinctive fragrance immediately gave her away. As the stranger approached, Bauji realized that she was beautiful beyond all his expectations. She had a pale, white, square face, surrounded by masses of long and dark hair, which fell below her hips. He thought her eyes were green, but he could have been mistaken in the poor evening light. Her nose and cheekbones were clearly chiselled on her face like the sculptures of Gandhara. She came like an apparition, and Bauji was afraid that she might disappear.

He immediately rose to his feet, and his tall frame overshadowed the two women. Bauji was big for a Punjabi Hindu and unlike his contemporaries he had not grown fat with age. His grey hair added to a physical presence, which could not be easily ignored even in a crowd. A glint of pride flashed in his dark brown eyes. It was not the pride of class, nor of worldly success, but a radiation called *raj-tej* by the Hindus. It was an energy radiated by a man of worldly power, usually a ruler. His long ungainly fingers caressed his moustache, the same fingers which could also caress the female body with extreme delicacy, as Bhabo well knew.

Tara introduced the stranger as Anees Husain, her teacher (and friend) from Lahore. Bauji offered her a chair. Tara explained that Anees' father was the DIG of Police in Lahore, but they had originally come from Kashmir. This explained her fair skin and the unusual colour of her eyes. She must be around thirty, he thought. But why wasn't she married, he wondered. He immediately placed her family since he knew many people in Lahore. He certainly knew everyone who mattered in Lyallpur but half of Lahore's society were also his friends. And the other half he had heard of.

Bauji made Anees feel at home. He recounted a brief meeting with her father in Lahore, where he had gone to defend a client at the High Court.

'Then you must have been on opposite sides?' asked Anees.

'Yes,' he replied with a smile.

'I'll go and bring us some fresh lime water,' said Tara getting up.

There was a brief uneasy silence after Tara's departure. Curiosity finally got the better of Bauji, and he asked his attractive guest if she had been near Kacheri Bazaar on a certain evening.

'It was I,' she said boldly. 'But I was wearing a burkha. How did you know?'

'Ah, that's my secret,' he said.

'Does someone always watch unsuspecting women in this manner?'

'If someone visits the wrong side of town at the wrong hour of the day, she must be prepared to be noticed, especially if she wears Chanel No. 5.'

'Oh, so that's how someone knows.' It finally dawned on her; she was impressed.

'Someone has a good memory for scents,' she said.

He smiled, acknowledging the compliment. There was a pause.

'I have sometimes wondered,' he said, 'how it feels to be behind a burkha—to be always a spectator, forever observing the world, and never acting, to be always tantalizing others, to keep them guessing, whether it is a woman of eighteen or of eighty.'

It was her turn to smile. She was struck by the unusual observation.

'I never thought of it in that way,' she replied. 'I have always worn a burkha on the streets. I was brought up to believe that it was the only way. But I don't like it. I envy Tara and other Hindu girls, who don't have to wear it. I don't want to be an observer, I want to be part of the world.'

Bauji was intrigued by her answer. He would have liked to pursue this thought, but she quickly changed the subject.

'Bauji, I want to talk to you,' the stranger suddenly became serious. 'It is about Tara.' Bauji now understood the reason behind their meeting. The fresh lime drink had been carefully arranged.

'She doesn't want to marry this man,' said Anees.

'I know,' he said.

'Then why must she?' asked Anees.

Patiently and gently, Bauji explained to Tara's friend why it was a good match. He was articulate and she was intelligent and open to reason. Gradually he convinced her that the match was in the best interest of Tara. Anees had argued strongly on behalf of her friend, but slowly she began to see the wisdom of the choice. From Tara's ally she became Bauji's, and in the end she even promised him that she would talk to Tara.

After he saw that he had the upper hand, Bauji was careful not to press his advantage to ensure that Anees did not feel that she was letting down her friend. Anees observed this—and she was touched by the sensitivity of this tall, proud man. Apart from his cogent and persuasive reasoning, Anees was impressed by his sincerity, warmth, and charm.

On his part, Bauji was obviously attracted to her. He let himself be drawn by the physical stimulus of the beautiful woman, and did not attempt to control himself. Anees seemed to be aware of the impression that she was creating, and she was excited by the obvious admiration that she was arousing in the older man. Her face became flushed and she became perilously attractive to behold.

Soon the fresh lime water arrived. Tara watched the two of them as they drank the refreshing cool citrus drink in the silence of the warm night. Tara was anxious to know the outcome of their conversation but she did not dare ask anything. They talked about small things—the summer heat, the moonlight, the smell of jasmine, the need for rain.

Tara finally became impatient, and told her friend that it was time to go back upstairs. However, Anees did not respond immediately; she seemed to be caught in the voluptuous torpor of the moonlit summer night. She was confused, and she could not move. The heavy scent of jasmine added to the threatening sensuality of the evening. Every jasmine flower seemed to promise an erotic delight.

Eventually Tara and Anees went upstairs, and Bauji was left alone with his thoughts. It took him a while to recover from the seductive spell that had been cast by the beautiful woman. He felt a sensual nagging. But he also felt a hint of guilt—that his own thoughts seemed to move in the wrong direction. The sensual impulse stung him and made him blush. Deep inside he wrestled with his acquired middle class scruples. He thought of his marriage and of Bhabo. Had he wronged her in his heart? He said to himself,

'I am weak it is true, but really, don't I deserve to do better? Bhabo and I have been married for too long. She has become a habit, has even begun to look old. And look at me: I am full of vigour and at the peak of my powers.' He felt sorry for himself, but he also felt ashamed. He could not help but envy his landowning ancestors in the village, who would have had a dozen women like Anees a hundred years ago. Yet neither could he overcome his feelings of shame, as he thought of himself flirting with the friend of his soon-to-be-married daughter. And that too a Muslim girl! The thought momentarily made him feel old. He felt a revulsion for the circumstances in which he found himself. But he quickly recovered as the pride of his Khatri blood reasserted itself.

He was diverted by the unanswered question—what had Anees been doing near Kacheri Bazaar that evening? She had not volunteered an answer and neither had he pressed her. A persistent intuition told him that she had been in trouble. He felt suddenly protective towards her.

After that evening Anees came to 7, Kacheri Bazaar every day. She was staying in Lyallpur with her uncle, who was a man of liberal views, and her visits to her girl friend did not arouse suspicion. Besides, it was the most natural thing for girl friends to spend their last days together before one of them got married and left. Moreover, the nightly singing amongst the girls was an established institution. Bauji hoped in his heart that Anees had other reasons as well. The daily arrival of the tonga, carrying a woman in a dark blue burkha, became the central focus of Bauji's day. He changed his routine, and came home earlier from the Company Bagh so that he would be sure to greet her in the courtyard. With sensuous anticipation he would wait for the happiness which came wrapped under the dark folds. He would tremble every time she came. She would not take off the burkha until she went upstairs to Tara's room. Thus he had to greet her without seeing her. He would look admiringly at the slim body inside the blue garment, and then anxiously at the veil, trying to pierce the concealed green Kashmiri eyes. She would linger slightly longer than was customary in the circumstances and then run upstairs to meet Tara. But she would leave the characteristic fragrance behind her, which was like a promise to Bauji of the delight that awaited him during the later part of the evening.

Thanks to Anees' persuasion Tara became more and more reasonable about her marriage and there were fewer scenes between father and daughter. Karan's absence also helped. Bauji was grateful to Anees for reconciling Tara to her bridegroom. Although the lively social life of the house and especially the folk singing upstairs—which went on till the small hours—provided an excellent cover for the intermittent meetings between Bauji and Anees, Tara began to suspect. Anees seemed to spend more and more time in the secluded part of the downstairs courtyard beside Bauji. At first Tara was confused. She was afraid to talk about it lest she might hurt someone. She also found it strange and exciting. Because of her romantic nature, Tara felt an instinctive sympathy for the relationship which seemed to be developing between her father and her friend. She did not judge her father or her friend. Their relationship seemed to address some of her own romantic but unrequited dreams. Instead of interfering she began to go out of her way to protect them from the inquisitive eyes of others, and cover up for them when required.

Anees and Bauji talked about many things, but Bauji always seemed to bring their conversations back to the Hindu-Muslim question. One evening as the clock struck eleven in the tower, Anees became uneasy.

'I must go,' she said.

'Stay,' he pleaded.

'But what must they think upstairs?' she asked.

'Please stay.'

'I don't want to go either,' she said. 'But I must.'

'No wait. I want to talk to you. Anees, what is happening? Look at us—I am old enough to be your father. My daughter is getting married in a few days. Here I am completely swept away. I don't understand. And you. . . you. . . .'

'Are a Muslim?' she said.

'No, I wasn't going to say that,' he said.

'You are older and wiser. Explain it to me, then.'

'It's got nothing to do with your being a Muslim,' he said with a touch of irritation.

'It is not safe for me to be here,' she said.

'In a Hindu area?'

'Yes.'

'You have been listening to bazaar talk again.'

'They are expecting trouble tonight,' she said.

'No, impossible! It is too soon after the Quit India riots. The police are still alert.'

'But it is true,' she said.

'Why?' he asked.

'To revenge the rape of the Hindu girl last week.'

'What is this madness, Anees, that is sweeping through our lives? Hindus and Muslims have lived together peacefully for centuries. I have always admired the Muslims for their Persian culture and Arabic learning. I have also found them hardworking, freer and open and more trustworthy in business matters. Muslim lawyers, although there are only a few of them, are more honest. I wouldn't trust a Hindu lawyer but I would a Muslim.'

'Oh no!' she said, interrupting him. 'We are not going to start on this Hindu-Muslim thing again, are we? That is all you seem to think about.'

'But nobody seems to give me an answer. You never want to talk about it. Why are the Muslims distrustful today?'

'Do you really want to know?' she asked after a long pause.

Bauji nodded.

'Then listen. It is we Muslims rather than you Hindus who lost in the British Raj. During the Mughal Raj we were the Zamindars and we had lands; we were the Kazis, the judges and the courtiers, and we had power. The English came and took away our positions. They substituted our Islamic law with English law, and Persian with the English language. We resented it. You Hindus were flexible: you quickly learnt English and adopted the new ways and filled the important posts which the British eventually opened up. We failed to imitate you and were left sullen and helpless. Independence worries us because in a democratic government you will outnumber us. For every Muslim there are four Hindus in India. For all the harm they did, the British at least kept a balance between Hindus and Muslims.'

'What kind of balance? You mean they divided us—in order to strengthen their hold,' disagreed Bauji.

'We can't hope to be counted in a free India,' she went on. 'Our intellectual backwardness makes us even weaker. We can't even hope to form an effective opposition. The representative system of elections will mean tyranny by the majority. That is why we are afraid. That is why we want our homeland.'

Bauji was stunned by this cogent and well articulated defence of Pakistan. He made as if to applaud, when she stopped him.

'Sh. . . they will hear upstairs.'

'Even though you argue brilliantly, I don't agree with you,

Anees. Your Pakistan means that I must leave behind everything I have created. Why must I? This is as much my land, you know.'

'Of course, it is,' she said, taking his hand in hers. 'You must live here. Pakistan doesn't mean that you have to leave.'

'But it would be an Islamic state. What would I do here as a Hindu?' asked Bauji.

'Now do you understand how a Muslim feels about living in a Hindu India?' asked Anees.

'Oh, but you are wrong. It will not be a Hindu India. It will be a secular India. Haven't Nehru, Gandhi and others constantly given assurances to the Muslims?'

'We don't believe in them,' she said.

'You are wrong again, Anees. Muslims and Hindus have so much in common. It is the British who have exploited the differences.'

'Exploited them, yes, but they did not create the differences. They were always there—our religion, our culture, history, dress, the food we eat, our laws, marriages, customs, language—they are all different. We don't even know about each others traditions: because we were educated apart—we in our *madrasas* and *tols* and you in your Sanskrit *pathshalas.*'

'It was true earlier. But not now. After the British Raj, it is the same. Both Tara and you have learned the same things in the same school.'

'Yes, about the West, but not about our own cultures.'

'The learning in modern India after the British leave will be modern and scientific. We shall create one secular culture. Why hark back to the past and to religious differences? Why? Why?'

'Oh, why are we arguing? We have so little time,' she said.

He put his hand in hers. Amidst the smell of the jasmine, they watched the moon, who was a familiar friend by now. They felt a kinship with the moon, the planets, and the stars.

The night before Tara's wedding, Anees came dressed in a pink and white garara, which seemed to heighten her Muslim identity, and made her stand out even more than usual. She told Tara and Bauji that she had to return to Lahore the next day and would not be able to attend the wedding. Both father and daughter were bitterly disappointed.

Anees was unusually vivacious and excited throughout the

evening. Everyone remarked how beautiful she looked, and she seemed to grow more and more distracted as the evening went by. Both Bauji and she seemed to feel the evanescence of the moment. Much as they tried to hold it, they felt that it was coming to an end. What one day brought, the next took away. They tried to make believe that it could be otherwise, but the feeling of transience seemed to prevail. For time was not concerned with their hopes; it hurried on with its business.

Tara came down at midnight, accompanied by Anees.

'Suresh is sick Bauji,' she announced. 'And there might be trouble in the city tonight. You will have to take Anees home.'

Bauji did not believe in predestination, but he did believe in good fortune. Otherwise, why should Suresh fall sick so opportunely? He felt that luck was not merely chance. It was somehow earned. Very few lived by choice alone. Everyone was placed in circumstances by causes which acted without foresight. It was a piece of skill to know how to guide your luck even while you waited for it. When fortune came, he believed that one must seize her, before she changed her mind.

Under the white light of the moon the land was flat and silent. Below the bright sky everything diminished. As a precaution Bauji and Anees had not gone through the city. They had taken a roundabout route, which took them by the canal, through the sparsely inhabited countryside. As they rode, snuggled up against each other under the moonlight, they were grateful for what they sensed was their last opportunity to be together. They stopped by the canal. The tall branching mango trees shaded an artificial pond and the ground below the grove was spotted with blurred moonlight. A temple stood nearby. Bauji directed the tonga towards the grove, and the horse on its own came to rest in the shade as if it understood their desires. There they stayed.

In the light and shade, Anees' soft black tresses appeared longer than usual, setting off her pale face and her striking eyes. The unusual light seemed to give her a fragile and iridescent quality. The same light shone on his rich brown skin, which stood out in sharp contrast to her Kashmiri hue. She looked at his brow, and the light revealed his authoritarian Khatri temperament, passionate and irascible, easily excited at the slightest hint of injustice. His eyes disclosed a quiet pride, but as she looked closer, she was disturbed by what she saw. It was an uneasy discontent. She had noticed it before. The disquiet seemed to be persistent, and Anees could not understand why this successful, tall, proud man should suffer so. What did it mean? Did he have a premonition of evil? She had tried to understand it the past week, but she had not been successful. There seemed to be a helpless feeling behind his anxiety. For a man used to controlling his destiny, this helplessness must be peculiarly painful.

As if it was in sympathy with her thoughts, the sky slowly became clouded and dark. There was a gust of wind, which brought welcome relief to the hot summer night. A light roll of thunder in the distance proclaimed a pre-monsoon shower. A few drops of rain fell on the mango grove and the sizzling ground. Anees shivered, and Bauji gripped her arm. It aroused a mutual onrush of desire. She reciprocated with a caress. After a pause she took his hand. The drops of water on the dry, thirsty ground released innumerable rich smells, which competed with the heavy scents from the trees. Softly she bent under his embrace. The smells were almost too strong—cloying and decadent. The wafts from the grove were erotic and they seemed to reinforce the surge of sensuality in the pre-monsoon air. The desire became a torment for the sensual urge had to be restrained. But the restraint upon it was also delightful for it seemed to strengthen the desire. In the moonlight, her eyes looked anxious, bewildered, and voluptuous. Gradually the storm passed and the sensual cyclone subsided.

Time flew by and soon it was the holy hour. A Brahmin boy came out of the temple, his thin body naked except for a dhoti and the sacred thread. He was not suspicious of the strangers in the tonga, thinking them to be pilgrims. As he went about his pre-dawn duties, an older Brahmin, probably his father, clad in a loin cloth and sacred thread also came out and went down to the long steps on the canal to bathe. With a brass jar he poured water over his fine slender body. They were struck by the elegance of his posture. In that solitary pose was stated the aim of being a Hindu: moksha or release from subservience and the contingency of life; detachment, irradiated by the realization of the Absolute; an awareness that life is an essential unity of objects and thoughts and the great communion with the Absolute is within this world, achieved inside this same living body.

An unexpected cry from a peacock jolted them out of their reverie; Bauji pulled the reins of the horse and they started. They were silent, their thoughts absorbed in the nearness of their bodies. Dawn was breaking in the distance and soon they could see

Lyallpur's main mosque in the foreground. It was an immense rectangle with tall octagonal minarets and a domed pavilion at the summit. Its beautiful pointed arch formed the facade and faced the Kaabah in the direction of Mecca. Flanking the central arch were two smaller arches and the impressive pair of white minarets. Its courtyard was surrounded by pillared cloisters. Bauji had always admired the mosque. He did not see it as a symbol of an alien faith; rather it was part of his definition of his city. He could not conceive of Lyallpur without it. It was gracious to look at and it gave him a feeling of cool serenity. Whilst to many Hindus it was a symbol of intolerance, to Bauji it was an impression of man's transcendence.

As they entered the Muslim quarter, Anees put on her burkha. Seeing her wrapped in the dark blue folds, Bauji was reminded of his initial fleeing vision of her in Kacheri Bazaar. This was how he had first seen her.

8

There were many weddings in Lyallpur that summer, but the one at Bauji's house was the most important, because of the family's social standing, the number of guests and the splendour of the arrangements.

Bauji was a man of the world, who had been successful in the world, and success had become second nature to him. Like most such men he had perfected the art of dealing with people and circumstances, so that without much effort they played to his advantage. He had an instinctive ability to delegate responsibility, and he was thus able to do many things at one time. Typically, on Tara's marriage day, he had organized matters well, and he had time to think of Anees, instead of worrying about hundreds of details.

Early in the morning, as he was passing by the stables, he found his syce's youngest child crying his heart out in a corner near the horses. With some effort and a good deal of patience he slowly discovered that the boy believed that 'someone was coming today to take Tara masi away.'

He put the boy on his lap and he said, 'That is not true. Tara is going to be beautiful like a princess tonight. A handsome prince will come on a horse with a gleaming sword and silver crown over his turban of golden braid. And they will marry. We will not lose Tara, we will win a prince tonight.'

The boy nodded, then slowly smiled and ran away.

Bauji's princely vision was not far from the truth. It was customary for the bridegroom to come dressed for the wedding as a Khatri king on a mount. And Bauji had made certain that the bridegroom would observe all these traditions. Being a good judge of men, he correctly guessed that his peculiar son-in-law-to-be, under the influence of the guru and spiritualism, might not observe all the traditions. He was also aware that the humble circumstances of the groom's family might force them to compromise. He had thus quietly organized the details for which the groom's side was responsible, without anyone knowing, least of all Bhabo.

The day before the marriage, for example, he had himself chosen a handsome white mare and made sure that she would be washed and groomed till her skin shone, and then saddled and caparisoned brilliantly. Similarly, he had selected the groom's gold embroidered robe, a pair of gold embroidered Kashmiri slippers with turned-up spurs and a deep yellow velvet scabbard with silver mountings. All these would be innocently sold to the groom at a nominal cost by dealers when he arrived in Lyallpur. The groom's party had been discreetly informed by post that such and such items were available more economically in Lyallpur. Prices had been sent in advance to save them embarrassment.

The sun had set and it quickly became dark. It was time for the groom to arrive at the bride's house. Under an arch of leaves and flowers, at the entrance to Kacheri Bazaar, stood the male members of Bauji's house, headed by Bauji himself, who looked handsome in the traditional pink turban, a cream-coloured double-breasted achkan, which flowed like a robe, emphasizing his height, and tight, cream-coloured churidars. Behind him obediently stood in order of seniority, his brothers, his brothers-in-law, and his sons— all arrayed in pink turbans. It was an impressive sight. They were anxiously waiting for the arrival of the groom's party. The women of the house adorned in silks and diamonds, stood at the back, eager to see the groom. The entire street had been closed for the occasion, and covered with a shamiana.

Traditionally, the groom's arrival at the bride's house was a moment of great triumph for the bride's father. It was symbolic of his hospitality and generosity; of a life well lived according to dharma; of a debt repaid to the community, of a job well done by the householder. Instead of savouring that triumph, Bauji was distracted. His mind was troubled by thoughts of Tara. He felt uneasy that her heart was not in the marriage. He acutely felt the absence of Anees. He worried about the unconventional nature of this marriage. All these weeks he had stood firm against Bhabo's and others' doubts about it, but now was assailed by the very same fears. The status of the boy's family, his novel occupation, the guru, the ashram—all these went against the wisdom of convention.

Adding to his distress was the unsettled political climate. Anything could happen in these times. Had Anees reached Lahore safely? He wondered if she would write. Strange as it seemed to him, he needed her at this moment. Without realizing it, he had come to depend on her, and he felt her loss sharply. Without her, his moment of triumph felt bland. He tried to imagine her standing amongst the crowd of women, in the familiar pink and white garara, her pale, square face covered with a smile, her dark, long hair flowing behind her. Why couldn't she have stayed for the wedding?

His mood had changed subtly but perceptibly. What should have been a joyful event was threatening to become a tedious worldly duty. He began to feel hot and uncomfortable in his heavy clothes. A cool shower, he thought, would be welcome. It would bring comfort from the tyrannical summer heat. But the thought of rain reminded him of his responsibilities; and he realized that it would spoil many of the open-air ceremonies. The idea of hundreds of people going hungry was mischievous, but it fit in well with his morbid mood. He was reminded again of Tara and that it was meant to be her day; and that decided the issue, as he decisively came out against the rain. As a precaution he began to enumerate in his mind the series of steps which would be needed in case the ceremonies were to be moved indoors.

These meteorological thoughts were soon forgotten as he spotted the procession in the distance. Headed by a brass band, lit by coolies holding gas lamps on their heads and accompanied by exploding firecrackers, the groom's party wound its way through the streets of Lyallpur. In the middle of the procession, Bauji easily identified his son-in-law, although he could not see his face: it was covered by the *sehra* of gold threads, jasmine and marigold flowers. But he was relieved at the sight of the white mare and the gold-embroidered coat. He also felt ashamed of himself for having given in to his self-indulgent and morbid mood. He must pull himself together. He had responsibilities. Hundreds of relatives, friends, guests depended on him. His family looked to him as a source of strength.

The procession came to a halt near the arch. The groom's father, also in a pink turban, came forward with a garland of marigolds. Bauji embraced him mechanically but impressively. They exchanged garlands. Bauji presented him with a saffron-coloured envelope containing money after twirling it twice round his head. The same ritual was repeated by all the pink turbans, and seemed to go on forever. Big Uncle, who had poetic pretensions, then read out a poem, in which he praised the groom and the members of his family and wished the couple a long and happy married life. The women were especially touched by the sentimental poem, and some of them had tears in their eyes. The poem confirmed Big Uncle's place in the hearts of the women in Bauji's large clan.

The groom alighted. The bride, led by her sisters and cousins, came forward. Her head was veiled by chiffon. In a heavy red sari adorned with gold threadwork, her hand elaborately painted, Tara looked the perfect image of a Punjabi bride. She garlanded the groom. This act of Tara's recalled to Bauji the ancient *svayamvara*, when a princess chose her own husband from a line of suitors by garlanding the lucky one. He smiled as he thought of the famous *svayamvara* of Damayanti, who was so beautiful that even the gods stood in line for her hand. Knowing that she was in love with Prince Nala, the gods assumed Nala's form. When she was ready to choose and garland her husband, the confused Damayanti found a dozen Nalas before her. But she was clever. She looked carefully at all the Nalas and noticed that only one cast a shadow. And she remembered that gods do not cast shadows. She stepped forward confidently and garlanded her human love.

The women who accompanied Tara, now surrounded the groom and led him inside the home. He was made to sit down next to the bride and went through an uncomfortable session in which he was quizzed and teased by the women.

'Why are you so late, sir?' enquired one of the women. 'We thought you might have changed your mind.'

'Ask my horse,' replied Seva Ram with a smile. 'I came as fast as my horse would carry me.'

The women laughed enthusiastically when they heard this. Tara, who was feeling nervous, also smiled.

'Won't you have a drink, sir?'

'I'll have a cup of tea, thank you.'

'Won't you have a stronger drink?'

'I'd prefer tea,' smiled Seva Ram.

It was plain to everyone that the groom was completely self-possessed. His composure had the same effect on the women that it always had on everyone. They calmed down and looked at him with sympathy. Tara was quick to detect in his manner a certain remoteness, even though he was cordial and charming. He continued to respond to the breezy chatter of the women. But she was conscious of a singular detachment about him, as though he were playing a part.

As the rest of the party sat down to eat under the canvas shamiana in the courtyard, Chachi grabbed Bauji's arm and led him to a corner.

'Well, you old fox, you did manage to get the boy,' she said with a wink.

'Thanks to you, Chachi, Tara is also being married.'

'What is the boy like?' she asked.

'He is a good boy, but too wrapped up in spirituality.'

'Yes, yes. At his age, he should play, enjoy himself, and think less of god,' said Chachi. 'Where is he posted, by the way?'

'Amritsar.'

'Ah, that's where Jean Fryer is also posted. I must ask him.'

From a distance Bauji greeted friends with his eyes and smiled charmingly at the ladies.

'Once he gets married, he will change. They all do,' continued Chachi.

'I suppose so,' he said mechanically. But he wasn't so sure. He felt mildly uneasy. He had heard that his peculiar son-in-law placed his spiritual life above everything. What if he was not flexible? Tara might have many lonely nights ahead.

This unpleasant thought was quickly interrupted by a burst of laughter from the opposite corner. Both Chachi and Bauji turned and their eyes fell on Karan, who was surrounded by a bevy of adoring young females in silk. He was relieved by the thought that Tara was safely tucked away inside the house.

'He's the one who needs to marry,' said Chachi. 'Eh, how did you get him out of jail?'

'I petitioned for his temporary release to attend this marriage.'

'You make it sound so easy. Dewan Chand's arm truly extends far in this city.'

'There's the plainclothesman guarding him,' Bauji pointed with his eyes. Before turning back to Chachi, he observed the dinner arrangements, and he was pleased that everything was going smoothly.

'How these people eat,' said Chachi, guessing his thoughts.

'They come to eat, Chachi.'

The wedding party was sitting in long rows on the ground and vigorously devouring food. Dozens of vegetarian dishes, cooked by professional cooks, were being personally served by members of Bauji's family with great attention and generosity. Only after the groom's side had finished, would the bride's side sit down to eat.

As Chachi left to talk to Bhabo, Bauji's gaze returned to Karan, who continued to reap laurels from admirers of all ages. Karan had become a hero in Lyallpur after his arrest two weeks ago. Instead of leaving town, he had led another satyagraha through the streets of Lyallpur, starting from the Company Bagh to the Clock Tower to protest against Britain's use of Indian soldiers in the War. Always popular amongst the young, tonight he inspired awe among the older people as well. He was clearly the centre of gravity of this gathering. However, Bauji noted with amusement, that his nephew's stock in Lyallpur's marriage market had plummeted. Those mothers, who a few months ago were desperate to link their daughters hands with Karan's, now found him ineligible. But the daughters themselves couldn't take their eyes off him throughout the evening. You admire heroes from a distance thought Bauji; you don't marry your daughters to them.

Bauji wondered how Karan found the experience of jail. As for himself, he had no taste for jails. He remembered with nostalgia the days of the Swarajists, when one could pursue a professional career and still play a political role through debate and discussion. Gandhi and later Bose had come and changed all that. Politics was now in the streets and in jail. Besides, the idea of gradual self-rule, which he had supported in the twenties, was also out of the question. It was all or nothing. Even he saw the naivety of his own stand in the thirties, when he had been enthused by the Simon Commission formula for limited self-rule leading to Dominion status for India. Australia and Canada were natural dominions for they loved the British sovereign, but who cared for the King in India? Even the Maharajas could no longer count on the loyalty of their subjects.

Chachi had gone up to the groom, Bauji noticed. She was talking to him, and he felt a hint of concern that she might scare him.

'And how is dear Jean Fryer?' asked Chachi of Seva Ram.

Surprised by her question, he looked puzzled and said he did not know.

'Oh haven't you met her. She is such a nice woman. She was always kind to us in Lahore when my husband was alive. Why didn't you go and see her?'

'The fact is I don't know her,' he said.

'Don't you?' she said as if she couldn't believe her ears. 'Why not? You are in Amritsar, aren't you?'

'Well, you know, to tell you the truth, we lowly engineers don't get to meet Commissioner's wives.'

'But she is such a sweet woman. I'm sure you'd like her.'

Among the guests, Bauji spotted several notables from the ashram and he went towards them. On the way, he stopped before the groom and his father; he courteously bowed to them. The ashram-dwellers greeted Bauji warmly and asked him if he was ready to be initiated by the guru. Bauji smiled back and replied that he was still thinking.

Bauji now made his way to the more Westernized group in the gathering. It consisted of local government officials, some professors, his lawyer colleagues and a retired English judge. Bauji had thoughtfully provided this upper crust of Lyallpur society with English liquor in his drawing room. In deference to the austere groom, liquor was not served under the shamiana.

As he neared the drawing room, he heard the hum of busy voices. At the door he took in the all-male scene. His guests were predictably formed into three circles—each determined by natural professional affinity—the academics, the bureaucrats and the lawyers. Each cluster was in animated conversation on the same subject: When would the British leave India? Would they split the country in two when they left? Should India support them in their war with the Japanese in the East?

When Bauji was spotted, many eyes turned to him in warm greeting, and the carefully glued groups began to loosen. Soon after Bauji, Karan also entered. As expected there was a rush towards Karan, and the conversation became livelier.

'Do you really believe the British will leave India?' asked Big Uncle of the English judge.

'Unquestionably,' replied the retired judge, who was well known for his pro-Indian sympathies.

'What about *you*, Judge? Do you look forward to returning home?' asked Bauji.

'Home? What home? India is my only home. I was born here, brought up here. Except for one miserable three-month visit, I don't know Britain at all.'

'Aren't you disappointed by our reaction to the war in the East?' asked Big Uncle.

'I think the surrender of Singapore in September was a staggering blow to British prestige in India,' said the judge. 'It opened up the Bay of Bengal to the Japanese navy.'

'And we don't seem to understand that *we* are threatened by the Japanese,' said Bauji.

'And why should you?' asked the judge. 'Indians are already under an alien ruler. Why should you feel that one foreigner is worse than another?'

'We don't support an Axis victory, Judge,' said Karan charmingly. 'We merely want to be neutral in a conflict that doesn't concern us. If Churchill were merely to hint at the unconditional freedom of India, we would be ready to fight the Japanese tomorrow.'

'With what?' sneered Big Uncle. 'Gandhi wants us to fight them with non-violence.'

'I am sorry to admit Sir, that I take pleasure at Britain's present discomfort in the East,' said Chachi who had just walked into the all-male gathering. 'I applauded the successive fall of Hong Kong, Philippines, then Malaya, Indo-China, Thailand. We were amazed at the speed of the Japanese advance. It means that the colonial empires are flimsy structures built on pillars of rotting clay.'

'The English people are weary of the Indian Empire. But Churchill continues to confuse them with the Muslim question,' said the judge.

'But there is a Muslim question, isn't there?' asked a silvery voice at the back. Everyone turned around to look at the distinguished Sir Mirza Khan, who was one of the few Muslims in the gathering. A soft-spoken, highly successful lawyer, he was one of Bauji's oldest friends. But Bauji had been disappointed to note a growing communalism in Sir Mirza's outlook over the past six months.

'It is partially our creation, I am afraid,' said the Englishman. 'The Hindu-Muslim problem became a problem as a result of the distinctions we began to draw in the last century. It worsened when your reformers and revivalists attempted to modernize India, and unintentionally they created a gulf, because each went back to his own philosophy. To counter the English challenge, the Hindus turned to the Vedas for inspiration and the Muslims to the Koran.'

'Yes, yes,' impatiently admitted Chachi. 'But why must you equate one-fourth Muslims with three-fourths Hindus? Or rather why can't you treat all Indians as one?'

'Islam says that Muslims should be ruled only by Muslims,' said Sir Mirza firmly.

'Come, come, Sir, we both know that the Hindu-Muslim conflict has little to do with religious tenets. The real basis is economic and social. It's a struggle for power and the opportunities which political power confers,' said Karan.

'No, young man. The differences are religious and cultural. The English are rightly concerned to protect the minority from the potential tyranny of the majority. We would prefer the English to continue in India rather than turn it over to the Hindus,' said Sir Mirza.

At this point, realizing that the conversation was on delicate ground, Bauji tried to intervene, but he was too late.

'I always thought that the Muslims were anti-national. But I didn't believe it till I heard it with my own ears this evening,' said Chachi provocatively.

'Look here, look here,' Bauji tried to placate the Muslim barrister, but the damage was done. All eyes were on Sir Mirza who smiled, bowed, and walked out. Bauji ran after him and caught up with him just before he reached the main gate. With his considerable powers of persuasion and the warmth of his personality, Bauji succeeded in inducing Sir Mirza to stay. Arm in arm the old friends walked towards the ladies under the smaller shamiana.

There Sir Mirza quickly merged with the silks and scents of a group of middle aged women, whom he had known all his life and who were willing to be charmed by his wit and easy manner. Bauji noted from a distance that his attractive silver-haired colleague had changed considerably in the past few months. As he had become more fanatic about his religion, he had lost his sense of humour. He had almost completely forgotten to laugh at himself, a quality that Bauji prized more than any other in his friend. Earlier, Sir Mirza was always ready to amuse and to be amused, often at his own expense. If this is what faith did to one, Bauji wondered, then he wanted to have none of it. Faith, to his mind was a stiffening process. It made one rigid and to that extent less human. Each human being was unique and thus his faith should be unique. Millions of people believed, but each one had to believe by himself. Above all, faith was a hope or a wish that god might exist. As with all wishes, why should not this one be special with each one. Where was the room in all this for organized religion? It was the continuous voice of one's own conscience and one's own reason that should make one believe, not that of others. In fact that which was believed by everyone, all the time, had every chance of being false.

Leaving his mollified friend behind, Bauji returned to the main shamiana. Bauji greeted friends and smiled charmingly at the ladies as he passed them. He was relieved to note that all was well: the wedding party was still absorbed in the serious business of eating the sumptuous feast; Bhabo was gossiping with the Khanna ladies on a sofa; people were moving about serving food and drinks with quiet efficiency; and two gaudily dressed Muslim musicians in a corner were unsuccessfully vying for attention with their shenais.

Suddenly Bauji thought of Tara, and he decided to go inside the house. He was astonished to find her sitting quietly all by herself in her room. She was absorbed in examining her painted hands.

'Why are you alone, child?' he asked. 'Where are the other women and all your friends?'

'I threw them out,' Tara replied crossly.

'A bride is not supposed to be alone on this day.'

'An unhappy one is.'

'What is wrong, my dearest?' he asked tenderly. He took her colourful, gaily-patterned hand, and he sat down beside her. She burst into tears and threw her arms around him.

'He is here,' she said, between sobs.

'Who is here?' he asked.

'Karan,' she whispered, and he understood the cause of her misery.

'He came to see me,' she said.

'In here?'

She nodded. There was a pause.

'I asked him to take me away,' she slowly added.

'You did what!' said Bauji incredulously. This was going too far, he thought. And he shivered.

'He said he had to go back to jail,' she said.

'Of course he has to go back. Do you think he has time for your romantic foolishness?'

'It is not foolish,' she protested.

'What else is it!' He found himself getting angry. 'A daughter of mine on her wedding day, behaving in this disgraceful way.' He looked into her tear-filled eyes. And he couldn't sustain his anger any longer. 'Hush, my dearest,' he said as he put his arm around her. 'Now put these impossible ideas out of your head. Remember he is your cousin and you must love him as a brother. Soon you will meet your husband and learn to respect and love him, and all will be forgotten.'

'I have just met him. And I don't like him.'

'You have merely seen him. There is a great difference between seeing and knowing. It has always been this way and in the end it is for the best. Trust me.' He got up to leave. 'I'll send in your friends.'

On the way out, he turned round, and asked, 'Does anyone else know? Did anyone hear you speak to him?'

She shook her head.

'Where is Anees, Bauji? I need her.'

'You know very well that she left for Lahore this morning, my child,' he replied.

'I need her to tell me that it is all right. I need her to teach me to like him. I need her to help me forget Karan. Why did you send her away?'

'I did not, Tara.' He wondered if she realized how much *he* needed her Muslim friend.

'How do I look, Bauji?' she asked suddenly.

'You look beautiful, Tara. A beautiful bride.'

A troubled Bauji emerged from Tara's room. He felt relieved that no one else had heard her speak to Karan. As a man of the world, he knew that it was important to avoid a scandal. However, he was also concerned about how Tara felt. It was bad enough for her to be marrying against her will. Certainly all the women he had known had been married in this way. The girl was obviously nervous and afraid to leave the house in which she had grown up. It was quite natural. This fear was understandably mixed with an anticipation over the first real relationship with a man. Girls from good homes were brought up to believe that it was the only way. Why then was Tara behaving in this manner? Was there something wrong in the way he had brought her up? She had obviously picked up these ideas in college. Bhabo had warned him not to give the girl too much education. But, surely Bhabo was not right. Tara had always been a spirited girl, and had invariably done what she believed in.

He was soon back in the main shamiana. He looked around and found that the festivities were going well. The boy's side had finished eating, and the girl's side had sat down to eat. People were animatedly talking and eating and enjoying themselves. It couldn't have been better organized. Instead of being satisfied by the success of his arrangements, Bauji could feel ill humour creeping slowly over him. The faces began to appear ugly, the arrangements grotesque, and the whole spectacle absurd. The incident with Sir Mirza, and his daughter's grief were beginning to affect him. Again he started to feel hot and weary. He wanted to get out of his stifling formal clothes, especially his tight-fitting turban. He felt a loathing for himself. He took out the gold watch from his pocket and saw that it was still early. He decided to go out for a breath of fresh air.

In the opposite corner, Bauji saw a group of giggling young girls, all distantly related, from his village. He was struck by their unhealthy pallor and sickly appearance. Unlike Tara's educated girl friends from the city, these girls were overdressed, and unsure of themselves; they were socially immature, and inclined to be hysterical. He couldn't blame them for many of them had been child brides, and had remained emotionally indisciplined. Since marriage they had lived within the confines of the joint family of their child husbands in a borrowed Islamic style purdah. Ever since they had arrived into their new and unknown families, they had been subjected to every form of humiliation until they had become pregnant. Since they were children, this did not happen for several years, and meanwhile they were taunted and unceasingly reminded by every form of innuendo that their sole duty was to conceive a son by their husbands. Their only response was passive obedience. Since they were not allowed to go out, they did not get fresh air and sunshine, and this explained their unhealthy colour.

As he was walking out of the shamiana, Bauji also noticed how utterly ill-made were the faces of his distant family members; even worse, how ill-shaped were their bodies. Because of eating roti and ghee, starch and fat, day in and day out, everyone over thirty was over-weight, and some were positively obese. Since they tended to put weight on their faces, they appeared even more deformed. And what he overheard from their bloated mouths was dull, commonplace and awkward conversation. His melancholy had changed to black gloom. He drank a glass of tepid water. Instead of refreshing him, it seemed to increase his bitterness.

He was relieved to be alone in the dark street outside. He raised his hand, but he could not feel even a hint of breeze. He thought to himself: what kind of land is this? Half the year round it is unfit to live in—you sweat all the time and the temperature doesn't go below hundred in the shade. If Indians find it hard, why do foreigners want to live in this inhospitable land? He was distracted momentarily by the thought of Mughal princes sensuously lounging about in shaded pavilions amidst their fountains, their languid women and their cushions. Indignation gradually displaced this fleeting Mughal vision, as he recalled the shameful way he pretended to himself on countless evenings that a breeze was blowing when he went for a walk. Instead of reviving him, the walks usually left him tired and sweaty. From March the hot season began, with the mean temperature rising at the rate of ten degrees per month. In May, when the thermometer ranged between 95 and 115, a desiccating, scorching wind started to blow. And there was no relief till the end of June when the south and east wind finally ushered in the monsoon rains. Both the Mughals and the English had disliked the Indian heat, and both had worked out elaborate ways to make themselves comfortable. The English built hill stations or built bungalows with extremely high ceilings and the Mughals surrounded themselves with gardens and running water.

These thoughts calmed him and he decided to return inside. On the way back, he passed by a group of his poor relations from the village, who sat quietly in a corner apparently not feeling the need to converse, and content to observe the festivities. Theirs was not an awkward silence (as it might have been with the drawing room crowd); they appeared to find happiness merely in being together with their own kin. He felt heartened by this observation, and from melancholy his mood slowly turned to compassion for his people. He saw faded aunts, stupid cousins, ambitious nephews and conceited nieces. Each one thrown into the world. Simple people trying to enjoy one night of frail happiness between their exhausting unhappy days. He felt protective towards them. They were all part of himself. His people seemed to give him strength and helped him fight off the last remnants of his gloom.

It was two in the morning and the pandit intoned, 'Om Swaha'; Bauji and the rest of the family picked up incense and threw it into the fire. The marriage ceremony was in progress. The girl's side and the local gentry had finished eating hours ago. Many of the guests had left soon after, and by midnight most of the carriages had departed.

The pandit was seated on the ground in front of the sacrificial fire. Across from him sat the bride and groom. Around the pandit were trays of incense, holy water from the Ganges, sacred thread, honey, flour, rice and fruit. The two families, and some close friends, sat a few yards away in a large semi-circle watching the marriage ceremony. The couple were facing east: the bride on the left, with the end of her phulkari tied to the groom's sword. Tara's head was covered by the red phulkari, drawn low over her face;

Seva Ram's face was hidden by the *sehra* of flowers.

The pandit had just explained to the couple that the wife was part of her husband. No man or woman's life was complete without marriage. No religious ritual could henceforth be performed by the man without his wife. Holding the bride's hand in his, the groom began to repeat in Sanskrit, 'I hold your hand for our happiness. May we both live to a ripe old age. You are the queen and shall rule over my home. I am the heaven, you are the earth. Let us marry and be joined together. Your heart I take in mine. Our minds shall be one. May God make us one.'

After this, the couple took the seven sacred steps around the holy fire. With the first step, the groom prayed for sustenance, with the second for strength, with the third for keeping their vows and ideals, with the fourth for a comfortable life, with the fifth for their cattle, with the sixth for their life through the various seasons of the year, and with the seventh step for fulfilling their religious duties.

The bride next mounted a stone, which symbolized the strength of their union. Together they gazed at the pole star, and prayed for constancy. They observed the seven stars in the Great Bear constellation, and told each other that like the stars in the skies, they too would never be separated. Tara then prayed to Agni, the god of fire, to witness their marriage for the prosperity of their new home. She sipped the water from the Ganges to wash away her impurities, so that she could start a new and pure life.

The pandit finally exhorted Seva Ram to practice the four aims of life: be righteous; earn sufficient wealth for well being; allow yourself time for love and passion with your wife; and strive for oneness with the Absolute.

Bauji sat with Bhabo in the front row amidst the spectators. Since he could not see Tara's face he couldn't tell what his daughter was feeling. More than likely she was a bundle of fatigue and nerves. He reflected on the strange ways of nature. He, the father of the bride, had an honoured role in 'gifting' his daughter in a *kanya dan*. Instead of feeling honoured, he was struck by the irony of the situation: for twenty years you gave your daughter love and everything you had and then one day you had to 'gift' her away. Suddenly she belonged to someone else. You told her that she shouldn't come back if she had problems, because this was no longer her home. She had a new father and mother. This was clearly unfair. But then life was not meant to be fair: it just was, he thought, as he tried to fight the melancholy which again started to envelop him.

His thoughts returned to his daughter. Did Tara know what was ahead of her? After the initial period of adjustment, she would be happy and in love. Soon boredom would set in and then the inevitable cares, children, and worries and slowly the romance would disappear. He did not feel like pursuing the script—let Tara be happy to be made into a woman.

It was dawn. The long Vedic ceremony had finally ended and preparations had begun for the biggest moment of the wedding, the departure of the bride in a palanquin. Bauji had broken his day-long fast with a glass of milk. Friends and relatives had complimented him for having done his duty: the daughter had been gifted.

While the dowry was being packed and loaded, and as the family was gathering for the departure, Bauji had gone into the study for a bit of peace and quiet. Just as he was beginning to feel better, having fought off fatigue and gloom, he received the news of a tragedy which plunged him into the greatest depths of despair. It brought to focus all his fears and forced him to face a reality which appeared inescapable.

His neighbour's son of twenty had been murdered in cold blood in the house next door less than half-an-hour ago. Bauji knew the boy well and enjoyed a relationship of mutual respect with his family. The boy had been fast asleep in his room, when he had been set upon by at least three people. The instrument used was an axe, and the boy had quickly bled to death. It was a 'communal killing', of a Hindu by Muslims, in return for a Muslim death by Hindus a few days earlier in another part of town.

Bauji's mouth began to feel sticky. He started to sweat. He took off his shirt. Nausea seemed to be coming over him, but he tried to control it. He went to the bathroom to wash his face. Instead he vomited. He rinsed his mouth and felt better.

Soon the stink returned. It was the same smell, he realized, that came from the corpse in the Company Bagh. He let the smell linger and slowly diffuse throughout the room. It was muted by the fragrance of languorous magnolia. For a moment he was almost enjoying it. He had recaptured that moment under the leechi tree when he turned the corpse over in the carnation bed. He could clearly see the boy's face covered in blood and vomit with his nails dug into the ground. He sat down on his carved teak chair and looked down at his legs. He saw life flowing through them. While the young die, he thought, life runs through the old. He could almost see the vital liquid rushing through his legs. He smiled ironically.

The fretted hands of the bronze clock on the shelf stood at five-thirty. He turned to the window and saw the deathly light of dawn. He looked back at the clock and slowly his mind began to clear. It is a perverted world, he thought, which divides people; it makes people feel exclusive and put their own community above the whole; and to prefer their own community's good to the good of all.

He felt a revulsion for all organized religion. The only thing that matters, he said to himself, is to be kind and decent to your fellow human beings. It is the only imperative. Religion can hang itself. This thought gave him strength. He recalled his past, and he was comforted by the reassuring fact that he had not formed religious attachments. There seemed nothing more to do in life but to live it out as gently and kindly as he possibly could; not to hurt anyone, not to worry and not to expect anything.

The stink gradually dissolved. He looked again at the clock and he was reminded of his duties. He rose, got dressed and left his study. Both families were assembled in the courtyard. Many others who had slept through the ceremony had now returned. Mercifully, someone had sent away the band after the news of the tragedy next door. However, the colourful palanquin bearers were ready and waiting. The palanquin was covered in purple silk. The parting of the bride from her family, a sad moment at the best of times was made sadder by the events of the past hour. As he looked at people's faces, Bauji thought the scene resembled a funeral procession. The weary Tara soon arrived in the courtyard, weighed down by jewellery and heavy silks. As someone began to sing the traditional song of departure, Bauji gently asked him to stop. Bhabo, Tara and her sisters embraced tearfully. Finally Bauji led Tara to the palanquin. He embraced her for the last time and blessed her. She screamed from within and the palanquin bearers knew it was time. Bauji folded his hands in farewell to the boy's parents and relatives, and Tara left for her new home.

Eventually the dam broke. Half-an-hour after their departure, Bauji started to cry in the privacy of his room. Chachi was the only one who knew. Either she was sensitive to his moods and his growing pain of the past twelve hours, or she merely happened to be around. Bauji was never quite sure. As he was weeping, she came and put her tiny arm on his vast shoulders and she said, 'Be a man, Dewan Chand. Don't cry like a woman! You have done your duty of *kanya dan*; you should be proud.'

9

Lala Dewan Chand had known a sense of loss for some time now. Ever since the evening when he discovered the Hindu boy's corpse in the Company Bagh, life had begun to escape him. Sometimes in moments of deep and intense worldly activity this continual sense of loss would disappear, only to reappear in moments of silence and introspection.

Five years had passed. The War was over. Britain was about to announce its departure from India and the partition of the Punjab in order to create the political state of Pakistan. While the world around him was bursting with activity and politics, Bauji stood paralyzed in his own private world. Every day it took more and more effort to catch the jasmine's scent or the koel's sound in the Lyallpur evenings. Even the most familiar sensations seemed to be slipping away. But it was not totally unfortunate, for with the loss had also come an increasing insulation from the evil outside. Every day there was news of riots, carnage and rape. He seemed to slowly become immune from their impact. His private partition had begun many years ago, when he had first experienced the wickedness of organized religion and politics in the Company Bagh.

It was a humid day at the end of July 1947. Bauji sat in the courtyard smoking a hookah in the early evening. If the scents of the early summer evening eluded him, the memories of the past did not. Much to his annoyance they came gushing out like a river in spate. For months he had stopped going to the Company Bagh as it was no longer safe. Besides, most of his Company Bagh companions had fled Lyallpur in anticipation of trouble. He listened to the servant filling up a bucket with the hand pump in order to water the courtyard. But he was a poor substitute for Mashkiya. Despite his best efforts, he could never bring forth the smell of the earth. Mashkiya had left two weeks ago. They had kept this information from him for several days, but it had finally spilled out.

Suddenly after a long time Bauji heard the welcome cry of the peacock; he smiled at the familiar sound and felt buoyed up. He remembered Anees. He had missed the peacock's voice for weeks. Just as he was feeling reassured, the cry turned into a harsh shriek. It slowly became more menacing. He covered his ears, as he saw despair approaching. Soon there was silence. Under the fading light of the evening, surrounded by his favourite jasmine which had ceased to smell, Bauji heard no other sound but that inner one of life gushing out from him.

The silence was broken by the amorous sounds of pigeons. He looked up and he saw the mischievous lovers, Heer and Ranjha, who were as usual up to no good, pecking playfully and flirting with each other.

'At least they don't have to worry about finding a new home,' he said enviously.

There, now it was said. He had been avoiding it all this time. Many of his friends had confronted the truth squarely and left to make a new life in the East. Bauji had not been able to face the prospect of leaving. To his mind, it was an ugly joke of the politicians—suddenly one day you were expected to leave your home and the life that you had lived for generations. Just like that. And for what? Go where? You were expected to cross a new border and look for a new home and a new life. And why? Just because one politician had promised a separate nation to the Indian Muslims? Why must they take his home away?

'I spit on all of you—Mountbatten, Gandhi, Nehru and Jinnah. If this is the price of freedom, I don't want it. Let us continue to be ruled by England. I want my home. I hate dreamers, especially if they are politicians. Mountbatten dreams of glory—of setting the second largest country free, of giving birth to two nations, not once but twice blessed. Gandhi and Nehru dream of winning freedom from the most powerful empire on the earth and that too by peaceful means. Jinnah dreams of being the father of the new nation of Pakistan.'

He wished there were more practical men in politics. They would think like him, and look to the needs of ordinary people. There were sorrows enough without dreamers making it worse. In the end only the mundane mattered: to live in your community with kindness and affection; to love those who loved you; to care for those who needed it; to support your neighbours, your friends and your relatives; to be a good son to your parents, a good husband to your wife, a good father to your children. The rest would take care of itself.

How dare the politicians snatch away his home! Years ago, with much love and pride, he had brought his bride to this house. His children and grandchildren were born here. It had nourished three generations. And now they expected him to calmly pack up and walk away from his beloved Lyallpur, where all his joys and sorrows lay. And for what? Some principle, he was expected to believe in: freedom, nation-state, self-rule? He was also being asked to give up the legal practice that he had built with hard work, his properties, which he had acquired with patience and skill. And go where? Go and roam the countryside across a borderline which an Englishman named Radcliffe was just then drawing on a map, while he smoked a Havana cigar, without a thought to the million emotions on both sides of the line.

Had it been an earthquake or an accident of nature Bauji would have found it easier to accept it. Yes, he would have raged against fate but he would have accepted it in the end. It was the insanity of men acting in the name of higher principles which he found hard to stomach.

His thoughts suddenly turned to the ashram. He remembered with nostalgia the atmosphere of the river, the peace and detachment. Despite the obvious charms of that way of life, he still found himself resisting it. He couldn't quite accept being a 'passenger through life'. His mind kept relentlessly wandering through the labyrinths of his heart. Where did this hatred of Hindus and Muslims come from? Was man by nature a hating beast under the cloak of reason and dignity conferred on him by his ability for abstract thought and the facility to verbalize moral dilemmas? Thus he questioned, momentarily forgetting his own spell of hatred and anger.

He asked himself whether he, a Hindu, hated Muslims? Yes, came the honest answer: he did. He instinctively disliked them. He knew he was wrong, but it was too late to fool himself. There was no sense in being hypocritical or 'liberal'. Now that it was out, he might as well understand it. Why did he dislike them? Because he supposed, they were exclusive; they could not accept him as an equal; he was an infidel in their eyes; their loyalty to Islam transcended all other loyalties; they were fanatical, violent and intolerant.

As he thought about Anees and his Muslim friends, he felt the need to qualify his feelings. He did not hate the person he realized, but he disliked what being Muslim did to people. He hated organized religion, which took away the ambiguity of life. Were the Muslims not after all mostly Hindus converted to Islam, one to twenty generations ago? If that was true, if they were like him, of Hindu ancestry, why did he hate them? Yes, the fault lay in institutions, not with ordinary people. A dangerously liberal thought, which he tried to dismiss. He suppressed a depressing laugh which left an aftertaste of sweetish nausea.

As a tolerant, worldly Hindu, who had lived all his life amongst Muslims, he could not understand why they wanted to be apart. He found it difficult to concede that the Muslims existed as a separate and independent community whose outlook was essentially different from that of the Hindus. He appreciated that many of their beliefs, traditions and even values were different. And certainly their dress, food and manners were unique. But they were Indians after all, with the same temperament and love for the Indian soil. Otherwise they would have left and gone to Arabia. Yet, sitting here, far away from Mecca, the hold of Islam on them was undeniable.

He found it hard to understand the power and loyalty of the Islamic faith. Its outlook was so different from the tolerant Hindu mind. He was reminded of his conversation with Anees five years ago. He had never seen her again, but she was often in his thoughts. He had never thought of himself as Hindu, but she had made him conscious of it that day. He instinctively knew that Anees would choose her faith over her love for a man. Not that he had ever been in a position to offer such a choice to her. But it frightened him.

He tried to reflect calmly on Islam. Surprisingly, he found it easier to get hold of than Hinduism, which was amorphous and vague. He remembered Anees telling him, 'Bauji, Islam is clear, stern and definite. A Creed, a Book and a Brotherhood: that is Islam. The Creed is that of the Prophet—"there is no god but God and Mohammed is his prophet." The Book is the Koran, which contains the dogma and rule of life. The Brotherhood is the equality of all Muslims before God and each other'. She had sounded almost angry as she had said this to him. Bauji felt that a Muslim accepted the world and tried to make the most of it, whereas the Hindu denied it, and sought to escape from it. For the Muslim, life was a probation for the next world; for the Hindu, it was *maya* or illusion, therefore, unimportant.

Although he had never thought of it before, now in trying to understand Islam it occurred to him that there was an attractive quality about the Hindu way of life. Hinduism was a sort of fellowship of faiths because it was willing to learn and absorb new ideas. For example, Buddhism had been born as a reaction against the power and corruption of Hindu brahmins, but it had been absorbed back into Hinduism a thousand years later. This explained the Hindu's free-thinking, catholic, easy-going temper. Why, he even knew rank atheists who could call themselves Hindus. It had few dos and don'ts and provided a whole menu of spiritual paths. Depending on one's inclination or aptitude there were many ways to the supreme end: the way of knowledge, of love, of deeds, etc. He concluded that he preferred the ambiguity and the 'humanity' of the Hindus rather than the boring and fanatical certainty of the Muslims.

'Who are these Muslims amongst us?' Chachi had once asked him. Before he could reply she had answered her own question. 'They would like to believe that they are "conquerors of India" in the past ages, but the vast majority are descended from Hindus. Many of them were converted by force. A few upper class Hindus switched because of the promise of power and wealth under Muslim rulers. But the largest number was attracted from the low caste Hindus. Islam held the prospect of improving their lot, a promise of brotherhood, and fewer taboos. They had nothing to lose by conversion.'

He was distracted by the smell of cooking in the earthen tandoor upstairs. It must be lunch time. Good, he needed a distraction from these thoughts. He got up slowly and walked over to the hand pump. A servant saw him and rushed to work the pump. The cool water brought comfort in the heat. His hands were almost burning, he felt. The water was cool because it came from their own well rather than the water pipes of the city. The girls were right about one thing. The sink at Khanna's was definitely a good idea. It prevented you from bending down and kept your feet and clothes dry. He too must instal one.

The servant handed him a freshly laundered towel which he luxuriantly enveloped around his hands. It was white and it smelled of the dhobi ghat. It exuded a familiar cool feeling which he had known for almost fifty years, for the same dhobi family had washed their laundry ever since he had come to Lyallpur. First it had been the father, now the son. His eyes fell on the label of the towel: 'Manchester' it said. The irony of using an English towel in a country which was the home of textiles did not escape him. It merely testified to the complete success of British colonialism. This land of ours, he mused, has been too hospitable to the foreigner. We have become accustomed to alien rulers who neither knew our religion nor our language. Otherwise how could we have coped with Turkish Emirs, Afgan viceroys, Mughal tax collectors, and English Sub-Divisional Officers. Now with the British leaving, how are we going to cope by ourselves? We are like orphans—but orphans who are thousands of years old and exhausted—who must suddenly rule ourselves. Not that we cannot do it eventually. Not that we do not have good people, but ruling takes years of learning. We are out of practice (by perhaps a thousand years). We have perfected the art of being ruled; now we must learn the skills of ruling ourselves.

The foreign rulers brought their full baggage of religion, language and culture. The Muslims built mosques, taught us Persian, and collected taxes. The British built churches, taught us English and collected taxes. We did not understand their religion or their language, but taxes we understood only too well. Because of the dreaded jazia tax many Hindus converted to Islam and now these same converts spit at us and want to divide our country. With this depressing idea he found he had arrived in the dining room, and he was happy to escape from his dreary thoughts. He realized that he had also carried the towel along with his thoughts, and he handed it back to the servant.

At five o'clock the next morning four Muslim boys armed with daggers, broke into Bauji's house. Bauji was asleep indoors under a fan. They headed for his room. Finding it locked, they tried to pry it open. Bauji woke up, and opened the door. 'Good morning,' said Bauji. 'Do come in. I'm sorry you dragged yourselves out of bed so early for my sake. I know you have come to kill me. And I am ready to die. But please do sit down. Shall we have a cup of tea before the ... um ... event?'

The boys were stunned. One of them who could not have been more than sixteen began to cry. The others looked visibly embarrassed. They had their heads down. All of a sudden their leader dropped down to his knees and begged for Bauji's forgiveness. Bauji pressed them again to have tea, but they declined the offer.

Bauji asked the youngest boy why he was crying. His older companion answered instead.

'He is a cry-baby, sir.'

'I am not,' protested the youngster.

'Every morning he comes back home and boasts to his friends how many Hindus he has killed. But at night he cries in bed. At least that's what his mother says. The other day he couldn't even kill a person properly. We were in Gol Bazaar, and he half killed this old man. The fellow lay in agony and I had to go back and kill him properly.'

'Boys, tell me, why are you killing Hindus?' asked Bauji.

'Because we will go to heaven. Our mullah says that a Mussalman gets seven beautiful women in heaven if he kills a kaffir.'

10

In the half-light of dawn of the twelfth of August, Lyallpur was deserted and forlorn. In the front of the tonga sat a huddled, pitiful
figure who could not be recognized as the towering man of yesterday. As he passed by each vomit-coloured house, Bauji saw the
refuse of human suffering accumulated along leprous walls. Even
the dogs trembled as they wandered in despair for a morsel of
human neglect. Once or twice a door opened and the smell of fear
spilled onto the street. By this pale half-dead light Bhabo felt the
foreheads of her grandchildren for symptoms of malaria. The
houses in Kacheri Bazaar were either empty or in mourning. He
saw carcasses of men strewn over the street and he heard the wail
of widows. He spotted two men on the road who gripped their
bodies in shame as they walked with heads hung low not daring to
look at anyone.

His humiliating journey had begun. Bauji was taking his family
and a few belongings out of Lyallpur. The tonga was on its way to
the railway station. He was vanquished and sore, like the defeated
horse leading his tonga.

On the ninth of August a train of half-alive Muslim refugees had
arrived in Lyallpur. They had told a harrowing tale of murder,
arson and rape on the other side. The Muslims of Lyallpur had
vowed revenge. On tenth August had occurred the great massacre
of the Hindus and the Sikhs of Lyallpur, in which two thousand
people were killed in twenty-four hours. On the morning of the
tenth of August, a meeting was held in Lyallpur's main mosque
where the Muslim clergy called upon all Muslims to kill non-
Muslims. Sikhs were especially singled out to pay for crimes in
Amritsar, Jullunder and Ludhiana. On hearing this, many Sikhs
immediately cut off their hair and shaved their beards, thinking
that a less conspicuous appearance might help to save their lives.
The barbers of Lyallpur in consequence had been unusually busy
that morning. At noon, the sweeper woman brought the news

about the mosque meeting to Bauji's family and it became clear to them that it would be impossible to stay on in their beloved city.

In the early afternoon, a Hindu mohalla behind Kacheri Bazaar was attacked by a mob, led by a Muslim Sub-Inspector of Police. Around four o'clock the National Guards of the Muslim League stormed Gol Bazaar. Fires soon raged in all major Hindu parts of the town. At six p.m. Bauji could see a huge wall of smoke and flame standing against the sky. Throughout the evening Muslim groups armed with guns, pistols, spears, hatchets, and lathis wandered about the streets attacking Hindus and Sikhs and setting fire to their shops. From the roof Big Uncle reported that he had seen their kirana shopkeeper, at the corner of Kacheri Bazaar, being dragged out by his hair. The official communique stated that twenty-five fires were blazing, of which eight were of a serious nature. By seven p.m. the Civil Hospital had received 856 dead bodies and 1680 injured.

Prices too betrayed the state of affairs. As the day advanced, panic buying by the departing Hindus pushed up prices higher and higher. The prices of gold, weapons, horses, tongas doubled every hour in the afternoon, while the prices of furniture, clothing, utensils and household goods kept falling equally rapidly.

At ten o'clock that night, Mr Hamid, the Muslim District Collector, came to visit Bauji. A doubles tennis partner of Big Uncle, he was a good friend of the family. He held Bauji in particularly high esteem. In turn Bauji's family had been impressed by his neutral and helpful attitude. With his indefatigable energy Mr Hamid had kept lawless elements in check for the past two weeks. Just a few days ago he had vowed that he would not allow Hindus to be harmed. Bauji and most Hindus had believed him and had not so far evacuated. Lyallpur was a prosperous district where most of the capital belonged to the Hindus. Apart from property, Hindu capital was invested in cotton ginning, weaving, flour and sugar mills. The Hindus of Lyallpur thus lingered on, desperately hoping that this madness would pass and peace would soon return. They had to believe in Mr Hamid, and they received his assurances unquestioningly. But the emotional wave of communal frenzy on the tenth of August was proving to be too much for him. The arrival of the Muslim refugees from the East, who had suffered at the hands of the Sikhs had made Mr Hamid's job near impossible.

Mr Hamid looked sad and defeated as he sat in Bauji's courtyard that night. The tragic happenings of the day had overwhelmed him.

Seeing him lose confidence—he who had been the source of hope and so much strength all these months—filled them with fear. They began to despair. Mr Hamid informed Bauji that it was no longer safe for a Hindu to stay on in Lyallpur. They must leave immediately. He offered to hide them in an evacuated Englishman's house in Civil Lines under the protection of a trusted Muslim servant until it was safe to leave the city. He gave them one hour to pack.

At midnight a police van came for them. As they piled in noiselessly into the van, Bhabo cried, 'Oh, wait! I forgot to lock the front door.' Bauji roared with laughter.

'What are you laughing at?'

'At you—locking the Muslims out,' he said.

They were transported to an innocent looking house in Civil Lines, where they stayed in hiding until the next night. At four a.m. on the twelfth, the servant knocked on Bauji's door and informed him that they had been discovered. The Muslim driver of the police van had apparently informed the Muslim League. Their life was again in danger. The servant had got hold of a rickety tonga, which would take them to the railway station before daylight.

Thus it happened that Bauji's fear-stricken family was riding out to the station at dawn on the twelfth. They were nine in a tonga meant for five. The tonga was smaller than usual and the footboard at the back was dangerously low. The wheels leaned inward as if their revolutions would make them come off. Each time Bauji looked at the horse, his heart sank. He was small and emaciated and he moved with his head dispiritedly low, almost between his forelegs. His back was raw with sores and harness galls and he breathed as no horse he had known.

'Not much of an animal, is he?' said the tongawalla. 'Looks like he'll die any day. But he's the best I could do. The Muslim guards stole mine yesterday. They would have killed me too had I not immediately dropped my salwar and shown them my circumcised penis.'

He turned the horse's slow feet eastward, and the wobbling carriage bounced into the rutty lane with a jolt that brought a stifled cry from Bhabo. Dark silent houses loomed on either side. The narrow street was like a dim tunnel with the faint red glow of the sky its ceiling. The smell of smoke became stronger. The shadows chased one another in the faint light. With the hot air, came a pandemonium of sounds from the center of the town, yells, the dull rumbling of a crowd. As the tongawalla jerked the horse's head and turned him into another street, a deafening explosion tore the air and a skyrocket of flame and smoke shot up in the east.

'That must be the police ammunition dump,' said Bauji calmly.

'Well, too bad for us,' said the tongawalla. 'I thought that by circling around the centre of town, we might avoid the fire and the drunken mob at the clock tower. But we've got to cross the tower now to get to the station.'

'Must—must we go that way?' Bhabo quavered.

'Wait,' said Bauji suddenly.

Springing down from the tonga, he disappeared in the faint light. He returned with a small limb of a tree in his hand. He pulled the reins from the tongawalla, and laid the wood mercilessly across the horse's galled back. The animal broke into a shambling trot, his breath panting and laboured. The carriage swayed forward with a jolt. The girls cried out as they bruised themselves against the sides. As they neared the clock tower, the trees thinned out, and tall flames flew above the buildings. There was a glow of sickly light which cast monstrous, twisting shadows. Bauji felt cold, and he shivered even though the heat of the flames was hot against their faces. He looked back. He would have liked nothing more than to turn back to the refuge of his beloved home on Kacheri Bazaar. In the abnormal glow, his dark profile stood out clearly and beautifully. As they dashed down the street, he applied the whip automatically. His face looked set and absent, as though he had forgotten where he was. His broad shoulders were hunched forward and his chin jutted out. The beat of the fire made sweat stream down his forehead.

Suddenly they were approaching an angry crowd. 'Mussalman!' shouted the tongawalla. Bauji pulled into a side lane, then turned and twisted from one narrow street to another until they were at the Clock Tower.

They were greeted in the square with the crash of a falling house. The cheering mob's attention was immediately diverted to this spectacle. As the children and Bhabo began to cough from the smoke in their nostrils, Bauji brought the tree limb down on the horse's back with a cruel force that made the animal leap forward. With all the speed the horse could summon they jolted and bounced across the square. The glare dazzled their eyes and the heat seared their skin. Ahead of them was a tunnel of smoke. They plunged into it, and abruptly they were in semi-darkness. They came out in a narrow street that led to the railway station.

But they never reached the railway station. As they approached they heard the sound of bullets and found Hindus pouring out in the hundreds from the direction of the station. Many were fleeing across the railway tracks. They learnt that the Muslim guards had taken over the station under the leadership of the Superintendent of Police, and they were indiscriminately shooting at anyone who tried to get onto a train. Not knowing what to do, Bauji's family joined the escaping Hindus who had formed into a *kafla* (foot convoy) and were heading out by the only road leading east towards Lahore.

After they had gone half a mile, they smiled for the first time as they observed at a distance a six-mile-long *kafla* of Hindus and Sikhs coming from Sargodha, under the escort of a Muslim Baluch regiment. In numbers they felt secure. There must have been more than a hundred thousand people, most of them on foot, but some seated in bullock carts, a few in tongas like Bauji's family. The Lyallpur *kafla* waited at the road junction as the Sargodha foot convoy passed and then joined it at the rear.

Among the refugees in the *kafla*, Bauji found a friend and a neighbour from Kacheri Bazaar. His name was Dr Des Raj. He had sometimes been called home on an emergency, although he was not their regular doctor. Dr Des Raj was in the habit of writing a diary, which he continued through this troubled time. His diary was recovered from his aunt's house in Delhi, a few years after his death. He wrote the following account of the Lyallpur *kafla*.

After joining the Sargodha *kafla*, we had gone half-a-mile when we had to slow down in order to pass a railway level crossing at Tarkabad, on the outskirts of Lyallpur. Three-quarters of the *kafla* crossed the railway line, when the gate suddenly closed. As if out of nowhere a mob of armed Muslims emerged at this moment, and fell upon the portion of the convoy left behind, and began a ruthless massacre. The mob must have been hiding in the fields and planned the massacre in advance. Pandemonium broke out. Screaming men and women and children began to run hither and thither in all directions. The Muslims cut down with axes and *chavis* anyone who came in their way. They looted the property from bullock carts. Since most of their valuables were carried by the women as jewellery, they stripped the women naked, and paraded them. They abducted the younger and prettier girls, and killed the older women. The Hindus looked helplessly to the Baluch military for protection, but the military merely watched, and in a few cases even opened fire on the scattering Hindus who appeared to be escaping into the fields. The assault continued throughout the morning, and by the afternoon the ground was strewn with dead bodies. The army then asked the able-bodied Hindu survivors to pick up the dead before the civil authorities arrived. They had them loaded into military trucks, to be thrown into the Chenab river.

Mr Hamid, the District Collector, arrived on the scene in the afternoon. He recalled the Baluch army, and under heavy police guard returned the survivors of the convoy to a refugee camp, which he set up in Khalsa College in Lyallpur. Among the survivors were Bauji's family and Dr Des Raj. They were alive because they had been far at the rear of the convoy; there were too many people to kill and not enough killers. Mr Hamid wrote a report censuring the Baluch commander and the next day he suspended his own SP for his activities at the railway station. In the confusion he did not see Bauji's family nor they him.

Dr Des Raj continued the account in his diary of the Khalsa college camp.

That night in the college camp the Muslim police in charge attacked the inmates. Sixty cases of rape were reported and another fifty Hindu girls were carried away. The police were observed to instigate the Baluch military to join in the attack. At first the soldiers were reluctant to do so. But later they succumbed to a police inspector's appeal, who eloquently argued that it was the duty of every Mussalman to kill the infidel. It was written in the Koran, he said. Killing the infidel was a legitimate way to reach heaven.

At about midnight, accompanied by the cry of 'Ya Ali, Ya Ali', the Baluch military opened fire on the helpless refugees. The refugees, many of whom were asleep, tried to scatter and run away. Some of them jumped in the well of the Khalsa College and were drowned. Approximately eight hundred people were killed and thousands wounded. Bauji was hit by a bullet in his thigh. The bodies of the dead were again loaded into army trucks to be thrown into the Chenab.

The mopping up of bodies was done carelessly, and the next morning when the DC arrived he found 150 bodies still lying in the camp. He immediately left to wire the Headquarters in Lahore for a Hindu Gurkha army contingent to replace the Baluch regiment. He removed the police entirely from the camp, and had the inspector arrested. He persuaded the military commander to disarm the soldiers.

In the afternoon, Mr Hamid went to the Lyallpur Club for lunch, where he learned that the attack had been pre-planned. The Muslim Agent of the Imperial Bank told him that he had overheard his police guard boasting the previous evening about a plan to attack the camp at night. Mr Hamid asked the Agent, 'Why didn't you tell me?'

'I didn't attach much importance to the talk. Besides I think the Hindus deserved it, don't you? We want to cleanse our country of infidels. Pakistan means "land of the pure", after all.'

Disgusted, Mr Hamid left his lunch uneaten.

Meanwhile, at the camp, Dr Des Raj had survived the attack, and he had been treating the wounded since the morning. He left the following in his diary.

> I had no medicines, nor instruments. I asked the camp commander to let me go out with an escort to my clinic or to the government clinic to bring my instruments, but permission was refused. Thus I had to perform major operations with second hand razor blades, which I obtained with difficulty, and use ordinary oil for dressing wounds. In place of guaze I used tailor's rags. Since there were no bandages, I had to leave the wounds uncovered. I worked throughout the day and took out bullets from tens of wounds. They were mostly big bullets from .303 rifles.
>
> I treated a goldsmith's wife, whose breasts had been lopped off, but she died the same night. There was another lady whose hands were chopped from her wrists and she had been thrown into a fire, as a result of which her lower parts had been burnt. During the firing, she had jumped into the well of the college along with her children; although the children drowned, she had escaped; she was a courageous woman and she survived my primitive treatment. I also treated a large number of men with circumcision wounds on their penises.
>
> There were no latrines in the camp. We had to defecate in buckets, and then carry the buckets out. I also delivered a number of babies, which came prematurely in most cases because of the panic, excitement, and discomfort felt by the pregnant mothers. Since there was no place to confine the mothers, the deliveries took place in the open before the public. I am sorry to say that since there was no soap and proper cloth, many cases became septic.

In the evening, Mr Hamid returned to the camp for an inspection. During the visit, he spotted Bauji's family from among thousands of people. He saw that Bauji had been seriously wounded, and he began to weep. He took Bauji's family and Dr Des Raj to the Civil Hospital, where they administered emergency treatment to Bauji. At the hospital Mr Hamid begged the Muslim doctors and nurses to go to the refugee camp, but all of them refused. Since he did not trust leaving Bauji in the hospital, Mr Hamid took them to his own house, where he fed and clothed them. He sorrowfully told Bauji about his inability to give them asylum at his own house, since it would strain his credibility with the Muslim populace. He took them that night to the Sri Ram Mills, where about five hundred of Lyallpur's Hindu gentry were gathered. They were under a heavy Hindu Dogra guard, and were waiting for a convoy of trucks to take them east the next morning. The striking difference between these refugees and the ones at Khalsa College was in their economic circumstances. But they shared the same fear in their eyes. Mr Hamid left after reassuring Bauji's family that they would be safer here than even his own house. He promised to return the next morning to see them off. Dr Des Raj added this account in his diary about the happenings at the textile mill.

No one slept that night. We heard drums beating all night long, and repeatedly the air was pierced by the dreaded cry of 'Ya Ali.' We were scared. At dawn when there was light and we could see, we suddenly realized that the guard had been switched. Instead of Hindu Dogras, we were under Sindhi Muslim constables. We discovered that the Muslim League had tricked our guard by sending fake transfer orders from military headquarters. There was general anxiety and a hush fell upon the refugees. We stood rooted and watched each other with vague foreboding.

At six o'clock a shot was heard. Swami Ram Rattan, who had been an active member of the Congress Committee, went outside with a green flag to talk to the police. They asked for twelve hundred rupees which we immediately paid. Fifteen minutes later they demanded another twelve hundred, which too was promptly paid. Then they wanted to search everyone. Many of the women began to cry, as they were carrying their family savings on their persons in the form of gold jewellery.

All five hundred of us were asked to come outside in the mill compound. We were told to remove all our valuables and gold. Swami Ram Rattan advised the refugees to comply. Soon there was a great pile of roughly four maunds of gold and more than five lakhs of rupees in cash. I had never seen so much money, but then there were a number of trading families amongst us.

It was still early. Our transport was not expected for another two hours. After carefully collecting the treasure, the policemen started to molest young girls under the pretext of searching them. Swami Ram Rattan objected; he was immediately shot down.

About five yards from where I was standing, the seniormost in the police party began to fondle the breasts of an attractive young girl in a blue sari. The girl's brother, who I think stood behind him, pounced on the policeman, and knifed him whereupon the police opened fire indiscriminately on the refugees. While the front ranks of the refugees were falling to the bullets, some of the Hindu and Sikh fathers at the back began to slaughter their own daughters to prevent them from being raped or abducted by the Muslims.

Fortunately there was a large peepal tree nearby. Bauji's family and I hid behind the tree as the bullets rained. When the attention of the police was diverted to the killing of the girls at the back, we ran to the adjoining wall, scaled it, and leaped on the other side. Unfortunately one of Bauji's daughters was hit by a bullet and got left behind. On the other side, a policeman who was standing on guard, saw us. He aimed his gun at us, but Bauji, who was very close to him, jumped and rushed at him. He tripped and Bauji snatched his rifle; Bauji struck him with the butt end with all his might, leaving him unconscious. We ran towards the fields, and hid under a haystack. Bauji was unconscious the whole day.

In the evening we stole into the adjoining Ganesh Flour Mill, where we found two Hindu girls hidden under jute bags. Luckily the next day we saw a Muslim friend of Bauji's pass by, who took us at night to a neighbouring village. He provided us with a bullock cart, and escorted us to another *kafla*, which was headed towards Lahore and the Indian border, under the escort of Gurkha soldiers. Bauji, who was in extreme pain, lay in the bullock cart. He was unconscious through most of the blistering trek to Lahore. I wasn't sure if he would survive. . . .

The monsoon came late to India that year, and the summer of 1947 was one of the hottest in people's memory. The Punjab blistered like a hot oven. Each day cirrous clouds moved deceivingly across the sky, casting tantalizing shadows, occasionally throwing a veil across the sun. But by the evening the skies were hopelessly clear again, and the sun set in a blaze of brownish purple. The standing crops of maize were parched, their seed wasted. The cattle bellowed from hunger because the grass along the village ponds and river streams had dried in the sun.

On the road, where millions were marching, there was no relief. The train of humanity ploughed along noiselessly, sinking to the hubs of the wheels, straggling through the soft, stifling, heated dust that did not settle even at night. A part of this dust impeded the movement of feet and of wheels; the other part rose in the air and hovered like a cloud of dust.

By eight in the morning, the body was wet with sweat, clothes were soaked, and the mind sapped by the fear that it would grow even hotter. The sun looked like a purple ball, dazzling blindingly. Not a breath of air stirred, and human beings suffocated in the quiet atmosphere. Those who survived filed past, column after column, miles and miles of tramping feet. They trudged along, covering their noses and mouths. If they passed a village, they rushed for the wells. They fought for water, and drank every drop till nothing but mud was left. But often what greeted them in the villages was a faint hot smoke that bore the smell of burnt bodies. With terrified eyes, the refugees would return to the convoy with dessiccated throats. They had to choose, whether to die of thirst or from the Muslim's sword.

The bright glare of the morning sunlight streaming through a clump of passing sheesham trees awakened Bauji. For a long time he could not remember where he was. He was stiff from the cramped position in which he had been sleeping. The sun blinded him. The uneven and jolting movement of the creaking bullock cart was unfamiliar; the hard boards of the cart felt harsh against a body used to sleeping between satin sheets. He tried to sit up, but he could not because a heavy weight seemed to be across his legs. Slowly he began to remember. As he turned his eyes downwards, he realized that the weight was that of his wound. He felt hot and thirsty. He also felt dirty and sticky and he smelled.

On the blinding road men seemed to go by like ghosts, their voices stilled; he only heard the muffled tramping of feet on soft dirt. There was a smell of death in the air. He turned his eyes to the road's edge, and sure enough there was a dead man lying by the side, ignored, swollen, covered with flies.

'Water,' shouted Bauji weakly.

'He's awake!'

He heard the sound of subdued voices.

'There isn't any water, Bauji,' said Bhabo, coming up to him. 'Soon, very soon, we shall be in Lahore.'

Bauji again lost consciousness. Dr Des Raj, who had stayed on in the *kafla* with Bauji's family, throughout the difficult trek to Lahore, continued writing in his diary:

Our *kafla* from Lyallpur to Lahore must have contained over fifty thousand Hindus and Sikhs. We walked twenty abreast, with men on the outside and women, children, and the sick in between. Carts and carriages also moved on the extremities. Many of the women were uncomfortably clothed in three layers of salwar-kameez in order to make rape more difficult. Some women carried a bottle of poison, which they were expected to drink in case they were raped. One ten-year-old boy who walked near me had been circumcised recently and renamed Yar Mohamad. He kept repeating 'Run, run, there is a riot.' We had to be constantly vigilant against attacks from the sides. As the crops were high, it was easy to ambush a marching column of refugees. The Mussalman attackers would hide in the crops until the last minute and suddenly pounce on a vulnerable part of the *kafla*. Despite the best efforts of the Gurkha escort to hold the refugees together, the victims would scatter in panic. Then the ambush party would move after them with swords and spears.

There were only two incidents of note on our trek upto Lahore, thanks to the good protection provided by our escort. And one of them did not concern our convoy, although we were witness to it. At the canal bridge at Salunjehal in Tehsil Samudri, the front part of our convoy was attacked by a Muslim mob. Despite the firing by our escort, about sixty refugees were killed. While the attack was proceeding, dozens of young girls were lifted by the attacking mob and raped in the field among the crops. Some of the women were stripped naked to see if they had any valuables. Many refugees jumped into the canal during the attack, thinking it safer. But some of them drowned. One woman strapped her three children to her waist and entered the canal; her two younger children drowned. A ten-year-old boy pleaded with his attacker, 'Don't cut my throat. You have already killed my Bapu and Ma. Take me with you. Don't kill me.' Fortunately we were at a considerable distance from this attack, and we were unharmed.

The second incident concerned a passenger train of Hindu refugees which was stopped by a Muslim mob by laying a tree trunk across the track. This happened not too far away from Lahore, I think between Shadara and Badami Bagh stations. Since the train track ran parallel to the road, I was able to get a good view of what happened. All of us in the convoy were frightened, but the mob was only interested in the train. As soon as the train halted, the mob cried 'Allah-o-Akbar' and attacked. About a hundred yards from me a well-dressed, middle aged gentleman was pushed out of the compartment. As he fell down, they first robbed him; next they stripped him till he was stark naked; then he was made to dance and they kicked him in the genitals; slowly he was tortured till he fell unconscious. But the mob could not do much damage to others on the train for our escort fired in the air. Like cowards they ran away.

Lahore was not the end of the journey for the refugees. It was merely the most important milestone on their long trek to safety, to the new border between India and the newly born nation of Pakistan. After a hundred-mile journey to Lahore, there were still twenty-five miles to go to the Wagah border checkpost, near Amritsar. The hearts of the refugees were set on Wagah, for safety lay beyond. No one thought about what would follow after Wagah.

The refugees approached Lahore with mixed feelings. The loss of the legendary city of Lahore had come as a rude shock to the Hindus, who owned eighty per cent of the property there. Their hopes had been shattered when they had learned that Lahore had been included in Pakistan rather than India by the Radcliffe Commission.

There was someone waiting for the Lyallpur *kafla* at Lahore. The person waited patiently in a police van, parked strategically on the outskirts of the capital, where the Lyallpur road met the famous Grand Trunk road. All Hindu refugees from Lyallpur had to pass this fork on their way to the Wagah border. The van was under a tree, and at an angle which gave a clear view of everyone who passed on the road. Seated at the back of the van was a medical doctor and a police officer; a driver and a lady sat in the front. The lady was covered in a rich burkha, and even in the dust and the heat, she smelled of an expensive but familiar scent. Anees Husain was waiting for Bauji.

It was late in the evening and Anees was feeling restless. She had been waiting at this spot for the past three days. But she had a strong feeling that he would come today. Mr Hamid's message had clearly said that he had joined the *kafla* on the fifteenth night. She also knew that he was wounded. If they had started on the *kafla* on the fifteenth night, she calculated that they should have arrived yesterday; perhaps they were moving slower because of his wound. At her insistence her father, the DIG at Lahore, had wired Mr Hamid for Bauji's whereabouts; thus she had traced him to the *kafla*.

She was getting worried now because it was beginning to get dark. Although they had torches, it was difficult to recognize people in the night. She prayed that he would be alive and he should reach soon. She had been waiting in the burning sun and she now felt tired and giddy after staring at thousands of faces. If he did not come today, she had to assume that he had been killed on the way. Even if he had died from the wound, Bhabo and the others would at least pass this way; they would tell her. As it became late, she began to lose hope.

Just as she had given up, and was about to turn the van, she spotted them. The police officer jumped out of the van and went up to Bhabo and the family. They were frightened at first. But the officer spoke gently and pointed to Anees, who had bared her face and was standing at the side of the road. They were in a daze and stared unbelievingly, thinking her an apparition. She immediately knew that Bauji was in the bullock cart. She went up and embraced each one in turn. The police officer and the doctor helped to move Bauji into the van. The first thing they wanted was water. Dr Des Raj advised everyone to drink it slowly. Then he helped Bauji to drink a few drops. Bauji remained unconscious.

'Is he dangerously wounded?' Anees asked Dr Des Raj.

'Yes.'

'How serious is it? Will he live?'

'Only He knows,' said the doctor, pointing to the sky.

Without another word, she helped them into the van, and they quickly drove off into the night. She took them by an inconspicuous unpaved side road to avoid sentries or crowds. Soon they arrived at her spacious home. Rooms were prepared, beds were laid out, baths were readied. She had clothes for everyone. Over dinner she told them that Tara and her family had left Lahore on the ninth of August, the day before the Great Killing in Lahore, and were at the ashram. She had personally seen them safely to the Wagah border check post. She also gave them the tragic news that Bauji's youngest daughter had died in the mill compound. Mr Hamid had wired the information. The refugees were dazed and tired, and fell asleep right after dinner. Bhabo had been crying ever since they had met, and kept thanking Anees and god alternately.

To maintain silence about the refugees, Anees personally made sure that the driver of the police van was locked up after dinner in a servant's quarter. The main gate was sealed so that no member of the household staff could leave that night. She felt she could trust the police officer and the doctor, who were allowed to go.

When everyone had gone to bed, Anees went into her parents' room. She had moved there to make place for the guests. Her father had been called back to police headquarters in the evening. There had been another communal incident in the city, and he was not expected back till the morning. Her mother was still awake.

'Is he seriously wounded?' asked her mother.

'I think so,' she replied. 'He hasn't come to yet.'

'Come Anees, change and go to bed now.'

Instead Anees went towards the window, and thrust her head into the warm moonlit night air. Her mother saw that her slender neck was swollen from the heat.

'It's so hot. How can I sleep?' said Anees looking at the moonlight.

Slowly she went to the bed and mechanically started to undress. She pulled the drawstring of her salwar. After she had put on her night dress, she curled up her feet and sat down on the bed. Pulling her long, thick hair over her shoulders, she began to braid it. Her long, slender fingers deftly unbraided it, and then swiftly braided it up again. She turned her head first to the window and then towards the door. Her eyes, feverishly open, gazed fixedly straight ahead. She put out the light, quietly dropped down on the sheets and buried her face in the pillow. But she could not sleep.

Anees listened to the sounds outside. From across the street she heard the shouting of drunken men. They lived in a quiet part of the city, and during normal days such noises, especially outside the police chief's house, would have been highly unusual. But these were troubled times, and she did not bother about them. What she listened for was sounds from the room next door where Bauji lay unconscious. Instead she heard her mother mutter a prayer and a sigh. Soon she could hear the familiar sound of her mother's steady breathing. Her bare foot peeping from under the bedsheet felt the warm air outside. A cricket chirped from a crevice. An owl hooted in the distance and was answered by one nearby. The shouts from across the street had ceased. Anees thought she heard a groan through the open window. She sat up in bed.

'Amma, Amma, are you asleep?' she whispered.

There was no answer.

Anees rose and slowly, cautiously set her light feet on the bare polished floor. She took a few steps towards the moonlight, and took hold of the brass latch on the door. Again she heard the groaning sound. She felt as if something heavy was knocking on the door. She was frightened until she realized it was her own heart beating. All evening Anees had lived in the anticipation of seeing Bauji. But now that the moment had actually come she was afraid. She did not know what she would see. Would he be badly mutilated?

Would he recognize her when he became conscious? She had not seen Bauji properly so far. In the bullock cart his face had been covered to protect him from the sun. Later at the house she had been too busy organizing for his family, while Dr Des Raj had washed and dressed his wound, and changed his clothes with the help of a servant. Bauji had gained consciousness, drunk some water, but had again become unconscious because of the terrible pain.

She went out into the moonlit veranda. As she opened the door of the adjoining room, she thought her bare feet touched someone sleeping. It was the servant, who had been kept on duty to look after the wounded man. He sat up and whispered something. He stared at the strange apparition of a young woman in night clothes in the wounded man's room.

'Shh! Go back to sleep,' she said to the servant. 'It's only me.' The tired man did what he was told.

As she moved towards the patient, she caught sight of an ill-defined mass in the bed; she took his knees thrust up under the bedclothes for his shoulders and she imagined a horrible mutilated body; she was again afraid and she paused. Soon she felt compelled to move towards him. However terrible he might look, she had to see him. She cautiously took a step, then another, and she was by the bedstead. She could now see him clearly, thanks to the moonlight which filled the room from the open windows. With his arms stretched out over the bedsheet, Bauji looked just as she had always known him. He was awake. His dark eyes gleamed in the strange light; despite his unbearable pain, there was no mistaking the pride that flashed in his eyes.

He recognized her immediately and smiled and slowly extended his hand to her. She took it. She leaned her head gently against his hand and she cried.

'Is it really you?' he said with difficulty.

'Yes,' she whispered.

'My dream in the burkha.'

She nodded.

'What happiness!'

At midnight on 14 August 1947 the British Raj came to an end, and India became free. On the same day, a new nation called Pakistan was born, carved out of West Punjab and East Bengal. A man named Sir Cyril Radcliffe did the actual carving in five weeks and the demarcation on the map came to be known as the Radcliffe Boundary award. It was announced on the seventeenth of August, and the partition led to an unprecedented transfer of population and rendered ten million homeless. An estimated twenty million Hindus moved out of West Punjab and East Bengal and eighteen million Muslims moved into Pakistan. As a part of this mass movement over half-a-million people lost their lives; there were twenty-two thousand reported cases of rape and kidnapping of women; two-hundred-and-twenty thousand people were declared missing.

Anees looked after Bauji and his family for two weeks. Bauji slowly recovered from his injury under Anees' affectionate and energetic care. Both he and Anees knew from the beginning the limitations to their relationship. There were the constraints of circumstances and there was no point hoping for more. So they lived those two weeks as if they were a lifetime, trying hard not to pretend that it could be otherwise. When Bauji's wound was healed and he could move, Anees transported them personally under heavy police guard to the Wagah border and to the safety of India.

During those fifteen days Bauji and Anees talked about many things, but the recent events were uppermost in their minds. They strove valiantly to understand the communal madness. During the first few days Bauji lay numb without thinking, but slowly his mind became remarkably clear.

'Who is to blame, Bauji?' asked Anees one afternoon, 'Your people blame Jinnah for breeding hatred between Hindus and Muslims because he wanted a homeland for the Muslims. I blame the Sikhs who started the killing in East Punjab. My father blames General Rees and his Punjab Boundary Force for their failure to keep law and order.'

'I don't blame anyone, Anees,' said Bauji after a long pause. 'The freedom of three hundred million, whose culture is older than ancient Greece, required a sacrificial purification in order to wash away the dirt of the centuries of foreign rule. We had to cleanse ourselves in each other's blood. Less than a million dead is after all less than a third of one percent of the people freed. It is merely the price of our Independence. Think of it as a great ritual blood letting.'

'And Punjab had to pay the price for the rest of India,' she said gloomily. 'How can *you* talk like this Bauji? You are a fighter. That's why you are alive today.'

'I am alive because of you,' he said.

'Well?'

'Well, what?'

'Well, who is to blame?' she asked.

'Mountbatten, I think.'

'Why?' she said with surprise.

'For rushing through with the transfer of power without adequate preparation. He is a soldier after all. He had set an objective, and he was going to achieve it.'

'How could he have known, Bauji, that we would behave like beasts?'

'The killings had started long ago.'

'But no one predicted that it would lead to this. . .this mass migration. Even Gandhi didn't know.'

'The bloodshed would have been less if Gandhi had been in the Punjab.' Bauji smiled ironically as he thought of Gandhi wandering on foot in the villages of Bengal, teaching brotherhood to Muslims and Hindus of Bengal. Thanks to his presence, Bengal and Calcutta had been free of violence.

'So you can't blame Mountbatten,' said Anees.

'No Anees. If Mountbatten had not been blinded by a sense of his own historical destiny as the liberator of one fifth of the human race, the bloodshed could have been avoided. People needed time to pack their bags and leave. Even Radcliffe needed more time. He had to rush and so a town was cut off from its river, a village from its fields, a factory from its raw materials.'

'But Bauji, no one knew there would be such a massive transfer of people. They assumed that people would stay on in their homes on either side, and owe allegiance to the new nations.'

'Yes, yes I didn't want to move. I wanted to stay on in Lyallpur,' he said beginning to get depressed.

'It's done now. Let's not look back; it's much too painful.'

As they were driving to the Wagah border, Bauji and Anees had tears in their eyes. Their hearts were heavy for they had to part once again. Bauji told Anees that he could comprehend people robbing each other or killing known enemies. He could even understand men raping women or stealing girls, because there was at least a moment's pleasure and power in that act. But to kill innocent anonymous old men and little children, that he could not understand. What conceivable pleasure or motive could men have in doing that?

Anees tried to explain to him the fanatical power of the Muslim or for that matter the Sikh faith. In each case, the certitude of faith was born in a martial context and the killing of the unfaithful was a mark of bravery and valour.

'I would rather be a coward and live in peace in that case,' said Bauji.

PART TWO

Simla

1

Everyone at the ashram was sad because the guru's old cow had died early that rainy morning. The princess of Rewas started to cry when she saw it being taken away on a cart. 'The cow is dead,' said the guru, 'but her soul is alive. She will be reborn today as a boy to Seva Ram.' Hearing this, Seva Ram took off for the railway station like a possessed man. He jumped into the first train for Lyallpur, where Tara was in labour.

Later that stormy night Tara gave birth to a boy, almost a year after her marriage. Seva Ram told them of the guru's prediction. The boy was hailed as providentially blessed, and the prophetic guru was seen as a true man of god. Bhabo proclaimed that the baby was born under an auspicious star and would have the guru's protection for life. Big Uncle made a joke about cows and men but nobody thought it very funny. Bauji was overjoyed to have a grandson from his favourite daughter. He dismissed the prophecy because he did not believe in reincarnation, but he insisted that the boy would grow up to be like him.

A few weeks later, Seva Ram was transferred to a canal colony in the wilds of Rohtak district in East Punjab in order to supervise the construction of an irrigation canal. He proudly took his bride and his child with him, along with all his possessions, which consisted of a jute charpai and a few trunks containing Tara's dowry. On the way, they stopped at the ashram so that the child could have the guru's blessings. Seva Ram explained to Tara that a true guru's eyes had the power to protect; his glance would give the child a spiritual start in life.

At the ashram, Seva Ram placed the child at the guru's feet and requested him to give the boy a name. 'Let us call him Arjun, after the most courageous Pandava,' said the guru. 'This boy will grow up to be confident and fearless like Arjuna, and he will be a seeker like him.' The guru smiled and continued, 'You probably don't know, but my cow was also spirited and brave. It is an appropriate name, don't you think?' and he laughed.

When Bauji heard about this he slapped his thigh with pleasure. 'Yes, it is a good name,' he said, 'Arjun, Arjuna, bold and gallant. I want him to grow up fearlessly, to right the wrongs of this world, and not seek after another world.'

In the backward wilds of Rohtak district, Tara was visibly unhappy. She missed her family, her friends, and the comforts of 7 Kacheri Bazaar. She was anxious because the baby suffered from diarrhoea and would not put on weight. Every day she would weigh him on the scales of the bania, who brought fresh vegetables and fruits to their little PWD cottage. She would place the baby in a rickety tin bowl on one side; in the other bowl, would go some coloured stones. And she would hold her breath as the bania tried to balance the two bowls with a fragile jute string. The bania was either too poor or too mean to own real iron weights and he had persuaded his customers that the different coloured stones stood for 'an eighth', 'a quarter', 'a half,' etc. Every time a new stone was added to the scale, Tara would be overjoyed. She would reward the bania immediately by buying extra fruit, and return indoors singing. The bania thus acquired a vested interest in Arjun's size.

Having grown up in a city, Tara found the dusty, flat, unbroken countryside very lonely. The vast and open treeless horizon scared her at times, especially in the evenings when Seva Ram was out on his horse inspecting the canal. She liked the canal, however, and she would sit on its banks for hours. Behind their house, the canal passed a lock, where the water fell a couple of feet, and she enjoyed listening to the sound of running water. The rushing noise had a romantic character, and she would sometimes stop amidst her household chores to listen. She wrote a long letter to Lyallpur, describing the romance of the canal. But she did not write about her loneliness.

More than the landscape, she was troubled by her husband's silence. Seva Ram was a shy and quiet person. He never spoke unless he was spoken to. He woke up before dawn, had a bath and sat down to meditate. By six he was out on horseback for the morning inspection. He returned at eight, had breakfast, and worked in his office till one. After lunch and a rest, he again worked till six or seven. In the evenings he would have liked to go for a solitary walk. But Tara insisted on going with him. He was a quiet, mild man, and she learned to do all the talking on these walks.

As a Sub-Divisional Officer, Seva Ram was the most important official of the Raj for miles around. His mission was to maintain his part of the canal. He made sure that water flowed efficiently through the main canal as well as the smaller distribution channels which watered the farmers' fields. He had also to see that water was provided fairly to all the farmers. This was difficult at times because some farmer or other would invariably divert his neighbour's water to his own field, and this led to quarrels, fights, and even murder. In such a situation, he often became a judge. Tara usually became interested in such cases, and Seva Ram discovered that she had a knack for suggesting a fair solution. 'After all, my father was a lawyer,' she would remind him.

Seva Ram was also in charge of the tiny canal colony, which was neatly and functionally laid out. Besides their bungalow, there were quarters for the overseers' families, a rest-house for visiting officers and two office buildings. All the buildings were of brick, with flat roofs and wide verandas in the PWD style, and they were white-washed inside. Since it had its own water distributory from the canal, the colony was green and shady with trees, lawns, and flowers in abundance, which were looked after by full-time gardeners—a dramatic contrast to the brown and arid countryside around.

Tara also tried to make friends with the other women in the colony. She found that she was the only one who was educated, and she could not resist the feeling of superiority. To her surprise she discovered, however, that she liked being the wife of an important official. She was proud that her husband was like a god in the eyes of the peasants, not only because he provided water for the crops, but also because he was incorruptible. The farmers overwhelmed her with gifts from their fields, but Seva Ram always returned them because he regarded them as bribes. Not to hurt the feelings of the giver, he would take one piece of fruit or vegetable from a whole basket or a glass of milk from a bucketful, and return the rest. Tara was annoyed when he insisted on returning a whole set of baby clothes which the village headman's wife had brought for Arjun. 'Can't we keep one?' she implored. He was adamant because he knew the price: he would have to widen the outlet of the distributory channel for the headman's field. The villagers, too, were surprised by Seva Ram's high standards. His predecessors had not only accepted gifts but had not hesitated in asking for cows and horses in addition.

Nine months later Seva Ram was transferred to the district headquarters at Rohtak, where he was given an administrative job in the irrigation department. Whereas he had been a *'burra* sahib' in the canal colony, here he was only a *'chota* sahib' on the lowest rung of the district's officialdom. At the top of the ladder was the Collector, followed by the district heads of police, medical services, railways, forestry, irrigation, and so on. Many of these officials were English, although the Indianization of the services had advanced quite far by 1943.

Rohtak was a typical dusty, colourless town on the North Indian plain. Its only claim to fame lay in its famous jail which was as strong as a fortress. Since it was close to Delhi, the jail had seen many eminent occupants, including both Nehru and Gandhi. Tara was happier here, although she continued to long for Lyallpur. After the canal post, she welcomed the conveniences of the town— the hospital, the bazaar and the educated company. She made friends quickly and even got a job in the local junior college for women. She got a chance to observe the unusual ways of the English officials, especially her husband's bosses. However, she missed the sound of the rushing water at the canal head, as well as the sense of importance which the villagers had bestowed on her.

One bright winter's day, a cream-coloured Hispano-Suiza pulled up in front of the Rohtak Canal Rest House. Out of it came a well-dressed Englishman, his wife and three children. He was Seva Ram's superior by two levels, a stylish Superintending Engineer (SE) named Parker, who had come from Delhi on an inspection tour.

The entire staff of the local Irrigation Department, including Seva Ram and Tara, was assembled at the rest-house, to 'pay their respects' and garland the SE with bright marigolds. Tara found this display embarrassing because 'after all, the man was here on official business'. But this was how it had been done for three-quarters-of-a-century.

During the ceremony, a bus arrived with the Parkers' domestic staff and baggage. To Tara's shock, out of the bus emerged fifteen liveried servants and thirty-one pieces of luggage. She counted everyone—the khidmatgar, the English cook, the Indian cook, the dhobi, the darzi, two jamedars, two ayahs, two chaprassis, two bearers, a hamal and a chokra boy. It was a brilliant spectacle to see them lined up beside the chrysanthemums, in their gleaming white uniforms, with purple bands on their turbans and purple cummerbunds.

After everyone was dismissed, the Parkers went inside the cool, high-ceilinged rest-house, and ordered fresh lemonades. Then they quickly changed, and went around to the dozen or so homes of the British community, starting at the top with the Collector. At each stop, they left their calling cards in little black boxes outside the bungalow. This was a sacred ritual of the Raj. Tara thought it odd that they had formally dressed for this occasion even though they did not expect to meet anybody—in fact Tara was told that it was socially improper for the hosts to notice them at the gate.

As soon as they returned to the rest-house, the Parkers were deluged by chits brought by bearers, containing enough invitations for lunches, dinners, teas, dances and tennis matches to last a fortnight. And the Parkers plunged into socializing with vigour. Their 'inspection week' was remembered by the little district town for months afterwards. Parker's only concession to his duty consisted of brief visits to the canal works with Seva Ram in the mornings. While he was out, Mrs Parker attended 'elevenses' with various Englishwomen.

The Parkers reciprocated all the hospitality they received with a grand formal dinner at the rest-house, which was remembered for the excellence of its menu. Tara was keen to get an invitation, but of course it was out of the question, not only because 'the races had to be kept apart', but also because Seva Ram was not high enough on the official ladder to merit one.

Tara wanted to meet Mrs Parker, and she broached the idea to Seva Ram. He was shocked, and immediately dismissed the idea as outlandish. She persisted. He became upset and the two quarrelled.

'Why do you want to meet her?' asked Seva Ram.

'I want to know what they are like. Besides it will help your career if they know that you have an educated wife who speaks English.'

'I don't want that sort of help, thank you.'

Despite her husband, Tara sent a message through a senior Indian official's wife, who had access to Mrs Parker. Much to everyone's surprise, Mrs Parker agreed. She broke protocol one afternoon and visited Tara at her little PWD bungalow, where she also met the wives of the half-a-dozen junior Indian officers in the department. They spent an hour drinking tea, eating pakoras and smiling. Tara got a chance to practice her English, but the meeting did not particularly satisfy her.

Inevitably, the talk turned to servants. 'I only have Hindi-speaking servants,' Mrs Parker said, 'because you can never trust those who speak English. Besides, I never need to speak to anyone except the khidmatgar and the cook. They run everybody else. Still, I'm glad I am learning Hindi. I have a munshi who comes every morning, but I'm quite hopeless at learning languages.'

Tara asked if there was enough work for all her servants.

'The Chief Engineer has fifty, my dear,' she replied. 'In recent years wages have gone up and one can't afford as many servants as one used to.'

After a year in Rohtak, Tara discovered that Karan had been shifted by the British to the Rohtak jail. He was lodged in a special wing for political prisoners. She did not tell Seva Ram about her discovery, and after vacillating for a week, she finally decided to visit him. Leaving her child with a neighbour, she took a tonga one hot afternoon in April. On the way her heart beat violently, and she almost turned back. At the jail, she was informed that Karan was permitted one visit on the last Friday of each month. She pleaded with the authorities, and since Karan had not had any visitors for the past three months, she was permitted to see him.

The jail felt cool after the journey under the hot sun. She was taken across a number of corridors to a special room which was divided by bars. After some time a dark bearded figure was led in. She immediately covered her head with the end of her sari. She was afraid and embarrassed. She did not quite know what to expect. He had lost weight, and his brown eyes stared at her. She noticed his willowy hands holding the bars. Even in prison clothes he looked handsome, she thought, but she was bothered by an unfamiliar irony in his eyes.

'How is our hero?' she asked hesitantly.

'He is a prisoner,' he replied in his slightly nasal voice, which seemed full of muted irony.

'How is the prisoner treated?' she asked.

'As the prisoner should be treated.' There was a mischievous smile on his face.

'Heroes are foolhardy,' she said.

'Bring me more fools, said the wise man.'

'Wise men have a head and do not suffer fools.'

'But fools have a heart,' he laughed.

'This fool has no heart! He is stubborn like a goat,' she said with annoyance. He glanced at her with affectionate irony.

'How are Bauji and Bhabo?' he asked after a pause.

'They are all right,' she answered mechanically.

'How is your husband?'

'He doesn't talk much,' she replied.

Sensing that he was on delicate ground, Karan changed the subject. He asked her about the canal life. She talked about it animatedly for a quarter-of-an-hour. She described rapturously the sound of the running water in the canal.

'So, my hero of the "Quit India" movement!'

'It failed Tara—it turned violent.'

'While you all are in jail, Jinnah is outside, nicely fanning the flames of communal hatred. I mean the whole of the Congress is in jail, isn't it? I tell you Karan, Jinnah is going to get Pakistan. They are going to cut up India one day.'

Soon their time was up, and she realized that she had not asked him many important questions—when he would be leaving, what his plans were, what he did all day long. . .

'Do you need anything?' she shouted as he was being led out.

'No,' he said. He looked back and his eyes twinkled with a smile. He was as enchanting as ever, she thought. Even prison had not diminished him. He continued to be amused and to amuse others. Bauji had rightly thought this to be his most endearing trait. To be amused had meant a great deal to Bauji.

On her way out, she thanked the English jailer, who confessed that he was charmed by Karan's unusual manners. 'He often plays the sitar for the prisoners,' said the Englishman. 'Since we have a large number of political prisoners (including some important figures) he is always appreciated. For hours together we can hear him practicing some raag, and it softens the harshness of prison life.'

The visit left Tara confused. It aroused painful desires that had been dormant for a number of years. Karan's memory mocked her. For days afterward the warm April air was filled with sensuality, and she found that she got aroused at the slightest pretext.

After a few weeks Tara got hold of herself. She was ashamed at allowing herself to lose her self-control. She realized that it was indiscreet to visit Karan alone. Although no one might ever know, she felt that she had diminished her honour by her reckless action. She felt genuinely contrite and she tried to make up by being extra good to Seva Ram and to see the positive side of his nature. She resolved never to meet Karan alone.

2

After eighteen months in Rohtak, Seva Ram was again transferred, this time to Lahore. Tara was thrilled to be finally 'going to civilization', to the cosmopolitan and cultured city where she had gone to college and where she had many sophisticated friends. However, as soon as they arrived in Lahore, Tara's excitement quickly turned to disappointment. There was a severe shortage of housing in Lahore. Seva Ram was not senior enough in the service to expect the government to provide him with family accommodation in the provincial capital. The few private houses available were either too expensive or unsuitable. So they decided that until a proper house was found, it was best for Tara and Arjun to go to Lyallpur. Meanwhile Seva Ram would stay in bachelor's quarters, and would visit them as often as possible.

Thus Tara returned to Lyallpur in the new role of a married woman and a mother. Everyone was delighted to have her back, and Bauji proudly asked her to move into the east wing of the house, which was especially painted and furnished with new drapes and upholstery in her honour. Here, Tara had her own sitting room, her bedroom and dressing room, a nursery for Arjun and an adjoining room for Arjun's ayah. She even had a small dining room which she never used except occasionally when Seva Ram visited them or when she wanted to eat alone with Arjun.

The day after she arrived, the house was in a flutter because Tara's youngest sister had her exams. 'Make sure she eats yogurt and rice,' Bauji shouted from the courtyard below. 'Yogurt and rice, yogurt and rice,' said Big Uncle, as he sat down at the breakfast table. 'It's exam time again, eh?' Suddenly Tara was transported to her schooldays and she realized how wonderful it was to be home.

Tara quickly discovered that she liked her new position in Lyallpur. Society accorded her a place of honour as a young wife and mother, and she spoke with authority and inexhaustibly about the 'mysteries of life' to her unmarried friends. She dressed charmingly and appropriately in pastel and light-coloured chiffon saris, thinking that sombre colours were too matronly, and that bright reds and florals were 'too youthful for a person in her serious position.' Despite Big Uncle's protests, she also discarded the salwar-kameez as being 'too collegiate and inappropriate'. She liked to wear her hair up in a bun like a society lady. As the senior daughter in the house, she took charge of running the house, controlling the household budget and the servants, a responsibility that Bhabo was more than happy to relinquish in order to devote time to her grandson and to temples. She even charmed Big Uncle's wife, who by protocol was the seniormost, and to whom fell the responsibility of keeping house, after Bhabo, but who was willing to let her sister-in-law assume the burden of running a large and chaotic household.

Bauji was richly amused by the self-conscious dignity and seriousness that Tara brought to her new status, and by the immense pleasure she took in it. He smiled to see her make general observations about life and destiny, which she did with the utmost gusto. He had been worried that she might still not be fully reconciled to her husband. He was afraid of a scene, and thus everyone had been carefully instructed not to mention Karan's name in her presence, even by accident. But his fears were belied. She conducted herself with such dignity that no one could guess how vulnerable she really was. Once or twice, Karan's name did come up accidentally with her friends, but she turned the conversation skilfully, and everyone was charmed. Bhabo's society friends felt cheated because they had looked forward to a grand scene. Once they tried to bait her in the bazaar but she was more than equal to the challenge. Amongst friends and family, she frequently used the phrase, 'Ah, such is life.' Each time that she did, she would open wide her big black eyes and her face would assume a grave look, as if she had acquired a deep insight into human affairs and destiny.

'You know how it is father,' she once said to Bauji, looking at the ceiling fan with a thoughtful air, 'Of course I have learned what life is like. One has to create one's own home and find ways to overcome dullness and boredom from within oneself. One can't be selfish. One has to uphold the family's honour. But life is like that, isn't it?' Bauji was filled with amused tenderness, and he wondered why she had begun to address him as 'father' and not 'Bauji' like everyone else.

Thus the days passed into months. Seva Ram had still not succeeded in finding a house in Lahore. Arjun was now three-and-a-half years old. He had the run of the house. It was his kingdom, and he felt its absolute master. He would run continuously through its vast expanses and its many recesses. He would climb the three staircases at least once a day, climb onto the roof and look out over the panorama of the city spread below. He knew the territory well: from the bed next to his mother's where he was allowed to sleep on special occasions to the feel of polished leather down in the stables, to the sorcerous dance of the sun's rays as they filtered through the blue bamboo chick blinds in the veranda during the afternoon while everyone slept. Sometimes the rays would fall from one angle on to the wall; then enchantingly from another on to the carpet; and still another time onto a broken column in a part of the house no one visited any longer. He knew which routes to avoid at which time. Everyone in his kingdom was well disposed to him.

Arjun's best friend in Lyallpur was Bhabo. He would sit with her on the tiled veranda in the winter sun as she chopped fresh mustard and spinach for the midday meal. As they were chatting one day, she noticed that the middle button was missing from his new red shirt. She slowly got up and brought her silver needle and thread box. She opened it, and discovered that she didn't have a red button. And since she could not think of substituting a different coloured button, Arjun was given a square, shiny two-anna coin and sent off on his first trip to the bania's shop in the neighbourhood.

Arjun stepped uncertainly out of the small wooden door, which was set into a more massive gate, and ran along the narrow, shining open drain. Outside the store sat a number of men on a charpai, drinking tea, smoking the hookah and enjoying the sun. He made his way around them towards the bania, who stood among sacks full of onions and chillies.

'Brother, give me a red button,' Arjun announced to the unshaven bania as he handed him the square coin. While the bania searched, Arjun stared longingly at the glass jars on the counter filled with English sweets. The bania finally handed him the button, and Arjun was about to run out, when the bania caught him by the arm and thrust the change in his top pocket. One of the tea drinkers laughed, but Arjun was not intimidated.

As he ran back, Arjun felt exhilarated over his successful entry into the world. Just as he reached the gate, however, he slipped on a banana peel and fell in the dust. He would have probably got up and continued had it not been for Big Uncle. He had been watching Arjun from his room and quickly came down the winding staircase to rescue him. As soon as Arjun saw him he began to cry.

Thanks to Big Uncle's rhetorical ability, the incident rapidly grew into an event. With much style he related the story of Arjun's misfortune over lunch. Bauji became upset, and swore at Bhabo for sending his grandson out alone. She, however, was unruffled, as she calmly continued to serve warm rotis, which puffed up as they came off the fireplace. Arjun sat smugly through the meal, eagerly displaying his bandaged knee for people to see.

After lunch, when everybody was having a nap, Bhabo brought her needle and thread box to the veranda and asked Arjun for his shirt. He brought it to her, and from its pocket she took out the button and asked him for the change. With anguish, he remembered that he must have dropped it when he fell.

'Doesn't matter,' she said, 'we shall look for it in the evening. You remember where you fell, don't you?'

She began to sew the button. Arjun was disappointed that Bhabo did not once ask about his knee. After a while, she said, 'We must fix this tightly, for you don't know when a strong button comes handy. A long time ago your great-grandfather's cousin, Hari Lal, went on a voyage. After a few hours on the sea, his ship was caught in a storm. All day and night the men worked to save it, but the winds were too strong. At last when they knew they couldn't save her, they abandoned ship and jumped into lifeboats. They took as much food as they could and prayed to god for mercy.'

At this point, the thread slipped out of the needle. Arjun quickly rethreaded it, since Bhabo's eyes were weak, and she continued.

'The lifeboat was thrown around in the storm all night. In the morning though, God was merciful, and the lifeboat was spotted by a great white ship. The rescuers found only one person in the lifeboat.'

'Who was it?' Arjun asked.

'Hari Lal,' she replied. 'But he was unconscious.'

'What happened to the others?' he asked.

'They were drowned.'

'Why wasn't he drowned?'

'Because his button got stuck on the edge of the lifeboat when it capsized. The button was fastened so strongly to his shirt, that he survived when the others were drowned.'

There was a long pause. She smiled and said she would wash his dusty red shirt and he could wear it tomorrow. She then lay down to nap beside him on the charpai. Before they fell asleep, she asked, 'Why did you cry when you fell? Hari Lal wouldn't have been saved by crying in the storm.'

To keep him out of trouble, Arjun was put into the nursery of the local primary school. But he got into trouble the very first week, when he insisted on correcting the master who tried to teach him his first English words.

'Thee apple,' said the master.

'No, thuh apple,' corrected Arjun.

The master picked up his cane but Arjun would not budge.

'Where did you learn to say that?' asked the master.

'My mother speaks like that.'

The master did not use the cane, in deference to Bauji. But he asked Arjun to stand up and he ridiculed him before the other boys.

In the evenings, Tara would take Arjun to the Company Bagh. While she gossiped with her friends in the 'Ladies Garden', Arjun would run about in the vast gardens. Once Arjun got lost in the Company Bagh. Tara was in tears, and everyone was deputed to look for him. They finally spotted him on the shoulders of a policeman. When Bauji asked him that evening where he had got lost, Arjun calmly replied, 'No, I was not lost, Mother was lost.'

So passed Arjun's and Tara's days in Lyallpur. After the winter came the unbearable hot weather, and finally to everyone's relief came the rains in early July. Tara would sit in the veranda and watch the rain fall gently over the plants in the courtyard. She would look up at the fluffy white clouds above and her heart would fill with romantic thoughts. The breeze brought the aroma of fresh summer flowers. The grass in the Company Bagh sparkled richly green. Even the huge sprawling mango tree in the main courtyard seemed to relax and enjoy the rain, after having delivered its harvest of mangoes to the family in June. The parrots were unusually active on its branches and the koel sang its heart out in the nights. Tara said that she missed Seva Ram, but at night she dreamed of Karan.

In this sentimental season, a scandal burst open suddenly at 7 Kacheri Bazaar. Arjun's ayah was pregnant. She was a dark and pretty Christian girl, whose eyes sparkled when she was addressed. She was pious, and moved quietly around the house.

When the discovery was made, she cried and cried and refused to divulge the name of her lover. For days the house was kept guessing about his identity. Big Uncle thought it was the syce, Tara believed it was the cook. Bauji threatened to turn her out along with the cook and the syce. But Tara came to the ayah's rescue. She accused Bauji of being heartless, especially when the girl needed medical attention. She blamed Bhabo for never having accepted the poor, non-Hindu girl. She was treated like a member of the lowest caste; she was not allowed to enter the kitchen or touch the pots and pans in which food was cooked. After some skilful detective work, Big Uncle announced over dinner that it was the cook. With much delight he read out the cook's confession, which Tara thought was in bad taste. Bauji wanted to forget the whole wretched affair which had been the centre of the household's attention for almost a week.

'But where did they do it?' asked Big Uncle, whose main point of curiosity was still not satisfied.

'In her room, you fool,' shouted Tara.

'But couldn't you hear them, Tara?' he said.

'Oh, you are impossible!' said Tara.

'How can you be so vulgar! Stop it,' said Bauji.

'This is the type of practical and useful information he needs, so that he can follow in the cook's footsteps,' said Big Uncle's wife.

It was the late afternoon of 20 August 1946. Arjun was in his mother's dressing room, watching Tara comb her hair. It was a rectangular room whose windows opened on to the veranda on the second floor. From the open window, Arjun could spy a potted palm. Beyond the veranda was a railing in the form of a grille made out of bricks from where one could look down on the courtyard. The chick blinds had been raised, which meant that the evening was approaching. Tara was sitting at an ornate and heavy dressing table made out of Burma teak, with an oval mirror. Its legs were carved in the shape of tiger's feet, which Arjun found amusing. Arjun was standing near the low table, absorbed in examining the toilet articles—combs, brushes, oils, etc. Tara was applying oil to her long, dark hair with the help of a maid.

Suddenly there was a sound of footsteps outside. They were quick and urgent steps coming up the small staircase. It was Bauji. It must be important, because he never came to this part of the house. He burst in and announced in an excited voice that Mountbat-

ten had been appointed the last Viceroy. The British were finally
going to leave India, he said. The British Raj had come to an end!
Tara nervously dropped the bottle of coconut oil.

'Look what you made me do!' she said to Arjun. She turned to her
father and she asked, 'At what cost, Bauji? Is the partition of Punjab
going to be the price for our freedom?'

3

Tara was crying by the banks of the Sutlej river. She was seated inside a tent beside her four-and-a-half-year-old son. She asked Arjun if the sound of shots could still be heard. He went outside to check, but she called him back immediately. It was only the sound of thunder in the monsoon sky, he said. It had been an especially rainy month. The killing had been heavy too.

It was the historic evening of 14 August 1947. At midnight, India would become free. Seva Ram, Tara and their families had become refugees like fourteen million others as a result of the British decision to divide the Punjab. But unlike many others, Seva Ram and Tara were fortunate to have found asylum at the ashram, where the guru had set up a camp with tents and makeshift kitchens for the refugees. Since it was in East Punjab, the ashram found itself in India according to the boundary line drawn by Mr Radcliffe. When the partition was announced in July, Seva Ram and Tara had been living in Lahore. With Anees' help they had escaped and they now felt safe and relieved to be at the ashram. But their journey was not yet over.

Tara had been crying the whole day. She had been thinking of Bauji, Bhabo and the rest of the family. She had had no news about them for two weeks. In the last letter from Lyallpur, Bauji was reported to be stubbornly insisting on staying on in Pakistan. She wondered if they were still alive and where they were. Seva Ram had gone to Jullunder, the nearest town and railway station, to enquire about their whereabouts and about his transfer order from the government.

When she first started weeping, Arjun would also cry. Now he began to resent her constant sighing and crying. He sat on a wooden box wondering if she would ever smile again. After a while he got up and went outside the tent. He looked into the darkening August evening, full of scared voices, monsoon thunder and the smell of the bloody night. His mother's bangles jingled softly and he went back into the tent. Her deep eyes appeared deeper in the light of the kerosene lamp. Soon she got up, and went to the stove with a towel in her hand. Suddenly she turned around, for someone had entered the tent. It was the guru. He stood tall and erect, his handsome face glowing in the strange light of the monsoon evening. Tara was startled. She pulled down the end of her sari to cover her head, and tightly clutched the towel in her hand. She felt confused in the presence of her noble host, but Arjun was delighted to have someone to talk to.

'When is my father coming?' Arjun said.

'Tonight,' replied the guru.

The child clapped his hands with delight, and the holy man put his hand on the boy's head. Tara, feeling more at ease, allowed herself a faint smile.

'You have been crying my child?' he asked her.

'My family, I have been thinking about them.'

'Don't worry, child. We all have to die one day, but only when our time has come. Neither before nor after. The time is predetermined,' he said.

'All this killing and death! I am frightened,' she said.

'Do not be afraid of death, my child. Learn to die when you are still alive.'

She looked puzzled.

'Learn to meditate and you will die every day. During meditation, concentrate your attention at the point midway between your eyes, behind your forehead, where your soul resides. With practice your soul will catch the sound of the Infinite, and leave your body at the moment of death. Thus you will conquer death.'

She continued to look confused. He smiled again.

'Ask Seva Ram and he will explain to you why the initiate is not afraid of death,' he said.

'I am angry with all religions, guruji,' she said suddenly, picking up courage, 'because they divide people and turn one person against the other.'

He laughed as he realized that she had a mind of her own. He liked her pluck.

'A saint comes into the world,' he explained, 'to show people the way. He does not come to create a religion. After he leaves, people turn his message into rites and rituals. They convert his teachings into an organized religion. They become bigoted, start quarrelling with one another. The real message of the saint is soon forgotten.

This was the fate of the Buddha, Christ, Mohammed, Nanak and others. Saints do not ask us to go to temples, churches, and mountains to seek the truth. The truth is within us, within our own body.'

Before she could say anything he had turned and disappeared into the sea of refugees sprawled out in the wet night.

Tara's mood was completely changed by the visit. Instead of crying, she began to hum happily as she prepared dinner. It occurred to her that she had not thanked the guru for giving them shelter. She was amazed by his calm manner. He did not appear burdened or harried by the task of organizing for two hundred thousand refugees. She felt deeply moved that in the midst of all his responsibilities he had allowed himself the time to talk to her and to console her.

Soon there were familiar footsteps outside. A lightly built man entered. With a cry, Arjun jumped up and rushed to his father's arms. Tara too went up to him and greeted him with her eyes. He took the boy in his arms. Bursting to ask him a thousand questions, she could only say, 'You must be hungry. Dinner is ready.'

He sat down and quietly waited for her to lay out the food. She, however, could not contain herself any longer.

'What is happening?' she almost screamed in anger. 'I thought we had accepted partition as the price for communal peace. Once Jinnah got his Pakistan, there was supposed to be no need for killing Hindus. Oh God, how could Nehru and others have been so out of touch with the people? Did they really think they would buy Hindu-Muslim peace by agreeing to partition?' After a pause, she sadly said, 'We lost either way—we lost our homes and the killings didn't stop.'

'True', he said. After a pause he added, 'It is sad, Tara, that for thirty years Gandhi preached non-violence. But in the end it did no good in the Punjab. We still behaved like brutes.'

'What is going to happen to us? Where are we going to go?' she asked.

'We have been transferred to Simla,' he replied.

'Simla!' she uttered incredulously.

'Yes,' he said without emotion. 'Simla is going to be the new capital of the Punjab, now that Lahore has been lost to Pakistan.'

'You mean the Simla—the one in the hills?' she repeated, still not believing him.

He nodded.

'But how exciting! I mean, wouldn't it be wonderful to live in

Simla? I went there when I was fourteen and I have never seen anything so beautiful.'

Her reaction was understandable, for a visit (let alone a posting) to the Himalayan summer capital of the British Raj was considered to be an unbelievable stroke of good luck. To live in the mountains of Simla was the fondest hope of every English family in India during the Raj. It was a mysterious pleasure forbidden to most Indians.

'Oh, the Himalayan flowers, the pine trees, the rhododendrons, the snow-covered peaks, and the cool breeze from the mountains—it is a city built by the gods!' she added excitedly.

Seva Ram had never seen her like this. She was like a child, and she infected him with her excitement. He too laughed. It had been a long time since the refugees had known happiness.

'The pretty little English houses, the glamorous shops on the Mall, the tiny train. . .'

Arjun jumped with joy, shouting 'Simla train, chook-chook train.'

'When do we leave?' she asked.

'When it is safer. In a week perhaps. I am going back tomorrow to see if I can bring out my father and mother from the other side.'

'But you will be killed!' Her face changed suddenly; her eyes became frightened again.

After dinner that night, Dr Sharma, a friend of Seva Ram's, invited them to his tiny brick cottage, where he had the rare luxury of electricity, so that they could listen to the radio. There were a dozen people huddled around the radio in the ill-lit room when Nehru began his historic speech to the new nation.

> Long years ago we made a tryst with destiny, and now the time comes when we shall redeem our pledge. . . At the stroke of the midnight hour, while the world sleeps, India will awake to life and freedom. A moment comes, which comes but rarely in history, when we step out from the old to the new, when an age ends, and when the soul of a nation, long suppressed, finds utterance. . .

Despite the suffering and the uncertainty about their future, the refugees were filled with emotion as they listened to Nehru's words. The national anthem of the new nation was heard for the first time. Most of the listeners did not recognize it. Dr Sharma was the first to stand up. Then one by one the other listeners got up, until everyone in the dusky room was standing at attention. When the reference came to the 'Punjab' in the song, the refugees looked at each other. There was helplessness in some eyes, a few were red with anger, others were filled with tears. Despite their travails, Tara and Seva Ram realized their good fortune in having witnessed the birth of their nation after centuries of domination by foreigners.

Midnight came and the rule of the British over India was over.

Their train had been standing still for six hours at Jullunder station. Seva Ram got up and went out of the train carriage to check again with the station master when the train would move. As he was leaving, Tara implored him to be careful and to return quickly. And she clutched Arjun's hand.

There was chaos at the station since no one knew to what schedule the trains were running. On both sides of the railway platform crowds of refugees were gathered. On the east side, Hindus and Sikhs sat waiting for the train. On both sides they were huddled together, believing that they were safer in a group. As soon as a train approached, the refugees would get up. Pushing and shouting, they would rush for the train. But the last four trains had not stopped.

Arjun was looking out of the train window. He tried to lean out, but the horizontal steel bars on the window prevented him. A tall Muslim policeman stood stationary on the platform. His face was strong-willed and handsome. Suddenly, there was movement and noise amongst the refugees. A train was coming from the opposite direction—from Delhi going to Lahore. Activity on the platform increased. The policeman was unaffected, and continued to stare straight ahead. Arjun saw two Sikh boys in their teens suddenly emerge from nowhere. They came from the back and thrust a dagger through the policeman from behind. He did not cry. He just fell down and died. Tara pulled her son back. She tried to shut the window, but it wouldn't close.

Screams were heard as the incoming train slowed down. There were sounds of bullets. Tara pushed Arjun down; she too lay on the floor of the carriage with her baby. They were shooting at the incoming train, which again speeded up. It was not going to stop either. There was more shooting, followed by more shouts and shrieks. The train full of half dead bodies passed by.

Soon it was quiet again. Tara could hear herself crying. 'Why doesn't my father come back?' asked Arjun. 'Hush!' she silenced him. She was frightened and haunted by the same question.

Half-an-hour later, an elderly Sikh gentleman forced his way into their compartment. Full of fear, clutching Arjun, Tara screamed, 'We are Hindus, don't kill us!' Then she saw Seva Ram, who came immediately after the Sikh. She rushed up to her husband. The Sikh gentleman sat down with a sigh. Seva Ram introduced the stranger. He was the richest landlord from his home town, and he had lost everything, including every member of his family. Seva Ram found him at the ticket window when the shooting had started. He had grabbed him, and both of them had found shelter in the toilet of the First Class Retiring Room during the trouble.

The stranger did not say a word but stared out of the window mournfully. After some time, Tara, who couldn't bear the silence any longer, asked her husband if the Simla train was running. The stranger unexpectedly snapped at her, 'Woman, is this the time to think of holidays in hill stations!' Tara quickly explained that she was not going to Simla for a vacation. 'My husband has been posted there by the government.'

The old Sikh began to cry. 'Last Thursday night Muslims rushed into my house with swords, screaming jihad,' he said. 'In an instant they cut off the head of my seventy-year-old father because he was closest to the door. Then they cut off my son's legs. My poor brave boy, he hurled an axe at them before he fell down. They struck at him again, and killed him while I, like a coward, I concealed myself behind a standing charpai.

'Next they broke down the door of the room where my daughter and my wife had tried to hide. They dragged out the two screaming women. Before my eyes, I saw one of them hack off my wife's breasts one after the other. They cheered as each one was lopped off. Then they cut her throat. Just before I lost consciousness, I saw the man, who had cut my wife's breasts. I saw him carry off my fifteen-year-old daughter on his shoulders.

'When I came to, it was morning, and there was a deathly silence throughout the house. I stealthily walked out and discovered that there was not a single living person in the entire neighbourhood. I inhaled the pungent smell of decomposing corpses, and I vomited.

'My only thought now was to escape with my life. Fortunately, I found a patrol of the Punjab Border Force. I hid in a truck manned by a Gurkha, who brought me to this train. And here I am now, shamelessly alive, with nothing to call my own in this world, waiting to go wherever this train will take me.'

4

The view from the tiny window of the miniature Kalka-Simla train was enough to refresh the most exhausted emotions. Before them stood snow-tipped crests of the world's highest mountain range. Their eyes feasted on the resplendent green of the lower Hima-layas—soaring pines, luxurious deodar, and delicate carpets of fern. This was heaven, after the tiring journey through unending dusty plains, withering in the Punjab's remorseless heat. The stench of death was left far behind at Jullunder station.

The train stopped at Barog. Seva Ram and his family alighted to have breakfast in the garden of the railway refreshment room, surrounded by dahlias, roses and heliotropes. Rosy-cheeked hill boys served them tea, which tasted like no other tea in the world. As they ate breakfast they were treated to an extraordinary sight: a beautiful white car on rails went speeding by. 'The rail car,' said the waiter, 'carries the rich and the busy, who don't carry luggage and who want to reach Simla in a hurry. It used to be only the white sahibs who travelled in it. Since Independence everyone is riding in it. Amazing, how quickly the brown sahibs have slid into their shoes!'

After they returned to the toy train, an old Anglo-Indian ticket collector came into their compartment to check their tickets. He sensed their excitement, and he said, 'Ah, this is a lover's train!'

'Lovers?' said Tara.

'There are 103 tunnels in a run of just sixty miles,' he said with a mischievous smile.

Each curve of the winding journey revealed verdant slopes with tiers of neatly and evenly cultivated terraces, which looked like hundreds of gardens hanging in the air. Between the terraces were belts of huge fir and pine trees. Tara pointed at a splendid waterfall, tumbling majestically down into the valley below. Its water shone like silver in the distance under the blue, cloudless sky. They passed a dense forest of deodar, surrounded by slopes clothed with rhododendrons. Towards the south, they could see the Ambala plains far below, with Sabathu and the Kasauli hills in the foreground, and huge ravines leading down into deep valleys. Northwards, were the confused Himalayan mountain chains, rising range after range, crowned in the distance by a crescent of perpetually snowy peaks that stood out in bold relief. At Shogi they glimpsed the first wondrous vision of Simla. From afar it looked like a beautiful green-carpeted hill garden dotted with red-roofed Swiss chalets. Their excitement mounted. They passed Jutogh, crossed Summer Hill, turned into tunnel number 103, and finally reached Simla's Victorian railway station.

Soon after their arrival they settled into a little cottage called 'Pine Villa', which was situated in a less fashionable part of town known as Chota Simla. They had a servant from Lyallpur, Babu, to help them settle down. Although it was tiny and icy cold at night, Tara liked her little house. It was situated in a handsome grove of oaks and deodars and from her veranda she had a spectacular view of the next ridge and many ridges beyond. From the narrow veranda she could step out to a little lawn; from the lawn there was nothing to step onto except fresh air for the ground suddenly dropped beneath one's feet as it often did in Simla.

The first days in Simla were exhilarating. They went out every day, walking about the six-square-mile town, seven thousand feet above sea level. They had never seen anything so beautiful: the Tudor belfry of Christ Church Cathedral with its massive brass bells; the elegant Victorian villas with their gardens bursting with dahlias, pansies and sweet-peas, the imposing architecture of the Raj, epitomized in the Viceregal Lodge; and the wide Mall, with its brilliant and fashionable shops. After all, Simla had been a grand bouquet to the Englishmen's fondest Imperial dream. For five months of the year, from mid-April to mid-September, it used to be the Imperial capital from where the British Viceroy ruled the Indian Empire (extending, administratively speaking, from Burma to the Red Sea). Every Englishman and woman in India used to yearn to be in Simla for 'the season', when it was one of the gayest places on earth. For all its vivaciousness and glamour, one was never allowed to forget that it was an Imperial capital. Until World War I, Indians were not even allowed to walk on the Mall. Later they were, as long as they did not wear sandals, a requirement which effectively excluded the majority.

There was no dust in Simla, which was a shock to Tara. Having been brought up on the Punjab plains, she couldn't imagine life without it. She was accustomed to dust storms, which periodically swept the Punjab plains from the deserts of Rajasthan. Neither was there dirt, unless you went to look for it in Lower Bazaar. Everything was immaculate and polished, as befitted the summer headquarters of the Raj.

From the southern side of her house, Tara could look down on a clear day at the brown and yellow plains below. It was an India that she knew only too well. She shuddered every time she looked down because it reminded her of the partition and left her feeling depressed. So she avoided it and preferred instead to escape into Simla's make-believe world of the English Raj. During the evenings, however, she could not escape from her nagging past. Seva Ram would turn on their new Murphy radio, and they would listen to special bulletins broadcast expressly for the refugees, announcing the whereabouts of missing persons. Her heart would pound as she listened for news of her family. From one such bulletin, she learned that Bauji, Bhabo and the family were safe in a refugee camp in Amritsar. She was happy and relieved. The next day she wrote them a long letter, the longest she had ever written. But this happiness was short-lived, as she learned the very next night that her own sister had been shot in the Sri Ram Mills compound in Lyallpur. She also heard that Chachi and her entire household, including all her servants, had been killed as they were crossing the bridge over the Ravi.

'I swear to you,' screamed Tara, 'I swear on my son, that if a Mussalman comes near me, I shall kill him.'

For days Tara cried and mourned. She could not sleep at night, but Seva Ram was always beside her. He talked about mortality, sorrow and the meaning of life. During those days her husband gradually grew in her eyes and she discovered that she had begun to depend on him.

'You know, I sometimes wonder Tara,' said Seva Ram, 'if there had been two Gandhis, it might have turned out differently. Gandhi has such an amazing way of restoring peace wherever he goes. He is like a one-man army. But there is only one of him and he is presently in Bengal and not in the Punjab.'

After three weeks, Tara finally went to the Mall and bought new clothes for the whole family. The next day, dressed in a new sari, she made Seva Ram take her to Davicos, the most fashionable cafe in Simla, which was famous for its tea dances. Although neither of them danced, Tara watched the dancers with fascination. From that day onwards, they started to go to the Mall every day, and she began to freely spend the little money that they had. They ran into old friends from Lahore and Lyallpur who were refugees like themselves. She discovered that every family had lost someone in the partition, and the mood of the refugees was to live for the moment. Pushed on by Tara, they started going to restaurants and cafes, and lived amidst laughter and gaiety.

Everything about Tara underwent a change—her look, her gait, her voice. She wanted to forget all that had happened in the past. She gave herself over completely to this new feeling, and made so little pretence to hide it that Seva Ram began to feel worried. Suddenly she started talking about 'the spirit of freedom' and 'how good it felt to be independent with your own government in Delhi.' She said that she felt a sense of belonging, a oneness with others, a basic identification with all Indians. She began to sound like Nehru on the radio as she talked about 'democracy, planning, socialism, non-alignment.' But her feelings were genuine. She felt proud of her new sense of identity. By her constant talk, she even infected Seva Ram with her optimism. He began to share her confidence in India's destiny, although occasionally he felt that her optimism might be naive and unwarranted.

Calm by nature, Seva Ram was not used to feeling, let alone displaying, strong emotion. He was aware of Tara's impetuous nature, which he believed she had inherited from her sensual father. Nevertheless, he was puzzled by her recent enthusiasms, which were new and excessive. He would have expected the more practical side of her nature to have acted as a restraining force. He was aware that she could be extremely cautious and even calculating when it suited her. It amazed him that she could forget the past so quickly. He tried to admonish her once, but she replied, 'The English used to say that all of Simla's women are beautiful and all her men handsome.'

Seva Ram was puzzled. He sought the explanation for the abrupt change in Tara's behaviour in the irresolute nature of all women. He did not have a high opinion of women. Like many Punjabi men, he believed that women were by nature weak, inconstant and arbitrary. By and large he thought they were not serious, and when they were, their talents were devoted to intrigue and other evil things. They could not be trusted, and their emotions, although deeply felt, were selfishly motivated. Tara's recent behaviour confirmed his prejudices.

Seva Ram's own calm reaction to the horrible events of the partition was not unexpected. He attributed the killing and the hate to the imperfection of the phenomenological world. The catastrophe was an enactment of god's moral justice, which mere mortals could not hope to fathom. He did not feel anger or outrage but rather compassion for the suffering people, who were misguided by organized religion and its priests. True religion was about man's private relationship with god, about the Atman's submersion in the Brahman, which was perfected in privacy through meditation. Religion was not a social activity.

When he had married Tara, Seva Ram had not quite known what he was getting into. Neither had he been instructed in the duties of marriage by his shy parents. He had married largely to please his guru, who felt anxious over his being alone in the world. Like most Indian boys and girls whose marriages were arranged, he had not loved his betrothed at the time of his marriage. But if he did not love Tara, neither had he loved any other woman. He had always been shy of people and did not form deep relationships with either men or women. Although he did not experience the usual sensations of what is called love in the ancient Hindu texts, he did feel a strong duty to protect and provide for her. He also admired her for her good education.

Because of his austere upbringing, Seva Ram did not miss anything in his marriage. Unlike Tara, he did not feel an emotional void, because he did not have expectations. He was always satisfied with simple things. He had reached the age of twenty-five without knowing the luxurious side of life. He had acquired the habit of economy from childhood, having devoted all his time to his studies and his meditation. Even during his college days when most men ripen and learn to broaden their paths, Seva Ram exhausted his youthful energy on books. He had never felt the need for leisure or idle pursuits or deep friendships. He was civil and polite to everyone, and he was highly thought of by his classmates, who regarded him as quiet, fair, and bookish.

One evening, about a month after their arrival in Simla, Seva Ram came home early from the office, and suggested to Tara that they go for a walk towards Mashobra, a village a few miles east of Simla. Tara would have preferred to go in the opposite direction, towards the Mall, with its glittering shops and fashionable society. But she readily agreed because she saw a strange brightness in Seva

Ram's eyes, which simultaneously frightened and attracted her. They went up the thickly wooded path from their house to the Chota Simla bazaar, past a wide avenue, where stood the handsome secretariat of the Punjab government, and eastwards towards Mashobra. The sun was about to set as they walked along the shaded road with huge, stratified rocks on one side and tall, straight pines on the other. Half-an-hour later they càme upon a flat field covered with short, wild grass. Tara wanted to rest a while, and they sat down and looked at the setting sun. The hill on their right was carpeted from top to bottom with deodar trees and sprinkled with rhododendrons. On their left were small rocks densely covered with wild flowers of great beauty, predominantly in mauve and yellow. The scene left both of them breathless and silent.

He looked at her, and he thought for the first time how pretty she was. He reproached himself for not having noticed it before. At the same time he feared this new, peculiar sensation. It was a pleasant feeling but it made him feel guilty.

She realized that he was looking at her and she turned away shyly. He had always presented a polite but impenetrable exterior, which used to leave her frustrated. Today he was clearly looking at her in a different way. Slowly she raised her eyes. She looked fixedly at him and she smiled tenderly. He touched her arm and he suddenly felt an unfamiliar emotion. He felt it so violently that tears came into his eyes. He turned away to hide his face.

In the cool dusk she was trembling in a light summer sari. He squeezed her to him to warm her. Her scented breath moved the hair on his forehead. Softly she bent in his embrace. It was an ecstatic moment, during which desire had become a torment, but restraint upon it was equally a delight. Although they had been man and wife for years, they were overcome by a powerful, unexpected and mutual onrush of desire. But the clanging of mules on the hill to their right brought them shyly back to the world. Their interlaced mouths disentangled for a smile, as they observed a string of mules laden with colourful clothes, bells tingling merrily around their necks, winding their way up the narrow hill trail.

She put her head on his chest. For the first time he felt that the person who had attached herself to his life was a distinct individual with her own bundle of thoughts and emotions, whose uniqueness he must respect. He felt astonished by this revelation.

Soon it grew dark and a heavy mist came on. They decided to get up. In the distance there was a roll of thunder, which added to the sensual agitation. The first drops of rain heightened the atmosphere of desire. Halfway home it started to drizzle, and the rickshaws that passed them had raised their hoods. But Seva Ram and Tara did not hurry. They clung to each other as they walked in the rain.

Like most Simla showers, it was brief. The sky cleared before they reached home. The trees looked refreshed. In the light of the dim street lamps, the raindrops sparkled on the leaves. Many years later, when they were old and uselessly wise, their thoughts would go back to this day with insistent regret.

Seva Ram was startled by these new feelings. That night he twice woke up. He looked at Tara as she lay asleep, and again he seemed to be seeing a new person. He felt the same uncomfortable sensation of pleasure and guilt. He got out of bed, walked to the next room and looked out at the dark night. He had touched a forbidden delight and he was astonished to be alive.

The next day he took her back to the same spot and he talked about himself. In the sharp, exhilarating air he told her about how he had first encountered the guru. 'It was during my college days in Lahore. I used to go for a walk by the canal. One morning I saw a tall, bearded man, dressed completely in white. He had a young companion with him. When he passed me, he smiled. It was a radiant smile full of warmth, which appeared to say, "Why haven't we met before? I have been waiting for you." It was like love at first sight. I was drawn by the goodness and serenity of his smile, and I followed him. It turned out that he was staying in a modest house not far away from my hostel. He went inside, but his young companion came up to me, and invited me to return at six o' clock that evening. Before I could say anything the boy was gone.

'Weren't you afraid to go?' asked Tara. 'Anything could have happened.'

'I was curious. Besides I was deeply attracted. So I went. I was led inside by the same boy, and I sat down on a cotton durrie. Soon the room filled up. There were about two dozen people, mainly middle aged, none of whom I knew. The guru came at six. After a long silence he spoke in a soft voice, as if he were talking to each one of us individually. He spoke for about half an hour. When he said something profound, he smiled in a self-effacing way. The room was filled with his serene presence. He quoted from a number of mystics of different religions—from Nanak, Kabir, Tabriz, St. Teresa. He said that the truth lay within us, and we did not have to visit temples or mosques or churches to find it. Nor did we have to renounce the world and go off to the Himalayas. We merely had to learn to control our ego. Meditation helped us to do that. When we acted without selfishness, then our actions were pure, and our soul or our separate self was freed to become one with the universal self. I did not listen very carefully because I kept watching him. I was struck by his friendliness and his sincerity. I felt that I had found a friend, and I was happy.'

There was a long silence. Tara had listened in rapt attention. She looked alternately at the sunset over the distant snowy ranges, and at the face of this short, earnest man at whom she had laughed when she had first seen him in Lyallpur. She was drawn to his warm, shy smile, which lit up his entire face. Inside that small frame she suddenly saw a very large man with powerful convictions, which could shake the world. If Simla was a little insubstantial, as all dream-filled places are, this man beside her she felt was certainly very real.

A few weeks later, on a biting cold evening at the end of January 1948, Tara and Seva Ram heard over the radio that Mahatma Gandhi had been assassinated. Tara looked at Seva Ram with tears in her eyes. Seva Ram was relieved to learn that the killer was not a Muslim, but a Hindu fanatic, incensed by Gandhi's continued pleas for tolerance towards Muslims. Had it been a Muslim, the country would have been plunged into another civil war. Soon Nehru's voice came on the air:

> . . . The light has gone out of our lives and there is darkness everywhere. . . Our beloved leader. . . is no more. . . A madman has put an end to his life, for I can only call him mad who did it, and yet there has been enough of poison spread in this country during the past years and months. . . we must root out this poison. . . The first thing to remember now is that none of us dare misbehave because he is angry. . . In his death he has reminded us of the big things of life, that living truth, and if we remember that, then it will be well with India. . .

5

In the evenings everyone in Simla went to the Mall no matter what the season. Between five and seven o'clock the thing to do was to get dressed and take a stroll from the Ridge to the end of the lower Mall in order 'to eat the air'. It was a delightful winding stretch of about a mile, along a gentle slope, with glamorous shops and smart cafes. One went there to be seen and to see others, and every evening was a veritable fashion parade where men, women and children vied with each other in the elegance of their clothes. The colourful display of women's silk saris was especially striking, but even the men strutted about in the latest cuts from London. The Punjabi on the Mall felt the same emotions that a fashionable Parisian must have felt when strolling on the Champs-Elysées (or Deauville) at the turn of the century.

Seva Ram used to often meet Tara on the Mall after work. They would meet at 'Scandal Point', which was everyone's meeting place, where the Mall divided into three avenues, the broadest one called the Ridge, leading towards the bandstand and Christ Church; a lower one which went past the Madras Coffee House to Cecil Hotel and the Viceregal Lodge; and a higher one which went to the magnificent timbered General Post Office and the Army headquarters. One evening as Tara stood waiting for Seva Ram, she heard her name repeated by a familiar voice. She turned around but could not immediately spot its owner. But the mocking nasal tone was unmistakable, and her heart skipped a beat.

'Karan?' she whispered to herself.

'Tara!' said Karan, emerging out of the crowd.

She was shocked at how much he had changed. He had shaved off his beard, and the gaiety in his eyes had been replaced by a more searching look. His oval face had rounded out at the edges. He had put on a little weight since she last saw him in jail, but he was still slim. His hair was shorter, and he was less youthful-looking. Although he had lost some of his earlier dash, the good looks were still there. The most dramatic change she thought was in his eyes. Instead of the earlier spontaneity, she perceived a subdued irony.

'What are you doing here?' he asked.

'What are *you* doing here?' she asked almost simultaneously. They both laughed.

'We are posted here in Simla,' she said blushing.

There was an uncomfortable pause.

'What about you?'

'Me? Oh, I am eating the air on the Mall,' Karan replied with a laugh.

'I don't mean now. You know what I mean.' She looked flustered, and she reddened as she noticed the unfamiliar, cold irony on his face.

'I teach philosophy. Six months here and for six months in a college in Delhi.'

Tara was shocked. She had expected him to have become a junior minister in the government or to have attained some equally exalted position, as many of the bright young men had, who had fought in the Congress movement. However, his cold, ironical manner prevented further questions. She felt sorry for him.

'I've missed you, Karan. I've often thought of you.'

'Have you, really?'

'Of course.' After a tense pause she said, 'I have a son.'

They exchanged family news. They talked about Bauji, Chachi, and the others. They spoke about the partition. Tara noted a surprising absence of the idealism which used to be such a marked feature of his life in Lyallpur. She kept searching in his eyes for a hint of his old mischievous playfulness. Instead she found a stiff, cold cynicism, which was cleverly disguised by excessive politeness. She thought he would say something about Independence, a cause for which he had passionately fought and even gone to jail. But he remained silent. Did something happen in jail? she wondered. What was he really doing in Simla? She couldn't believe that he had given up everything to end up as a lowly academic.

'Isn't it terrible about Gandhi?' she said.

'I was there,' he said, trying not to make a big thing out of it.

'Tell me, what happened?' she asked, full of excitement.

'I was at the prayer meeting at Birla House. Gandhi was always punctual and the meetings began promptly at five p.m. But he was ten minutes late that day. As he walked towards the congregation, accompanied by his two grand-daughters, the crowd parted to let him pass towards the dias. A young man stepped forward from the crowd, folded his hands and bowed to him. Then he pulled out a revolver and fired three shots in quick succession. At the second shot Gandhiji fell, with the words '*He Ram*' on his lips. Within minutes he was dead.

Tara had tears in her eyes. As she wiped her eyes, she said, 'I must confess to you Karan, that I found his constant preaching of Hindu-Muslim unity a bit irritating. I know he was "India's greatest son since the Buddha", but what about us, who have lost our homes and our relatives because of the Muslims? Chachi was shot by a Mussalman. Do you think I can forget that?'

'Let's not look backwards, Tara.'

'I know, I know. Karan, isn't it great to be free? I feel such a sense of hope in the future.'

A quarter-of-an-hour later Karan left just as unexpectedly as he had arrived.

The chance meeting with Karan had an unsettling effect on Tara. But it was not as profound as it might have been. Initially she was in a daze. He had again woken a dormant sensuality within her. As unrequited feelings surfaced, she again felt restless with desire. However, the excitement quickly subsided, and she was proud of not losing control of herself. This encounter she felt was different from the previous one in the Rohtak jail. She did not feel the same kind of pain. He had aroused pleasant feelings in her, certainly, but she was not tormented as she had been at Rohtak. She attributed this difference both to a change in Karan as well as in her transformed relationship with Seva Ram. Whereas at Rohtak Seva Ram had been a stranger, now he was a familiar figure, whom she was learning to love and respect. He still irritated her, and he was too distant to call a friend, but there was no longer any question of her loyalty.

Tara felt pleased with herself as a consequence, for this meant she could see Karan without feeling guilty. She had found her moorings and they appeared to be sufficiently strong. Nevertheless, she was sensible and did not rush into another meeting. She allowed three weeks to pass in which she thought further. She resolved in the end that she would not see him alone. She wanted Seva Ram to get to know Karan and to like him. She wanted him to become a 'family friend'. Having cleared her mind, and having gained confidence, she wrote him a letter inviting him for lunch the next Saturday.

Karan arrived early on Saturday. He came before Seva Ram returned from his office and Arjun from school. Tara felt nervous and there was a certain uneasiness between them during the first few minutes. He behaved like a stranger, and this infuriated her. He was stiff and extremely proper. She even detected a hint of superiority in his attitude, and a derision for her humdrum middle class life. Gradually, however, he relaxed and she went back into the kitchen as he pulled up an easy chair into the gentle sunlight. While she prepared lunch inside, he sat savouring the intricate sounds of the Himalayan mid-morning. Soon Arjun arrived and Karan quickly made friends with him.

'Sh. . . hear that?' said Karan.

'What?'

'That sound.'

Arjun was puzzled.

'Listen!' whispered Karan.

Arjun shook his head.

'Listen again,' said Karan urgently.

Arjun's face lit up this time, and he nodded. There was no mistaking the honeyed notes which went up and down the same scale.

'That is the Himalayan cuckoo,' said Karan triumphantly. There was a pause. Just then the bird flew to the next tree. Both of them watched it carefully.

'Do you know that tree?' whispered Karan.

Arjun shook his head.

'It is a deodar tree,' said Karan and he smiled.

They were silent again. Arjun went back to playing by himself on the grass. Karan's eyes moved, glancing from Arjun playing at his feet to the sunlight playing on the deodar's branches, and beyond to the motionless contour of the hills. Each of them was absorbed in his own world, yet quietly united by their nearness. Karan seemed to relate better to younger people. The ironic mask seemed to drop away and he became more spontaneous.

Their silence was again interrupted, this time by a humming sound. Both of them looked up, and Arjun pointed to a swarm of bees in the wisteria flowers. Karan said, 'If you learn to listen, you will hear the sound of the universe.'

Soon Seva Ram arrived, and they sat down for a leisurely meal outside on the lawn. Although he said little, Karan seemed to be at ease. Tara too began to relax. He seemed to be interested in Seva

Ram, although the conversation did not flow easily. She watched Karan's exquisitely shaped aristocratic hands as he talked. She noticed that when the conversation turned to himself, he looked amused and laughed in an ironical, self-effacing way, and gently steered it in a different direction. She watched his black, expressive eyes. Although he had lost some of his threatening good looks, he was still very handsome. He gazed intently at Seva Ram. It was a searching gaze, as if he expected to find some answer. She sensed that he wanted to ask her husband about his spiritual life, but he was reluctant to do so.

'What do you do all day long?' she asked him.

'I have my lectures.'

'And?'

'And I read,' he said.

'And?'

'And I play the sitar.'

'And?'

'And that is all.'

They laughed.

'But who do you meet?'

'Oh, I have a few friends, but mostly I spend the time by myself.'

She could tell that he did not want to talk about his friends. 'What do you read?' she asked instead.

'I have been reading the Upanishads.'

Seva Ram was impressed.

'Doesn't it get boring?' she asked.

'No,' he said with an ironical smile.

'But what is it going to lead to?'

'Wisdom, I hope,' and he laughed.

'It doesn't seem very practical,' she said.

'You sound just like your father. It reminds me of our conversations in Lyallpur,' he said in a tone of carefully disguised scorn.

The mention of Lyallpur suddenly transported Tara into the past. She pictured Karan sitting beside Bauji in the courtyard of their house, and she ached at the memory. She felt the tears rising. He sensed her discomfort and changed the subject.

'You are right, though. It is not very practical, but it is very exciting.' Suddenly his face became animated. 'You cannot imagine the thrill, Tara, of reading the Upanishads in the original. It makes you feel as if you are walking on air.'

He had got up and begun to pace up and down. Tara noticed that

Karan's ironical manner seemed to recede for the first time. This was the old Karan, she felt. She looked into his eyes and glimpsed a hint of the earlier sparkle as the mask was lifted momentarily.

'But can you spend your whole life doing this?' she asked.

'A whole lifetime may not be enough to know what I want to know.'

'What do you want to know?'

He smiled, and continued in a quiet, matter-of-fact tone, 'I want to know what happens to us when we die; I want to know whether there is a god or not; where we came from and where we are going; whether we decide our own actions or if they have been decided for us.'

'But people have been asking these questions for thousands of years. How will you find an answer?' she asked.

'Seva Ram has found an answer,' he said.

'Then why don't you ask him? He will tell you.'

Seva Ram smiled and looked away uncomfortably. There was a pause.

'When are you going to find a proper job?' Tara asked. 'It is all right to talk like this when you are in college. But now you are grown up. You should think of having a family and earning a proper living.'

'But I have a job,' he said.

'I mean a proper job. We are a free country now and there are so many opportunities for a bright young man. So many things to do. This is the land of hope. The future is in our hands, Karan. It's not right for you to withdraw into ancient philosophy.'

'What do you suggest?' he asked coldly.

'You could still sit for the IAS. You were in any case going to sit for it before partition when it was called the ICS. I don't know why they need to change names. It still means joining the civil service and ruling the country. The only difference is that earlier you had an English boss, now you will have an Indian politician.' As Tara began to sound more and more like Bauji, Karan gently withdrew. He became subdued. The mask of the cynical man of the world returned. Tara knew that he had inherited money from Chachi. There was thus no pressing need for earning more, but it didn't seem right to her that Karan should be stuck as a provincial lecturer.

'With the English gone, there are many shoes to fill. And many more jobs will come with Nehru's socialism. You don't want to remain a college lecturer for the rest of your life. A man must not do less than what he is capable of.'

Karan laughed. However, it was not the natural, expressive laugh of his youth. It was the affected and formal response of a cultured socialite. Tara suddenly felt embarrassed. His manner made it clear that he thought it inappropriate to continue this conversation.

Tara suggested they all go for a walk, and the men readily agreed. Saturday afternoon walks were now a part of the routine of their life in Simla, and Tara wanted to show Karan the picturesque spots around their house in Chota Simla.

The town of Simla occupied a spur of the lower Himalaya, and ran in an east-west direction for six miles. Chota Simla was situated at the south east end of Simla, sloping directly south of the Monkey Peak of Jakko. It was sparsely inhabited and thickly wooded. Around Chota Simla they had two favourite walks, one of them with fine views of the mountains above, and the other leading off in the opposite direction overlooking the plains below. The former went towards the village of Mashobra. Tara was tempted to suggest the Mashobra walk, but for some reason she did not. Instead, they took the opposite walk along a rivulet, which was dry except during and after the monsoons from July to October. They wandered amongst the deodars with the afternoon sun penetrating through the trees. They stopped to look at a stray poppy here and an aristocratic rhododendron there. The winding path narrowed. They passed strangers on the way, people whom they did not know, but with whom they exchanged smiles. They met Tibetan women with high cheekbones and slit eyes who were adorned with gold and silver nose-rings and ornaments made of goatskins, which they plaited into their hair above their foreheads. Their men looked wild and unkempt, with long hair falling over their sheepskin jackets. They met hill traders whose mules brought honey, nuts and apricots from the drier lands beyond the Sutlej river. They were as happy and carefree as they could get as they walked on that lazy Saturday afternoon.

'Tell me, Karan,' said Tara. 'You knew these people. Why did Nehru, Patel and others agree to Mountbatten's plan for partition? Is it true that they felt they were getting old and wanted a taste of power before they died? God knows they deserved it after struggling for thirty years. But couldn't they have held out for a united India?'

'The only alternatives were to accept a divided but independent

India or to hold out for a united India and follow Gandhi into the political wilderness. Tara, I think they also had a conviction that once Pakistan was conceded the reason for communal violence would vanish. Patel used to say that once the cancerous growth was surgically removed, health would be restored to the body politic.'

'He should have realized that such an operation leaves the body weak and susceptible to the slightest infection.'

They walked a little further and found themselves back on Cart Road. Before them stood the imposing half-timbered house of the Mehtas, in whose upper-floor windows they glimpsed a brilliant reflection of the western sky.

'You have heard of the Mehtas, haven't you, Karan?' she asked. 'They had woollen mills in Amritsar, but they lived in Lahore. Bauji was always talking about them.'

Karan nodded.

'It's too bad, isn't it,' said Tara, 'that both father and son died. It must be lonely for the grand-daughter, in this big house, alone with her mother. She is growing up to be a real beauty. I saw them both on the Mall last week. The mother was wearing a beautiful Madras temple sari. They are among the most fashionable people in Simla, I hear.'

'As a matter of fact. . .' Karan started to say when he was interrupted by Arjun, who had caught a butterfly and was shouting for attention. Seva Ram asked him to let it go. After some cajoling, Arjun reluctantly complied, and the butterfly flew away.

'You were saying?' Tara asked Karan.

'Oh nothing,' said Karan.

While they were talking, Karan noticed that Seva Ram had been silent.

'You are quiet,' said Karan, turning to Seva Ram.

'I prefer to listen,' Seva Ram replied.

With a serene face, Seva Ram seemed to listen from far away, and not with his ears but with his eyes. He seemed to participate in the conversation, but without being involved.

On the way back, in the fading light, Karan carelessly stepped on a *bicchu* plant, and was stung in the leg. His leg swelled up and he was in pain. Arjun and Seva Ram promptly collected the spinach-like leaves of a plant that was always found growing next to the *bicchu* and served as its antidote. Tara gently rubbed the leaves on Karan's swollen leg. Karan found the leaves cooling, and the swelling slowly subsided.

It gave Tara a pleasurable sensation to touch Karan's body. His proximity and his smell again took her back. It was his very own, unmistakable smell, which she remembered from Lyallpur. Touching him awakened her half-buried desire for him. He watched her as she rubbed his ankle and his calf, but she looked away in the direction of Seva Ram and Arjun who were picking the antidote. She steeled herself to regard this experience as only another trial to reconfirm that she could be friends with Karan, without the pain that was always associated with seeing him in the past. She could live with the pleasant feelings which he aroused in her, because she no longer felt the need to possess him.

6

Arjun's earliest memory of Simla was of waking up suddenly on a
frosty overcast morning. It was just after dawn and he was only half
awake. It had been raining. Along with the wet there was a rawness
in the air, and he could hear the wind blow. He got out of bed in his
pajamas, and he ran to his mother's bed. She stretched out her arm
and he nestled by her side. With her warm hands she felt his body
and pressed him closer to her.

'Did you have a bad dream, my son?' Tara asked.

He did not answer; he was content to feel her warmth.

'Go to sleep, child.'

In his mother's warm, large bed, with her soft arms around him,
Arjun felt protected. He smiled, and he cuddled against her, and in
a moment he was blissfully asleep.

Soon after their arrival in Simla, Arjun was put into a Jesuit
missionary school. He cried on the first day when his mother left
him in the headmaster's office. The headmaster took him to the first
grade, where Arjun stood shyly behind the door. He was shorter
than most of the boys, and his hair was cut square and parted in the
middle like a peasant's. He was ill at ease in a new shirt which
pinched him under the arms. His khaki-coloured shorts braced up
tight around his thighs, and on his feet he wore a new pair of sturdy
Bata shoes, which Tara had bought the day before on the Mall.

The children began going over the lesson. Arjun was all ears, as
he sat at his desk at the back, not daring even to cross his legs. When
the bell rang at three o' clock, the master had to remind him that he
could go home.

The daily two-mile walk to school along Cart Road framed his
new life. In the mornings he was a rushed and nervous boy as he
hurried along to school, his hair still wet, combed down and parted.
In the afternoons in contrast, he would dawdle back home. He
would linger among the pine trees, eat wild berries that grew along
the road, drink water from the spring and arrive home kicking a

pine cone. At home Tara, who had missed him all day, would make up by feeding him home-made biscuits and milk. She would cut out pictures from magazines for him, tell him stories from the Hindu epics and regale him with playful but melancholy chatter.

There was nothing striking about Arjun's school life. He played during recess, worked in study periods, paid attention in class, studied hard when he had to, enjoyed sports, and managed to stay comfortably in the middle of his class. He learned to speak English early. Like other young Indians who acquired English at a young age, his idiom was natural and virile, freed of the imitative taste of London fogs and Oxford chapels. In contrast to the mimicry of the pre-Independence generations, his was a confident speech which emerged under the bright sunshine of the subcontinent.

Despite the politicians' exhortations to the middle class to give up its unholy attraction for the colonial language, and learn Hindi instead, Tara shrewdly knew that English would remain the basis for entry into the professions for years to come. She had also heard that the very same politicians secretly sent their own children to English-speaking schools while they hypocritically vilified it in Parliament. On the rare occasions when Nehru chose to speak English on the radio, in his gentle and aristocratic Cambridge accent, she would get tears in her eyes. She felt that Nehru too must be secretly ambivalent about English; she forgave him his public posture, which she felt he had to adopt as a politician. In any case, for her part she was determined that Arjun should speak, read, and write English well. In her loneliness she gathered her ambitions and centered them upon his young head. She had visions of greatness for her son, seeing him a grown man, handsome and intelligent, representing his country as an ambassador or a man of power and status.

Karan taught Arjun to fly a kite. He remembered the first time when he got it up in the air. Karan was holding up the kite and Arjun held the string on a spindle. He nodded, and Karan let it go; Arjun saw it swim into the air; he felt the tug that it gave to his little hand; he was thrilled as he released more string; the kite had caught the breeze. He felt a sense of power as he watched it soar towards the clouds as if he were bending the winds of heaven to his will. His triumph was cut short, however, as the kite soon snagged in a pine tree.

As Arjun's school was on his way, Karan would sometimes unexpectedly meet Arjun after school on Saturdays, and they would walk home together. They would talk about the trees, the Upanishads, and sports. Arjun enjoyed listening to stories from the Hindu epics. One day, Karan and Arjun enacted the following dialogue from the Chandogya Upanishad, and it thrilled Seva Ram.

'Bring me fruit from the tree, Arjun.'

'Here it is, Sir.'

'Divide it.'

'It is divided, Sir.'

'What do you see in it?'

'Nothing at all, Sir.'

'Thus, Arjun, from the essence in the seed which you cannot see comes this great tree. This very essence is the spirit of the universe. That is reality. That is Atman. That is you, Arjun.'

'Tell me more, Sir.'

'Tat tvam asi, thou art that.'

'Tat tvam asi,' repeated Arjun.

Karan created a stir on Arjun's eighth birthday. He arrived early in the afternoon as the preparations were underway. Tara was busy in the kitchen and the servant had gone off to the bazaar to fetch sweets from the Bengali shop.

At four o'clock, rickshaws started to arrive, bringing Arjun's young friends, who were accompanied by their mothers or their ayahs. As they trooped in, carrying their colourfully wrapped presents, Karan suddenly realized that he had forgotten to bring anything. He quietly slipped out to Mario's, the Goan bookseller on the Mall.

As they were finishing tea, Karan appeared with a large package, which he quietly put aside in one corner. His attempt to be unobtrusive failed, because everyone wanted to see his present, and it was opened with much ceremony. Out came three massive books: Plutarch's *Lives*, Homer's *Iliad*, and Tulsidas' *Ramayana*. Everyone burst out laughing. One mother snickered, 'Imagine, to bring such books to a little boy!' Another lady advised him to have children of his own to learn what kind of presents were suitable. Karan turned red. Tara consoled him by saying that Mario would gladly exchange the books. However, Karan resisted any such idea. He insisted that John Stuart Mill had these books at the age of eight. Seeing his discomfort, Arjun protested that he liked the books and did not want to change them.

A few years later at Mario's, Karan saw Arjun absorbed in some photographs of Simla. Mario displayed them in his shop window because they were attractive to tourists, and like picture postcards, they sold well, and profitably. Karan asked Arjun which picture he liked best, and Arjun pointed to one which showed the Simla cathedral from an unusual angle, with the Himalayas in the background. They went to the back, and looked through Mario's collection of old prints, until Karan found a nineteenth century engraving which approximated the angle of the photograph. When Arjun protested that it did not look as nice as the photograph, Karan replied in a voice full of affection, 'Arjun, my boy, you will tire of the photograph in a week, but this print will give you pleasure for a long time.'

Although Arjun came under the unusual influence of Karan, he wasn't allowed to get close to him. Karan remained a remote and shadowy figure. There was a mystery about what he actually did with himself for he was away for months at a time. But when they did meet Karan educated Arjun in the world of the senses. As Bauji through his example had taught Karan and Tara to enjoy the world, so Karan imparted the joy of sense-experience to Bauji's grandson. Arjun learned about flowers, trees and birds. He learned to recognize them from their smells and colours and their sounds. As Karan was much better read than Bauji, he educated the boy equally in the world of reason. He transmitted to Arjun his own sceptical outlook, rich with questioning. Arjun learned to have confidence in his own reason rather than in the opinion of others. He learned to distinguish between the excellent and the mediocre, the good from the bad, the just from the unjust. This sometimes led him into arguments with his mother, who was quite willing to accept society's conception of right or wrong.

Tara used to talk to Arjun about what was happening in the country, but Karan always changed the subject when it came to politics. Tara was filled with all the hopes of post-Independence India and infected by the dreams of Nehru. She told Arjun about the virtues of centralized planning, democratic socialism, and a large public sector—all the catchwords of the day. But he sensed that she had lingering doubts about the wisdom of this course. She used to sometimes wish that someone could tell her if they were doing the right thing in Delhi. Or were Nehru and others being led astray by the 'Russian miracle' and the Fabian ideas (under which they had grown up in the twenties and thirties)? Reflecting Bauji's old liberal prejudices, she used to express her fears that Nehru might land them into a huge and inefficient bureaucratic jungle. It was hard to refute socialism because it was intellectually so attractive and made such a good election slogan, she would say. Seva Ram refused to be drawn into these discussions. He was too aloof and too austere. Even though he was physically present, he kept to himself. Arjun could not think of a single instance when his father raised his voice, let alone scolded or thrashed him. Nor could he remember when his father had ever laughed or played with him. There were long silences when the two were together—silences in which Seva Ram was comfortable and Arjun uncomfortable. Seva Ram would disappear twice a day into his room to meditate. At such times he was not even physically available to his son. Nor did Seva Ram try to initiate his son into his faith and his beliefs, thinking that Arjun was too young to begin meditation. Arjun admired his father and was continually reassured by his sweet smile, but he also found him boring. When he wanted to talk he turned instead to his mother.

7

At about this time Bauji and Bhabo came to Simla. Tara had been inviting them for many years and thus it was a big event in Seva Ram's home when they finally came in the summer of '55. Seva Ram offered them their own bedroom, but they would not hear of it and settled down in the smaller adjoining room for a month's stay. The weather was perfect and Bauji's reaction to Simla was very similar to Tara's. Bhabo was delighted to be reunited with her grandson and she poured on him all the maternal love which had been gathering inside her through the years. Tara found in Bauji the friend that she had been seeking. With the passing of time, Bauji appeared in her eyes less the mighty patriarch of the Lyallpur house, and more an ordinary person she could get close to and confide in. The events of the partition and the eight years that had passed had reduced the gulf that separated the young girl from the middle aged father and they were no longer conscious of the disparity of age or the father-daughter relationship between them. Karan decided to absent himself from Tara's house during these days because he knew that Bauji was angry with him. Neither could Tara talk to Bauji about her feelings for Karan.

'I am happy, Bauji,' she said vivaciously as they sat alone in the garden in the morning sun. 'He has been a good husband. He's very sweet. He is kind to us. D'you know he's never said a harsh thing to Arjun or to me all these years we've been married.'

'How is his work?' asked Bauji.

'It's alright, I suppose. He works hard I know but he never talks much about it. But then he never talks much about anything. I am usually the one who does the chattering when we are together. Sometimes I feel I am talking to a wall. He is always so remote.'

'Yes, I remember he was always aloof.'

'But I do wish he were more ambitious. In a worldly sort of way, I mean. If he had tried we could have got a bigger house, and that too in a more fashionable part of town. For example in Benmore.

Some of his equals at the office have already moved twice, and here we are stuck in Chota Simla. And they don't even work as hard as he does! I think it's unfair.'

'But how would he have got a bigger house? I thought it was allotted by the government.'

'Yes, of course. But the government is a person, isn't it? All he needs to do is become friendly with Mr Ahuja of the Housing Department. We should visit them in the evenings and send them sweets at Diwali.'

'You mean, he is unwilling to lick boots,' Bauji laughed.

'No, don't put it that way, Bauji. This is how things are done. He won't get anywhere like this. He refuses to call on his boss in the evenings. I have told him so many times, "let's go and see them." His wife likes having the wives of junior officers drop in on them and flatter her. But no. He thinks it's not right. And I can't go alone.'

Bauji was amused. The more his daughter talked about her husband the more he liked him. Of course he himself was very different and would have probably behaved like Tara in the circumstances, but now sitting under the blue sky he felt an admiration for his unusual son-in-law.

'People are differently constituted, Tara. He's just made that way.'

'I sometimes think it's plain selfish of him. If he doesn't want these things for himself, what about Arjun and me? I would certainly like to live in a more fashionable part of town. It would be closer to Arjun's school too. All he thinks about is his meditation and of his guru. He hardly spends time with Arjun.'

Bauji made a gesture of impatience.

'I think he is one of those men, who are possessed by an urge so strong to do something that they can't help themselves, they have got to do it. His spiritual urge is of that nature. I can bet he would sacrifice anything to satisfy that urge.'

'Even the people who love him, his family, I'm sure,' said Tara with a rueful laugh.

'Perhaps. It's a long, arduous road he's travelling, but it may be that at the end of it he'll find what he is seeking.'

'What's that?'

'God.'

'God!' she cried. It was an exclamation of incredulous surprise. Although she vaguely knew of his intense search and his relationship with the guru, she wasn't prepared for this bold answer in the middle of a sunny day. Seva Ram was very private about his meditation and she had never dared to ask him about it. Tara immediately grew serious and Bauji sensed in her whole attitude something like fear.

'Why do you say that?'

'I can't be sure. And you should certainly know better, having lived with him all these years. But I think he is filled with a sense of the transiency of life, and he believes his inner search is a compensation for the sorrow in the world.'

Bauji could tell that Tara had not thought about any of this. He could also see that she didn't like the turn the conversation had taken. It made her feel shy and awkward. It was understandable that she did not want to think of her husband in this way.

'One should take the world as it comes,' she said decisively. 'If we are here, it is to make the most of it. When he wants to, Bauji, he can be a warm, lovable person. I have seen him like that, and that is good enough for me.'

Bauji shrewdly turned the conversation at this point. He told her about his own and Bhabo's life in Hoshiarpur, where he had settled and made a life after the partition. They had been writing to each other constantly and so there was little new that Tara learned. She told him that she had recently received a letter from Anees, and she noticed an immediate quickening of his interest. He could not stop asking her questions about her friend in Pakistan.

Looking into his eyes, Tara felt that her father had lost none of his youthful vitality. He was nearing sixty but she could sense the same sensual spark that she had felt in him when he had first met Anees. She watched him as he sat erectly, savouring the Himalayan morning. She followed his eyes as he looked beyond to the panorama of ridges and peaks in the distance. There was confidence and optimism in his look. Yet this was the same man who had been totally broken by the partition eight years ago. It amazed her how he had firmly lifted himself up out of that abyss. For her too, the partition had been traumatic, but she had been young and her life had been ahead of her, and Seva Ram's job with the government had eased the transition. In her father's case everything was lost. He had crossed the border with nothing except the clothes on his back. It was a high heart which could bear adversity and not run away from it—for in bearing it shone the beauty of the soul.

She remembered that the challenge of housing and feeding his family had pulled him out of his depression at the end of '47, even before Gandhi's death. He had restarted his law practice right in the refugee camp. He had begun by documenting the property and other assets which the refugees had left behind in Pakistan. For the next three years he had fought for their claims with the newly created Refugee Rehabilitation Department of the government. Eventually he had succeeded in recovering between ten and twenty per cent of the lost assets. In those cases, where he thought the government had not been fair, he had filed a suit in court and thereby succeeded in getting the proper share for his refugee clients. In his own case, his share included a quaint old-fashioned Muslim house in Hoshiarpur, a small town across the border in the East Punjab plains. It was remarkably similar in design to the house in Lyallpur, and he lived there now with Bhabo. They had planted jasmine and gardenia bushes in the smaller courtyard and hung identical blinds in the narrower veranda, and there was a powerful illusion of 7 Kacheri Bazaar. By the time India adopted her new Constitution in January 1950, Bauji, and many of his refugee clients, had moved out of the camp, and were well settled.

Bauji's success in settling refugee claims had made a name for him and had also made him well-off again. He had a car with a chauffeur and several servants to look after the house. In the early '50s, urged by friends, he stood for elections to the town's Municipal Committee. And he still continued to play a leadership role in the town government, although he had allowed his legal practice to slowly diminish. Bhabo continued to visit temples and feed holy men daily at noon. A visible change in their life was the breakdown of the joint family. In the tents of the refugee camp, the various members of 7 Kacheri Bazaar decided that they no longer wanted to be a burden to Bauji and they chose to go their separate ways. Although he had always found his son infuriating, Big Uncle's departure for Delhi was poignant and it had left a real void in Bauji's life. Nevertheless, Bauji and Bhabo had slowly got used to living alone. Having always lived in a house full of dozens of children, relatives, friends, and friends of friends, the solitude was the most difficult to cope with especially for Bhabo.

Bauji felt that the story of his life after partition was not unlike that of most refugees who had trekked penniless across the border. He told Tara that it was a testimony to the human spirit. After having fallen in the abyss, the refugees had pulled themselves out from the depths, made a new life of their own and risen up again. In many ways they had shown more initiative than the people who were not refugees, that is the people who were already living in the towns and villages to which the refugees went. That is because they had to work harder to pull themselves up than their more fortunate brothers who had been of the right religion on the right side of the line which Radcliffe had drawn. And for this the refugees were naturally resented. Bauji had heard from his son that the refugees had practically rebuilt the bazaars of Delhi in five years. Anees wrote the same thing to Tara. She said that the Muslim refugees who had come from India had made a remarkable life for themselves in Pakistan. Bauji said in a philosophical vein that a man really doesn't know his own strength until he has met with adversity.

There was a more practical reason why Bauji had come to Simla. It concerned the division of his property and it resulted in a big fight between Tara and him. Seva Ram and Bhabo were caught in the cross-fire and were embarrassed to be witness to strong language exchanged between father and daughter. 'Bauji, how could you? You're a bigot,' said Tara. 'And you are greedy for money, my daughter!' replied Bauji.

One of the first acts of Nehru when he became head of the government was to ask for a reform of the Hindu family law in order to bring about greater equality between men and women in marriage and inheritance. Nehru was an idealist and this fit in well with the spirit of those early years when Nehru and others saw themselves building a new nation based on principles of democracy, liberty and equality. The spark as usual had been Gandhi, who before he died, had tried to bring about an awareness among the masses for the need to improve the position of women. He would constantly tell the people, 'treat your daughters and sons as equals for otherwise you are less than human.'

Nehru had a strong ally in his Law Minister, B.R. Ambedkar, who was just as keen to abolish dowry, allow women to divorce and remarry, and divide the family property equally between sons and daughters. They introduced a bill in the Constituent Assembly to achieve these reforms. But they had not counted on tough opposition from the tradition-bound members of the Assembly and many leaders of their own party. Rajendra Prasad, the President, warned Nehru that the legislation would arouse bitter feelings and would affect the chances of his party in the next election. Patel, the Deputy Prime Minister, felt that these ideas were foreign and they would 'cause disruption in every family'. Because of opposition from his own party, Nehru was checkmated and he reluctantly backed off and Ambedkar resigned in frustration.

A few years later, Nehru again revived the legislation. Patel and Prasad were gone by then. Nehru now staked his political career on it saying, 'My government will live and fall on this.' And in 1955 by the sheer weight of his personality Nehru pushed through the celebrated reform which came to be called the Hindu Code Bill.

The whole nation participated in the drama. Newspapers covered the long debates extensively. Tara avidly read the press accounts every day in the *Tribune* and echoing the reformists she proclaimed 'My God, this is the most revolutionary change in Hindu society since Manu.' She immediately wrote to her sisters to demand an equal share of their inheritance from Bauji. This act of hers really hurt Bauji, who was more conservative in his sentiments and who was opposed to the Bill. According to Tara, she was upholding a principle and money was not the issue. Bauji, in any case, had lost his property in the partition she argued. That he had rebuilt a modest future after '47 was not lost on her, however.

'Why did you write to your sisters?' demanded Bauji.

'It was to make them aware of their rights under the new law,' Tara sheepishly said.

'Did you think I was not going to honour their rights?'

'No, no. Well yes, I thought you would leave everything to my brother.'

'And so you made me out into some kind of villain.'

'No, I didn't mean to do that.'

'You created disunity in the family.'

'No.'

'What else did you achieve? What are you trying to do Tara? The family is already broken with everyone gone their separate ways. It's lonely enough for Bhabo and me as it is. Why are you making it worse? My own daughter going against me, it is too, too sad.'

'I am not going against you, Bauji. It is a principle I am upholding.'

'This is what one gets from one's children at the end. What is the principle anyway?'

'Well, of equality.'

'Didn't you get your share with your dowry?'

'No, dowry is different. Besides dowry is illegal now.'

'How can these people think they can abolish dowry by legislation? Idealistic fools! No daughter in this country will be married without dowry. Just because there is a law, do you think people will do away with centuries of custom?'

'Surely you don't support dowry. It is like selling your daughter.'

'That is not the point. If you wanted my money you should have come to me directly. I don't like this underhand way of writing to your sisters and creating disunity.'

Tara was in tears. She ran away to her room and stayed there till Seva Ram came home in the evening.

'Why don't you tell Bauji that we don't need his money—that you are concerned with the principle for the sake of your sisters,' advised Seva Ram. 'We are well-off and don't need any more money, do we?'

'What do you mean?' said Tara. 'Of course we could use the money. Do you have any idea how I run the house? Do you know how difficult the last week is before the monthly salary comes? If we had some money we could get nicer furniture. Arjun could go to Bishop Cotton School. So much we could do.'

'Then I suggest you stop talking about principles and talk about cash.'

'Will you speak to Bauji?

'You must be crazy!'

'Well, he's angry with me. Maybe you could explain to him nicely.'

'I don't want his money, thank you.'

'Oh, you are hopeless!'

'In that case I suggest you avoid the subject,' said Seva Ram.

During the remainder of her parents' stay in Simla, Tara followed her husband's advice. As if by tacit agreement she and her father tactfully avoided the subject. They talked incessantly about politics but the subject of the Hindu Code Bill was skilfully skirted. The days passed quickly and before they realized it, it was time to go. Exactly a month after they came Bauji and Bhabo left.

8

By the time he was eighteen and in his final year in school, Arjun often used to go alone to the Mall in the evenings. He used to go up on the Ridge, the highest point on the Mall, and stand along the railing near the bandstand and look down at the procession of life below. He would gaze down and be filled with wonder over the countless different individual lives down there. And each moment of each person's life was unique, rich and would never occur again. The world seemed to be full of all kinds of people and strange happenings. He wondered why men and women lived together in families, and where the animals and birds came from. What, he asked himself, was the relationship of the stars and the moon to our destinies?

Walking on the Mall, he observed that one met the same people a number of times in the same evening, as everyone tended to walk back and forth along the same familiar stretch. The first time one met one's friends, one stopped and chatted for a few minutes. The second time one folded one's hands in greeting from a distance and continued on one's way. The third time one smiled conspiratorialy from a distance. The secret smile meant that both people belonged to a select group, and knew that three was about the right number of times to meet. And if there were a fourth or subsequent meetings in the same evening, both looked at each other embarrassed by the realization that one had nothing better to do than to 'eat the Mall air'.

One day Karan spotted Arjun wandering alone on the Mall. Arjun must have looked lost, for Karan immediately put his arm around him and took him into the exclusive Amateur Dramatic Club (ADC). Although he had never been inside, Arjun knew it as the fashionable meeting place of high society, where all of Simla's gossip and scandals started. Karan signed Arjun as a guest at the entrance, which was adorned with potted palms in polished brass planters. A hall porter in livery greeted Karan by name. Arjun was led past the library and the smoke-filled card room towards the Green Room. It was full of young people and laughter. They sat down at a small table and ordered tea and samosas. Arjun looked around the room (which was in fact painted green), and he was filled with awe. Bearers in starched white uniforms with green cummerbunds and green sashes and tassels in their turbans were gliding gracefully between the tables. Karan asked him if he wanted to act in a play, as the Club was casting for its next production. Arjun shook his head shyly. Karan explained that the Club had started in the 19th century as an addition to the Gaiety Theatre next door. The rehearsal rooms had soon become such popular meeting places that they were expanded, and the club acquired its social character. It still did a comedy every six weeks during the season.

From his wanderings on the Mall, Arjun recognized a number of people in the room whom he associated with the 'smart set'. Everyone was stylishly dressed and vivaciously absorbed in his little group. He noted that Karan was popular, as a number of people at different tables smiled at him or nodded to him in greeting. Karan excused himself to deliver a message to someone in the billiards room. Arjun looked around and thought 'So this is the place where all the smart people of Simla meet.' Meanwhile the bearer brought the tea, along with gleaming forks, knives, and white cloth napkins. Arjun felt nervous and hoped that he would not have to eat the samosa with a fork and knife. He was not adept with these instruments, as he ate Indian food with his fingers at home. He associated knives and forks with highly Westernized Indians.

Soon Karan returned, and Arjun was grateful when he saw Karan eat a greasy samosa with his fingers and then casually lick them afterwards. Karan chatted away, but Arjun was tongue-tied. To put him at ease, Karan hailed a group of young people from the next table.

'Priti, come and meet my young friend!'

Priti smiled, and skipped over to their table, bringing some of her friends with her. Karan introduced Arjun to them as his 'nephew and dearest friend'. Priti gave Arjun a vivacious smile, and Arjun marvelled at her complete lack of self-consciousness.

Priti poutingly turned to Karan, 'When are you going to play the sitar for us? Mother has been anxiously waiting to hear you play since your famous concert in Delhi. The whole world has been talking about it.'

Arjun looked incredulously at Karan, who blushed. Karan made polite sounds and gently changed the subject as he always did when the talk turned to him.

Arjun recognized one of Priti's friends at the table. She was Neena, the daughter of Rao Sahib, the successful director of a British company, whom his parents also knew. He kept looking at her, hoping she would recognize him. But she did not. In fact she completely ignored him, as if he were invisible, and he felt hurt.

The talk turned to popular Bombay movies. Karan excused himself again, leaving Arjun in Priti's care. Arjun was impressed with the sophisticated way in which everyone spoke about the films playing in the four cinemas of Simla. They all predicted that a particular film would break all records. Arjun was at a loss since he had not seen any of the films.

Arjun's eyes kept returning to Priti's lean face and her long, gleaming black hair. She had a habit of tilting her head in an audacious way, which gave her an imperious air. Her body was small, and she had striking, dark eyes. Whenever they met his, she smiled, and Arjun's heart skipped a beat.

Suddenly, Priti and her friends were speaking in hushed voices. Arjun heard someone say, 'Dabbu Ram was black-balled last Friday.' Everyone knew Dabbu Ram. Even Arjun knew him as the fat, rich, balding owner of a new saree shop on the Mall. But he didn't understand what had happened to him. He looked puzzled, and Priti explained that being 'black-balled' meant that he was refused admission to the club.

'The Committee members vote with white and black balls. White means "yes" and black means "no",' she explained.

'Why was poor Dabbu black-balled?' whispered the girl whom they called Veena.

'Because he is a trader, silly,' replied Neena. 'They don't want traders in the club.'

'But there are other business people in the club, aren't there?' asked Veena.

'Yes, but they are not shopkeepers.'

Arjun's eyes kept meeting Priti's. Every time they did, she smiled.

'Where do you live?' she asked.

'Pine Villa', he stuttered.

'Where is it?'

Instead of simply saying 'in Chota Simla', he blushed and started giving a round-about explanation, which someone interrupted.

'Isn't that in Chota Simla?'

'Yes,' he admitted meekly.

'Why didn't you say so in the first place?' Priti asked with a teasing smile, as she tilted her head the other way.

'Well, it's not in the bazaar, but below it,' he defensively added, since Chota Simla also referred to a small market street full of shops.

'Of course it isn't. Any fool knows that. Only shopkeepers live in the bazaar,' replied Priti impatiently.

The conversation turned to fashionable people unknown to him, and Arjun felt that he had made a fool of himself. A confident 'Chota Simla' would have been much more effective. He had sounded as if he were trying to hide something, which in a sense he was. He felt that he must be an object of scorn in Priti's eyes. He did not know about movies or fashionable people, and now he had committed the one sin that mattered in her society: he had tried to be something that he was not. He could not lift his eyes to face Priti's the rest of the evening.

Meanwhile Karan rejoined the group. Arjun was grateful that at least Karan had not witnessed his embarrassment. But he was afraid that Priti would tell him. He could not bear the thought of the two making fun of him. As he looked around the glittering room, with its animated chatter, he felt that they were all aligned against him, including Karan, who spoke charmingly and who seemed to belong so naturally to these people. When he spoke, everyone listened. Arjun suddenly felt alone. He wanted to run away. Yet, a magnet-like force drew him to this crowd and held him there.

Mrs Maira, the mother of the girl they called Veena came by to fetch her daughter. Karan and the only other male in Priti's group, a boy named Rishi, gallantly rose to greet her. 'Hello-ji, hello-ji,' she said gushingly. She spoke a little louder than necessary. Everyone smiled back at her. Arjun realized too late that perhaps he too should have risen. Priti must think him an uncouth peasant, he thought.

"Hello-ji, hello-ji,' mimicked Neena after Mrs Maira had left.

'What an odd thing to say. Either you say "hello" or you say "namaste-ji". You don't mix them up,' said Rishi laughing. The others joined in the laughter, except Karan.

'Her father, you know, worked so hard to become as English as possible,' said Neena in a conspiratorial voice. 'He even Anglicized his name from Mehra to Maira. And now look at her... The old man must be turning in his grave.'

Their attention was suddenly diverted, as the dashing young Major Chadha appeared at the door in uniform, sporting a baton in his right hand.

'Isn't he handsome!' said Neena.

'I like his moustache,' laughed Priti.

'He is a show-off,' interjected Rishi. 'Why does he need to carry a swagger stick into the Green Room? Obviously lacks confidence, poor chap.'

The handsome Major smiled at Neena, who smiled back.

'Entirely too many Army types in Simla,' said Priti.

'But they are such fun,' said Neena.

'They don't think very much,' said Priti.

'They are soldiers after all,' said Rishi.

'But they love life,' said Neena.

'And they are honest,' said Karan.

Everyone looked at Karan, as if he had said something odd.

'They are honest and fun-loving because they know they are probably going to die before any of us.'

'Who is honest? No one is honest!' interjected a tall and distinguished looking man, who had silver grey hair at his temples.

'Hello, Rao Uncle,' said Priti warmly.

'Hello, father!' said Neena.

A. N. Rao, Neena's father, was a boxwallah, and one of the first Indian directors of a British company based in Bombay. He sported an ascot and a tweed jacket; he was the sort of person who spoke Hindustani with an Oxford accent. He was the son of a senior civil servant, and everyone knew that his success in the Anglo-Indian commercial world had been due to his Anglicized ways and his father's connections.

'Priti, I say, are you coming to the picnic on Friday to Narkunda? There will be Sita and Chippy, Dinky, Neena, Bubbly and Flukey and Rishi, and all your friends,' said Rao Sahib.

'But why Narkunda? It is so far away.'

'Don't you know that one about Narkunda, my dear?'

'What?' asked Priti.

Rao Sahib began to recite in a thick British army accent.

There lived a small puppy in Narkunda
Who sought for the best tree to bark under

Which he found and said, 'Now,
I can call out Bow-Wow'
Underneath the best cedar in Narkunda.

Everyone laughed. Karan shouted 'bravo!' and Rao Sahib continued.

There was an old man of Narkunda
Whose voice was like peals of loud thunder
It shivered the hills
Into Colveynth pills
And destroyed half the trees of Narkunda.

There was clapping. Rao Sahib took a bow.

'Well done!' said Karan. 'A little help from Kipling can persuade the most reluctant picnicker.'

'Well, Priti, are you coming? Father has even arranged for the Governor's Rest House, in case it rains,' said Neena.

'I say, come to think of it, one never sees you on the Mall these days.' said Rao Sahib to Karan.

'And why should one see me on the Mall?' said Karan, closing his lips in an ironical smile.

'But what else does one do in Simla—except go to the Mall in the evening; find your friends eating ice cream at Scandal Point; drag them to the Green Room for the latest gossip and samosas; rush to the Rivoli for the newest picture; plan picnics to Mashobra and Narkunda; and throng to the Sunday morning bingo and beer?'

Rao Sahib had to stop to take a breath.

'Bravo!' said Karan clapping his hands again.

'Uncle Rao, you should act in the play that they are doing,' said Priti.

'Oh, but he doesn't need the Gaiety Theatre. He is always on stage,' said Karan.

With that Karan rose from his chair. He looked enquiringly at Arjun, who also got up.

'You are not leaving, are you?' protested Priti. 'Oh, you always leave early, just when we are getting started.' She smiled and tilted her head again. Arjun thought she looked ravishingly beautiful when she did that.

When Karan and he were parting on the Mall, Arjun picked up enough courage to ask, 'Who is Priti?'

'Priti Mehta. Her grandfather knew Bauji, and I knew her father well.'

'Oh, you mean that big house with the green fence on Cart Road? Does she live there?' asked Arjun.

Karan nodded.

'The one we used to pass on our Saturday walks!'

'She is pretty, isn't she?' said Karan with a sly smile.

Arjun's head was spinning when he returned home. He felt intensely excited after this first encouter with an inaccessible and forbidden world. He was intoxicated by the glamour, the clothes, and the sophistication of manners and language. He imagined these people living in big houses, surrounded by tall hedges, with many servants, living a life quite unlike his own.

The discovery that he had known all along where Priti lived, left him breathless. He had passed by her house on the way to school every day and he now realized that he had seen her on occasions when he peered through the hibiscus hedge. Priti's house, which had been merely an impersonal landmark on his daily trudge to school, now acquired a special character. He tried to recall her face again. He could clearly visualize her sparkling brown eyes, her gleaming dark hair, her thin face, and the extraordinary way she tilted her head. All these combined into an enchanting image. The more he thought how desirable she was the less accessible she seemed to become. Half the men in the Green Room must be in love with her, he thought. And they were all handsome and worldly!

When he reached home he felt depressed by the contrast of his drab everyday life with the brilliant world of the ADC. He hated his room, his clothes, his books. To make matters worse, Tara was upset because he had returned late. Arjun decided to keep his visit to ADC a secret. He also felt that Karan would not want him to talk about his life in society, as he himself never spoke about it.

9

In the following weeks, Arjun tried to find out everything he could about Priti and her family. This was not difficult because they were well known. But it was not easy to hide his feelings when he mentioned her name. Gradually he became adept at steering the conversation over family dinner so as to learn more about her. His parents may have guessed that something was afoot, but they said nothing.

What Arjun learned seemed only to extend rather than diminish the gap between Priti and himself. That their grandfathers knew each other was the single reassuring fact he could fall back upon. He wondered how close Bauji had been to Sir Sanat Mehta. Did Priti know about Bauji? Even if she did, would it matter to her? Probably not. He tried to picture Bauji and Sanat Mehta talking in the courtyard at Lyallpur. But his memories of Lyallpur were vague and the picture blurry. Nevertheless he visualized the two men sitting under the shade of the mango tree, and Bauji offering papaya to his friend. Bauji used to offer fruit to everyone.

Bauji had lost everything in the partition while the Mehtas had not been affected. For one thing, their mills had been in Amritsar, which had come to India under the Radcliffe award. Whereas Bauji had invested in property in and around Lyallpur, Sanat Mehta had spread his real estate investments in Delhi, Simla, and as far away as Calcutta. Even his mansion in Lahore he had sold off during the '40s, having guessed that the partition of the Punjab was inevitable, and that Lahore might go to Pakistan in the partition plan.

Apart from their house in Simla, which Sanat Mehta had bought from a departing Englishman in the '30s for a fraction of its real value, he had made an impressive investment in an apple orchard in Kotgarh, about fifty miles north of Simla. He had got it virtually for nothing, although he had been called a fool at that time. After Independence, California-style apples had become popular and the orchard was now worth a fortune. Although their money was old, the status of the Mehtas was not due to their wealth alone. It also owed to the fact that Priti's father had been active in the Congress movement in the '30s and '40s. During the freedom struggle, famous figures including Gandhi, Patel and even Tagore had visited their house in Lahore. Nehru had been a regular guest during the famous Simla round table conferences with the Viceroy. Karan knew Priti's father from his days in the nationalist movement.

With his khaki canvas school bag slung on his back, Arjun passed Priti's house twice a day. As he approached, his heartbeat would quicken. Even before the three-thirty bell, which announced the end of school, he would begin to think of her. When the bell rang, he would quickly gather his books and run out before any of his school friends decided to walk home with him. A round red post-box—a proud symbol of the British Raj—stood a hundred yards from her house, and it became a familiar landmark. When he reached it he would slow down his galloping pace, take a deep breath, and walk with measured steps towards the pleasure that awaited him.

Having reached Priti's home, Arjun would first look in through the latticed gate, which gave a view of the side of the house and of the flower-lined path leading up to it. From this angle he could tell if the Mehtas had company. He could observe the servants going back and forth from the house to the lawn with the tea service. As Arjun moved towards the front of the house he had to be careful not to be seen. He became skilled at hiding behind a giant deodar tree on the other side of the road, which was at a slightly higher level. From here he could get a complete view of the lawn and a partial view of the house. He was grateful that the hibiscus hedge was cut low.

The house itself had a long gabled front of red brick, but years of Simla's wet weather had mellowed it, with creepers growing abundantly around the windows and on the walls. Its wide veranda overlooked an acre of finely cut lawn, ending in the north in the dense shade of great old deodars and pine. Beds of colourful pansies, dahlias, asters, and a dozen varieties of roses bordered the lawn. The riot of flowers was surrounded by a low hedge and a green fence.

The Mehtas always seemed to have company. Full of fascination, Arjun would watch them having tea on the spacious lawn in the golden light of the sun. Afternoon tea at their house was obviously a well-practiced ceremony conducted with a gentle leisureliness. Arjun was struck by the Englishness of the scene. It seemed to come straight from a picture of an English country house which he had once seen in a magazine.

He imagined Priti living in these exalted circumstances which he could never hope to be part of. On his 'lucky days' he would spot Priti on the lawn, either swinging on a wooden swing, talking to her friends, or playing badminton at the south end of the park. He would be filled with longing. He would have given anything to be a part of her unreachable, magical world.

One day he saw her close up. She was in light blue and she sat on the grass, just a few feet away from the fence. She was surrounded by two other boys and a man of indeterminate age. They were listening while she talked. Her head was unmistakably tilted. Suddenly she looked towards Arjun. Her dark, lively eyes seemed to mock him. A shiver ran through his body. He moved back behind the tree. He did not think she had seen him, but he could not be sure. After some time they moved away, and Arjun got ready to go home. As he was leaving, the same man, whom he had seen with Priti, called out to him from the fence above.

'I say, young man, you shouldn't stare at people like that.'

Arjun was mortified. He walked away quickly so as not to be recognized. He heard Priti shout from a distance, 'What is it?' The man replied, 'Oh, it's nothing, just a street urchin peering through the hedge.' Despite his shame, Arjun felt soothed and healed by the sound of her voice. It had a melodious ring, which haunted him at night.

It was the same with her name. The words 'Priti Mehta' had acquired a magical quality for him. Once his school friend had uttered them, and it had left a warm and pleasant sensation inside him. Similarly, when his mother mentioned 'the Mehtas' he felt an unusual pleasure. He wondered about the power of words. He began to see why the ancient Brahmins were so particular about the configurations of sounds in a Vedic chant. His father did the same when he meditated by repeating a mantra. If they could invoke the gods with words, he would bring himself close to the Mehtas by the repetition of her name.

As the days went by, the daily walk to and from school became the chief pleasure of Arjun's life. His moods alternated daily. He was ecstatic one day, sad another. When he was joyous, life seemed to surge in him, like springtime Himalayan grass. He enjoyed the breeze and the lovely weather. He looked up at the azure sky, and received the light into the expanse of his soul.

At about this time, Big Uncle came up from the plains to spend a holiday in Simla. Bauji's eldest son had settled in Delhi after the partition. He had tried to make a go of his legal career, but had failed, and joined the government instead. He was now a department manager of the cottage industries programme which encouraged the development of village handlooms and handicrafts, mainly for export. Although he had not risen far in life, he had retained his sense of humour. When Tara asked why he had not brought his wife and children along, he replied, 'A family and fun don't go together. After seeing the same faces for eleven months, a man wants something new in the twelfth month.'

The day after he arrived, Big Uncle quietly gathered everyone's shoes and hid them in the attic. It created a real commotion in the morning, when Arjun had to go to school and Seva Ram to work. 'When will you grow up!' said Tara, not amused.

Big Uncle brought much life into the household. He teased Tara's maid, and even Seva Ram laughed at his constant joking. He went to the smartest tailor on the Mall and had a new wardrobe stitched. He strutted about in his fashionable clothes, as if he were the most handsome man in Simla. In fifteen days he found or made more friends on the Mall than Tara and Seva Ram had in fifteen years. He took Tara to the movies and to cafes, where she had not been for years. But most of all he loved to sit and gossip with Tara. Like two old maids they would talk for hours about the family over tea. Sometimes the talk would turn to Karan.

After all these years Tara still felt strong emotion for Karan. She would have probably characterized it as 'concern' or 'affection'. But her heart still ached whenever she thought about him. Or if she unexpectedly ran into him, her whole being was suffused with joy. However, she did not dare to admit to herself that there was anything improper in her feelings for her cousin.

'I get sick thinking about it,' said Tara. 'He had such a brilliant future. And look at him now. It is sad, isn't it, that a man should do less than what he is capable of.' She sighed.

'What exactly is he doing?' asked Big Uncle. 'Still lecturing in the college?'

'No, he left that some years ago, I suspect, because they did not promote him. But don't tell him I said so.'

'He has joined the Advanced Institute,' said Seva Ram.

'You must have heard about the new Institute in the papers. It got a lot of publicity. It is located in the old Viceregal Lodge,' said Tara with emphasis, and Big Uncle was suitably impressed. 'But they have no classes,' she added.

'Then what does he do?' asked Big Uncle.

'He is writing a book,' she said. 'I don't quite know what it is on. He is so secretive. One is never quite sure,' said Tara.

'It is on the origins of Carnatic music,' said Arjun.

'What a shame!' sighed Tara.

'There is nothing shameful about writing a book,' said Big Uncle with a smile.

'I don't mean that,' she said. 'He was capable of so much more. All those good-for-nothings who went to jail in the '40s became ministers. And the rascals put on such airs when they rode in government rickshaws.'

'Don't you speak to him about all this?' asked Big Uncle.

'I get tired of it. You know how he is. He just laughs.'

'Some people are just lucky. I wouldn't work either if Chachi had left me a fortune.'

'What!'

'You mean you didn't know?'

'But I thought Chachi died during the partition.'

'Yes, but she had cleverly transferred her assets beforehand. Karan was named as the beneficiary if her own family members died.'

'Which they did. Ah, so that explains a great deal.'

'I heard he gave a sitar concert in Delhi,' said Big Uncle with a strange smile.

After a pause, Tara suddenly lowered her voice, 'I too have heard rumours about concerts. And he uses a different name. They say the papers carry reports of his performances, but I haven't seen anything.'

'It is common to use another name among artists,' said Big Uncle.

Arjun was anxious to tell them that it was true. Karan was a famous artist, who performed in the big cities of India, and even abroad. He was a coveted member of the ADC, and all the rich and the powerful people were his friends. How could anyone feel sorry for him! Instead of saying all this, he merely smiled ironically like Karan.

'He is away from Simla for months, but it is no use asking, because he never tells. Anyway, that is no way to live, giving concerts in public. It is all right to perform once in a while for your friends but to perform for money, that is another thing.' After a short pause, Tara added, 'Ah, I wish he would marry and settle down.'

'Why don't you find him a girl, Tara?' said Big Uncle seriously.

'In fact I did receive a number of offers, but I felt they were below his social level,' she said, again lowering her voice, 'I also once tried for a girl for him. Good family from Pindi. They knew Bauji. But when they learned that he was a college teacher, they ran away. If only I had known about his inheritance from Chachi.'

'Alas. . .' said Big Uncle, smiling in mock sympathy.

'It is not natural for a man to remain a bachelor. He is not getting any younger. He should have someone to cook for him and to look after him. And he must have children to care for him when he is old.' Tara sounded genuinely concerned.

'It is our karma. We have to live out our karma,' said Seva Ram philosophically.

'Artists often don't marry,' said Arjun.

'Why don't *you* speak to him,' said Tara to her husband.

'No, no,' smiled Seva Ram shyly. 'Keep me out of it. I am no good at these things.'

'Seriously, tell him what the guru told *you* when you did not want to marry.'

'What?' asked Big Uncle.

Seva Ram reddened. 'The guru told him that marriage is a duty to mankind and civilization,' said Tara smugly.

Arjun thought this conversation strange. He smiled secretly at the thought of all those desirable women who had smiled at Karan when he entered the Green Room. Even Priti, he vividly remembered, the way she had looked at him as she implored him to come and play the sitar for her. Was there anything more in those deep, dark eyes of his than showed on the surface? He wondered and he felt a trace of jealousy.

During Big Uncle's visit to Simla, the Rivoli, which was a tiny cinema below the Ridge, announced a matinee showing of all of Guru Dutt's films for a full week. Tara, who was a devoted fan of the great director, asked Big Uncle to take her, since Seva Ram was not keen to go, and besides he was working at that time. As it did not require much persuasion to make Big Uncle go to the movies, both of them could be seen at the Rivoli every afternoon, crying their hearts out through each tragic scene, or laughing their heads off during the comic sequences. During the evenings they would sing songs from the films and dissect them scene by scene.

With their heavily charged sensuality, the films summoned all of Tara's middle class romantic dreams, which were also the dreams of the new nation that was still being led by the dreamer Nehru. Like Guru Dutt's heroes, Tara too was thirsty for affection, fame and romance. She identified with their search for the pure and the innocent, unscathed by the compromises of society. Unrequited love which led to self-inflicted suffering was a constant theme, and Tara put a little bit of herself in every film. She thought of the innocence of Seva Ram even if he was aloof; she thought of the cynicism of Karan even if he was attractive. She believed literally in the Mughal gardens surrounded by breath-taking lakes, bumble bees, sweet flowers and torpid breezes. But she did not go along with the desolation and despair at the end of the films. Her dreams for Arjun's future were safe in the real world. She believed in Nehru's hopes of democracy, socialism and secularism. She had long forgiven him for his miscalculation of the partition. Even though she thought he was an idealist, she liked his dreams. Besides she trusted Nehru because he had proven himself by liberating the Hindu woman. As far as she was concerned the Hindu Code Bill was the most important legislation enacted in the Indian parliament in the '50s.

With Big Uncle, Tara tried to avoid the subject that had caused such unpleasantness with Bauji several years ago. But somehow she couldn't help it. In referring to the Code her brother said, 'You can't be so naive, Tara, to believe that you can change people's behaviour merely by legislation.'

'I know that, but it affects us too. I don't worry so much for myself, but we have two unmarried sisters. They must get their proper share. And do you know what I think? Bauji is too much of a conservative. I don't think he is going to do the right thing for his daughters.' Big Uncle dismissed her fears. 'Wait, you don't know Bauji as I do,' she said. 'Besides, you are an interested party, and it suits you to look the other way.'

'Look here, look here,' Big Uncle protested, but Tara was not to be stopped.

Arjun got a chance to meet Priti again for the second time at the Dasehra celebrations at Anandale.

Since Dasehra fell on Saturday that year, Tara had planned a special festive meal. Karan came as usual, but he wanted to take them all to see the fair. 'Come, come,' he insisted, 'it will be great fun to see Ravana burning, with all his ten glorious heads going up in flames, one by one. And we shall celebrate his death by eating chaat afterwards.'

Tara was afraid of the crowds, but Arjun and Big Uncle were equally insistent. So they decided to go. After an early lunch, they walked up to the rickshaw stand on the corner of Cart Road and Chota Simla bazaar. There they took rickshaws, which transported them over the little hills of Simla down to Anandale. It was the only large flat ground in Simla, situated in the north end of town, at least a thousand feet below the level of the Mall.

Big Uncle wanted his rickshaw close to Karan's so they could talk. On the way Karan told him that the Simla rickshaw had been invented in Japan in the 1870s, and had rapidly gained popularity all over the East. The British had brought it to Simla; however, it did not catch on anywhere else in India. Perhaps because it required four people to wheel one passenger.

As they passed Lower Bazaar their nostrils were invaded by the smells of grains, spices, fowls, and fruit. Then they turned and came upon an unusual view of Christ Church.

'Have you ever been inside it?' asked Karan.

Big Uncle shook his head.

'You must come with me one day. I will show you a lovely chancel window with a fresco surrounding it which was designed by Kipling's father.' After a pause, he added, 'We can also see the grand bells, which were cast by the English from the brass that they captured from the Sikh cannon during the Anglo-Sikh wars more than a hundred years ago.' Karan smiled in his typical ironic manner, which seemed to say, 'Look here, this is really not very important, just trivia to pass the time.'

They crossed Scandal Point, and started moving downwards, towards a cream-coloured, many-towered, red-roofed building called Gorton Castle. It reminded Big Uncle of a castle in a fairy tale with dragons and captives. 'In fact it is the secretariat of the central government,' said Karan. 'And the clerks are the captives and the officers are the dragons.' Big Uncle smiled. 'Next to it is the old secretariat, which had burnt down and was later rebuilt on a fire-proof plan—all iron and steel skeleton, by far the grimmest building in Simla. A fit place for the captives, don't you think?' said

Karan.

They soon crossed into the countryside. Arjun pointed out a splendid view of the green valley with snowy ranges in the distance. As they descended further, it became darker, for the Anandale valley was shaded by pines, fir and giant deodars that sometimes grew to 150 feet. They went through a thick forest and heard the deep, low, hollow sound of running brooks. Before their final descent, they passed a small bazaar, where Tibetans and Paharis were squatting on their haunches, smoking in small groups of friends, among the smells, flies, pariah dogs, and other attractions of the bazaar.

They arrived in the middle of the afternoon on the lovely natural plateau when the fair was at its peak. There were innumerable stalls, and hawkers selling trinkets, novelties, and everything imaginable. It was a great gathering of all classes, castes and communities, with plenty of pushing and shoving. The simple hill people were dressed in their holiday best; their red cheeks glowed in the autumn sun. The bigger Punjabis were more boisterous and gaudy in pinks and purples. Some of the Sikh Akalis wore gleaming swords over their long blue robes. In the middle of the green field was a hundred-foot effigy of Ravana stuffed with firecrackers. A number of merry-go-rounds were revolving all at once, swinging men, women, and children round and round through the air. There were snake charmers, performing monkeys, and even an elephant, caparisoned beautifully.

Dasehra, was the autumn festival, which signalled the beginning of the holiday season. It was inspired by the epic, *Ramayana*, which told of the bad but brilliant king, Ravana, of Lanka, who stole Sita, the wife of the good king, Rama. Rama waged a war and won Sita back. On Dasehra, people burnt the ten-headed Ravana to celebrate the victory of good over evil.

As they mingled in the crowds, Arjun suddenly spotted Priti. His heart leapt. By happy chance she turned around at that very moment and looked him directly in the eye. He smiled nervously. She waved to him, smiling back warmly, as if it was the most natural thing to see him there.

Karan led them through the crowd towards Priti and introduced Tara and Big Uncle to Priti's mother. 'Amrita dear, these are Lala Dewan Chand's son and daughter. You know, I grew up with them. Bauji was like my father, and Tara is like a sister.'

'Of course, of course, I used to hear my father-in-law speak of

Lala Dewan Chand. How wonderful!' said Priti's mother greeting them.

While Karan was introducing the families, Priti asked Arjun, 'When are they going to start burning him?'

Arjun was tongue-tied, and could not answer.

'And this bright young man is Dewan Chand's grandson,' Arjun heard himself introduced.

'That means that our grandfathers knew each other,' said Priti, beaming at Arjun. His heart was pounding fast. 'Why don't you stop and play badminton with us on your way home from school?' she said, and tilted her head characteristically.

'Where do you live?' he asked.

'I say, you *know* exactly where we live,' said Priti indignantly. 'I even know the deodar tree behind which you hide and watch us.'

Arjun's face reddened. He was filled with shame, and he wanted to run away.

'Why do you just stand out there?' Priti continued.

'B. . .b. . . because I like to watch you play,' he stammered.

Instead of being angry, she surprised him by renewing her invitation. 'Why don't you come and play with us, instead of just standing there?'

It took a few moments before the stunning news penetrated. Then all was not lost, Arjun thought. He felt like a dead man who had been revived.

She turned to say something to her mother, but Amrita was deep in conversation with Tara. He was consoled by the fact that the older people were busy talking amongst themselves, and that no one had heard about his shame. He was also relieved that none of her Green Room friends were present to make fun of him. He looked up and saw her lovely profile against the late afternoon sun. She looked beautiful, he thought, standing on the Anandale plateau, surrounded by soaring deodars, pine and fir.

Meanwhile the actors arrived. They were to play the army of monkeys which had helped Rama conquer Lanka. Rama was at their head. He let off a lighted arrow. It struck one of Ravana's heads, which immediately blew off with a great bang. Priti jumped, and excitedly pointed it out to Arjun. Her hand brushed his shoulder, and he felt a spark go through his body. He shivered. Slowly, the remainder of Ravana burst into flames, to the cheering of the crowd. One by one, all the heads dropped off.

At the end of the spectacle, Priti and her mother left. Before leaving, Amrita invited them all to her house for a reception at the end of the month. Priti told Arjun that she was going down to the plains for a week, but she would be back by then. 'You must come!' she told him as she looked deep into his eyes.

Karan took the others to one of the stalls to eat chaat. The chaat-seller ceremoniously handed out cups of dried sal leaf to everyone; he punched a hole in the hollow wheat balls, and inserted mashed potato, tamarind juice and spices; then he dipped them into an urn of water spiced with cumin seeds, mint and tamarind and served them one by one into their cups. They took turns and kept eating till they were full. Next, they ate flat chips of fried white flour, dipped in whipped yogurt. Arjun's mouth started to burn from the spices. He drank vast quantities of water, and he felt sick. Seva Ram hardly ate anything at all.

After they returned home, Tara went on and on about Amrita, saying how elegant and charming she was. Big Uncle remarked that Amrita wore her sari in the old fashioned way.

'Did you notice how she covered her head with the end of her sari?' asked Tara.

'Yes, just like the princesses of royal families,' said Big Uncle.

Seva Ram joked that Tara was invariably impressed by people who were socially above her. Arjun asked Big Uncle about Ravana's heads.

'How else do you think he became so intelligent,' replied Big Uncle.

The next day Big Uncle said to Tara, 'Well, you don't have to worry about Karan. He seems to know all the right people, my dear.'

'I suppose so,' said Tara and she grew thoughtful. Big Uncle tried to make light-hearted talk about the Mehtas, but Tara did not respond. She was preoccupied and she answered his chatter in a perfunctory way.

'I say, are you still in love with Karan?' he said finally.

'How dare you say that!' she almost screamed.

'Hold it, I am your brother. I'm not Bauji. You can be straight with me.'

'I wish you wouldn't say things like that. It's not a joke, you know. I am very happy with my husband and my son. He's kind and gentle. And he looks after us well.'

'But that's not the same thing as love.'

'Well I can do without love.' She had tears in her eyes.

'Look, I didn't mean to make you cry.'

'It's just that I have this pain at the bottom of my heart when I think of Karan. As long as I don't see him, it is all right. But when he comes it starts again.'

'Don't you think it would be wiser not to see him?'

'No, I can't help it. Besides you know what he is like. He is here one day and then he vanishes for months together.'

As he watched his sister, Big Uncle was struck by the change in Tara's appearance. He remembered her before the partition as a pretty, bouncing girl who ran the risk of getting fat. But now she looked slender. Her dark hair made her look young. She wore saris which were not expensive, but she wore them with the careless confidence of a woman to whom it is second nature to dress well. Her features had become finer with age. There was not a line on her forehead or under her dark eyes, and though her skin had lost the first bloom of youth, its texture was as fine as ever. All in all, from an exuberant girl she had become an attractive woman. It was a shame, thought Big Uncle, that she did not go out into society.

A few days later Big Uncle's vacation came to an end, and he left for Delhi, taking his jovial heart with him.

10

The rail car came out of the long tunnel into the Himalayan country. Tunnel number sixteen was the dividing point between the plains and the hills. Under the early evening light the earth was covered with pastel shades of green. The white car pulled up at Barog station, and everyone, except two passengers, got out to have tea.

A girl who had been sitting on the other side came over and opened the window in front of Bauji. The cool air poured in. 'Chinese Set to Grab Our Land,' screamed a newsboy. Leaning far out of the window, the girl called out to the boy. She spoke louder than necessary, as if he were a great distance away.

The boy, weighed down with books, papers and magazines, hurriedly walked over to her. His face was partially buried in a scarf. It must be cold, thought Bauji. And here was this boy burdened by the useless rhetoric of politicians. It was good to be free and a democracy, but the politicians were a price that had to be paid for this privilege. The girl bought a newspaper and a copy of the *Illustrated Weekly of India*.

'It's getting cold, isn't it?' she said to the boy as he handed her the change. Bauji was bothered by the melancholy news of the Chinese, but he tried to put it out of his mind. Instead he thought of the girl. He thought that she had a beautiful young voice, but it was also a little sad. From the material and the cut of her coat, he surmised that she came from a wealthy family. Her youth and her manner suggested that she was unmarried; her tone of voice was that of someone who was used to getting her way.

The girl shut the window, and pressed her hands to her slightly red cheeks. She moved back to her seat. The tea drinkers returned from the dining room, and the rail car pulled away from the station. It had begun to grow dark outside and soon the lights were turned on inside the car. As a result the windows were transformed into mirrors, and it created a strange atmosphere of forced intimacy. Putting his face against the window, Bauji tried to look out. The sky behind the mountain carried red traces of the setting sun. Individual shapes on the dusky landscape, although still visible, were becoming harder to distinguish. The train climbed the northern slope of the second range into another long tunnel. They came out at the other end in a mountain valley. Sudden faint bursts of colour appeared from the chasms between the mountain peaks.

His gaze returned to the girl, who was now absorbed in the magazine. He was looking at her from an unusual angle, and peculiar emotions welled up inside him. As he stared at her long neck, bent slightly to one side, he seemed to feel the vital memory of the woman he had left behind in Pakistan. However, the more he tried to call up a clear picture, the more his memory failed him. She seemed to fade far away, leaving him with nothing to catch or to hold. In the midst of the clouded past, the neck of the girl in front reappeared—it was damp—and it seemed to push him forward into the future. Suddenly Anees' eyes floated before him. He gasped in astonishment. The figures and the background were unrelated, sometimes vivid, other times dim, melting together in a strange combination of the past and the present. A light from the outside unexpectedly flashed on the girl's face, and Bauji felt his chest rise at its strange beauty. The face in the mirror-window moved steadily across the landscape.

He woke up with a start. As he came to, he realized he must have been dreaming. The reflection of the girl in front was still there in the window. He hastily lowered his eyes, feeling guilty for having stared at the stranger. To cover up his embarrassment, he put his face to the window and looked at the darkness outside. At the next moment, he pulled out a large white handkerchief, and cleared the steam, which had gathered on the window.

The bewitching stranger continued to read. From the way her shoulders were gathered, Bauji sensed an independence of nature. The peculiar angle at which her neck was tilted suggested more, perhaps a touch of arrogance. There was a fierce intentness in her eyes, which did not permit her even to blink. It was a cool, piercing beauty, which exerted a strange, unreal power in the mirror-window. Feeling startled, Bauji lowered his eyes again. Although he knew it was improper to stare like this, he consoled himself with the thought that there was no way for her to know that she was the object of his attention. From where he sat he could see what she was reading. Having just completed a short story, she was now skimming over an article on Nehru's China policy. The man sitting next to her also saw her reading it and he could not contain himself.

'How dare the Chinese cast eyes on our land!' he said to her with outrage in his voice.

'Well, it is disputed territory, isn't it?' said the girl.

'Disputed, my foot! They have tricked us. First they talk of friendship and *Hindi-Chini bhai bhai* and then they want to take over our soil.' Before the girl could answer, he turned around to face Bauji, hoping to find a more sympathetic listener. Bauji did not want to talk to the man, but he changed his mind because he thought it might be a way to get to know the girl.

'It is Nehru's fault for believing them,' said Bauji. 'He is too much of an idealist and forgets that the pursuit of the nation's self-interest is the only responsible course for a leader. Moralizing must take second place. He feels let down by the Chinese because he trusted them. And there's no room for trust in these things.'

Not finding Bauji sympathetic to his point of the view, the man grunted and turned around in a huff. The girl did not get a chance to say anything because of the abrupt way the man closed the subject. Or more likely, Bauji thought, she did not want to get into a conversation with strangers. The rail car again became silent and Bauji went back into his own private world.

Bauji was startled when the rail car reached Simla. He saw the girl rise. He had been lost in thought for three-quarters-of-an-hour. His private battles against Nehru as well as his secret romance in the mirror-window had disappeared in the reality of the brightly lit platform. Suddenly he spotted Tara and Seva Ram in the distance. He did not wait for them to approach, but stepped out of the carriage with a resolute step. As soon as Tara reached him, she flung her arm around his neck, drew him rapidly to her, and embraced her father warmly. Bauji's eyes sought out the attractive stranger, who was now on the platform, surrounded by several equally well-dressed people. She obviously belonged to the best society. Standing there, he thought, she was not beautiful, but rather there was a youthful elegance and grace about her whole figure. As he looked around, she too turned her head. Her shining, dark eyes, that looked darker from the thick lashes, rested with cold attention on his face (as though she were recognizing him) and then she promptly turned away. In that brief look, he noticed a suppressed eagerness, which flitted between her brilliant eyes and a faint smile that curved her lips. It was the look of a young lady who is sure of her own beauty, and like all such women a little cruel.

'She's very sweet, isn't she?' said Tara.

'Sweet? Do you know her?'

'Yes,' replied Tara, as she waved to the girl, who waved back enthusiastically. There was a bustle in the station as the evening train from Kalka was approaching, several hours late. The black and white signal indicated 'down', and there was a rush of porters, attendants and people meeting the train. Through the vapour could be seen ill-clad workmen crossing the rails. The engine whistled in the distance. Seconds later the platform was quivering, and with puffs of steam hanging low in the air from the cold, the engine rolled up, the lever of its middle wheel rhythmically moving up and down, and the figure of the engine driver stooping low.

In the confusion of the arriving train, the girl had disappeared in the crowd. 'Can you guess?' asked Tara.

'What?'

'Who she is?'

He shook his head.

'Your friend Sanat Mehta's grand-daughter. She lives here with her mother.'

'What is her name?'

'Priti.'

11

It was the day of the Mehtas' reception. Since morning, Arjun had been in a state of wild excitement. As he was combing his hair in the mirror, he was overcome with despair. He thought he was not good looking. He imagined there could be no happiness for one with such long ears, such a broad nose, thick lips, and brown eyes as his. He would have given anything for a handsome face so that he could appear attractive to Priti.

Karan came promptly at seven to collect them for the reception. He had informed the Mehtas that Bauji would also come. When Karan saw Tara, his eyes widened and he remarked that she looked beautiful. She felt flattered because she had gone to considerable trouble to put up her hair in a special bun, which was considered fashionable at the time. Arjun too was proud of his mother, and thought that she looked lovely in her Madras silk sari. So rarely did they go out that Arjun felt it strange to see his mother all dressed up. He was proud that her thick hair was still black, and the bun showed her long neck and her ears to advantage. She wore her sari in modern style, comfortably and not too tightly, with a nicely cut blouse, which focused on her attractive bosom and gave her a lean and youthful look.

Karan invited Bauji to ride in his rickshaw but Bauji refused. He was still upset with Karan. Thus father and daughter rode together and Arjun rode with Karan. As they rode to the Mehta house in the raw chill of the Simla autumn, Arjun tried to imagine the brilliance of the grand reception that awaited them—the brightly lit drawing rooms, the splendour of the clothes, the sumptuously laid food, the dignitaries and important people. Karan had said in an off-hand way that a Cabinet Minister and the Governor would be coming, as well as several members of the diplomatic corps who were visiting Simla. While Arjun was lost in the spectacle of his imagination, Tara was preoccupied in safeguarding her hair and her silk sari.

As they approached the Mehta house, they were impressed by

the brilliant lights which blazed from the numerous windows of the mansion. A police guard stood at the brightly lit, carpeted entrance. As the rickshaws drove away, new ones took their place. From the rickshaws descended beautifully dressed women. Before Arjun realized what was happening, they were in the mirrored vestibule, taking off their coats, helped by a liveried servant. Arjun tried to assume a dignified manner appropriate to the occasion. He glanced into the mirrors, but he could not see himself clearly. He seemed to be a part of one glittering whole. As they reached the door leading to the main drawing room, a continuous sound of voices and glasses and the rustle of silk saris greeted them. Amrita was at the door, and she smiled at them. She greeted Bauji with special warmth.

'Now *you* better introduce them to *all* my guests,' she said to Karan. Turning to Tara, she added, 'I can't think of a better person, because he knows my guests better than even I do.' She put her arm around Arjun's shoulder. 'Priti is somewhere about. I am sure she will be delighted to see you.' Arjun felt a thrill both at the mention of Priti's name and by her mother's touch. He felt that great happiness awaited him that evening.

'Karan, do you really know *all* these people?' asked the wide-eyed Tara when they were well inside the room. Tara was greatly impressed, but Karan in his usual way dismissed her question and fell silent.

'But at least tell us who some of them are?' implored Tara, who was dying to meet people.

'There, that is the British High Commissioner,' said Karan, directing Tara's attention to a tall pink man with silver grey, closely trimmed hair. He was surrounded by a group of ladies, all of whom he had just set laughing by some joke.

'To his left is Sita, the princess of Chamba,' said Karan.

'Ah, she is beautiful' said Tara.

'She is also a delightful woman,' said Karan. 'She can say the exact opposite of what she is thinking. And she always speaks in such a simple and natural way that even the most careful and experienced people are taken in. Er... would you like to meet her? Let me go and bring her. She needs to be rescued from His Excellency's jokes, I think.'

They watched with fascination as Karan confidently walked up to the British diplomat. He bowed to the Englishman, who smiled back. Karan quickly put his arm around the beautiful hill princess, and the diplomat winked at Karan as he saw the most attractive part of his audience being stolen from him.

'Come, let us sit down here,' said Chamba, after Karan had introduced her to Seva Ram's family.

'It's been an unusually damp October, hasn't it, especially after such a lovely summer. I really wonder whether it is worth staying on so late in Simla,' she added as everyone sat down. Saying this the princess leaned over and exposed her ample bosom through her low-cut blouse. Paying no heed to people sitting across the room who were trying to catch her eye, she smiled and confidentially said to Tara, 'I must get to know you and your handsome son. Amrita and Priti have told me about you.'

Tara blushed when she heard this and smiled back gratefully. Arjun beamed with pleasure at the praise from this grand lady, who had till then seemed completely inaccessible. As they began to talk, drinks and *hors d'oeuvres* were brought in by a fat bearer, whose enormous paunch was covered by a blue cummerbund. The princess selected Scotch whisky, while Seva Ram's family took fruit juices from the tray. Karan drank a glass of plain soda and avoided conversation. He stared unashamedly at Chamba's exposed breasts, not with any desire or lust, but as if her anatomy were an aesthetic object.

Arjun's eyes were roaming. Suddenly, he noticed Priti in a sari, leaning against the fireplace. She had her back to him, but he immediately recognized her by the mass of raven hair, and of course the imperious tilt of her head. As soon as he was aware of her, he became nervous. She turned her face around, as if she sensed that she was being watched. She looked at him squarely with her impetuous, dark eyes, and he blushed. She came across the room to greet him and his family. Immediately she recognized Bauji as her companion in the rail car, and she smiled at him.

'Ah, here is our beautiful hostess,' said the Princess of Chamba. 'I can still remember her as a tiny, little girl? Even then she had those dark, alluring eyes under her bangs, and she used to squeal with a wild, merry laugh. But look at her now!'

Arjun looked at her in a daze. He stood there with his breath taken away, and could even feel the veins pulsing in his temples. She seemed to be excited. He wondered afterwards if it was due to her animated state that she looked so beautiful. Arjun tried to make a few clever remarks, but conversation did not flow easily, since he did not seem to have much to say. She pretended that she was interested in what he said. But Arjun could tell that she listened carelessly, and her eyes seemed to wander to others. He was nervously aware that he was not amusing her.

Bauji looked at Priti and then at his grandson with an affectionate irony which age accords to youth. He understood the situation immediately, and his heart went out to the young man. So this cruel beauty was the descendant of his old friend from Lahore! The grand house and the style of life it represented were a blow to his pride. Sanat Mehta had obviously done better by shrewdly scattering his investments, while he had been a fool to concentrate his property in and around Lyallpur. Whereas he had lost everything in the partition, the Mehtas had emerged unscathed. Now the granddaughter's looks added to the wound. But the old war horse that he was, the call of feminine beauty found him ready to forget his pride, and he turned to Priti with a gracious tone. 'How lucky for me to have had the pleasure of your lovely presence during the train journey, even though we did not speak. I hope we shall make up for it now.'

'Thank you, Bauji. You are so kind. And how wonderful to know that you knew my grandfather. You know, I too said to myself on the train, "Who is that nice man?"'

To disguise his nervousness Arjun had resumed listening to the princess of Chamba without taking in a single word that the ample lady said. As Priti turned to talk to Tara, Bauji again began to regret the past. With Priti's neck perilously close to his face, he consoled himself with the thought that he was fortunate at being old enough, to escape the suffering, which was the inevitable lot of a young man of Arjun's age. Yet he was not so old that he could not envy the chances open to the young man who would possess this creature. The impulse of lust stung the civilized lawyer of sixty-five so sharply that it made him blush. Touched by his middlé class scruples, he felt ashamed. To divert his mind, Bauji turned to look at the gathering.

'How is my darling?' boomed Rao Sahib, as he came around, and put his arm around Priti. He bowed civilly to the others. He was acquainted with Seva Ram's family, but he did not wish to acknowledge it. He was a snob, and his interest in a person was in direct proportion to his social position. He turned towards Chamba, and said confidentially, 'I say, Sita, do you know that Rekha Kapur has left the old man?'

'Where has she gone, Bunty?' asked Chamba.

'Naughty, naughty! One doesn't ask such questions, my dear. Don't mention this to Colonel Kapur, I say.' He paused to observe the reaction among his audience, and refilled his whisky from the bearer passing by.

'And if the Colonel is not in his best third burra peg bum-bum-ho-ho mood, then. . . .'

'Shame on you, Bunty, gossiping like this,' interrupted Amrita. 'Come help me. I think they have arrived,' and she pulled Rao Sahib and Priti away. Chamba smiled, shook her head, and said to Karan, 'He is the life of every Simla party, isn't he?'

Karan looked distastefully at Rao Sahib's back as it disappeared in the crowd, and he smiled ironically by compressing his lips in a peculiarly delicate way. 'He is the son of a heaven-born ICS.'

And in that short phrase, Karan summed up the social structure of Simla, where one's status was dependent on one's father's rank in the civil service, and on the official order of precedence. Neither wit nor wealth could help one break that iron barrier, which Indians had acquired intact from the English superimposing on it their own caste system.

'Who was that horrid man, Tara?' asked Bauji.

'Shh. . .' said Tara.

There was a general stir near the entrance and it became clear that the Governor and the Cabinet Minister had arrived. The people who had crowded near the entrance were pushed back by officious plain-clothes policemen. A whisper ran through the gathering. All eyes turned to the entrance, and the crowd divided into two rows, between which came the two important guests with their wives, pompously led by Rao Sahib and followed by Priti and her mother. Both the political figures bowed and smiled to the left and to the right. Several people in the crowd had anxious faces, as they wished to be recognized by the VIPs. The crowd quickly closed around the drawing-room door. The Cabinet Minister, who was the more distinguished of the two dignitaries, recognized the Chamba princess and Karan in the crowd, and immediately came forth to greet them. Arjun and Tara were both thrilled as they were introduced to the famous statesman, who looked handsome and powerful in an elegant silk kurta, an embroidered waistcoat and a Gandhi cap. He was alert and enthusiastic. His vivacity was infectious, and the conversation suddenly became very animated.

Priti chatted with Arjun, explaining who was who in the room. 'That is Brigadier Thapar with his daughter Usha—isn't she beautiful! They are stopping here briefly on their way to a reception in honour of a visiting General from Delhi. And the young and round lady sitting in the corner is from Mandi. She wears the best jewellery in Simla. Do you think she has a glow? That's because she is expecting. She doesn't attend big parties any longer, but only drops in at small, informal gatherings. Mother is flattered that she came today.'

Arjun's eyes were fastened on Priti, and he neither heard nor saw anything that was happening at the party. He felt irrevocably drawn into this strange, grand world, which was so far removed from his everyday life. It was impossible for him to know what was right or wrong, what was reasonable or foolish. He stood beside Priti, oblivious of everything else. She returned his gaze with her brilliant eyes; he blushed, and she gave him a tender smile.

Bauji had wandered off to see if he knew anyone in the gathering. He was soon deep in conversation with a group of men, who he realized were refugees like himself, from the old Punjab. He was amazed at how well they had all done in life. Not only had they quickly rehabilitated themselves but they had actually prospered and were now better off than before. What accounted for their success, Bauji wondered? Hard work and inventiveness, certainly. But it was courage more than anything else, for they had despised death when life was more terrible than dying, and they had dared to live.

'Do you know the curio shop on the lower Mall?' Priti asked Arjun.

Arjun shook his head.

'The one which displays prayer wheels from Tibet, turquoise necklaces, incense jars and a big bronze Buddha.'

Arjun nodded.

'Well, it belongs to that mysterious man in the glasses. They say he is a Russian spy, but Mother thinks that he is the best astrologer in Simla. He can mesmerize you too.'

'Mesmerize?' asked Arjun.

'Hypnotize you—put you in a trance—so that you don't feel any pain or anything.'

Priti's eyes wandered. Arjun watched her eyes as they closely followed Karan, who had just walked across the room. Every time Karan turned his head, people recognized him and gave him a smile. Everyone seemed to know him and to like him.

'He is a great favourite!' said Priti, guessing Arjun's thoughts.

Suddenly, she left him and·skipped over to Karan.

Seeing Karan as the centre of attention, a peculiar sensation stirred in Arjun's heart. As sometimes happens at significant moments in a boy's life, it was a confused feeling. On the one hand he felt pride in Karan's success and on the other envy, because he felt insignificant in comparison. One day perhaps he too could occupy such a favoured position, he hoped. But there was no getting away from the feeling that he was awkward and ungainly. He looked at his hands, and they were broad and dense compared to Karan's, which were long, fine and aristocratic.

Karan had been stopped by the grey-haired Governor. Arjun noticed that Karan did not glance around from one person to another as everyone else did. He looked intently at the man he was talking to and gave him his full attention. Neither did he shift from one leg to another, nor did he hurry with what he was saying, although he was aware that Priti was standing close by waiting to talk to him. He seemed to speak quietly and deliberately, as if he had all the time in the world. After he had finished talking, he turned to Priti, and gave his full attention to her. It seemed to Arjun that the two spoke forever.

Bauji found it distasteful that such a lot of fuss was being made over the Minister. People had crowded round him and were hanging on to his every word. It did not seem right that great privileges and power should be attached to politicians in a democracy.

He was amused with the thought that when it came to power it was remarkable how easily Indians had slipped into British shoes. Independence had come and gone and Indians had substituted one set of rulers for another. These new rulers enjoyed the privileges just as much as the old. They must be secretly happy, he thought, that Gandhi was not around to spoil things. With his yen for austerity he would certainly not have approved.

But why shouldn't they enjoy themselves, he asked. After all they had made sacrifices enough, spent half their lives in British jails. Bauji did not grudge them a few moments of pleasure. As it is there is so little of it to go around. But he was uncomfortable with their hypocritical protestations. They not only covered their actions in a Gandhian cloak, but worse, they justified everything in socialist rhetoric. He wouldn't have minded if it was only rhetoric, but many of them, including Nehru, believed in it. They were under the mesmerizing spell of socialism, and that worried him.

At this point the Minister bumped into him, and he made a show of a profuse apology, even thought it was probably Bauji's fault since he was not looking where he was going. Rao Sahib raised his nose in the air and glaring at Bauji, he icily asked his neighbour, 'I say, who is that crazy man?' Meanwhile the Minister continued in his eloquent defense of Nehru's policy towards China, a subject that was uppermost in everyone's mind; no one wanted a war with China and they were hoping that the Minister could tell them how it was to be averted.

During a pause in the Minister's monologue, Bauji quietly said, 'I think you are all out of touch. First, you lead us up the garden path of Indo-Chinese friendship, forgetting our own self-interest, and now you talk about "throwing the Chinese out". Isn't it a bit naive? Dreamers are dangerous, especially if they rule nations. I was thinking of your boss, Mr Nehru, sir. No offence intended to you.'

'Well, what do *you* suggest we do?' asked the Minister.

'What our young hostess suggested the other day in the rail car,' and he smiled at Priti, who had also joined the crowd around the Minister. She beamed back, acknowledging the compliment. 'I think the sooner we admit that the border is disputed territory the better off we will be. And just as quickly we should sit down with them and negotiate.'

Rao Sahib returned to the sofa near Tara accompanied by Chamba and Priti. 'I say the cheek of the man. Who the devil is he?'

'He happens to be right, Uncle Rao,' said Priti.

'You are a snob, Bunty,' said Chamba.

'No, I merely happen to know who has precedence,' said Rao Sahib.

'He is the father of this charming new friend I have made,' said Chamba and she smiled at Tara.

'Oh I say, I say,' said Rao Sahib uncomfortably.

'Look, there's your friend, Dinky Chopra,' Chamba said rescuing Rao Sahib from his discomfort. She pointed with her eyes to the figure who had just come into view.

'Did you know, my dear, that I caught Dinky on the Mall last Friday?'

She looked at him blankly.

'Wearing sandals! Poor man, he was mortified when he saw me. I went up to him and I said, "Could I buy you a pair of shoes, old man?"' said Rao Sahib, roaring with laughter.

'Stop it. You are vicious, Bunty. But you have a certain vicious attractiveness about you.'

At this point Chamba's eyes met Tara's; Chamba smiled, and as if by a common signal, they turned to look at Karan, who was again talking to Priti.

'Ah, so you know him from childhood,' said Chamba to Tara. 'Karan is the most irresistible man in Simla.'

'What nonsense! He merely plays the sitar well and that gives him a certain. . .' said Rao Sahib.

'You are jealous, Bunty,' said Chamba with a charming smile. 'How do you account for his close friendship with Nehru, and the greats of the world? He has actually stayed with Nehru in Delhi!'

'That's easily explained. He got to know Nehru in jail,' said Rao Sahib. 'I don't understand the fuss over a half-employed sitar player who is lucky to have a few friends in the world. The Maharaja of Gwalior had a half-dozen musicians, and they were treated like servants.'

'It is you who refuses to understand, Bunty,' said Chamba, shaking her head. 'It is none of these things. It is his personality, what he says, that makes him so attractive to everyone.'

Both Tara and Arjun were in a trance on the way back home. Tara had seen Karan in a new light that evening. She felt the irony in feeling sorry for him when he enjoyed such success in society. It was a shock. Until now she had viewed him merely as an unmarried and obscure academic. She tried to reconcile the contradiction in her mind, and then understand the reasons for his lofty position in society. Clearly, Karan was talked about, people were interested in him, and everyone was anxious to see him. She felt confused and hurt. She had believed that she was alone in the way she felt for him. Tonight she had discovered that there might be many others. She also could not understand how a sarcastic and ironical person could be so attractive, and socially so successful.

Before going to bed Bauji paused a moment before the window of his bedroom. The shadowed garden lay sunk in sleep beneath. In the strange light the trees were like images in a Chinese brush painting. From the overhanging roof came the elfin hoot of an owl. The sky was clear of clouds and the stars shone brightly, their rays sharply penetrating the icy air. Bauji's soul yearned out towards them, their frozen reaches beyond human time; they gave joy to him, without asking for anything in return. He looked down and thought that the earth was also once a star and it too had shone.

It had not been a good evening; he realized it now, not only from the acidic pressure at the top of his stomach, but from his deep disappointment at the way his favourite, Karan, had turned out; by the threatening beauty of that girl, Priti; by the opulence of his old friend's house, compared to his own humbler status today; by the way the politicians were treated in a democracy. 'Enough,' he said to himself. 'To sleep now.'

12

Soon after Amrita's reception began Arjun's education in badminton and love—a phase at once more pleasurable and painful than any previous one in his life. Through the excuse of lending himself as a fourth in badminton, he became a familiar visitor to the Mehta household. He used to arrive punctually at a quarter-to-four at Priti's gate. He would first peep in hesitantly, and if he saw Priti in the garden, he would open the gate, set his schoolbag on the verandah, and join in the badminton game in progress. An hour later Priti would leave for the Green Room. He seemed to fit neatly into that idle hour of her busy social day. While she went to the Club he trudged home to his gloomy schoolbooks. Dusk came to mean loneliness and defeat.

Every morning, as he woke up to go to school, he would think: would she be there today? If it was rainy or overcast, his hopes would be dashed, for he knew in advance that there would be no badminton. On these days, Priti would usually go off to visit a friend. The weather thus became an important ally, and he prayed for every day to be clear.

Sometimes, however, even on a perfectly sunny day she would go visiting. Or her mother might pick her up directly after school and callously take her away to a tea party or to go shopping. When this happened, Arjun would walk around her house once or twice to make sure that she was in fact not in, and then sadly return home.

The next day when he asked her where she had been, she would coldly answer, without a hint of regret, that she had gone to a birthday party at such and such a friend's house. He would be curious to know about the party and she did not mind talking about it. She would tell him who was there, what they said, what they wore, where they 'fitted', and many other things—with the result that he felt he had been at the party. In this way he slowly got to 'know' her friends, but more importantly he began to share her confidences. Gradually he got to know whom she liked and whom she disliked. He was thrilled by this new world. But he also felt envious and sometimes despondent that he did not belong to it.

Arjun asked his mother one evening why they did not belong to the ADC.

'Your father and I don't play cards and we don't drink. So what's the use of going to the Club,' Tara replied.

'But don't you want to *meet* people?' he asked.

'Every evening we go to the Mall. That's where we meet our friends. After sitting at the office all day long, your father doesn't want to go and sit at the Club again. He and I relax by taking long walks in the evening.'

He sensed her disapproval.

'Besides, the Club is expensive and we can't afford it,' she added. With this she effectively closed the subject, because it was obvious to him that she ran the house on a tight budget.

Priti usually returned from the Club in time for dinner. But occasionally she came back early to dress, when she had to go out. These evening parties were brilliant affairs to which Arjun was of course never invited. Priti generally went to them with her mother. The brilliance of the party was determined by the clothes and jewellery that everyone wore, because the people who were present were usually the same. Since she had just started to wear a sari, after her eighteenth birthday, she was even more conscious of clothes. The standard by which the 'brilliance' of the parties was measured was the Governor's Ball, which was the closest thing to the grand Viceroy's Ball of the old British Simla.

Arjun sat at home during these evenings, thinking of Priti laughing and flirting at these glamorous parties, and he was filled with longing to be a part of her privileged world. But if the Club was inaccessible for economic reasons, these parties were out of bounds for social ones. Arjun's family could have aspired to a higher social position because Seva Ram had a high enough job in the government. But they would have had to work for it; technocrats were still regarded a notch lower in the hierarchy than generalist career civil servants. Many of Seva Ram's colleagues did rise socially, but they did it through social accomplishments such as tennis or bridge or frequent entertaining. Seva Ram of course had no social ambitions, much to (first) Tara's regret, and now to Arjun's despair. Arjun's family merely lived the ordinary life of a modern, educated, decent family. They were the representatives of a growing, urban middle and upper middle class that had rapidly developed after Independence.

Priti's family on the other hand, belonged to 'society' because they were rich and famous. Although with her father's death they had lost the possibility of power, they were still well off, and of course they were considered an 'old Simla family'. Bauji told Arjun and Tara that Priti's great grandfather had founded the family fortune in the 1860s. He had made a 'killing' in cotton during the American Civil War. When the cotton from the American South got cut off during the War of the States, Priti's ancestor had stepped in to supply Indian cotton to the mills of Manchester. He later invested the profits from the trade in one of the early Indian textile mills. His son, Sanat Mehta, who was even shrewder, set up woollen mills in Amritsar, and was knighted by the British for donating one lakh rupees to the World War I effort. During the depression of the '30s, he had bought the house in Simla and the apple orchards in Kotgarh at throwaway prices. Bauji had admired Sanat Mehta for his business acumen, and represented him as legal counsel in several court cases.

A small decline in the family fortunes set in with Priti's father, who was more interested in the Independence struggle against the British than in the family mills. While some of the textile mills had to be sold off, he added lustre to the family name because of his political work. He had known Karan in the '40s when they were together in jail. Soon after Independence he had died in an accident, leaving behind his widow, Amrita, and his daughter, Priti. Since his death the financial affairs of the family were capably managed by a trusted and competent family accountant, and the family business had looked up.

Arjun was attracted to the entire Mehta household. He was drawn to Amrita, he liked the servants; in fact he was enticed by everything inside that house. Everyone surrounding Priti had acquired a special significance. He was particularly fond of two middle aged maid servants, who were warm and considerate towards him, who seemed to sense his feelings, and wanted to make small gestures to make him feel comfortable. In the Mehta house Arjun saw the working of an old, cultivated, wealthy and honourable family. All the members were covered with a mysterious veil, which permitted him to remove their defects and clothe them with perfection. Even the scandalous Anglo-Indian governess, who taught French and the piano to Priti, was invested with lofty sentiments in Arjun's heart.

One evening Priti did not go to the club. She asked Arjun to stay on after badminton. He happily agreed, although she was preoccupied with getting ready for the Governor's party in honour of the British High Commissioner. After she was all dressed in a white sari, she came out and asked him how she looked.

'Come, you may ride with me to Raj Bhavan, if you like,' Priti said, getting ready to leave.

Arjun looked puzzled. He was thrilled by the invitation, but did not understand how he could just go along. Priti noticed his confusion.

'Silly boy, I am not inviting you for the party. Only the Governor can do that. But you may ride in the rickshaw with me. After it drops me, it will take you home and come back for me.'

'But. . . but it's a long way to take me home,' said Arjun nervously.

'It's all the same, I say. The rickshaw has been hired for the evening. Come, come!'

To ride sitting close to Priti was an unbelievable stroke of good fortune. As he got in with his schoolbag, she warned him to be careful and not to crush her new sari. The Simla rickshaw was a stately but intimate carriage. He smelled the luxurious padded leather seats and arm-rests and the oilskin hood. Priti leaned back as if she was on a comfortable reclining armchair at home. He sat up, with his bag between his legs, trying to be careful not to touch her clothes. The carriage rested on bicycle wheels, with two men pulling it from the front and two pushing it from the back. As the coolies picked up speed and began to run, Arjun felt as though he were flying along the slopes of Simla, past mere mortals, accompanied by the soft pit-pat of eight human feet.

'In the British days, we had our own rickshaw and grandfather had made a beautiful blue and white livery for the coolies,' said Priti. 'All the best English families had their private carriages, you know, and their coolies wore their family's coat of arms on the breast of their uniforms. Only the Viceroy's could wear scarlet rosettes. One mad Scotsman actually put his coolies in plaid kilts!' She laughed. After a pause she continued, 'Now, mother says, it is too expensive to maintain a rickshaw. So we hire one when we need it. But we use it so often that this one is with us all the time.'

Just before they started their ascent, Priti pointed to the sunset over the snow-covered mountains in the distance. It was a thrilling sight. He asked her to look in the opposite direction, towards the

valley below, which was covered with masses of wild red rhododendron trees, surrounded by brilliant scarlet blossoms. 'It is like a
carpet of scarlet and green,' he said.

She stopped the rickshaw. They got out, and walked down along
a path with wild flowers and fern under their feet, alongside the
moss and the ivy on the trunks of the oak and the pine. He looked
at her as she walked with her hands holding up her sari. His eyes
travelled from her sari to the purple shadowy valley below which
was covered with dark and dense woods. He found it difficult to
describe the delicious feeling inside him. Suddenly they came upon
a mass of wild red rhododendron trees, at least forty feet high. The
rays of the setting sun fell among their branches, making the trees
seem even taller, highlighting their trunks with their slanting
beams. The two of them stood there speechless for a long time,
moved by the vast stillness of the scene.

Soon they were back in the rickshaw, and as they ascended,
Arjun pointed out other trees—more rhododendrons, majestic
deodars, oak, pine, fir, and the magnificent Himalayan horse-
chestnut.

'I say, you certainly know your trees,' she said, visibly impressed. 'I never looked at them till this evening.'

He was happy because for the first time he could tell her
something that she did not already know. He explained that in the
lower Himalayas one found mainly deodar and white oak; in the
middle, spruce, fir and green oak, and at the higher levels were the
silver fir and the brown oak. 'You sound like a regular forest
officer,' she said. He took that as a compliment, and he felt exhilarated as they climbed further, and the air became sharper and
lighter. Soon a heavy mist came along and it became dark. They felt
drops of rain. The carriage suddenly stopped with a jerk. Arjun was
thrown back against Priti. Her long brown plaits softly brushed his
cheek, and he felt an exquisite thrill. The rickshaw coolies pulled
forward the wooden frame on which was mounted the oilskin
hood. They were just in time for the rain suddenly became stronger.
The carriage started to move. There was a glass pane fixed on the
hood, and they could see the rain outside. Inside, they were
perfectly dry and it felt cosy and romantic. There was a sudden
intimacy between them. His arm accidently touched hers but she
did not bother to remove it. He trembled. She looked at him
unselfconsciously with her striking, dark eyes, and pointed to the
raindrops on the glass pane. Her face looked fresh, and radiated a

warming glow. He noticed that her cheeks were red, full of the healthy colour of the mountains. Arjun was enchanted, and he felt undeserving of such intense happiness.

Slowly, the rain subsided, and they noticed below the town's lights being gradually turned on. It was a dark night and the lights created a festive feeling, but the stars were bright and low on the horizon as they often are in the hills. Arjun remarked that the stars and the lights seemed to touch each other, and you could not tell the difference between heaven-made and man-made stars.

Soon they arrived at the Governor's House. Priti got up. As she was getting out she took his hand and pressed it gently. She alighted quickly and was soon lost in the confusion of the fashionable and glittering guests who were all arriving at the same time. The rickshaw turned around. He looked back and thought he spotted her in the crowd. She suddenly seemed to smile at a familiar-looking man, who was tall and lightly built with straight, black hair. It seemed that he put his arm around her. It was Karan, he realized with a shock. But the picture was lost as the carriage moved out of view.

On the way back home, he began to feel jealous. Gradually, he reasoned that it could not be Karan. He must have made a mistake. Or perhaps it was not Priti. It must be another girl wearing a white sari. He tried to believe this, and slowly he felt reassured. The rain had stopped and the hood came down. The raindrops sparkled in the light of the street lamps. There was a strong smell of the earth and the grass. He was happy again. He felt a thrill as the rickshaw flew along the slopes. He had grown up believing that one walked in Simla, and it seemed an extravagance to hire a rickshaw all the way to Chota Simla, almost five miles from the Governor's House. He had inherited this practical and miserly reflex from Tara, who had got it in turn from Bauji. In Lyallpur, Bauji did not mind owning two tongas but he would think ten times before he hired a public carriage or a taxi.

Dark thoughts slowly returned. He looked ahead and he thought about the coolies who were pulling the rickshaw. It did not seem right that just because a coolie was born in a poor family that he should spend his life carrying someone who happened to be born in a rich house. But Arjun's mind could not stay away from Priti for long and the coolie was quickly forgotten. His agony lay in knowing that Priti was somewhere else, enjoying herself where he could not ever hope to be. Although he tried to dismiss it more than once, the picture of Karan putting his arm around the figure in white kept intruding. It couldn't have been Karan, he thought. Why would he put his arm around Priti? She was so much younger than he. What was he, in fact, doing at the Governor's party? Karan found such affairs boring and tiresome. Perhaps it was only an innocent gesture—what an older man would naturally do to a younger lady—and there was nothing more to it. However, there was something in her eyes which worried him. On the other hand, had she not pressed his hand before leaving? At the thought of her touch he was transported into a happy world again.

13

Arjun woke up the next morning determined to find out what had happened the night before, and if Karan had been present at the Governor's party. He was distracted all day in school, thinking of Priti and Karan. After school he rushed to her house, where he discovered, alas, that she had left early to visit a friend. One of the servants mentioned, however, that she planned to go to the Club at her usual time. He resolved immediately to go to the Mall and wait for her there.

Since he knew she would pass that way on her way to the Green Room, he arrived early and waited for her near the entrance of the chemists', Sahib Singh & Sons. At last, after a quarter-of-an-hour, he saw Priti, and eagerly went up to her. She wore a striking red sweater. It was clear that she was not pleased to see him.

'Hello, Priti!' he said. 'I knew you would come by, and I thought I would walk with you to the ADC.'

'I haven't got much time, since I told Neena I'd see her at 5.30.'

'Do you mind if I walk with you?' he implored her.

'If you want to,' she said indifferently.

He walked with her without saying a word. He felt hurt. He tried to think of something to say before asking about the party. But he could not. She did not bother to say anything either. She walked rapidly as if she wanted to be rid of him. He felt ashamed. He hated her. Soon they came to the gate of the ADC and she walked in without saying goodbye.

He stood at the entrance for a long time, feeling miserable. He should have gone home, but he could not. His feet felt heavy as if they were glued to the spot. He decided to wait till she came out. The doorman looked at him suspiciously at first, then ignored him. While he was hanging about waiting for her, he thought he saw someone who looked just like Priti. His heart leapt and he hurried to catch up with her. As he was about to speak to her he realized that she was a total stranger. He blushed and apologized for his mistake.

An hour-and-a-half later she came out. He saw that she was alone, and he was relieved. When she saw him she turned away her face. But he went up to her and asked if he could walk home with her.

'If you want to,' she said. 'Why did you wait for me?'

'Because I wanted to.'

'I say, don't you have anything better to do with your time?'

He looked at her as they walked, and could think of nothing to say. He again sought desperately for a remark which might amuse her, and draw her to him. She turned around to see if anyone was looking, almost as though she did not want to be seen with him.

'Did anyone see you waiting for me?' she asked.

'Are you ashamed of me?' he asked boldly.

He wished with all his heart that she would like him. He seemed to constantly humiliate himself. They walked on quietly. He had a sudden thought. Perhaps if he made her feel that he was from a rich and important family she might be more interested in him. He concocted a story about a rich uncle who had hordes of servants and jewels, a fleet of cars and even an elephant. He let his imagination run as he described his uncle's meetings with Maharajas and Ministers. By the time he finished, they had reached her house.

'So, you see, we are well connected,' he said.

She smiled.

'You don't believe me.'

'No,' after a pause she said, 'Goodbye! I am going down to Delhi to spend the Diwali holidays with my cousins. You need not stop here anymore.'

'Will I see you again?' he implored feebly.

'Perhaps.' And she turned to open the gate.

'Wait,' he shouted. She was surprised at the vehemence in his voice. He had tears in his eyes. 'Priti, why are you being beastly with me?' he asked.

'I don't like to be surprised,' she answered coldly, and she tilted her head audaciously.

'I must know something: was Karan at the party last night?'

'Perhaps,' she said. 'Were you spying on me last night?'

'No, no. I thought I saw him as I was leaving,' he said reassuring her.

'And what if he was? What difference does it make?' she asked.

'No, nothing whatsoever,' he replied. 'You were so kind to me last evening. Why are you angry now?'

'I don't like spies or surprises.' And she went in.

He slowly walked back home. He felt miserable. It seemed to be the lowest point of his life. How could he allow himself to be humiliated like this? He should have gone away after greeting her outside Sahib Singh's. How could she respect him if he kept thrusting himself upon her like this? On his way home he re-enacted countless ways by which he could have made a better impression on Priti.

When he lay in bed that night, he continued to see her walking into the ADC. He pictured her sitting in the Green Room drinking tea, and being admired by Karan. He thought drowsily of her long face, her rosy skin, her dark, sparkling eyes, her full mouth and the tilt of her head. It was obvious that she did not like him. She was clearly ashamed to be seen with him. Why had she changed just like that? Why couldn't he just forget her? Why must he allow himself to be so desperately unhappy? Yes, this was the end. He must resolve never to see her again.

But the next moment he wanted to be with her; he wanted to look into her eyes; he wanted to touch her. He wondered if this was what the books called love.

He had not thought of love, although he had read about it in European novels. It had been a mysterious, forbidden thing. In the books it always seemed to bring happiness and ecstatic bliss. To him it had brought only unhappiness and grief. He yearned for her all the time. It was a painful hunger in his heart. He wanted her to be his. He was jealous of Karan. Each time he left her, there was only misery. He wondered how he was going to endure his pain. He turned on his pillow and he thought of ways he could get through the hours that lay ahead before dawn.

14

Twenty days after Dasehra came Diwali, the festival of lights. It celebrated King Rama's triumphant return home to Ayodhya with his wife, Sita, after fourteen years of exile. The last episode in this exile was the defeat of Ravana in Lanka. The exuberant people of Ayodhya greeted their great monarch's return by lighting their houses.

Seva Ram's family like everyone else recreated this event every year on Diwali by placing hundreds of clay lamps, filled with oil, along the perimeter of their house. After illuminating their home they went around the town to deliver boxes of sweets to their friends, and to look at the lights of the other houses. It was a thrilling sight to watch hundreds and thousands of twinkling lamps light up the dark night. After returning they watched from Pine Villa the skies of Simla dazzle with brilliant firework displays. When he was younger, it used to be the most exciting day in Arjun's life. For days on end he would talk about it. Diwali also coincided with the Hindu New Year, and that meant new clothes, pocket money, and school holidays.

This year Arjun had mixed feelings about the approaching Diwali holidays. He was older and increasingly indifferent to the lights and the fireworks. He was happy about the end of the school term, but he dreaded the term report since he had done poorly in his exams. Most of all he felt irritated, restless, and miserable because he could not get Priti out of his mind. He wanted to possess her. It was a ceaseless hunger, the like of which he had not known before. Despite the constant pain and the humiliation which he suffered, he could not do without her. He was depressed at the thought of the Diwali holidays because he would not get to see her for two weeks.

The last day of school was cold, wet and desperate. He was walking home quickly to avoid getting wet. His heart was heavy because of the miserable report card in his bag. There was no hope of seeing Priti after yesterday's humiliating scene. Sick with misery, he did not notice that he had passed the round post box, which was a prized signal that Priti's house was round the corner.

Suddenly, she was before him. She stood framed in the main doorway of her house. She was wearing a pink raincoat and hat and black gum boots, but her face was wet. She had a distant and wistful look, and she appeared to be waiting.

When she saw him, she ran down to the gate. She opened the gate and asked him to come inside. She took him to the kitchen and gave him hot milk and biscuits.

'I was rather beastly with you yesterday,' she said. 'You know, I did not expect to see you, and it came as a surprise.'

'It's all right,' he said.

His heart suddenly felt lighter. He sensed that a painful burden had been lifted. He was thankful for any kindness from her. He wanted to express his gratitude, but could think of nothing to say. He wanted to tell her how much she meant to him, but he could not.

She took him upstairs to her room. There was a log fire burning in the fireplace, and Priti's face glowed in its reflection. She went across to the window, and he followed her. She pointed to the rain outside. As she did so, her wrist and arm brushed his, and he felt that her body was smoother and softer than anything he had felt before. She suddenly looked straight and hard into his face as she had done the first day they had met at the Green Room. He felt nervous and uneasy. Then she smiled in the same way.

'You may kiss me if you want to,' she said.

He was confused.

'Have you ever kissed a girl before?' she asked.

'No,' he replied.

'Do you know how to kiss?'

He shook his head.

'I can show you if you want.'

He nodded nervously.

'Close your eyes first.'

He did as he was told. He felt her draw closer. Her breathing was heavier. He felt her hands on his shoulders. He waited, but nothing happened.

'Open your eyes. You look so odd with your eyes closed.'

He opened his eyes and stepped back. He saw her brown eyes surrounded by long, brown lashes, thick braids, her soft skin and her red cheeks and red lips.

'Come near. Nearer,' she whispered. 'I won't hurt you.'

She grabbed hold of his shirt and her face became flushed. He looked eager and apprehensive.

'You may put your arms around me,' she softly said.

Obediently he bent over her, his arms clumsily around her neck. His heart beat violently. She raised herself and threw her bare arms around him, tossed her hair back with a quick motion of her head, and kissed him on the lips. Then she slipped away to the other end of the room. She smiled faintly. His heart was beating anxiously. He was desperately keen to please her.

'You do like me, don't you?' she said.

'Yes,' he said hoarsely.

She turned around and ran downstairs. As he was leaving the house she said, 'It is Diwali tomorrow. We are having some people for tea, including Karan. Mother asked me to invite you. So be sure to come.'

When he returned home that evening, the rain had stopped. The grass was wet, and there was a strong smell of the earth. A nightingale sang in fitful snatches from below. The same road to the house on which he had walked hundreds of times seemed transformed into a magical path. He looked up at the partially cleared sky. The moon had risen. He did not deserve such happiness, he felt.

15

The next day was Diwali, and Tara and Seva Ram were reluctant to let Arjun go out alone to Priti's house. Diwali was a family affair. Arjun persuaded them, however, by saying that he would return early; besides Karan would be there too. Tara gave him a box of sweets to give to Amrita.

'Be sure to bring Karan back with you,' said Tara as he was leaving the house.

He nodded.

'Shall we pick you up on the way to the lights?' she asked.

'No. . .no, it is a party, Mother. You cannot just drop in.'

'But it is Diwali, Arjun. Everyone visits each other on Diwali,' she said.

Tara would have liked to visit the Mehtas, but she let it go when she saw how embarrassed Arjun felt. From Arjun's clothes and manner, and his strange behaviour of the past weeks, she guessed something was going on. She had meant to speak to him about his school marks, but she did not want to spoil his Diwali. She told Seva Ram that she would wait until after school opened. She was secretly happy that Arjun was welcome at the Mehta house, since 'they belonged to the right society'. She felt that he would make the right friends and learn the right manners, and who knows, even make the right contacts that would be useful in the future when he went out to work. From Bauji she had learnt that contacts meant a great deal.

Tara dreamed that Arjun would grow up into a well-bred, handsome and intelligent man who would be good at games and studies. She wanted him to go to a fine college in Delhi like St. Stephens, where he would acquire the necessary intellectual equipment, but not necessarily become a scholar. Then he would be ready to join the civil service or one of the professions, or industry or any of the pleasant niches for which the post-Independence Indian bourgeoisie groomed its young. After Arjun was settled she would marry him to a good Punjabi girl with the same background and education. He would join a club, and thus be fit to become a member of the establishment, to rub shoulders with the intellectual elite of the land. And she hoped he would want to repeat the same process with his children. It was important to her that he should have more money than they did, so that he would be able to send his children to boarding schools like Mayo or Doon, and if possible to a good University abroad, such as the Ivy League colleges in America or Oxford and Cambridge in England. This was Tara's recipe for an enviably happy life.

Soon after Arjun left the house, Tara and Seva Ram settled down before the fireplace, he to reading the newspaper and she to her knitting. Seva Ram was nearing his forty-fifth birthday and Tara was in her late thirties. Neither had altered visibly, apart from the normal changes brought on by age. The Himalayan air had suited them and they both looked healthy. Seva Ram continued to comb his curly hair backwards, as he had always done, except there were fewer hairs to comb each succeeding year. His round eyes peered sincerely from behind his spectacles, and his prominent nose stood out as much as ever. Because of a digestive problem, he was not able to put on weight, and continued to appear small and frail as he had always done.

Tara, although never beautiful, was still attractive in her middle years. She had looked after herself. She was especially proud of her jet black hair. The soft expression in her dark, brown eyes, her pretty, curved upper lip, the fine, oval-shaped face, and a healthy colour on her cheeks from the Himalayan air, all these made her look like a much younger woman. Her face shone by the light of the lamp beside which she was knitting.

Giving her husband a sidelong glance with her eyes, she asked, 'Well, shall we go to the Mall and look at the lights? We can also drop in on the Dewans and the Paltas and deliver their sweets.'

Seva Ram looked comfortable before the fire. He unenthusiastically replied, 'Without the children, the lights are not much fun. But if you want to give the sweets. . .'

'I can always send the sweets with the servant,' she interrupted. 'It's too bad that Arjun has to be away on Diwali evening,' she added with a touch of sadness.

'Well, he insisted on going to the Mehtas' party, and . . .'

'And we are here all alone on Diwali evening,' she said.

After a pause, he said, 'Why did Bauji have to leave before

Diwali?'

'Some urgent work came up in Hoshiarpur, I think,' she replied curtly. Besides, he probably wanted to be with Bhabo on Diwali.' After a pause, Tara said irritably, 'Oh, I wish you were not so anti-social. We could do so much with our evenings. There are such interesting people in Simla. You don't even care that we don't receive invitations from Raj Bhavan. All our friends in the department do. When Asha Vasudeva discovered that they had not been invited to the last "At Home", she made Lekh go to Government House and get an invitation from the Governor's ADC.'

'I wouldn't do that,' said Seva Ram.

She sighed and said, 'Ah, I would love to be at the Mehtas' with Arjun this evening. The lights, the silk saris, the glamorous people—how lovely!'

'And totally unsuitable for a schoolboy!'

'But think of the people he meets. I want him to have the social life that we never had.'

'You are allowing him to be spoiled, Tara. They are the wrong kind of people,' he said angrily.

'But they are so cultured.'

'He is learning bad habits. They drink, they smoke, they eat meat.'

'Good heavens, the whole world eats meat,' she said with a laugh.

'Well I don't want him to acquire the animal's karma, and carry that burden along with all the other karmas he will have to bear through life.' After a pause he added, 'They are not our type of people, Tara.'

'And what are *our* type of people, may one ask?' said Tara with irritation.

'Well, god-fearing people, who love the guru and visit the ashram.' he replied defensively.

'Just as I thought. In short, boring, dull, smelly, lower middle class clerks.'

'There are others too,' he said weakly.

'They may be *your* type of people but not *our* type of people.'

'I still feel he is in the wrong company, Tara. You know, I would rather he spent his free time playing sports and games with other boys. At his age, I only had thoughts of studies and of the guru. Arjun is a *brahmachari*, and he should think only of studies and god. Look at the clothes he wears! He wants to join the Green Room; he wants to learn skating.'

'But good heavens, he is growing up,' she smiled again. 'It is normal to want these things. He wants to have the opportunities that you and I did not.'

Seva Ram rose up abruptly. He began to pace the floor. His face became more animated. So far he had been speaking in an even, natural way. Now for the first time that she could remember, he raised his voice, and Tara became a little afraid.

'That Mehta girl is corrupt, Tara. She has turned his head completely. Is it surprising that he is doing poorly in his studies? She is toying with him. The other day I saw them walking on the Mall. He was walking behind her, pleading with her about something, behaving like her servant. I tell you, Tara, the poor boy is going to get hurt. He is out of his element.'

Seva Ram sat down abruptly. There were tears in his eyes, and he turned his face away. Such an outburst was uncharacteristic of him, and he was ashamed of himself. Tara was moved. In twenty years of their marriage, she had not heard him raise his voice. Her heart went out to him. He had looked handsome as he sincerely tried to tell her what was wrong. And the thing was that he was right. She too had the same fears about Priti.

What a jewel of a man her husband was, she felt, as she realized that he had never raised his voice before. She had not been aware of it until he did. And he cared deeply for his son. She was touched. She thought about all the husbands who were constantly nagging their wives and their children. He was tolerant in comparison. He had never tried to force his strong religious beliefs on them. Nor had he ever insisted that she visit the ashram. True, he still sent a fourth of his salary to the ashram and that remained an irritant between them. But that was a little thing before his other virtues. She had sometimes wondered whether he really cared for them. He had seemed so quiet and completely removed from everything. Over the years he had changed. Now she was convinced that he did care. As she saw him sitting there, looking quiet, humble and sincere, she felt a freshness which was the exact opposite of the cynical and effete feeling that Karan inspired in her. She seemed to understand her husband for the first time. He was not cold but merely remote. He was sincere but aloof. He seemed to listen from far away, and he seemed to listen with his eyes. The only word to describe him, she felt, would be 'saintly'. Filled with tenderness, she went up to him and embraced him. She put her head on his shoulders and she wept.

she went up to him and embraced him. She put her head on his shoulders and she wept.

16

Like everything else, Diwali too was celebrated on a grand scale at Priti's house. For the past two weeks, Arjun had noted a great deal of activity at the Mehta house. As Diwali approached, the servants began the annual ritual of house cleaning: they beat the carpets. The tailor came to make new curtains. Everyone was in a hurry, and for days the house was filled with excitement. The cook, the gardener, the watchman, the bearer, and the maid—all of them got new clothes. The postman, the milkman and the washerman got money. There was much coming and going and confusion. Whereas Tara bought her Diwali sweets from the bazaar, Amrita engaged a halwai for three days to make sweets at home. While Tara gave sweets to a few select friends, Amrita distributed them to half the poor in the town, plus all the workers at her orchards.

Between Dasehra and Diwali, between Amrita's reception for the Cabinet Minister and her Diwali party during that autumn of 1962, more melancholy news came of Chinese incursions on the Indian border. Nehru regarded the Chinese action as a personal insult, and it left him in a depression from which he never recovered. Many Indians similarly felt the Chinese action to be a betrayal, and the conversation in Amrita's drawing room was no different from what was being said in homes all over the country on that Diwali evening.

'After years of friendship and "*Hindi-Chini bhai bhai*", why are the Chinese suddenly angry?' asked Amrita of Kanwar Krishan Singh, the dashing young Minister of State who was on a week's visit to Simla with his petite Nepali wife.

'Because you take everyone in Asia for granted,' interjected his Nepali wife. 'You are so preoccupied with what is happening in Washington and London that you forget your neighbours. It won't do to look at the world through English spectacles. Look at the way you treat us Nepalese.'

'Come, come, you are putting it too strongly, my dear,' said the young Minister, who wore a rose on his closed collar coat, in the fashion made famous by Nehru. 'We may be guilty of forgetting Nepal, but we certainly don't take the Chinese for granted.'

Amrita had a great talent for having the most interesting people at her informal get-togethers. Society in Simla agreed that the success of her evenings lay in her apparent lack of effort. People somehow came together, and invariably found at her house some new and interesting or powerful person who was often from the world of politics. He was usually a friend of a friend, and was visiting Simla briefly in order to escape the heat and dust of Delhi. Amrita's friends were always rewarded by being able to get the latest reading of the political thermometer in Delhi or to find out about new trends in art and literature.

Arjun had arrived early and was standing in a group which was dominated by Rao Sahib. He was nervous and in awe of the magnificent company and the flower-filled drawing room. He wore a new sweater, which Tara had knitted for him for Diwali, and he had promised his mother that he would not get it wet in the damp evening. He kept looking around the room for Priti, but she had not appeared as yet in the brightly-lit drawing room. Nor had Karan arrived, and Arjun was paralyzed by an insurmountable timidity.

'I think people silly who want to stay home rather than go to a party,' Rao Sahib was saying to the bald-headed Justice Khosla. 'You must remember an important rule in Simla's society is that if you are not seen everywhere you are forgotten.'

'Come, come, Bunty, that is a cynical view of people,' laughed the judge. 'Hardly something to teach this bright young lad' and he looked directly at Arjun, who smiled nervously. 'If you are inclined to think the worst of your fellow men. . . .'

'Look at Chamba,' interrupted Rao Sahib in his smooth Oxford accent. 'Ever since he abandoned society he has been forgotten.'

'Did I hear my name?' asked the fascinating princess, who was sitting nearby on a sofa with Amrita. The men immediately turned around to face her and her ample, exposed bosom.

'Not you, Sita dear, but your extraordinary husband,' replied Rao Sahib.

When her husband was mentioned, the princess put on a dignified expression, which was most becoming on her. It was no secret that the two were not getting along, and the princess was in fact relieved when her husband left one day to become a yogi in the

Himalayas. Ever since he had left, everyone in her glittering social circle felt sorry for her. She responded to these solicitous remarks appropriately as the injured party. As with all things, she managed her 'dignified expression' with her great talent for tact and social diplomacy. And her success lay in her appearing tactless and naive and perfectly natural, as though she did not realize the significance of that expression.

'I always thought he was cracked,' said Rao Sahib sympathetically. It was not uncommon to criticize Chamba behind his back. People who had never said a bad word about him suddenly became critical, hoping in this way to come closer to the lovely princess. She was unanimously regarded as the most beautiful woman in Simla, and she had turned the head of many brilliant men. Rao Sahib had openly flirted with her, but with no apparent success. Her attraction lay in the mystery of her private life, and no man had been publicly linked with her name.

'I too think he was peculiar, but his only flaw was that he was too independent,' said Amrita. She was not as hearty in condemning an erstwhile guest, who had been a regular feature, albeit an odd one at her parties. 'He certainly had a mind of his own,' she added. Amrita had in fact liked him. She had a feeling that the marriage was not going to succeed, since he had a revulsion for society, whereas Sita couldn't do without it.

'I say, don't speak to Sita about him. It is too hard for her.' said Rao Sahib, and he turned towards Justice Khosla. 'Ah, she is such a charming and unhappy woman.' He said this to the judge, but loud enough for the princess to hear.

Arjun looked around him, trying to spot Priti. He walked a few steps to the right, and at once he knew she was there. He knew by the rapture and the terror that seized him. She was standing in the alcove talking to Neena, Rao Sahib's daughter, and to Rishi, the anaemic boy, whom Arjun remembered from the Green Room. There was nothing particularly striking in her sari, which was a tasteful maroon silk and which she wore with confidence, nor in the way she was standing and chatting. But to Arjun she would have been easy to spot anywhere. He wondered if he ought to go close to her and greet her, or whether he should wait till she came up to him. Then his nerve failed him and the place where she stood appeared unapproachable. He had to master himself and to remind himself that he was her guest after all, and that it was Diwali, and he had nothing to fear. He was filled with envy for Neena and Rishi, who could speak freely with her.

Priti noticed Arjun at this moment, smiled and waved to him. The world brightened up for him because of her smile. But she was distracted suddenly, and Arjun followed the direction of Priti's gaze, which went to the entrance, where she had spotted Karan arriving. Through her eyes he saw an extraordinarily handsome man, who moved gracefully, with an air of easy assurance and confidence. Arjun noticed that Priti blushed and became excited and happy, and perhaps because of her aroused state, looked beautiful.

Arjun's eyes were fastened on Priti, and thus it came as a shock when Karan came up to him, and put his arm around him. Karan gently took Arjun with him. Amrita beamed happily when she saw him. All eyes in Amrita's group turned to Karan. Amrita got up and introduced him to the Minister of State and his Nepali wife, who recognized him from one of his concerts in Delhi.

The conversation in the group had steadily continued on Indo-Chinese relations and had just turned to the madness of the coming war. General Thapar spoke authoritatively about Chinese military capability. He argued that although the Indian soldier was not inferior in bravery he was less prepared to fight in the Himalayan terrain, both because of lack of experience and an ineffective supply line. Karan listened attentively to what was being said, and politely waited for the right pause in the conversation. While he waited his turn to speak, he glanced several times at Priti, who smiled back each time he looked at her.

Amrita led the conversation towards a more general note about the place of power and war in men's affairs. She did this in order to hear what Karan had to say. After a few minutes Karan spoke. He attributed the behaviour of the Chinese to their desire to be regarded as the supreme power in Asia. He felt Nehru was insensitive to them, and by walking in boots too large for himself, he had brought the two countries to the brink of war.

Clearly this was an original point of view, and Karan held everyone's attention. When he finished, he was applauded by the Minister and his wife, although the nationalistic sensibility of the General was hurt. Karan looked around and was rewarded by a smile from each person whose eye caught his.

Priti now joined their group. Arjun observed that she was aware of the impression that Karan had made and was delighted by his triumph. Arjun hoped that he would now be able to talk to her. She seemed so perfect in every way, as she stood close to him. To Arjun she was a creature far above anything earthly, and it was inconceivable that she would regard him as worthy of her. But Priti's eyes were fixed on Karan as if she were under his spell. Arjun tried to catch her attention, but he was unsuccessful. Suddenly Karan smiled back at her, and she took him away towards the alcove.

Arjun watched them with torment in his heart. He noticed that as they were talking, Priti did not once take her eyes off him. She unashamedly stared at his oval face, the centre parting of his hair, his lean neck, and his slim arms. Karan was wearing a comfortable pair of baggy khaki pants, a white cotton shirt, and an equally loose fitting sweater. Nothing remarkable in itself, but the effect produced was of comfortable elegance. Arjun was left in no doubt about Priti's feelings for him.

It was more difficult to decipher Karan's feelings. Despite his puzzling ironic look, Arjun felt Karan found her agreeable. Arjun was equally troubled by the way Karan looked at her naked shoulders and arms and exposed midriff below her blouse. He wondered why they did not limit their looks to each other's faces as normal people did when they talked. As they were staring at each other, Arjun had a terrible feeling that a barrier of modesty, which is always present between Indian men and women in society, was suddenly down between Priti and Karan. Without being able to explain this strange and uncomfortable sensation, Arjun was conscious that Priti and Karan were on dangerously intimate ground. If Karan were to place his hand on her bare arm, or even her neck, it would be the most natural thing to happen between them, thought Arjun. They were speaking about simple matters, but Arjun felt there was a hidden intimate meaning in everything that they said to each other. Suddenly he felt embarrassed. He became conscious that he was spying on a private conversation. He felt guilty and turned away.

As he looked away, his eye caught Amrita's, who was busily engaged by General Thapar. Arjun's imploring look seemed to ask: What does all this mean? Oblivious of the torment in his soul, Amrita smiled back warmly from afar with a look which seemed to say, 'I hope you are happy. I am so glad you're here. Do enjoy yourself.'

Arjun was disturbed, and the cause of his agitation was across the room from him. Despite his best efforts, he couldn't help looking at them. Just as he turned towards them again, he saw Priti squeeze Karan's arm above the elbow. Karan looked startled. Priti blushed, and her brilliant eyes looked deep into him. Arjun shivered as Karan gave her a tender smile. She took his hand and led him outside.

Not until a few minutes later did Arjun realize all that had taken place. He was horrorstruck. He groaned inside himself. And he was irrevocably drawn outside to follow them into a strange, mad world and to await the next development with terror.

It was a bright moonlit night, and he had to be careful not to be seen. He walked quickly and stood behind the closest deodar trunk. He saw them nearby on the lawn. They kissed. Karan looked at her, a joyous light flashed into her eyes from the reflection of the moon, and a smile of happiness curved her lips. Karan seemed to make an effort to control himself, to cover his delight with his ubiquitous irony. But a strange look came on his face. His usual resolute, self-possessed manner and the carelessly calm expression had vanished and Arjun saw a look on it he had never seen before. Karan appeared bewildered, humble and submissive.

They kissed again, and Arjun escaped from behind the deodar tree and from the Mehtas' Diwali party.

17

Bauji smoked his hookah and thought about the pride of his inheritance. He looked at his grandson, and he saw a worthy successor to his line (even though, alas, it was his daughter's son). The proud sensuality of which this boy was presently a victim was also his heritage. Momentarily, a frown came upon Bauji's brow as his mind was distracted by a film song on a loudspeaker somewhere in the neighbourhood; he thought with mild distaste of the vulgar ways of the new class. But it was a temporary lapse, the frown disappeared and his thoughts returned to his grandson, who sat nearby on a low stool skilfully preparing the next chillum to replace the dying embers of the one he was smoking.

Arjun had been with him for two weeks. But he had not said very much. His accursed pride kept him mostly to himself. The only thing he seemed to have succeeded in doing in this time was in learning to prepare the hookah. He would go out to the bazaar on a bicycle and carefully select the raw tobacco, which he helped Bhabo to cure at home with molasses and malt. He knew the right level at which to fill the water in the brass base; the exact angle at which to place the stone on the silver chillum in order to prevent the tobacco from falling through; and the correct amount of tobacco to fill in the chillum. Finally he would carefully place the smouldering dried cow-dung cakes above the tobacco, and his grandfather's hookah would be ready.

A week after Amrita's Diwali party, a scandal had exploded in Simla which kept that society talking for years. Not since Nehru's name was linked with Lady Edwina Mountbatten on the first Indian Governor-General's visit to Simla in the spring of 1948, did society have as much to talk about. Priti had run away with Karan. No one knew exactly where they were. Some said they had gone away to Delhi, others said to Bombay. A few like Rao Sahib maintained that they were in hiding somewhere in Simla. Most of Amrita's friends and acquaintances were shocked. Some women, who envied Amrita for her pre-eminent place in society and who were weary of constantly hearing of her virtues, were secretly pleased to see their rival fall. They were waiting for a turn in the public opinion from the sympathy which her plight immediately drew, in order to pounce upon her with the full weight of their scorn. But a large number of older and middle aged members of the establishment were genuinely grieved at the scandal, and wanted to help Amrita and protect the Mehta name.

Tara was horrified. Even before schools broke for the winter vacation, she persuaded Seva Ram to give Arjun two hundred rupees and sent him down to visit Bauji in Hoshiarpur. Although Arjun did not say much, both Tara and Seva Ram were aware of his pain and could think of nothing better to do for the poor boy.

The chillum had been prepared, and grandfather and grandson sat soaking in the winter sun. They could smell the cooking of mustard greens and corn bread in the kitchen, and slowly they began to get hungry. The day Arjun arrived in Hoshiarpur, Bauji suspected something was wrong. He told Bhabo, 'What's bothering this boy is a woman!' and his eyes twinkled behind his spectacles, and his moustache curved imperceptibly. 'And I know her.'

Arjun had held out for ten days, but finally the dam had burst. He had sobbed uncontrollably. Bauji's large fingers had stroked the top of his head. But he had not allowed the fire of Arjun's rage to mute to self pity. It had taken time for the grandfather to gain the grandson's confidence. But in the end Arjun's faith was complete, and he was certain that Bauji would understand. And Bauji had understood his passion. In consoling his grandson, he did not make light of Arjun's feelings. He seemed to know what a mighty pain it was to love. And mightier still it was to love in vain. At first Bauji's pride was hurt—that a grand-daughter of Sanat Mehta should reject his grandson. But when he saw the defenceless boy's pain, he regarded it a very serious business.

'If you have to love a woman, my boy, she might as well be good-looking. At least you will have the memory of a nice face,' Bauji said. And Arjun had smiled for the first time.

'In the evenings, I sometimes see boys and girls from the Government College pass by. Ah, those girls, they keep me alive, my boy. One, in particular, is a dark-haired beauty. She came here the other day. She came with a petition. Don't mention it to Bhabo, but she took my breath away. She was tall and well-made, and her skin had the flavour of freshly made butter. Under a mass of raven hair, curling in gentle waves, her dark eyes gleamed motionless like a statue. . . .'

He suddenly stopped as he caught Arjun's eye, smiling with affectionate amusement. He blushed. The direction of his thoughts stung him suddenly and made him blush. He felt ashamed of himself for harbouring thoughts not befitting a gentleman in the seventh decade of his life. According to Hindu scriptures, he was in the fourth or the renunciation stage of a man's life, and he should be well advanced in detaching himself from the world's delights (and its sorrows) including the fragrance of jasmine in his garden and the smell of mustard greens and corn bread cooking in the kitchen. To leave all this and go off to the Himalayan woods in search of his soul—what could be more ridiculous, he thought.

'What was in the petition?' asked Arjun.

'They want to change the name of the road outside our house. It is called Lawrence Road; they want to call it Netaji Subhash Chandra Bose Marg. I have resisted this change on the Municipal Committee.'

'But why don't you let them change it?'

'They want to change it in the name of nationalism,' said Bauji.

'What's wrong with that?'

'My boy, I hate abstract ideals. Such ideals are always too simple to fit the facts. Ideals and instructions must not be imposed. They must be allowed to grow and come alive. I don't grudge the British for having stayed on perhaps twenty years longer than they should have. It gave our nationalism an opportunity to penetrate deeper and to flourish. The limited elections in the '30s gave us a chance to experiment with new institutions and practice democracy.'

'What does that have to do with changing a name?'

'We must be reverent both to our new and old institutions. We must nurture them. A clever politician can easily destroy, in the name of the common good, an old institution which has worked well and which has time, familiarity, and habit behind it.'

'But then there wouldn't be any change at all,' protested Arjun.

'We must change gradually, a little at a time. My boy, in India we have traditions of the family, of the village, of the caste. Each man feels the need to be a part of something larger and more enduring than himself. We have a history and customary ways of acting. And the British Raj is part of our history. Although they came as conquerors, they gave us some of their best. It is now a part of us. We must not discard it easily, for the good might be lost with the bad. The same goes for our Muslim history.'

At the mention of 'Muslim' Bauji's face suddenly twitched. He rarely mentioned that word.

'If they want to have a road named after Bose, they ought to build a new one and so name it. But why rewrite history by changing the name of an existing road?'

'It is an alien name "Lawrence", Bauji,' said Arjun.

'Do they know who Lawrence was?'

'Lord Lawrence, the Governor-General, wasn't it?' said Arjun, remembering his history text.

'No, this one was his brother, Henry Lawrence, who was the first Resident in the Punjab and who was very fond of India and Indians.'

'So what's going to happen, Bauji?'

'They are bringing a procession here this evening to persuade me to change my mind.'

'Aren't you afraid?'

'Of what?'

'Why, something might happen,' said Arjun.

'Bhabo is afraid, and she's not even sympathetic to my point of view,' said Bauji.

The procession of students came and it went. It was led by the same dark-haired beauty who had the complexion of 'freshly made butter'. Bauji openly flirted with her, and it unsettled her considerably. He was charming and conciliatory, but he told her and the others the same things that he had told Arjun that morning. He recited the life of Lawrence and sent them to the college library. She and the others were amused, but they remained unconvinced. Bauji too knew that he was in the minority and that it was a losing battle, but he enjoyed himself. The students were disciplined by and large and there was no serious incident, except when they were dispersing: one of them threw a stone which broke Bhabo's bathroom window.

Bauji consoled Bhabo saying that it was a small price to pay for one's convictions.

A month later came the twenty-sixth of January, a holiday, to celebrate India's becoming a Republic. In Hoshiarpur, Bauji, as the President of the Municipal Committee, was asked to speak at a flag unfurling organized by the local Lions Club, and Arjun agreed to accompany him.

Arjun watched with pleasure as Bauji sprinkled scent on his

handkerchief, a signal that he was almost dressed. He pulled down his starched cuffs, inserted gold cuff links, and deliberately fastened his gold watch with its double chain to his pocket. It was one of the few possessions he had brought from the old Punjab. Feeling clean and fragrant, he took his old, carved walking stick, and with a swinging gait went towards the waiting car.

'The trees are different from Lyallpur,' said Bauji, pointing to the tall simbal trees, which produced silk-cotton for soft pillows. 'During the monsoon they are covered with brilliant red flowers. And the chutney from their blossoms is delicious!'

As they passed the Hoshiarpur Club, a frown came over Bauji's forehead. With distaste he looked at the crumbling, betel-juice-stained walls of the sprawling old club which had been lovingly built by the English, and which had now been completely taken over by the new rich class of traders and small industrialists. He could still remember the time (soon after '47) when the same walls were impeccably white-washed and always covered with masses of bougainvillaea. Now they seemed to spend more money on the club, but on the wrong things invariably.

Bauji told Arjun, 'I rarely go there because so few speak any language except money. They play bad bridge, with stakes that are too high. They sit at the bar, flashing hundred-rupee notes, speaking loudly, and drinking too much whisky. The rule that you never paid cash (because your credit was good) is observed in the exception, because the new rich want to spend their black money as rapidly as possible. The last thing they want is a receipt lest the income-tax officer gets wise to their real income. You were never allowed to tip in the old days, but now you can't hope to get a bearer's attention unless you tip in advance. You are surrounded by 'Hello-ji! How-are-you-ji?' They can't speak one language properly and insist on mixing two. It's much too depressing, my boy.'

'I know, the telephone operator is Exchange-ji,' said Arjun.

'The other night on the bridge table an aggressive lady suddenly switched to English and shouted 'I am demanding you. I am demanding you.' When her partner gently corrected her (inserting the "from" in the sentence) she screamed an obscenity that would have made a Sikh truck driver stand up.'

Bauji's speech at the Lions Club was a great success. It was brief and witty. He could not resist a few jokes at the expense of the new-rich class, which was amply represented in the audience. But like all targets of such jokes, not one of them took exception, thinking that it was his neighbour who was the intended butt.

There was a problem, however, when it came to unfurling the flag. Twice Bauji tried. He raised the flag, but it would not open. The Lions in the audience roared, insisting that the flag be opened, the flowers taken out, and the flag raised without the flowers. It was the practical and efficient thing to do, proclaimed the efficient businessmen. But Bauji politely insisted that it wasn't the way to do things. He patiently untied the knot, and tied a new knot. Then he raised the flag, pulled the string, and the flag unfurled, showering hundreds of marigold petals to the ground.

Next on the agenda was a speech by a local politician which predictably was long and windy, and the Lions started to get fidgety and embarrassed; the Chief Lion on the dais first hinted, then gestured, and finally tried to pinch the politician to make him sit down. At this point Bauji intervened and gently pointed out to the gathering that it was after all Republic Day; it was a celebration of democracy; and a central idea of democracy was the right of free speech; therefore, the politician should be allowed to speak for as long as he wished.

Eventually the function ended. The restless crowd started to disperse quickly. As they were leaving, Bauji noticed a little girl crying. Someone had accidentally bumped into her, and her string of beads was broken. The beads had scattered in the crowd. Bauji, with Arjun's help, bent down and began to pick them up. The Lions, seeing what their Chief Guest was doing, also started to help. And as soon as the beads were gathered, the Lions handed them to the young girl and smugly went on their way. But Bauji and Arjun stayed behind till they had beaded the string. Eventually they put the necklace on the little girl, who wiped her tears, and gave them a smile.

As the days went by, Arjun felt that little by little the confusion in his mind was clearing up, and the shame and the discontent were passing away. In the company of Bauji and Bhabo, he began to feel himself again. He discovered that it was not necessary to be anyone else. He decided that he would never allow himself to come under the complete influence of another person. All he wanted now was to be himself. If that meant that he would have to give up hopes of an extraordinary happiness, so it had to be.

PART THREE

Bombay

1

Arjun's first and most enduring impression of Bombay was of water. He arrived on the island on a monsoon day. The damp streets shone from the rain and the city's air was dense with wetness. The yellow and black taxi from Bombay Central station drove him through soggy quarters, carelessly bouncing over puddles, splattering water over the roadside. It was an early evening in August and the streetlights glistened on the moist asphalt. That night he saw fifteen-foot-tall waves of the Arabian Sea shatter thunderously against the rocks below his window. The southwest wind whistled through the tiny cracks between the shutters. The rain advanced from the deep sea like the disciplined forward line of an army.

The monsoon went away in September but the smell and feel of the Arabian Sea stayed. Arjun settled down in a 'paying guest' flat in Colaba at the southern tip of the narrow island city, near an ancient fishing village of the Kolis. From his window Arjun could see the nets of the Kolis spread out in the sun, their brightly coloured sails fluttering on their beached boats, their huts of thatch and woven matting surrounded by the smell of ageing Bombay Duck. Sometimes in the evenings he would watch the boats, many of them equipped with motors, go out floating with the tide as the full-breasted Koli women waved from the shore. His cleaning woman was a Koli. She had an attractive, dark body which she adorned with gold jewellery, and she wore her colourful sari tightly hitched up to the knees, twisted around her thighs, and pulled tautly between the cheeks of her buttocks.

Arjun had come to Bombay to make his fortune. After completing school in Simla, he spent four years in college in Delhi, where he read a great deal, mainly history and economics. But his academic results were not distinguished. He was not unintelligent, it was just that he could not get excited by the rote method of exam preparation. After college both Tara and Seva Ram wanted him to sit for the civil service exam. If he got in, they argued, he would be set for life with a secure career ahead of him. In the 1960s, a government career was still a part of the Punjabi middle class dream.

But Arjun had different ideas. He wanted to go far away, he wanted to see the world, and he did not want to work for the government. There were endless arguments. Tara was worried. Arjun sulked, and Seva Ram remained quiet. The truth was that Arjun did not know precisely what he wanted to do. Since he was idle for months, Tara had visions of an unemployed, unsettled son. She felt let down by Seva Ram, who did not seem to show particular interest in talking to the boy. Seva Ram answered her nagging with 'Let the boy decide! He is grown up now.'

Then one day Arjun surprised everyone. With a flourish he pulled out a letter from his pocket. It was a job offer from a firm in Bombay. Neither Tara nor Seva Ram knew quite what to think. But the pay was good. It transpired Arjun had quietly answered several advertisements, got himself interviewed in Delhi, and landed the job. He was excited, but Tara and Seva Ram were sad to see him go so far away.

The company which Arjun joined made consumer products in a factory in a northern suburb of Bombay. It was part of a large diversified commercial house, which owned trading and manufacturing companies all over India, dealing in everything from tea, textiles, and jute to engineering and consumer goods. Arjun started out in the sales department as an 'Officer-Trainee' under the charge of a sales training officer. The particular company he was assigned to manufactured toilet articles, such as hair oil, talcum powder, a skin-whitening cream, and over-the-counter drugs—a pain balm, an antiseptic for cuts and wounds, etc.

From the very first day on his job, Arjun had problems. His training officer, B.V. Rajan, a South Indian of the old school who had trained dozens of recruits, was an honest man, without any regional bias against Arjun. Yet he felt uncomfortable with him. As he explained to a colleague, 'I think he asks too many questions.'

Although Arjun knew practically nothing about the business world, he had an inquisitive mind. Other trainees might be willing to accept the way things were done, but Arjun wanted to know 'why'. No one had ever questioned the basic rules and procedures in this manner and after three months the training officer was at his wit's end. He reported to the company that as regards Arjun a mistake had been made. Reluctantly, the company agreed with his recommendation 'not to confirm' him.

However, the Advertising Manager had watched Arjun and talked to him several times. He sensed that Arjun had something in him. When he learned about the company's decision, he called in Arjun. He gave him a newspaper advertisement and asked him for his opinion. The headline of the advertisement said, 'For headaches, cuts, insect bites and colds, use Bombay Balm.'

'Do you like it?'

'I hate all advertising,' replied Arjun.

The Advertising Manager was taken aback. He began to understand why this boy was in trouble. Not wanting to be drawn into a discussion on the social value of advertising, he persisted with his original question.

'But if you want to sell more Bombay Balm, how would you improve this?'

Arjun thought for a while. 'I would sell the balm for only one ailment, not for everything.'

'But we would lose the customers who buy it for other problems.'

'You would more than make up, I think, by having people believe that it really works for that one thing.'

'Which problem would you sell it for?'

'What do most people buy it for?' asked Arjun.

'I don't know, but I think for aches and pains.'

'What kind of aches?'

'Headaches, I suppose.'

'We could find that out by talking to a hundred customers.'

'Yes, I suppose we could.'

'I think if I stood for a week at a chemist's shop like Kemps, I could meet a hundred customers.' After a pause Arjun asked, 'For which sickness does it really work best?'

'I suppose it works best for aches and pains, but it also relieves colds, and cuts and. . .'

'If it is best for aches and pains, let us sell it only for that.' After another pause Arjun added, 'Before we do so, shouldn't we check with some doctor or medical person if it really works on pains?'

'Young man, doctors don't like us because we cut into their business. They'll never give us proper advice.'

'Then let's try to find one doctor who is not biased. Let me try. I know of one. I'll go and ask him.'

That evening Arjun went to meet Dr Khanna. Tara had given him an introduction to the general practitioner on Malabar Hill. 'You will be a stranger in the big city, son. Go and pay your respects to Dr Khanna; he will introduce you to people.' Dr Khanna was a distant relative from Lyallpur, who had settled in Bombay after the partition and made good.

Arjun told Dr Khanna about Bombay Balm and asked him if it was effective for headaches. The doctor laughed. 'All your patent remedies are useless.' But Arjun was not disheartened. He showed the good doctor the balm's label and asked him to explain to him what each ingredient did. The doctor looked at the formula. He became serious suddenly and he said, 'Yes, yes, I think it has some good ingredients. Yes, yes, it could help a headache. Yes, yes, it also has camphor and menthol, both useful counter-irritants. But you could improve this formula, you know, by adding another analgesic, yes, yes.'

Dr Khanna and his wife insisted that Arjun stay on for dinner. 'Yes, yes, Bombay is the only real city in India!' Dr Khanna told Arjun over dinner. 'Delhi has too many bureaucrats, politicians and Punjabis. Calcutta, despite its boxwallas, is essentially a Bengali town. Madras belongs to the orthodox Hindu South, yes, yes. But Bombay belongs to no one. Muslims, Parsees, Hindus and the British—all of them made it into what it is today. And now people from all over India come to make their fortunes here. We all have a 'native place', as we Bombaywallas say, and we all dream of returning to our homes in the heartland. But the city mesmerizes us and we never return. Yes, yes, ancestral attachments fade away and we begin to call Bombay our home.'

The Khanna noticed that the boy's mind seemed to run along a single track. He kept coming back to Bombay Balm. But the doctor admired Arjun's inquisitive nature. It did not escape them either that he was an eligible bachelor, from a good family in their community, who was earning twelve hundred rupees a month in an established company. The visit set off a stream of letters to the Punjab to relatives with marriageable daughters.

Arjun sat down in bed that night and wrote out a dozen different advertisements for Bombay Balm. He also wrote out a short proposal on what was needed to be done to improve the product, its image, its advertising, and its sales. In it he suggested that the product be called 'Bombay Pain Balm for Headaches' rather than merely Bombay Balm.

The next morning Arjun arrived early at the office and left his proposal on the desk of the Advertising Manager. At eleven o'clock he was called in by the Sales Training Officer. As he walked into Rajan's cubicle, he noticed that his boss looked uncomfortable. Rajan stared at the fluorescent light overhead and then at his olive-coloured steel desk. Finally he asked Arjun to sit down. He cleared his throat and began to speak mournfully. It took him a long time to get to the point that Arjun was being fired.

'But why?' asked Arjun.

'Well, eh. . . you don't seem to fit here.'

'What have I done wrong?'

'Ah, nothing wrong, you just don't seem to fit.'

'But why?'

'There you go. You are always asking questions,' he said with annoyance. 'It's ah, your attitude. You can collect, ah, one month's salary this afternoon with your other dues. And you, ah. . .need not come in tomorrow.'

When Arjun went back into the hall, he thought all the clerks were staring at him. It seemed everyone knew that he was fired. He could not stand it, and instead of going back to his desk he went out into the street.

He felt incalculably sad and defeated as he walked towards the harbour. He looked at the gritty, impossible city. He passed by a row of warehouses and soon reached the great natural harbour, with its miles upon miles of deep, sheltered water. Scores of merchant ships were moored there, waiting to unload. It was a clear day and the mainland of India was visible in the distance. The vast scene was coloured by his unhappiness. He shivered as a flush of wind blew past, and he looked up at the hot midday sky. His thoughts returned link by link along the chain of memory to the two brief months in which he had inhabited the callous city. How could he have mistaken it for a careless, happy place? He felt wounded in his body, and in his mouth he detected the taste of camphor.

In the afternoon he returned to the office and immediately went to the cashier on the third floor to collect his wages. As he waited at the cash window, the Managing Director brushed past him with his nose buried in a file. Since the corridor was narrow, the Managing Director almost tripped over Arjun.

'Excuse me,' said Arjun stepping back.

The Managing Director looked at him and said, 'Not your fault, I should be looking where I am going. My name is Billimoria.'

'I know,' said Arjun, 'You are the Managing Director. I was

introduced to you along with the other trainees two months ago. My name is Arjun.'

The MD's eyes widened.

'Will you please come into my office?'

Arjun followed him. Billimoria's office was cool, dark and spacious. The walls were panelled in wood, and there was a thick carpet on the floor. At the back was a window overlooking the harbour. On the desk Arjun noticed a copy of the proposal which he had penned the previous night.

'So you are the young man who wants us to sell Bombay Balm for. . . let me see. . . for headaches.'

'Yes, sir.'

'Good. We'll do it. But *you* will have to do it.'

'But sir, I have just been fired from the company this morning.'

'What!'

'Mr Rajan called me this morning and said that I need not return from tomorrow. I was collecting my notice pay when you bumped into me.'

'Get me Rajan on the line,' Billmoria told his secretary on the intercom. 'Hello! Yes Rajan, what is this about the young trainee, Arjun? . . . What? Yes. . .Why? Yes. . .By why? Asks too many questions? No, let's keep him. Transfer him to Advertising, and um. . . confirm him. Tell Nimker we won't need to fill that vacancy of Assistant Advertising Manager now. Yes. I'll talk to Personnel. And Rajan, the next time you find a person who asks too many questions, send him to me before you fire him. By the way, I'll send you a copy of a proposal that this young man has written. Do read it and put it in his training file. You'll also understand why we can't afford to let him go.'

Billimoria turned to Arjun. He looked at him sternly. 'You'll have a new job tomorrow. In thirty days I want a progress report on the relaunch of Bombay Balm for. . .um. . .headaches.'

'Thank you, sir.'

After Arjun left his room, Billimoria called in the Advertising and Personnel Managers in order to regularize his decision. The Personnel man thought that Billimoria was making a mistake. Billimoria asked him to read Arjun's proposal and then comment on his decision. The Advertising Manager, whose name was Choudhary, was delighted to have him.

'He's the most refreshing thing to walk through these doors in years,' he said.

'After he relaunches the balm,' said Billimoria, 'he should naturally return to complete his sales training. We can shorten his training to half the period but he must travel. We may need support in reformulating the product. I'll inform PD. And Choudhary, give him plenty of rope. . . he's a bit odd, but creative. And watch him. . .um. . .two years from now he might have your job.'

Like every Northerner, Arjun did not like Bombay at first. It seemed crowded, noisy, and chaotic after the wide open spaces of North India. He had to learn to negotiate the tangled traffic, the beggars and the pavement sleepers. He found it all squalid and dismal. He complained about the smoke from the mills in Parel, especially in the rain when it seemed to become like exhaust vapour. Amid the harsh nakedness of industrial India, he sorely missed the Himalayan birds, the trees and the grass with which he had grown up in Simla. When he looked at the mill workers, he saw empty faces, eyes without expression of life. There was no beauty in the lives of the industrial masses, he thought.

From the suburban train he could see the urban stain spreading, eating away at peaceful old villages, driving back the coconut trees, smothering the once-calm lives in lazy bungalows with chemical fumes and dotting the shores of creeks with slums. Because it was an island, joined at the top with the mainland, Bombay's dormitory suburbs lay to the north; on the other three sides there was only water. In the northern reaches stretched mile after mile of urban sprawl, with sordid apartment blocks, already dirty and crumbling, although only recently constructed. In between he caught a glimpse of a green field here and there, scattered palm trees, an occasional blue mountain. But more often the view was of dull shanty towns with mud huts pushing one against the other, covered with tin or plastic sheets, sometimes only with rags. Exposed suddenly to this horror, Arjun felt ambivalent about industry and 'city living'. He imagined the island city one day being swamped by a dangerous tide of humanity, and crumbling into the sea.

After the initial shock wore off the city slowly began to grow on Arjun. The wind from the Arabian sea, sent as if by Bedouins from the other side, had the power to banish all uncomfortable thoughts and soothe the palpitant body. Waking up in the soft morning air to an entrancing view of the sea, shining like a brilliant turquoise stone, became a daily pleasure. He delighted in walking on full moon nights in the dazed air of Hanging Gardens alongside the gulmohar trees, watching the clear night sky above the Queen's

Necklace. Even negotiating the gales on Marine Drive during the monsoons held a certain adventure. Arjun was gradually won over by the city, in whose daily life whole centuries coexisted within every passing moment. He admired the city for its great heart. Bombay was a miniature India which opened its arms to people from all over the country. It contained an infinite number of social worlds, intricately woven, yet separate, which moved back and forth, over the same long strip of island.

Even Arjun's ambivalent feelings about industry underwent a change as he got slowly caught up in the romance of the commercial world. He worked in the heart of the business city, surrounded by the port, the stock exchange and the commodity markets. On his way to work he passed by warehouses, business houses of limited companies and shipping agents. Gradually he adopted Bombay's heroes as his own. His eyes would grow misty when talk turned to the merchant princes like the Sassoons, Wadias, Tatas, and Birlas. He began to use phrases like 'capital accumulation', 'growth markets', and 'competitive strategy'. Instead of viewing industry with disdain, he began to see it as the life blood of the future and a symbol of prosperity. He believed that if the engineering industry had not succeeded the old textile industry, and if petrochemicals and chemicals had not succeeded engineering, Bombay would not have continued to be a source of strength, employment and taxes for the country. Yet, at the back of his mind, he was bothered by the dilemma that prosperity and squalor seemed to grow equally.

A month after he joined the company, Arjun was sent out into the field to learn the trade. Billimoria was a great believer in learning in the bazaar. Carrying a brown salesman's bag, Arjun arrived on a dusty winter morning at Ratlam, a rail junction on the main line between Bombay and Delhi. The coolie carried his bedroll and trunk a hundred yards to Sri Krishna Lodge, situated opposite the railway station. The pink-and-green, ten-room hotel was popular with salesmen and other commercial travellers. As it was 'house full', Arjun had to share a room with another salesman. He was grateful for a bed, and did not mind the flies or the open drain outside his window. He walked out to the small balcony outside his room and looked down at the street. The movie theatre diagonally across appeared forlorn. A cycle-rickshaw pulled up beside a tea-stall. Its driver, with a long scarf around his head, lit up a beedi as he waited for a hot mug of tea. Another rickshaw passed, top heavy with half-a-dozen school children balanced precariously. Arjun walked back to the corridor, stained by betel juice. He waited in a queue outside the wet bathroom, which was shared by the four rooms on his floor. He bathed noisily out of a metal bucket, using a brass mug to pour water over his head. After breakfast he called for a rickshaw and went to the market.

His first call was on the company stockist, Messrs. Malwa Traders. Malwa Traders was the leading wholesaler of patent medicines in town, and for a five percent commission had served as the stock point of Arjun's firm's products for two decades. The local retailers and some wholesalers, who catered to rural retailers, bought their supplies from here. Arjun was greeted by the short, dust-covered and unshaven proprietor, Kewal Ram. He was cleaning his teeth with a twig from a neem tree, and had not changed from the lungi he had slept in. The shop was equally dusty. The open jute bags of grains and chillies sent Arjun into a fit of sneezing.

Kewal Ram ordered tea from the tea stall in front of his shop while Arjun got busy checking stock. Over tea they chatted about wholesale rates. 'The market is depressed,' said Kewal Ram mournfully. Seeing that Arjun was a novice, Kewal Ram decided to take him under his wing, and lectured to him on the devious ways of the wholesalers. Meanwhile, two salesmen arrived from a thread-making company. Kewal Ram was an important wholesaler of theirs but not their stockist. They sat down and tea was again ordered. They too were new men. Shyly they opened their order books, and took an order. Soon they were ready to leave, but the tea had not yet arrived. They asked to be excused as they were in a hurry.

'Ah, but you *must* have tea,' insisted Kewal Ram.

'No, no, heh, heh, thank you, you are so kind.'

'No, you *must* have tea!'

'Well, if you insist. But we have to catch the noon train, and many shops still to cover.'

'Hey, what happened to the tea?' Kewal Ram roared at the tea stall, lifting his finger indignantly. 'Bring two glasses of your best special. And quickly.'

After waiting ten minutes, the salesmen got restless, and wanted to leave, but their host was insistent. Again he shouted across the street, admonishing the teashop with his finger. Another five minutes passed. The salesmen finally left, while the wholesaler continued to curse the teashop. As soon as they were gone, another cup of tea promptly arrived for Arjun.

Later that evening in the hotel, his room-mate threw light on the tea episode. 'Kewal Ram is both a stockist and a wholesaler. His policy is to serve tea only to the representatives of companies whose stockist he is. But he doesn't want to appear less hospitable to the others. Therefore, the lifted finger is an old, established signal between him and the teashop. If he orders tea with a lifted finger, it is understood that tea is not to be served. The old timers know his ways, but these thread people must have been new. Anyway everyone gets caught the first time.' Arjun wondered how Kewal Ram benefitted from his foolish penny-wise tea policy at the cost of losing the goodwill of his suppliers.

Despite the heat, the dust, and the occasional 'house full' hotel, Arjun enjoyed his field training, and meeting new people. Everyday he worked diligently from morning to evening and learned to outsmart wily traders. He grew accustomed to the narrow, congested streets, full of pedestrians, bicycles, handcarts, and garbage dumps. After visiting the local stockist each morning, Arjun would call upon the major retailers in the town, accompanied by a 'poster man' and a tricycle filled with the company's products. While he took orders, the tricycle driver delivered stock and collected cash, and the poster man plastered the shop with advertising. It was an efficient division of labour, even though the poster man sometimes put the posters upside down.

Lunch was always a leisurely meal since the bazaar closed for the afternoon. He couldn't get used to sleeping in the afternoon, and would read a book instead, sitting on his hotel bed under a fan. At night, if he didn't have to catch a train for the next town, he would walk down to a nearby cinema, check the advertising commercials of his company, and watch the latest Hindi melodrama. Occasionally he would be expected to hire and supervise schoolboys and girls who would sample and demonstrate his products either in the bazaar or at schools and other gatherings. These demonstrations were in accordance with the promotion plans laid down by the Advertising Department in the Bombay office. They were meant to supplement the meagre reach of mass media in the particular town. The stockist usually contributed half the cost of the promotion.

By and large his fieldwork went off uneventfully, except in a little trading centre called Katni, near Jabalpur, where he was bitten by a snake one night. He was carried off by the hotel staff, not to the local hospital, but to a Parsi cloth merchant.

'Stand!' shouted the Parsi, as Arjun wobbled before him.

While Arjun tried to stand erect, the grave merchant recited a mantra.

'Stamp your foot!' bellowed the Parsi.

Arjun obeyed, and again the Parsi repeated the mantra.

'Stamp your foot, twice!'

A minute later Arjun walked out of the merchant's shop without a limp, fully cured.

2

'Before I die I want to see my grandson and I want to see the sea'.
Bauji told Bhabo one day early in 1972. A few days later, his eyes
twinkling with excitement, he held up a set of keys and a pair of
train tickets. He said, 'There is a servant in Lala Surya Narain's
house but let's take ours as well.' Bhabo protested, 'Bauji, three
months ago you were on your deathbed, and now you are ready to
go to the other end of the world. The crow who goes travelling
comes home just as black.'

'I have already wired Arjun. Tell the servant to pack,' he said.
Bhabo knew when she had to give in.

'Why can't we stay with Arjun?' she asked. 'The boy has been
pleading with you for years.'

'He is a young man in the city. We don't want to be a burden to
him. Besides, Lalaji is going abroad with his family. The bungalow
will be empty and we shall have it to ourselves.

'And why has Lalaji become so generous all of a sudden?' asked
Bhabo.

Bauji parried the question at first, but he finally admitted, 'I
imagine he's grateful for my help with the court case last year.'

Bhabo was tempted to ask, 'And why are we accepting hospitality from someone whom you daily abuse as a "black marketeer", a
"tax evader"?' But she did not say anything.

Arjun was waiting at Bombay Central station to receive them.
He was at first disappointed that they were not to stay with him, but
when he saw the bungalow at Juhu beach he was reconciled. It
seemed to be a more sensible place for them to be, rather than being
stuck in his small flat all day long, and besides, it allowed Bauji to
be near the sea.

Arjun looked the figure of confidence and Bauji was proud to see
his grandson. In the past five years Arjun had done exceptionally
well at his job. As Billimoria had predicted, he had become the
Advertising Manager, not in two years, but in four. He was also

regarded as one of 'Billi's blue-eyed boys'. As a consequence of Arjun's rise, Choudhary had been pushed up to Sales Director, and still continued to be Arjun's immediate boss. Billi had once told Choudhary, 'If it were not for Arjun you wouldn't be a director today. Surround yourself with good people, I always say. They will push you up in the world, as long as you resist the temptation to interfere with them daily.' One of the reasons for Arjun's quick rise was the success of Bombay Pain Balm. He had worked indefatigably to get the product improved and to get the advertising copy right. He had tested and retested his idea with the consumer before he took it to the market place. His strategy had eventually paid off. People did begin to perceive the product as a good solution for headaches rather than a general, multi-purpose balm. With the new positioning the product gained credibility in the public mind, and sales shot up to the point that the company had to instal another production line at the plant. Because Arjun's promotion was based on visible performance, no one could accuse Billimoria of favouritism, although there was much envy among Arjun's peers. After he was promoted, Arjun was much in demand socially by the glamorous advertising agency crowd. He was constantly asked out for lunch or dinner. But he did not let his new-found social success go to his head, because he was aware that his sudden popularity was in proportion to the size of his advertising budget.

'Tea number one,' ordered Arjun when he met Bauji on the veranda of Bombay Gymkhana the next day. 'As long as anyone can remember, "tea number one" has always meant Darjeeling tea with overdone buttered toast.'

Bauji smiled and turned to look at the imposing Victorian edifices across Azad Maidan. 'Ah Bombay! It is truly a free city, Arjun, built with patience and hard work by men of trade.' After a pause he added, 'But it seems to me that the one great defect of your city is that it dwells too much in the present, and is not aware of the past. Look at those buildings there. They have been around for over a hundred years. But, my boy, they still have an alien quality.'

Arjun looked quizzically.

'Because the English were as alien to India at the end of their Raj as at the beginning.' As if he were talking to himself, he added almost in a whisper, 'Maybe they didn't want the races to mix.' After another pause, Bauji pointed to the Municipal Corporation. 'Look at it! I suppose you'd call it Gothic-Muslim or something. Whatever else it may be, it certainly is aloof.' There was another pause. 'Mind you, I admired the English for many things. But I never forgave them their remoteness. Rulers are expected to be proud and arrogant, Arjun; they can even be cruel and oppressive; but to be so cold and unfriendly, that is hard.'

'Detached, objective, and fair,' said Arjun. 'This is what the British Raj prided itself on. Wouldn't you rather have that from a ruler, Bauji, than friendship and injustice?'

'But why do I feel more comfortable when I visit Delhi? There too I am surrounded by monuments left by foreign rulers. Muslims also came as conquerors, but they assimilated into India. What they left behind—whether it is Urdu, or the Qutub Minar—it is a synthesis of ours and theirs. They don't feel alien like these buildings.'

There was another pause, while Arjun thought about the choice between British fairness and Muslim empathy.

'Enough!' said Bauji abruptly. 'I want above all to know what you are like, your views and your beliefs, what you have become and what life has taught you.'

'And all in one sentence!' said Arjun with a laugh.

As Bauji listened to Arjun talk easily about his work and his life, he had the ressuring vision of someone who would proudly carry on his line. Arjun seemed to have both intelligence and ambition in abundance. He had fresh confidence, an assured manner, and a good instinct about people, Bauji thought. He would do well and bring honour to himself. As the guru had predicted at his birth, Arjun had grown up into a fearless young man, like his namesake in the *Mahabharata*. Bauji noticed that his cheeks were flushed when he became excited. His wide eyes, still boyishly earnest, were framed by long lashes and sharply defined brows. Success at thirty was a delightful thing, felt Bauji—you meet the great, you are attractive to beautiful women, you enjoy life.

Bauji himself belonged to the first generation in his family to acquire a Western education in the early years of this century, and he had become a lawyer. At that time the law was almost the only profession open to young Indians. He had married off his daughter, Tara, to Seva Ram, who had been part of the second generation, which had gone in for technical training. Seva Ram had become an engineer, because the British had realized that roads, canals, bridges and railways had to be built in order to rule and exploit the country. Now here was Arjun, who represented the third generation, which aspired to managing private enterprise in a scientific manner in a free country. It was new and it was good. Despite the changing occupations of the three generations, Bauji could feel a continuity. Despite great social changes that had taken place during his lifetime, he could still detect the unbroken and enduring thread that linked one generation to the next.

Before returning home, Arjun took Bauji to see an exhibition of paintings at the Jehangir Art Gallery. Quite unexpectedly Bauji liked a 'modern painting', showing three female figures in green and blue colours. Upto now he had only seen unveiled imitations of Western paintings or crude copies of the Ajanta frescoes. This was something quite new, with sharp, bright colours and a feeling of animality, which was akin to his own sensual temperament. Looking at it, he felt the old feeling of ecstasy returning. He decided, on the spur of the moment, to buy it, even though it was more than he could afford.

When they reached home Juhu was dark. Bhabo was worried and upset because they were late. She also thought the painting too expensive. At dinner Bhabo did not touch anything. She began to cry and then the truth came out. She had eaten lunch cooked by Lalaji's servant, who she later discovered was of the 'untouchable' caste. She had immediately vomited, and had taken a bath. On her face Arjun saw deep disgust, an almost physical revulsion. She had felt soiled by the contact with the casteless man. On hearing this Bauji became embarrassed. He shouted at her. 'I am ashamed of you, woman! How can we call ourselves a democracy when we have this going on.'

After dinner Bauji wanted to get away from the house and he suggested a walk on the beach to Arjun. 'Be careful,' said Bhabo as they went out. Bauji took a deep breath and inhaled the sharp breeze of the Arabian sea. The darkness and the silence were broken by the uneven lapping of the white waves on the deserted sand.

'So strong is the pride in one's caste, it is easily wounded,' said Bauji. They walked on silently. Arjun recalled that Bhabo had once told him that in her village when she was young even an untouchable's shadow was not permitted to fall on a brahmin. Their casteless sweeper used to creep stealthily into the brahmin's house from the back, clean the toilets and sneak away. If by chance he saw a brahmin on the road he had to hide till the brahmin had passed.

3

'Arjun!'

Arjun stopped and looked behind him. Priti was sitting in a cane sofa in the Bombay Gymkhana, her hands folded in her lap. She was facing the green playing field and the Victorian buildings on the horizon. He had passed by without noticing her.

'I had heard you were living here,' she said.

'And what are *you* doing in Bombay?' he asked.

She opened her empty hands in her lap in a futile gesture, and looked up slowly. 'Nothing—hoping perhaps to find a job here; hoping to escape from myself.'

'Escape? Can one ever escape?' His lips curled into a smile, and he looked at her with a playful expression.

'You've changed,' she said.

'Doesn't everyone?'

'Most people don't,' she said, and she tilted her head in her characteristic way. 'They stop in their twenties and stay the same all their life.'

She was still a good-looking woman, he thought.

'Stay awhile, if you are not pressed,' she said, looking intently at him.

He sat down beside her.

'What will you have?' He rang the shiny brass bell and a bearer appeared.

'What does one have in this remnant of the British Raj?' she asked.

'Fresh lime soda?'

'Of course,' she said.

'Chutney sandwiches?'

'No, I'm not hungry.'

He signed for two fresh lime sodas.

'What are you doing at the Gym?' he asked.

'I am waiting for Neena. She is playing tennis. I always seem to be waiting these days.'

Priti wore a plain, handloomed cotton sari with a quiet pattern, which enhanced her profile. Her sleeveless blouse drew attention to her handsome neck and finely framed shoulders. In the late afternoon sun of Bombay, her 'cotton look' appeared graceful and made her stand apart from the other women in the club, who mainly wore saris of synthetic materials. Her long hair was brushed back into a bun. Her body, although still small, was now more rounded—just like her personality, which appeared to be friendlier and mellow in comparison to ten years ago. She seemed frank and almost humble in the way she spoke.

The bearer returned with two bottles of soda, a bucket of ice, a jug of sugar syrup, a container of salt, and two glasses containing fresh lime juice. Priti added sugar and salt to her drink. Arjun drank his more austerely, without ice, salt, or sugar.

As he took a sip, Arjun's mind went racing back ten years to that evening in Simla when she had asked him to kiss her. He could not believe that this weary, serious-looking woman was the same one who had caused him such agony. The memory of her framed in the doorway of her house in Simla came back to him: he saw her in the rain in a pink raincoat and hat and black rubber boots, her face wet, waiting for him with a distant, wistful look on her face.

Now here she was ten years later, and Arjun wished that he could reciprocate her confidence and give her some token of acceptance. But he felt there was little in his flat, intensely work-filled life that was worth talking about. He spoke, instead, of Bombay, lightly and amusingly. But he was not very good at small talk, and the conversation faltered.

He pointed out in the distance the splendid Municipal Corporation, with its extravagant domes and minarets. Nearby was St. Xavier's College. Behind it, he told her, was the J.J. School of Art, where Rudyard Kipling was born, a hundred years ago when his father ran the school. 'Victorian Bombay at its exuberant best!' he exclaimed. 'And if you go back another hundred years all you had here were coconut and palm trees swaying to the breeze of the Arabian sea.'

'So you like this city?' she asked.

'Yes. It's fine place where a lot goes on, and there are chances for all. I can put up with the overcrowding and the dirt for the sake of being a part of it. I love the energy and you can almost smell the money in the bazaars.'

'You have changed, Arjun. You are wiser in the ways of the

world. Not at all the frightened boy who used to come to our house in Simla. Tougher, too.'

'You're gentler,' he said.

'And more patient,' she added.

And sadder, he thought.

'I don't think I am as good as I was ten years ago,' Arjun said.

'Women don't usually like men for their goodness.'

'But once they do like one, they believe only him to be good.'

'You are not really bad, are you?' She looked up with a smile. Her dark eyes sparkled as they once used to. They both laughed. They talked thus lightly and easily. She must be close to thirty, he thought—the eleven months difference in their ages which seemed terribly important then, had ceased to matter. Her tilted head, which he had once thought was not quite connected to her body, seemed now very much a part of her.

In the intervening years he had heard that the Mehta fortune had collapsed because of mismanagement, and the family had become bankrupt. Their grand house in Simla had been sold. He had also learned that Priti and Karan had broken up after a few years. She spoke lightly about some of these things, but he could tell that she had suffered. Occasionally there was discouragement on her face, but it also gave it a new character which he found attractive in its way.

He stayed listening to her for a long time. They had another round of fresh lime. In the breezy late afternoon they watched the buildings in the distance suffused with a yellow glow from the setting sun. She watched his eyes as he looked out to the green stretch before them, not consciously seeing it, absorbed in his own thoughts. Long strips of mellow light fell on the playing fields and among the rows of commuters as they crossed along the narrow track beyond the green field to catch the Western Railway line from Churchgate or the Central Railway line from Victoria Terminus. The rich, long shadows touched the great buildings in the back.

'Will you have dinner with me?' he asked.

'I've promised to go to Neena's house.'

'Then what about tomorrow?'

'Why don't you come to Neena's?' she asked.

'I don't think she likes me,' he said with an innocent smile. She laughed.

'You are amused?'

'No, your smile.'

'What of it?'

'It fills your whole face, Arjun. You've got it from your father, haven't you? My mother used to talk about his smile.'

Neena arrived with Rao Sahib and Arjun got up. Rao Sahib shook his hands warmly and invited them for a drink in the bar. Seeing Rao Sahib after a decade, Arjun had a strange feeling of going backwards in time. His clothes, his manners, his bearing had not changed, and Arjun could have sworn that the frayed blazer and the faded ascot were the same ones he used to wear in Simla.

'Oh, I say! How he's grown!' said Rao Sahib as he sat down at the bar.

'How have you been, sir?' said Arjun.

'Yes, I hear you've done very well. Good!'

'Oh Neena, there you are!' came a voice from the crowd. It was Dumpy, a young and rotund executive with a British soap company. He was distantly related to the Jaipur family, had gone to Doon School, but had got into the firm on his own merits. He came up to her. 'Hello Dumpy,' said Neena. 'Meet Priti. She is staying with us. And you know Arjun.'

Dumpy nodded to Arjun, and immediately turned to Priti. 'I say where have you been hiding all this time?'

'Well, I've just arrived in Bombay.' said Priti.

'How is the soap business, Dumpy?' said Rao Sahib.

'People are still bathing,' said Dumpy with a boisterous laugh, which had an aristocratic public school ring to it.

'I thought with the recent price control on soaps, you chaps would be in the dumps.'

'Yes, I know "Dumpy in the dumps".'

'Ho, ho, ho,' roared Rao Sahib.

As Dumpy turned to talk to Priti, Rao Sahib said to Arjun, 'Be a good chap, will you? Do you think you could fix up Flukey? My nephew, you see. I dare say it's time he settled down.'

Looking at this anachronism, Arjun wondered if this was the same man who had appeared such an exalted human being ten years ago in Simla. How could he begin to explain to Rao Sahib that a whole generation of MBAs had entered industry since he had retired, and you didn't 'fix up' nephews in management jobs over polite drinks at the club any more? People like Rao Sahib were the only true 'English' left in the world, Arjun realized. The species had vanished in England, and the only surviving specimen were to be found in the old clubs of India.

As he settled down over a second peg of Scotch whisky, Rao Sahib began to speak of his connections with Cambridge in his exaggerated upper middle class accent. He quoted from Shakespeare and Coleridge, and he spoke wistfully of the Court Circular in *The Times* of London. He was proud that he was more familiar with the geography of London than of Bombay. But the twenty-five years since the end of the Empire had robbed him of much of his plumage and left him a somewhat ragged figure of fun. Even the once imperial Bombay Gym had changed. The Gym today was vibrant and humming with confident young Indian managers, who had been educated at the institutes of technology and management and were refreshingly free of the baggage of the old Raj. Having retired from his job in a British company, Rao Sahib was only comfortable with old school types like Dumpy, who were becoming increasingly rare. While he tenaciously clung to the attitudes of Kipling's India, and carried on with his mock English country squire's life, new classes and new powers were emerging daily. There were elected legislators, entrepreneurs, and farmers who had prospered with the 'green revolution'—about all of whom he was quite oblivious.

A week later on Saturday afternoon, an artist friend took Arjun to the Jehangir Art Gallery to see an exhibition of Amrita Sher Gil, the extraordinary painter of Punjabi-Hungarian parentage. He was absorbed in a painting of three women, when his artist friend tapped him on the shoulder and said, 'Come quickly before she changes her pose.' They went past the crowd rapidly and arrived in time to see Priti leaning against a wall, looking dreamily at a painting called *Woman Resting on Charpoy.*

'There, isn't she a sight!' said his friend. 'Look at the way the melancholy head reclines on the shoulder. And the flame red sari against the white wall! I'd like to paint her just as she is. And those dark eyes!'

'For God's sake, I know her. Don't stare like that, she will see us.' said Arjun.

She did see them. But instead of being angry, Priti gave Arjun a smile which was full of innocent goodwill, unmixed with vanity. Seeing him seemed to shake her out of her self-absorbed discontent. Her face looked more open and youthful than before.

Arjun flushed and shyly introduced his artist friend. She smiled at the artist and naively asked both of them to explain the painting to her.

'I am ignorant about painting. I feel stupid when everyone is admiring something, and I don't know why.'

To the artist this was a perfect opening and he launched on a rapid exposition on colours, forms, moods, as they walked from picture to picture. Arjun and Priti listened quietly. The artist was extremely articulate and well-informed and Arjun felt a shade jealous.

'She was one of our first painters, who responded directly and non-intellectually to visual impressions around her,' he said. 'Don't take "intellectual response" as a term of blame or approval. It's just a habit of the mind; some people have it more than others, and good or bad use can be made of it. Anyway, that is why you see groups of women sitting and talking, hill people standing. As a sophisticated city person, she could use the material of folk art without making it cheap or diluting its power, and also say things about the present moment.'

'What about your own work?' Priti asked.

'Me? Whose opinion do you want? Let's see, the papers and the professors call me Western, rootless, alienated, confused, imitative and sterile. I am told to choose between Eastern and Western art. They deny my right to be modern, because they think that to be Indian is to be traditional or folkloric. They question my right to paint, to comment on the present. And they hit below the belt saying "When people are starving, what are you doing with a brush?"' The artist was not finished; in fact he was just warming up to his favourite subject when he was suddenly called away by one of his admirers and Arjun was relieved to be left alone with Priti.

'He explains things wonderfully, but I wish I could feel the beauty of the pictures directly,' said Priti.

They decided to have tea at the Samovar, a smart bohemian cafe in the garden behind the art gallery. There wasn't any awkward shyness between them and they both felt that the meeting was natural.

'There is such a lot of talk about art,' she began. 'I don't think it matters all that much, really, does it? Isn't it more important to live? I should like my life to be a work of art.'

Arjun looked at her questioningly.

'I mean I should like to make my life beautiful. Art seems to lie outside of life. I know that I am inside life, or life is inside me. And I should like to make what is alive beautiful.'

'And how would you do that?'

'I shall tell you some day,' she said with a smile.

They started to talk about the people they had known. He discovered that she was not interested in people in the way most people were—about what they were doing or where they were living or the gossip about their lives. She was seeking to find some kind of truth about them. She was searching in each life for some general principle which she could apply to her own life. She spoke rapidly, almost feverishly, as though she had been starved for someone to talk to. As she talked, Arjun got the feeling that she knew all there was to know about men. After she had finished speaking, she shook her head slightly and a faint blush spread over her face.

Priti told him about many people, but she did not speak of Karan. Neither did Arjun press her. She spoke fondly of Simla and her childhood as though she were turning the pages of a nursery book. They spoke of Amrita, of Rao Sahib and her friends at the ADC, and they recalled sunny picnics amidst the rhododendrons. There was a haunting unhappiness about her which spoke straight to his heart.

Before long it became dark outside, and the waiters were relieved when they got up to leave. Arjun suggested a walk along Marine Drive. They took a cab to Churchgate. Through the glass doors of the Ambassador Hotel they could see Arabs lounging in the lobby, looking fat and bored. At the hotel entrance the handsome Sikh doorman in livery had the air of a ceremonial guard. He looked straight ahead without moving his eyes, contemptuously ignoring passing pedestrians, his attention single-mindedly focused on the black limousines which pulled up one after another at the door. From Kamling, the Chinese restaurant next door, they heard loud laughter. A bright streetlamp shone through the trees in front. A red double-decker bus stopped momentarily to let off a passenger. More laughter was heard from the open windows of Kamling. In a dead-end lane between Kamling and the Ambassador, Chinese cooks in short pants were sitting on stools, cutting vegetables in the open air. A paanwala under the peepal tree smiled at them, his red betel-stained teeth glistening in the night.

As they turned onto Marine Drive, they were welcomed by a gust of salty air from the bay. The sea was dark and several fishing boats could be seen, lit with hurricane lanterns and rocking gently in the water. Against the western night sky were spread the brightly lighted flats of the rich on Malabar Hill. As they walked along Marine Drive, the sea seemed to grow more sombre and the little date palms on either side cast scrawny shadows. The black and yellow taxis rushed noisily.

Having talked all evening, Priti and Arjun were content to walk quietly and look at the city. They decided eventually to sit on the smooth cement sea wall. They stared beyond the sea at the dimly lit stars which hung in the cloudless night. The water was smooth and dark. It hardly made a sound against the sea wall. A white-haired man holding the hand of a young girl passed by. Two slim boys, arm in arm, followed them, speaking loudly in Marathi.

Priti leaned against his shoulder but continued to look away. Her hair blew across his eyes. Through her hair he looked again at the bright string of boats swaying rhythmically on the water. She sat still leaning gently against him, her face now pressed against his cheek. He gathered her into his arms.

'Bauji, Priti is here in Bombay.'

'Priti?' asked Bauji absently. His mind went back to the rail car journey from Kalka to Simla ten years ago. He could picture the cool, piercing beauty who had exerted a strange, unreal power in the mirror-window.

'Sanat Mehta's grand-daughter, Bauji,' said Bhabo.

'I met her a few weeks ago.'

'What is she doing here?' asked Bhabo.

'Looking for a job, I think.'

'Who would have thought it would come to this—their mills closed, their property sold. And this poor girl's mother now lives in a single room in old Delhi. They say this girl and Karan broke up after a few years and. . .'

'Stop woman!' interrupted Bauji. He looked apologetically at Arjun.

'It's all right, Bauji. After all, it was ten years ago,' said Arjun.

'I knew their accountant was a rascal,' said Bauji.

'I'll bring her to Juhu to meet you,' Arjun said.

Bauji raised his eyebrows.

'Yes, I've met her several times.'

'You be careful boy!' said Bhabo. Bauji too felt apprehensive at the idea of Priti's reappearance in his grandson's life.

Next Sunday, Arjun asked Priti out to Juhu. After a nervous meeting with his grandparents, they went out on the beach. Fortunately it was cloudy, and in every way a perfect day to be outdoors. Barefoot they paced along the beach close to the water. Priti had hitched up her sari in the manner of Koli fisherwomen. The sand was smooth and hard and it made walking easy. It was early and there were few people out except for coconut sellers, who had nowhere else to go. The beach was strewn with ordinary white shells and round thin ones which looked like wafers. The waves beat rhythmically beside them and the salt wind blew into their faces. They walked in the breezy calm, and each faint sound near or far seemed filled with meaning. Priti soon felt pleasantly giddy from the salty air.

The beach ended at a creek. They crossed it with care and spotted a large, shady banyan tree behind a white stone wall. They went and sat in the shade, resting their backs against the wall. The clouds had cleared, the sun beat strongly against the sand and the water, and the shade was welcome. They looked at the sea without speaking. A pair of shrieking seagulls flew past. In the distance they saw the white sails of a fishing boat. The waves formed a white wall of foam on the blue water. The sound of the waves mingled with the murmuring of the banyan leaves and the smell of the salt air had a powerful effect on them. After continuously thrumming in their ears, the breeze suddenly died, and they looked at each other pensively.

'Will you be going away soon?' asked Arjun.

'No, why?' she said absently.

'Nothing. I didn't know how long you were staying,' he said.

He scooped up a fistful of sand from between his feet and watched it trickling out of his fingers. She appeared lost in her own thoughts.

'Look, I have come here for a job. Nobody seems to believe me. Or they don't think I'll find one,' she said cheerlessly. She looked deeply unhappy. She described a series of unsuccessful attempts so far. She had spoken to his heart, and he gently took her hand.

'How can I give up? I must find a job.' She sounded determined but her tone was forlorn and unsure.

Arjun hailed a coconut boy. They bought two green coconuts, which the boy cut open with a sharp sickle, and they drank the juice directly from the shells. Next he scooped out the 'cream' from inside the shells. Priti had never tasted green coconut before. She discovered that she liked it.

Moving closer to Arjun and speaking in a low voice, Priti began to talk about the past. As he listened, Arjun watched three boys a long way off at the sea's edge, picking up shells. He gently leaned against her, and began to idly comb the sand. Her eyes were lowered, and her long lashes quivered as she continued to talk.

'You were such a mocking, spoilt thing, don't you remember?' he said.

'Was I?' she said with surprise.

'Making fun of everyone. Thinking everything frightfully silly. Enjoying seeing people at your feet. . . .' He suddenly stopped. Her lips trembled as she turned towards him. He saw her distressed look. She said softly, 'Arjun, you were wrong to think of me so. I was equally vulnerable. I was at someone else's feet.' This was the closest reference she had made about Karan. She smiled sadly and ran her fingers through his hair.

'You know, I'm beginning to like your city,' she said.

They returned to the house for lunch. Afterwards they sat lazily with Bauji. Pointing to a seagull flying past, Bauji remarked, 'He is much older than us, and in nature's eyes he is a much bigger success.'

Arjun looked up enquiringly.

'Long before man came and began to feel superior to other animals, the seagull was set in his ways, and he has never varied them. Unlike us, Arjun, he allows nature to be his guide, and he doesn't do anything against the interest of his species. So he endures, and that is a big thing. In our pride we have forgotten that there is a virtue in mere survival. If we let nature have her way, she will reward us with peace and security.'

'But Bauji,' said Arjun, 'It is precisely the questions we ask about our existence, and the demands we make which make life worth living.'

'I am weary, my boy, of human instability and discontent and violence. Couldn't we at least learn some social virtue from these creatures? Learn to live selflessly and together for the sake of our fellow man.'

'Bauji, would you really exchange your life for that of this seagull?' asked Priti.

'Alas, that is not a choice open to me. No, Priti. Much as I admire the seagull's social virtues, I also realize that what makes me cling to life is the same quality that makes me want to protest, and which makes the regularity and peace of the seagull's life impossible for me. Yet, the seagull over there is wonderful because he doesn't ask what he gets out of life, or why he should make a sacrifice. He prepares his nest and his young are born. He nourishes them, defends them, and teaches them, and when the time comes he dies quietly. The important thing is not self-fulfillment but that life should go on.'

Bauji turned to look at the sea. The sun was still high. Even though they sat in the shade, it felt hot. They watched the seagull without speaking. The waves beat quietly in the low tide. The humid air was calm. They could almost hear their thoughts in the restful silence. In the quiet Arjun looked at Priti's face, and wondered if his chief function was merely to see that life should carry on after he had lived his busy and futile life. He did not feel comfortable at having to accept this fate. It amused him to think that man is also the only animal whose existence is a problem which he has to solve.

4

The black and yellow taxi went up Malabar Hill, rounded Teen Batti, and climbed onto Ridge Road. They passed the gulmohar trees and a bus standing near the WIAA Club, and turned towards Little Gibbs Road. Arjun and Priti were sitting apart, but they were thrown close together as the taxi turned sharply. The street was dug up and some workmen were pushing a drainage pipe into the ditch. Priti's pale face glimmered under the street light. In the semi-darkness Arjun noticed the long line of her neck, but her features appeared less sharp. He couldn't make out the expression on her face.

'I don't want to go to the party, Arjun. Let's go somewhere else,' Priti said, abruptly.

He asked the taxi to turn towards Hanging Gardens. Her bun had come undone and her black hair was flying in the breeze. They stopped at Cafe Naaz. They sat like strangers in the cafe and looked down from the top of the hill as the Queen's Necklace lit the curves of Marine Drive below and beyond towards Nariman Point. From above they saw lights being switched on in different parts of the city and the clear night sky was slowly filled with faint stars. A thrilling flush of wind from the Arabian sea grazed their bodies.

'Shall I ask you something?' she asked.

'Yes, of course.'

'Kiss me.'

'Here?'

She nodded her head.

'Before everyone—waiters and all?'

She nodded.

'It isn't done, not even in Bombay.'

'Do it. Please.'

He quickly leaned over and kissed her on the cheek, and looked around and reddened. She laughed.

'Why do you laugh?'

'That wasn't a kiss,' she said.

Both of them were quiet for some time, absorbed in their own thoughts, as they watched the lights and the water, and smelled the aroma of the gardens below.

'It is lovely here. Such beautiful stillness, the sea alive yet so quiet,' she said. 'But it's chilly here and I want a proper drink. Let's go somewhere else.'

They decided on the Bombay Gym bar. She sat erectly in the cab, and he put his arm against the back rest on her side, just behind her. As they started she leaned back and her body touched his arm. Coming down towards Kemps Corner, it was dark again and she kissed him. Their lips met momentarily. But she quickly turned away and pressed her face against the window.

'No, no,' she said.

'What is it?' he asked.

'I can't bear it.'

'Oh, Priti!'

'I cannot.'

'Don't you like me?'

'I don't know.'

They were quiet for a while. The taxi cruised on Marine Drive, and turned on the flyover into Princess Street.

'I feel happy when I'm with you,' he said.

'What do you mean?'

'Happy. It's a nice feeling.'

'Nice? No, it is not.'

'Don't you like it?'

'No. I hate myself.'

'Still, it's good to be with you.'

'Is it?'

The taxi stopped at the red light near Metro Cinema, and she noticed for the first time pictures of holy men hanging on the dashboard of the cab. There was Christ, Guru Nanak of the Sikhs, Lord Krishna, Zarathustra of the Parsis, and even a plaque with an inscription from the Koran.

'You protect yourself well,' Priti said to the taxi driver, with an unnatural laugh. 'What are you?'

The cab driver remained silent.

'You have covered all the possibilities, eh, driver?' she insisted.

He looked back at her but he did not say a word. Soon they arrived at the Gym. When Arjun was paying the fare, the cab driver said matter-of-factly to Priti, 'There is only one God, and He is the same in all religions. Now you tell me what I am?'

'Bravo!' she clapped her hands. 'A secular Indian at last.'

They found many friends at the Gym bar. It was noisy and boisterous. Some rugby types were singing by the piano.

'I want a drink,' Priti said.

'Oh Priti, there you are!' came a voice from the crowd. It was Dumpy. He pushed up to her.

'Ah Dumpy,' she said.

'Priti, I want you to meet someone famous, the Nawab of Ronepur. Come.' An elegantly dressed man in his thirties materialized from nowhere.

'Hazur, let me introduce a dear friend, Priti Mehta.'

'You're the tennis star, aren't you?' Priti said.

'Was,' said the Nawab. 'How long have you been here?'

'A few minutes.'

'I mean Bombay,'

'A few days.'

'And how do you like our city?' asked the Nawab.

'Don't say "our city" in that patronizing way, as if it was Rampur or Rajpur or wherever you are the Nawab of,' she said.

'Well, I have lived in Bombay most of my life and I feel I belong to it,' said the Nawab.

'Well I have lived here a few days and I feel I belong to it too,' she said.

'That's what's wonderful,' roared Dumpy. 'It is everyone's city.'

The Nawab nodded to Arjun, but clearly he was more interested in Priti. Arjun and the Nawab were passing acquaintances and in fact Arjun had once been to his flat to attend one of his famous parties. The Nawab was a slender man with a deep waist like a woman's and long, arched, beautiful hands. His handkerchief, with which he was always wiping his forehead, smelled of expensive eau de cologne. His main interest in life was women, and he spoke about them from rich experience. The succession of female visitors to his flat was known to be endless, and rarely did one see him with the same face twice. He had a sleepy look, which Arjun supposed women found attractive.

Arjun stood for nearly half-an-hour by the bar observing the Nawab, Dumpy and Priti slowly getting drunk. At one point Arjun caught a glimpse of Priti, her head bowed as she stared into her glass. The Nawab tried to get her attention, and spilled his whisky on her sari; while attempting to repair the damage, he accidentally touched her breasts. No word was spoken. But Arjun, feeling left out, decided to go home.

'Goodnight, Priti,'

'Must you go?'

'Shall I see you?'

'When?'

'Call me.'

Arjun left the bar. As he was walking out of the veranda, someone waved from afar. He could not make out who, but he raised his hand perfunctorily. He wanted to get home. He came out by the Mahatma Gandhi Road entrance and walked towards the Fountain. Normally the busiest part of the city, it was now deserted. Pundole art-gallery-cum-watch-shop had its shutters down. The boys inside Pyrkes Cafe were stacking chairs on the marble tables. The row of shops opposite the University were also closed. At Kala Ghoda he got a taxi and went to his flat in Colaba.

Tucked underneath his door were some letters. One was a bill from his tailor, near the Fountain. He looked at it, without reading it, and after a while put it away. He had already paid for the two khaki trousers, one of which had been stitched badly. The other letter was from his company salesman in Orissa, whose son was getting married. He hardly knew the man; why did a man want to tell the whole world that his son was getting married?

He picked up the morning paper, turned to the sports page and read about a local tennis tournament. It reminded him of the Nawab, and he felt angry. He put away the paper.

He undressed slowly. He opened the dresser and indifferently pulled out the first pair of pajamas he could find and changed. His bed was between two windows. He opened both of them. He switched on the ceiling fan and tried to sleep.

But he could not sleep. A bus went by. His mind would not rest. He was back in Simla. Again it was the scene of the rainy day, with Priti standing in the doorway, with the pink raincoat and black rubber shoes, gazing into the distance.

His mind jumped from one thing to another. But his thoughts kept returning to Priti. He could not think clearly. It was all quite confused. He felt miserable. Another bus went by—this one was a double-decker, he could tell from the sound. Until Priti came back into his life he had not realized that he was lonely.

Two days later Priti dropped in at Arjun's office. She walked right in, unannounced.

'Nice office you have, but it's a bit cramped isn't it?' she said. 'You aren't *really* busy, are you?'

'What do you think?'

'You are.'

'What have you been doing?' he asked.

'I had to see you.'

'Why?'

'Oh just like that.'

'What's happening?'

'I was with the Nawab and his tennis pals again last night. But I got tired.'

'The Nawab is certainly one of the most distinguished men of our city.'

'He wanted to sleep with me.'

There was a pause.

'And?'

'I said "no".'

'Why?'

'He smelled terribly.'

Arjun stared at her. She laughed.

'I told him that I was in love with you. Poor fellow. It hurt him. But he was nice about it. Don't stare at me like that. He has invited both of us for dinner at his house tonight.'

'Do you want to go?'

'Yes. Will you come?'

'If you want me to.'

'I'd better be going now.'

'Why?'

'I just wanted to see you.'

'Have lunch with me?'

'I can't. I promised Neena.'

'Wait. I'll see you down.'

They walked down the airless stairway. He hailed a cab outside Handloom House. She kissed him on the cheek and left. He suddenly felt embarrassed. He turned around to see if anyone was looking. Did she do it to shock him, he wondered. Whatever the reason, he liked it. All afternoon, the feel of her kiss lingered. He was swept by the feeling that maybe she did really care. About four o'clock he felt so happy that he decided to go for a walk to the Oval Maidan. The sky seemed bluer than usual, the weather unusually fine and everything shone brightly. It took his mind off his work as well. He had been feeling low because he had failed to persuade Billimoria and the others that morning to introduce a companion version of Bombay Balm, positioned for colds and coughs. He had told them that it would contain menthol and eucalyptus, which were useful in relieving nasal congestion. Basically it would be a milder version of the pain balm. He said that it would be particularly good for rubbing on children with colds, especially at night time to allow them to sleep.

'I can even picture the advertising commercial,' Arjun had said excitedly. 'Little Raju comes home sniffing and wet with a cold which he has caught while playing in the rain with his friends. At bedtime his mother lovingly rubs Bombay Colds Balm on his nose, throat, chest and back. While Raju sleeps, the vapours of the balm work all night to open his clogged nose and relieve his cough. He wakes up the next morning, his cold gone, and he runs off to school.'

'I don't know if people want another rub,' said Billimoria to the Sales Director. 'What do you think, Choudhary?'

'I'm not sure if dealers will stock a second Bombay Balm. We already have a problem in this recession of getting enough shelf space for one.'

'Look here, it's a simple idea,' Arjun had argued. 'In the beginning we used to sell Bombay Balm for all kinds of ailments from headaches to colds to insect bites. We reformulated it, positioned it strictly for headaches and bodyaches, and called it Bombay Pain Balm. And we were successful. We have since learned by talking to consumers that the pain balm is used mainly by older people, because it is too strong for kids. Mothers have also told us that they would welcome a safe rub for their childrens' colds in place of the pills which they take. Thus, all I am suggesting is that we further segment the market: Bombay Pain Balm for adults' headaches and bodyaches, and Bombay Colds Balm for childrens' coughs and colds.'

Billimoria had turned to the Finance Director who raised his eyebrows at the high advertising budget which Arjun had proposed, and made some noises about the company's poor cash flow and the long payout of the project.

Finally Billimoria had turned to Arjun and had said, 'Look here, I don't want to er. . . kill the project. Why don't you go back and check the numbers to see if you can introduce it with lower advertising and give us a quicker payback; and check with the trade if they would be willing to handle another version of our balm.'

'Why don't we at least test it?' Arjun had pleaded. 'We could try it out in a small town with real people and real dealers instead of making judgements in an airconditioned conference room.'

Billimoria had quietly stood up, and had walked out.

Arjun and Priti thought they were late, but in fact they arrived early at the Nawab's house. Dinner was rarely served before midnight, and often as late as two. The Nawab lived at the top of a smart building off Carmichael Road on Cumballa Hill. They were led to the main drawing room which was immensely tall with a round glass dome. The extravagant apartment was an odd mixture of styles, with many galleries and high rooms closed in by arches and verandas. It had been built at great cost, but for many months of the year it remained empty, except for the ancestral servants, because the Nawab was away either in Europe or in Bangalore.

The Nawab's enormous fortune was legendary in the city. Even though Mrs Gandhi had recently abolished the princes' privy purses, people said that his family could live in luxury for another five generations. He did not care for money, except to spend it. Being so wealthy, he actually disliked it, and never carried it on his person. His credit was good everywhere in the city and his debts were scrupulously honoured by the family clerk. Yet despite his condescending attitude to money, he had an uncanny ability to make it. Although he appeared indifferent to commercial matters, not a single detail of his family's investments or businesses escaped him. He spent no more than an hour a day on business, and usually confined himself to a single major issue. But when the transaction was completed, it sent waves through the entire financial district. He never dealt directly with the broker in the commodity or the stock markets, or with a buyer or seller, or even a banker. He operated through front men, who themselves did not know on whose behalf they were acting; only the ubiquitous clerk knew. For this reason no one could tell what the Nawab owned or when he had entered the market.

The Nawab sat cross-legged on a richly embroidered matress in one corner. Dressed in a silk kurta, he was smoking and listening to a vocal raga from an expensive sound system. Countless Bukhara rugs lay sprinkled across the floor. Several guests sat beside him leaning against silk bolsters. The guests appeared to Arjun to be provincial, unctuous and dreary people. Although the setting was pretentious, the Nawab himself was a man of considerable education, who genuinely loved music and theatre and even Western opera. He had many cultivated friends in all parts of the world.

Arjun and Priti were particularly struck by a fair, young woman, who was serving betel to the Nawab's guests. She couldn't have been more than thirty and certainly did not look fully Indian, although she could have been Kashmiri with her light eyes and broad cheekbones.

'Hello, I am Sakina, Nawab Sahib's wife,' she said coming up to them. She was graceful and spontaneous. She took them to the balcony, from where they got a full view of the sea. The water was dark below and there was a small sliver of a moon above.

'You must be the Nawab Sahib's latest find,' said Sakina to Priti. 'He is terribly fond of women, you know.' She laughed showing off her youth and high spirits, not to mention her brilliant teeth. 'His only other abiding interest is Indian classical music, especially vocal music.'

'He certainly must feel like a monarch up here,' said Arjun looking at the magnificent scene.

Soon they returned to the drawing room, and Priti went and sat beside the Nawab.

'Where is Dumpy? And the tennis players?' she asked.

'They are such bores, my dear. They can't stand my music and almost never visit me at home,' said the Nawab.

The Nawab was an excellent story-teller and he entertained Priti and his guests with witty anecdotes and Urdu couplets. His guests applauded him even though they did not always understand some of the Persian phrases. Apart from Priti and Sakina only two other women were present. Both were fat and middle aged, with rolls of midriff bulging out of their georgette saris. They looked stony-faced, except for occasional furtive glances around.

Around midnight Dumpy and a half-dozen merry-makers strolled in. They had been drinking since the evening and were in high spirits. They were mostly school friends of the Nawab, and they all worked as managers of foreign companies.

'I say Hazur,' said Dumpy to the Nawab, 'Isn't it absolutely feudal that Rekha here has to be approved by Arun's boss in ICL before they can get married. I mean we live in 1972 after all. I know it was done in the '40s by Shell and the others. But no one should allow it today.'

'Rekha, is that why you are here in Bombay?' asked the Nawab.

'Yes,' giggled Rekha.

'To be approved?'

'Yes,' she giggled again.

'Well?' roared Dumpy.

'Well what?' whispered the Nawab.

'Do you approve?' said Dumpy.

'Of course I approve of Rekha,' said the Nawab and he gave Rekha a bewitching smile.

'No I mean the idea of. . . .'

'I don't like your choice of words, Dumpy. "Feudal". After all, you do belong to the Jaipur clan, albeit distantly, and they are as feudal as they come.'

Eventually dinner was ready. Priti watched as a never-ending stream of elaborately cooked dishes was brought into the dining room, followed by brightly lit candles in coloured glass chimneys and bottles of French wine from the Nawab's cellar. For some time Priti had been watching Arjun who was at the other end of the room. She was struck by the extraordinary contrast he presented to all the decadence about her in the Nawab's house. The impression which he conveyed to Priti was a wonderfully clean and fresh one, as though he must be immaculate to the hollows of his toes, and she wondered whether she was worthy of his friendship.

She marvelled at how Arjun had grown. From Simla she remembered him as not particularly good-looking, with a broad nose, thick lips and common brown eyes. Now as she looked at him, she realized that the same broad nose revealed sincerity; the thick lips were powerfully sensuous: and the brown eyes suggested a spiritual strength that she found attractive. So moved was she by this realization that she ran up to Arjun. She took his hand and she said, 'You appear so clean and strong and above this company, Arjun. How can you stand all this? Let's go away.'

Arjun was bewildered. He grew concerned that she might be sick. He also thought that it would be rude to leave before dinner; the Nawab would be hurt.

'How I love the smile on your face! It is irresistible,' she said. 'Hang the Nawab. Let's go.'

She came with him to his flat, uninvited and unopposed. As soon as he closed his door, she came up to him. He glanced apprehensively. She turned her face and moved slightly away. Suddenly he saw a tear fall on her shoulder. His heart melted, and he put out his hand and laid his finger on her forlorn shoulder.

'I'm confused, Arjun. You're too good for me.'

'You mustn't cry,' he said. Softly, shyly, he kissed her cheek.

She covered her face with her hands. She tried to dry her eyes with her shoulder. He put one hand on her shoulder, closed his other hand softly on her elbow, and drew her to him. Gently, he caressed her. He seemed to grow confident and she felt his reassuring warmth. He felt her shoulders, her back, her hips hidden by her sari, and her round buttocks. He had little experience with women, but by instinct his hands moved up her body. Shyly and softly he stroked her breasts.

'Let's lie down,' she said.

He moved towards the bed.

'No,' she said, 'let's lie on the floor.'

They lay down on the cool mat of long, thin reeds. He looked at her face, but could not make out what she was thinking. His hand felt her body again. It stroked her face soothingly and gently, he touched her lips. She kissed him, more ardently. Timidly he reached out and touched her knee through her sari. Then his fingers slid to her thigh. He could feel her skin quiver beneath his fingers. She lay quite still. His hand climbed up to her bare midriff and touched her navel. He felt the front of her body next to his. It felt urgent against him. He reached for her high, arched buttocks. She gripped him in a tight embrace, her knee gently but insistently pressed against him.

As if by a common signal they both sat up and removed their clothes. With a feeling of reverence he touched her soft naked body. She snuggled close to him as he moved his lips and tongue along the hollow of her shoulder and neck. He circled her nipples with his tongue, not touching, until she impatiently thrust them into his mouth. He kissed her breasts softly, taking the nipples in his lips in tiny caresses. She put her arms around him and felt his naked flesh against her. Both felt drowned in sharp pleasure as she guided him inside her. For a moment he was quiet. Then he began to move upon her. She lay still, feeling his motion within her. His movement became more passionate. Soon it was over. He clung to her for a long time as if he were unconscious. At last he drew away.

They lay in a mysterious stillness, disturbed only by the rustle of the coconut trees outside. A sea breeze had begun to blow, and it gently caressed their naked bodies. What was she feeling, he wondered? What was she thinking? She lay there with his arm around her, her body touching his.

Eventually he roused himself and drew away from her. He covered her with the cotton bedcover, and threw a sheet across his own body, and went out on the terrace. The sky was full of stars. The sea was in shadow, almost in darkness. He could hear the dark waves softly rising and heaving. The breeze continued to stir the coconut trees. He looked at the stars and wondered what was beyond the great vastness. He turned again to the sea and thought of the fate which had brought him and now Priti to this anonymous city, so far from the vast plains of his ancestors.

He went to sleep beside her, and was wakened by the stifled roar of the first double-decker bus carrying the earliest morning passengers from Colaba to Mahim. He woke Priti from a troubled doze and explored her mouth and eyes and fine hair with a sensuality mixed with curiosity. 'I must be going,' she said. Awkward and a little shy, they breathed quickly between kisses; they knew what they wanted of each other, and they were drunk with the sea air, which was an ally in furthering their marvellous, unexpected intimacies.

They dressed languorously and in silence and made their way down the gloomy staircase. On the street they walked together like a pair of accomplices. They did not dare link their arms, but their hands kept meeting involuntarily. They had not shaken off the spell of the night and could not bear to be separated. They parted speechlessly as Priti got into a taxi on Cuffe Parade. She looked back and gave him a long, lingering look.

Walking along Cuffe Parade, Arjun felt the whole city ringing in his ears. He wandered aimlessly about the streets of Colaba and was amazed by how many new buildings there were, and how much that was familiar had changed. It struck him with fresh, wild force that he belonged to the city. He felt as if heaven lay close above Bombay, and he was between them both.

5

One Saturday afternoon during the break in the monsoons, Arjun caught an unexpected glimpse of Priti walking idly on the street below his flat. She wore a light gossamer sari, almost white, with white sandals. The pale lengthening rays of the afternoon sun fell on the curves of her body, heightening them in the waning light. A taxi went by, carrying a Parsi priest in a familiar black cap. She gazed darkly at it. As she walked past below his terrace, she smiled as if from some private satisfaction. It was a sad, quick smile, one which he rarely saw. There was also something touching and pliantly feminine in it. Soon she disappeared into the exhausted streets of Colaba and he was left forlorn.

Priti was right in believing that the monsoons would change her fortune. She had finally got a job in the traffic department of Air India. It was a comedown from her earlier dreams of journalism, and not even as good as copy-writing in an advertising agency, but it was a job. At the last moment, she had almost lost to a girl from a 'backward caste', who had political influence. But even the Finance Minister of Maharashtra could not help when the backward caste certificate turned out to be fraudulent. Bhabo's reaction was that Priti's mother would never have worked for an airline. Bauji said that Amrita would never have worked at all. Soon Arjun helped Priti find a room in Colaba, near the Radio Club, and she moved out of Neena's house. Being financially independent did not make her less moody. She seemed to be searching constantly for something, but Arjun had no clear idea what she was after.

Half-an-hour after he'd seen Priti on the street his doorbell rang. He opened the door and there she stood on his gloomy landing. She gave him a look of terrifying honesty and weariness. He inhaled the warm afternoon smell of her skin as she stepped in. Taking off her sandals, she washed her feet under the tap in the bathroom, and sat down on the cool, tiled floor. Arjun joined her on the floor.

'You look unhappy,' he said.

'I am neither unhappy nor happy,' she said.

On the polished, red terracotta tiles she felt the cooling touch of the earth penetrate her body. And in that afternoon light she was possessed by a desire to open her heart to him. Soon their conversation was infused with intimacy. Her head tilted, she talked, and he listened. He took her confessions as a lucky omen of friendship. Her ideas were fresh, but later when he tried to recall her conversation he remembered only the pattern but not the substance. He leaned on an elbow as he listened to her and the afternoon became filled with the marvellous healing power of her words. She seemed prematurely exhausted by experience. It gave him an odd pleasure to discover her weakness: her concern for the opinion of others, especially servants and shopkeepers, her small vanities, her total lack of interest in money, her inability to face the unpleasant, and her willingness to accept any superstition that came along.

Now she lay beside him, breathing lightly, and staring at the wooden rafters and the ceiling fan with her large, brown eyes. His eyes took in her shining, brown skin and dark hair, which glowed against the whiteness of her sari. Suddenly he was conscious of an unusual silence in his little flat; he could hear the bathroom tap dripping. She turned upon one elbow and lowering her neck she gazed into his eyes for a long time. Finally she smiled; it was the same sad, feminine smile he had seen many times before. He was about to say something when she pressed her warm hand to his mouth, and she took off her sari and her blouse. He too shed his clothes. They lay on the floor watching each other, eye to eye, their bodies touching and healing temporarily at least the symptoms of sadness, while the languor of the waning afternoon filled the room. He felt her strong mouth on his own, and his arms closed upon hers.

After they had made love, she lay lightly in the crook of his arm, her hair blown across his mouth by the sea breeze. She yawned. Sitting up on the floor she clasped her ankles with her hands, and started to speak. She talked with a desperate urgency as if she had to get it out before someone silenced her. Arjun listened intently. She appeared to be seeking something outside their love, something bigger. Arjun also observed that their behaviour, their attitudes, even their passion was in some ways a response to the luminous, sea-swept city. The one sure clock in their life was the sea and its tides, at which they continuously gazed from the terrace of his flat, or when walking on Marine Drive or along the harbour towards the Gateway from her room. Constantly they drank in the

blues and the browns of the seascape among the Gujaratis, Mahar-
ashtrians, Keralites, Sindhis, Parsis, and all the peoples of India
who inhabited this cosmopolitan city.

Arjun watched his lover's face with passionate concentration as
it was reflected in the benign light of the faded evening. He
suddenly remembered one of their first kisses by the sea. It was a
kiss broken by her laughter, but later she had placed her hand in his
as if to make amends. They had idled arm in arm on the beach the
remainder of the afternoon and later had lain for a long time side by
side in their wet bathing suits, oblivious of the hawkers and the
passers-by, till the last pale rays touched their brown skins in the
delicious evening coolness. It had been an overture to a ravenous
and possessive sexuality. How did they allow it to come about?
Priti certainly was more experienced and seasoned by the disap-
pointments of love. Now in Arjun's mind the lean figure of Karan
still loomed large. Arjun felt that Karan seemed to be watching
them. Priti was aware of this obsession of his, and tried to reassure
him.

To take their minds off Karan, they went outdoors. Priti wanted
to ride a Victoria, and Arjun hailed one on Cuffe Parade. As soon as
they got in, Priti's face flushed with excitement. She felt gay and
exultant.

'Let me drive, Arjun. I want to go sit up with the driver.'

'Please, Priti.'

'Whoa driver!' she shouted. 'Wait. I'm coming up beside you.'

Arjun held her by the arm to stop her from falling. The carriage
sped onward. Her forehead wrinkled slightly as she tried to see
better ahead of her.

'Ah,' she said as she sat back and relaxed on his arm. Her head
came close to his, and he recalled for an instant the warmth of her
body under her sari. The city looked entrancing in the monsoon
twilight. A gentle wind from the sea grazed their cheeks. They
heard the wail of a siren as they went past Sassoon Dock. From the
Gateway the sea looked unusually blue, unlike the grey that they
had got used to.

They drove past Walkeshwar and up Malabar Hill to Hanging
Gardens, where they got off to walk. After some time, they sat down
on a bench. A traffic policeman in familiar blue and yellow walked
passed wearily on his way home. Other passing faces had a shiny,
blurry quality, as they hurried by.

'Arjun, tell me about your father?' said Priti.

'What?'

'I mean what is he like?'

'What *does* one say about a father?'

'I remember him vaguely from Simla. He is a good man, isn't he?'
Arjun nodded.

'Very quiet?'

Arjun nodded.

'Tell me about his religion. It is true that the guru gave you your
name?'

'Yes.'

'And that you were the guru's cow in an earlier birth?'

'If you want to believe that sort of thing.'

'I do. I really do. And I want to meet your father and his guru.'

On an impulse they decided to go out of Bombay. They both felt
that they needed a change, and they agreed to visit Karla caves in
the Western ghats. They met at Victoria Terminus early the next
morning. She wore a cotton sari. In spite of her plain clothes, he
thought that she stood out in the crowded station. She looked
younger and happier, like a schoolgirl. In a plastic bag she carried
their picnic lunch.

The Poona train was not crowded. They were in a carefree mood,
eager to be satisfied by the smallest pleasures. The very names of
the suburban train stops echoed the poetry of their journey: Byculla,
Dadar, Sion, Kurla, Ghatkopar, Thana, Kalyan. Soon they were out
of the city and the countryside was like a carpet of green. It drizzled
lightly and Arjun stuck his face out to feel the rain falling on it. They
alighted at Khandala and took a tonga. Arjun felt moved as they
walked up the hill to the two-thousand-year-old caves. He read to
her from a guide book about how Buddhist monks used to live in
these rock-cut monasteries. Priti was not much interested in history, but she seemed delighted by the outing. Arjun continued to
read aloud about the master rock-cutters who had made the caves
in the first century BC.

As they entered the caves, they suddenly became quiet. They
stood gazing reverently at the great stupa in the large vaulted
prayer hall. They walked around the stupa several times, but they
found themselves slowly pulled towards the colossal free-standing
pillars surmounted by lion insignia. Each pillar was fifty feet high
and stood on a wide cylinder of rock with a group of stone lions
supporting a large wheel. Behind the lion columns was a vestibule
separated by a rock-cut screen. They passed through a horseshoe-

shaped archway and approached the tiers of carvings in rock. Below the railings were panels filled with figures in relief, and, alongside, a series of life-sized elephants, each carved in relief. They walked out of the central hall through doorways, into square cells, which were used as apartments by the monks. There were numerous cells and the cliff side was honey-combed with them, like the nesting burrows of birds.

They sat quietly in one of the cells, overlooking the plain, and Arjun's mind was filled with the beauty of the colonnade, the lion insignia, and the wonderful carvings. He thought about the rustle of monks' feet in procession, thousands of years ago, echoing through the colonnade of the prayer-hall. And he was filled with admiration for these men who, urged by their devotion to the Great Buddha, conjured such a majestic place of worship out of the bare hillside.

Arjun looked at Priti and wondered at her lack of enthusiasm. She seemed to be lost in her own world. She did not look bored, merely detached. Arjun felt excluded and hurt. They had their picnic quietly on the hillside. Down below, on the other side of the hill, they spotted a lake.

'Let's go and have a look,' he said.

'If you wish,' she replied.

Her indifferent tone suggested to Arjun that she had lost interest in everything. What had happened, he wondered. Was she looking for something else? He had noticed this before, several weeks ago, and it made him uneasy. Perhaps, he thought, that she had experienced everything at too early an age. What was she really after, he asked himself.

At the landing on the lake, Arjun negotiated with a fisherman. He unfastened the rope and they got into the smelly, dilapidated fishing boat. He pushed an oar against the stone landing and the boat gently glided off. The calm surface of the water reflected the green hills. As the ripples rose through the brilliant surface, Priti's mood visibly changed. She said that she felt liberated by the thought that this day, this moment would never return and that something was slipping away irrevocably.

'Shall we go to the other end?' he asked.

'What's at the other end?' she said.

'Come on, let's go look,' he said and he rowed with vigour.

The late afternoon sun shone through the clouds. It was a peaceful, uneventful time of the day. There was only one other boat on the pond. They reached the other side and climbed up to a grassy clearing. They lay back on the grass to stare at the monsoon sky. The rough grass pricked their backs, making Priti feel uncomfortable. It gave Arjun, however, a pleasant sensation of a prickly pain that spread out in a fragmented way throughout his back. Out of the corners of his eyes he saw a heron sitting on the back of a buffalo at a distance. The bird's supple, curved beak was silhouetted, stretched against the sky.

'After the lion columns and the great stupa, the boat ride, and you here, it's almost perfect. In all my life, I haven't had many such days,' said Arjun.

'Are you speaking about happiness?'

'I didn't say anything about happiness.'

'Well, that's all right then. I'd be much too scared to talk as you do. I don't have your courage.'

'Look, Priti, what more do you want than a day like this? What are you after?'

'I don't know,' she answered wearily. With that, she gently rolled over on the grass. Lying on her stomach, she lifted her head and stared across the water.

'Arjun,' she whispered mournfully after a while, 'last night I dreamt that I was dead. I lay still in the middle of an empty room with large windows. It was just before dawn, and outside the light was deep blue. A young man clung to my bed; his long, black hair fell on his shoulders, and his head drooped. I wanted to see his face, but I could only make out his graceful forehead. Instead of the smell of incense and sandalwood, the scent of ripened mangoes filled the room.'

There was a long silence. Arjun watched her intently. Her cotton sari inadequately disguised the roundness of her hips, which were surprisingly large for her slim figure. All at once he felt unsettled, his mind like the lake of clear water was suddenly clouded by a disturbance below the surface.

Soon they had to return because it began to drizzle. On the way back to the station it rained hard and the tonga got stuck in the mud, but they were well in time for the last train to Bombay. Priti took out a handkerchief and dried Arjun's forehead and hair. A feeling of happiness coursed through him. It was as if the rain had washed away the tension between them.

As they dried themselves in the tiny waiting room at Khandala station, Arjun remembered their first encounter in Bombay at the

Gymkhana. Despite knowing her intimately for many months, he was still shy, and looked away as she dried herself with a towel. She, however, felt at ease with him. The air inside got thicker and hotter, and Arjun opened a window. On the roof they could hear the rain beating down. The waiting room had a strangely uncozy atmosphere, but they were determined to make the best of it. Arjun ordered a pot of tea and some biscuits. From an overflowing gutter the water poured down in a steady stream onto the platform. It sounded like a waterfall in some faraway Himalayan village.

'I suppose the people in the station think we're married,' said Arjun.

She laughed and he was happy to see her smiling face. On the roof the rain was still pattering down, but the force of the storm was over; only a trickle now issued from the gutter. Arjun sighed softly.

'Look, Priti,' he said after a pause. 'I've never asked this before, but do you still love Karan?'

'No, not anymore.'

6

Bauji felt that his time was coming. He had been sick in bed the whole week. It was an indefinable malady, its only symptom being a mild intestinal flu, which the doctors did not think serious. He could not eat. He quickly became weak and his interest in life waned. He began to feel that his cramped bedroom was suffocating; his suffering was aggravated by the humidity and the mustiness of the ill-dusted furniture as well as the medicinal odours emanating from the large number of bottles on the night table.

When Arjun arrived Bhabo was in tears. She complained that Bauji would not allow the windows to be opened, the room to be dusted, and he was in a terrible mood. As Arjun opened the shutters, a blinding light entered, reflected from the metallic sea. With the help of the servant Arjun moved a divan out to the shady veranda. Leaning on Arjun's arm, Bauji dragged himself out and lay down on the divan. He put his head against the bolster so that he could look at the coconut and casurina trees. Gradually he felt better; it was the kind of feeling he had had when he sat in the Company Bagh after a particularly difficult day at the courts in Lyallpur. Bauji smiled at Arjun and took hold of his hand.

Arjun kept holding his hand and talked to him. He spoke easily and enthusiastically about his work; he explained the projects he was involved in. He commented on political developments; he told Bauji about a particularly savoury scandal that had just broken out in the state government. Bauji was grateful. But after a time, he ceased to listen. His mind drifted into the past and he began to make a general balance sheet of his life. To a man of the world, familiar with business and commerce, to think in terms of credits and debits came easily. He was naturally drawn to the credit side. There were some happy moments, such as the birth of his eldest son. That Big Uncle did not accomplish much did not matter, the original moment of triumph was real. He remembered a saying: he who conquers a country doesn't get the same pleasure as a common man who sits in the sunshine watching his first-born suck his toe. Then there was the first awareness of success in the British-ruled establishment of Lyallpur in the early '20s. He had enjoyed the power and the prestige which had accompanied his early professional achievements. There were voluptuous moments just before Tara's marriage, when Anees briefly entered his life; till today her memory, caught in the heavy scent of jasmine flower, could still make his thoughts wander along a decidedly erotic path—that this could happen when he was seventy-five and dying made him alternately blush and smile.

Ruminations on the balance sheet were temporarily suspended because a snake charmer had stopped beside the house, mistakenly thinking there were foreigners about, and had started playing his pipe. Arjun hastily went up to the gate and threw him some coins and waved him on in the more profitable direction of the five star hotels on the beach.

Arjun, yes, he was certainly on the credit side of the ledger. First it had been Karan; but not only had Karan not lived up to his potential, he had revealed a dark and alien nature, which Bauji had found abhorrent. Arjun, on the other hand, brought sunshine to his last days; it was a pleasure to watch him manoeuvre through life; the affection and sincerity of his character were heart-warming.

There were other credits too: to have seen his country win freedom from foreign rule during his lifetime; to have watched Nehru place the country on the right path of democracy, secularism and social justice. There were smaller and more intimate moments: the smell of the fragrance of the wet earth mingled with jasmine in the courtyard of the Lyallpur house after the Mashkiya had watered it; being shaved and massaged by the family barber while playing bridge with his friends in the men's courtyard; glimpsing the first wondrous vision of the snow-tipped crests of the Himalayas on the rail car to Simla.

There were other little satisfactions which mattered only to him: the delight in wearing a new silk coat; the smell of a new leather chair; the desirous smile on a beautiful woman's face; and the first realization that she found him attractive; a few moments of frenzied passion before the marvellous yet also ridiculous act of sex was over.

Slowly his brow clouded over as his conscience reminded him to look towards the other side of the ledger. For every credit there seemed to be a half-a-dozen liabilities. He was almost afraid to start enumerating the debits because he might lose control, plunging into depths from which it would take days to surface. Just as he was about to begin to bravely count the debits and embarrassments, Bhabo rescued him. She called out to say that lunch was ready. His train of thought was broken, and he amused himself with the thought that it was just as well to let the positive side of one's life 'hang out'.

He had felt this way for a fortnight or so, ever since he had become aware of a sensation akin to a pair of shears approaching the vital chord of his existence from afar, ready to snip it off at the end. This sensation was not linked to any physical discomfort. Nor was he afraid; it was merely disagreeable to a man used to celebrating life. Still, with his strong pride, he did not let this sensation diminish him. On the contrary he felt a secret recompense in being privy to a secret while everyone else around him was absorbed in his petty daily routine. He felt a sense of participating in high universal drama in which the truths of life and death were unfolding.

He was accustomed to consoling friends and relatives when they suffered the loss of someone close. He had become adept at repeating at countless mourning ceremonies, 'Now, now my dear, we must remember that we all have to die some day.' Today he suddenly felt the irony of that mundane statement. For it was now transformed to 'I am dying'. The obvious had become real. As a sensitive man he felt the irony acutely, because observing the death of others had not prepared him in any way for his own. Each person has to face his own death alone, he realized. He wondered if this knowledge of his dying could have any meaning or significance. Could he, for example, live his life any differently, knowing that he did not have long to live? Could this anticipation of his own death make his last moments more real, more honest, and more free?

He had his whole family around him now, but no one seemed to sense this grand drama and mystery. Certainly not his own children. Not even Bhabo. They seemed all trapped in the everyday world of small talk and mindless preoccupations. He tried not to feel sorry for them.

Sitting in the divan, Bauji looked out at the Arabian sea. The sea breeze blew familiarly through the casuarina and coconut trees. His legs were wrapped in a blanket. He could see several shapes sitting on the beach. The rounded waves came rolling towards him, and broke into rich white foam before they could reach him. He picked up some sand in his hand and let it sift through his closed fingers. It sent a sensuous quiver through his body. Again he felt the shears approaching.

In the corner of the beach house was a ragged looking banyan tree, which had never quite had a chance. Beside it was a stone lamp that Bhabo was now lighting. The oil wick burned feebly as she performed the *sandhya*, and the evening slowly welcomed the night. The evening star was low against the horizon, and Bauji felt he could almost reach up and touch it.

On a clear evening after the monsoons an attractive, middle aged lady confidently stepped out of a cab. The sky in the west was filled with brilliant shades of violet and crimson. She lightly crossed the empty street. Before her were a dozen identical low-built Mangalore-tiled houses and she became confused. On the corner she saw a noisy group of young men and women. They looked like students. One of the girls burst out laughing. Anees asked them for directions. There was a free-spiritedness about them, which was in sharp contrast to young people in her own country. A girl in a bright Rajasthani sari knew the house. She looked the 'arty' type from the way she had slung a cotton bag across her shoulder. She guided Anees to the gate.

The house was surrounded by trees and a lawn of crab grass. The side facing the street was covered with an awning of dried coconut leaves. Anees walked right in, directly to Bauji, who was sitting among the trees facing the sea.

'No, it cannot be! It cannot be you!' exclaimed Bauji. His eyes were filled with tears.

'What a beautiful evening!' said Anees, sitting beside him.

Bauji looked at her smooth, delicate skin, almost untouched by age, and he was filled with sentimental longing. A quarter-of-a century later she was still beautiful, he thought. Her pale white face was older, but her nose and cheekbones were chiseled on her square face. Her hair was still dark. The texture of the exotic light hanging over the distant shadowed sea changed from moment to moment on her face. Presently the shadows began to deepen and the evening was bathed in a wan light. The casuarinas stood out darkly against the sky.

'From Tara's last letter I realized you were very sick. I knew nothing would come of it, but my soul thirsted to see you.'

Anees turned her head and looked at the coconut trees.

'How old are they, Bauji?'

'Who?'

'These trees.'

'Twenty, maybe thirty years old.'

'Inside them is the empty memory of all the years we have remained apart.' She felt an inward sob. She looked piercingly at his eyes and they were filled with yearning.

'I have longed to see you once again. But I was always a little afraid. I have kept in touch all these years through letters from Tara. You never wrote.'

'I wanted to, but it didn't seem right. How have you been?'

'I left my husband a few years ago, and I was immediately ostracized by my family, by the neighbours, even by my children.' She laughed sadly. 'I suppose what I had done was inexcusable in Islamic society.'

'I am tired of the mullahs and the generals in Pakistan, Bauji,' she said with a sigh. 'I don't believe that to be a good Muslim I have to live according to the wasteland of the mullah's mind. They won't leave me alone, constantly reminding me of my "sins". Oh, how I envy the breeze of freedom that blows in your country! Each time we try to break free, the mullahs ask the army to take over.

'The mistake we made in the 1940s, Bauji, was to believe that just because we were Muslims we belonged to a separate nation. India didn't have to be divided in 1947. And we cheaply sold away the birthright of the Indian Muslim. In fact the Muslim majority areas which became Pakistan were the ones which least needed to be protected from the Hindus. It was the Hindus in these areas, on the contrary, who needed to be protected.'

'And Muslims in little villages all over India were the ones who needed protection,' said Bauji.

'We got swayed by Jinnah into believing that Muslims couldn't survive in India. Look at the Arab world: one religion, one language and a dozen nations. And if Jinnah himself had believed in it he wouldn't have left forty million Muslims behind in India.'

'There were many mistakes, Anees.'

Listening to her, Bauji recalled the spirited defence that Anees had made for Pakistan during the days preceding Tara's marriage. He laughed, but it was at his own expense. He felt irony in the average Indian's zeal for the form rather than the substance of his religion. A Hindu would recite the Sanskrit mantras scarcely comprehending their meaning; similarly a Muslim would recite the

Arabic prayer five times a day with fervour and an equal lack of comprehension. This dedication to formal religion with little regard for the humanism and the charity that the two religions preached had made a bigot of the average believer on both sides. Subconsciously, a Hindu felt affronted by the muezzin's call for prayers, while a Muslim was irritated by the tolling of temple bells.

Anees stayed in town at the Taj Mahal hotel, despite Bauji's protests. But she came to see him every day. Arjun would sometimes pick her up from the hotel and take her to Juhu. He liked visiting the hotel, which was distinguished like its namesake, and expressed the rich confidence and splendour of another age. It pulsated with the life of the city's rich, and was a meeting place where big deals were struck in which millions were won and lost. Through its doors walked princes, prime ministers, and film stars with pet poodles. Built by the famous industrialist, Jamsetji Tata, at the turn of the century, it had a distinctly Victorian pomposity with terracotta tiled domes, fretted windows, and stately spires. Inside were chandeliers, shining brassware, and dreams. Occasionally, Anees would offer Arjun tea and they would sit on wicker chairs in one of the turretted balconies and watch the winking harbour.

On one such visit Arjun discovered a santoor in Anees' room and he persuaded her to play it at Juhu. She must be a serious player, he thought, as he carried the Kashmiri string instrument to the car. She had shown none of the artificial shyness about playing, which was characteristic of amateurs.

Once at Juhu she settled down to play without a fuss. One of the strings snapped as she plucked tentatively at the instrument. With a firm, confident touch she changed the string and tuned the instrument.

She began to play. Bauji felt a powerful sensation as the first notes swept into the air. He shivered. The sounds of the santoor went deep inside him. After initially feeling startled, he listened to the music with reverence. Although filled with feelings of loss and regret, he gave himself to the sound, to the pleasure of being swept away by it.

Anees had a sure touch. He could not believe how very good she was. She sat cross-legged on the veranda, and played steadily, oblivious of anyone around her. Sitting rigidly upright, she seemed to be in a spell. As the sound rose higher, Bauji became aware of her loneliness. Practising alone day after day, unaware of the world, she had made this instrument her companion. Her music seemed to have conquered her sorrow.

'The tone is different by the sea,' Anees said. The rich and vibrant notes rose up and gently went out into the clear evening. Bauji, unlearned in technique, was conscious only of the emotion in the sound. He followed the musical ideas purely through the feeling contained inside them.

From that day on the instrument was kept at Juhu, and Anees played every evening. People went about the house, doing their work, and she did not feel inhibited, or concerned about an audience. Bauji relaxed and gazed at her face as the voluptuous softness of the music filled the air day after day. Her face seemed to become younger, the smooth lips and moist eyes shining, as she played and Bauji felt closer to her than ever before.

One day, late in the evening, Bauji went alone for a walk on the beach. There was no moon and it was pitch dark. The sky was full of stars. There were almost too many of them. They came forward brightly as if they were an offering to be accepted. As they approached the sky retreated into the night. The indistinguishable constellations seemed to merge into each other, and the whole of the night scene came together in a unity and a celebration.

The cluster of stars called Rohini flowed above Bauji's head in the direction in which he was walking, and seemed to bathe his head in its light. The light pierced the sky and pointed directly ahead. Bauji was entranced and followed it.

Bauji looked again and again at the constellation, and the light seemed to come down and wrap itself around his body. The light flowed through his body, shining like a great primeval glow, and stood at the edge of his feet. He was astonished at the splendid scene.

Bauji looked up again and he felt himself floating into the vast constellation. Its radiance was so close that it seemed to take him into it. Rohini seemed to hold the sea in a naked embrace. He felt rapturous. Rohini stood apart from the rest of the sky, and its limitless depth pulled his gaze into it.

He returned home, and sat on his usual chair in the garden facing the sea. He continued to gaze at the constellation. Suddenly his head fell back, and the light flowed deep inside him with a roar. He was dead.

7

A few months after Bauji's death, Arjun took the lift up to his office in Ballard Estate and sitting down at his desk wrote the following words, 'My dearest Mother and Father, Priti and I have agreed to marry. I would never do this if I thought it would compromise in any way either the affection you have for me or. . . .'

Suddenly appalled by the thought that this was an unspeakably cowardly way to behave, he tore up the note and folded his arms. Whatever he might write would sound defensive and inadequate. As he sat staring at the polished desk, he decided to act. After another moment of thought, he picked up the telephone and asked the travel department of his company to make arrangements for a visit to his parents over the weekend. He would fly to Delhi on Friday night, then take the overnight train to Nangal, via Ambala. He told his secretary to telegram his parents that he would be spending the weekend with them at the ashram.

His self-assurance now left him suddenly and he felt acutely shy, unwilling to face his mother directly and confront her with his intentions. He knew she would disapprove. She had refused to meet Priti a couple of months ago when she was in Bombay because of Bauji's sickness. Each time Arjun had brought up the subject, she had quietly skirted it. As far as she was concerned Priti was irrevocably tainted by scandal. He looked out of his window at the harbour. The waiting foreign cargo ships formed a brilliant pattern of reflections in the water—brushstroke images of swaying masts and rigging and international flags. The play of light with colour created a resonance upon the surface of the sea. Several ferries connecting the mainland with the city glided in the harbour scuttling in and out among the great ships. Towards the south lay brooding the white silhouette of a warship of the Indian Navy parked in Lion's Gate. A flock of glittering seagulls flew past, turning their wings to the light. This was Bombay, he thought, a city which could unconsciously make poetry and history out of commerce.

He turned his back on the panels of the brass-framed window to study his problem anew. He was puzzled by this disagreeable new feeling of shyness for he had always been close to his mother; although they did not often meet because of the distance, the affection was deep and mutual and often did not need words for understanding. He had always been special to her, as she had been to her own father. It was to him that she had turned when Seva Ram had decided to take early retirement from the government at age fifty-five the previous year in order to settle at the ashram. And she had accepted his advice to go with her husband for she felt that her son instinctively understood the sweetness and the sorrow of her life with Seva Ram. If ever Arjun had felt shy or awkward it was with his father, never with her. And now why did he fear facing her? Even though she would disapprove, he also knew that he would eventually prevail, and she would acquiesce. Why then should he feel inhibited? Curiously, the thought of his father's reaction did not enter his head. Perhaps this was because Seva Ram had remained as saintly as ever, and matters of this world did not merit strong reaction. Not that he did not care for his son. But Arjun understood that this father's passions were reserved for other matters.

Seva Ram's decision to retire early had been traumatic for Tara. It had been taken several years ago at the peak of his career, when he had reached the rank of Chief Engineer to the Punjab Government. There were many perquisites that went with the position which Tara found useful and even delightful—a retinue of office staff, a big house with a garden and servants to look after it, an office car with a chauffeur. All of these were also symbols of power, and that summed up what was so delightful about her new life. She was now a somebody. She enjoyed the prestige and the status which his new position provided in the state capital. Suddenly she found sycophants visiting them at home and even though she could see through their flattery, she nevertheless enjoyed it. Socially she was now in demand, and she began to cultivate a new set of friends. There was a new gaiety in her life. And the prospect of leaving it all was altogether too depressing. And for what? A quiet life at the ashram, where nobody would care who she was nor where she had come from. No, no it would not do. She was willing to consider that sort of life when they were sixty, when he would have to retire by the rules of his service. But she must be allowed to enjoy the next few years of her life especially when she had waited so long for it.

Seva Ram's own reaction to his elevated status was predictable. He was not even aware of the flowers and the shrubs which Tara had lovingly planted with the gardener's help in the new house. He found the sudden growth in their social life an interference to his evenings which were meant for long walks and spiritual meditation. He found their new 'friends' false and boring. Yes, perhaps his work was more interesting, because it now involved motivating younger engineers to perform. His juniors responded to him because they realized that he was not political, and that he genuinely cared for the work. But his desire to move was influenced by the guru, who felt that his spiritual progress could be enhanced by moving to the ashram. Besides there were a number of projects which Seva Ram could undertake once he was at the ashram. For instance he could help to reclaim and irrigate the lands around the Sutlej. The river had changed course in the past twenty years and left a great deal of waste land between the river and the ashram. He could also help build a hospital, which had been on the guru's mind for some time, as there was no suitable medical care for the surrounding villages; he could help construct rest houses and a new dormitory for visiting devotees who came from as far away as America.

Seva Ram liked the prospect of being close to the guru and doing all these things, and he announced his decision to Tara. When she realized that her husband was serious, she was furious. It was no use arguing with her husband, who seemed to her to be stubborn as an ox once he had made up his mind. So it was to Arjun that she came running, and cried her heart out. She thought her husband unfair to take her away from the world of society and power that she had recently found. She thought the guru was selfish to use her husband for his own ends. The spiritual life was an excuse she felt; the guru really wanted the free use of her husband's experience as an engineer.

Mother and son spent several weeks together, at the end of which Arjun persuaded her that the motives of both her husband and the guru were honest. Talking to Arjun, she also realized that she did not have to 'renounce life' and live in complete austerity. In the end she returned home and agreed to go to the ashram provided that her husband built a comfortable house there, where she could cultivate a garden, keep her electrical gadgets and her furniture and live a 'normal' life.

The train arrived at Nangal just after dawn, and Arjun saw from his compartment the short figure of Seva Ram standing on the platform. He threw up an arm in an awkward gesture of pleasure as he saw his father, and stepped out of the train with a beating heart.

'Arjun!' Father and son, so unlike in physique and looks, embraced with feeling after Arjun had touched his father's feet. But there was an awkward shyness about them which was always present when they were alone without Tara. A porter with a white beard came forward to lift Arjun's luggage.

The father, shorter and slimmer than the son, wore the rural working dress. His rough, woollen shawl covered a thick long shirt and baggy pants held up by a string. Arjun noticed his father's nicely shaped hands and curly hair. His eyes were the same—innocent, sincere, and remote. Seva Ram led his son towards the waiting tonga.

The tonga driver was a familiar face, an old disciple, who had known Arjun from childhood. He folded his hands with a humble smile and then got busy loading the luggage. Arjun went up to him, shook his hand western style, and then embraced him. There were tears of happiness in the old man's eyes. Seva Ram was touched by his son's easy, feeling gesture full of camaraderie.

'And mother?' said Arjun in a low voice as they settled in the tonga.

'Is well,' said Seva Ram. 'Your telegram worried her. But telegrams always worry her.'

'There wasn't enough time for a letter.'

'Precisely what I told her. But she is a worrier.'

'How does she like it here?'

'She doesn't as yet. But the new house is ready and the grass and the garden have come up. It's much smaller of course. But then this is an ashram after all. She stays busy with the flowers.'

The tonga now took them along a network of irrigation channels. On both sides were rich fields, bursting with young, golden wheat. Arjun always loved this ride for it evoked his many visits during childhood. He looked proudly at the wheat and thought that this is what they called the 'green revolution'. Guessing his thoughts, Seva Ram said, 'It's not the canals and tubewells alone, but the new dwarf varieties that have done it. Look, look over there! See, how much smaller it is. Small and prolific.'

The sun came up on the other side of the river. Arjun's face was filled with pleasure, watching the bountiful fields and the Sutlej. It was a fine morning, and people were already busy in the field. He could hear the new sounds: tractors had replaced bullocks; there were tubewells instead of Persian wheels. Here and there they passed a hamlet, whose old, flat houses of unbaked mud were giving way to brick and cement, but the stacks of the monsoon harvest still covered the flat roofs. More and more people were on bicycles now, he noticed. Seva Ram turned his sparkling brown eyes to stare into the dark eyes of his son.

As they approached the ashram, there were suddenly more trees. Arjun knew that the guru had a modern mind: he believed in reforestation and reclamation. On either side of them were wooded lands and Arjun could see eucalyptus plantations, and acacia and palm. Before he realized it they were at the rusty gate of the ashram, half-smothered in bougainvillaea. Seva Ram jumped down and opened the gate and climbed up again. The tonga moved through bylanes, past the water tank of the old colony, which was much the same as it was thirty years ago when Bauji had visited to offer his daughter to a canal engineer. The tonga came to a halt at the western periphery of the ashram near the river. The modern house, which Seva Ram had built for Tara as an inducement to live in the ashram, fitted in well with the architecture around, although it was clearly more functional, and had a garden on the outside, as well as the benefit of trees which had now grown tall since the guru decided to first plant trees along the perimeter years ago. As Arjun looked up at the soaring eucalyptus, Seva Ram said proudly, 'We planted one lakh trees this year.'

Arjun entered the cool house. He noticed pictures of the guru on the walls, and walked straight out into the garden at the back. Tara was sitting in the sun, waiting for him. He touched her feet. They embraced with such trembling tenderness that looking at them Seva Ram laughed, as he tasted the joy of Tara's love for Arjun.

Holding hands they sat down together in the winter sun. Seva Ram brought out a pitcher of buttermilk. Tara questioned her son on worldly matters with those dark, clever, and still youthful eyes which looked steadily into his. From time to time she nodded vigorously in a determined way, while the father watched them both, admiring the simple, concise way in which Arjun expressed abstract ideas.

Tara had maintained a lively interest in politics, despite Seva Ram's complete apathy toward public affairs. Three newspapers on the side table attested to the fact that she was not about to abandon her secular interests in favour of an uneventful country life at the ashram. Nor did Arjun perceive any sign that she intended to embrace the spiritual life. Although she did attend the morning discourse of the guru, it was, she hurriedly clarified, to help her wake up early, and it gave a nice beginning to the day. She admired the guru she admitted. 'He says and does so many things that make so much sense in the modern world.' Arjun concluded that underneath her calm, which fitted nicely with the peaceful hermitage, a fire still burned on. She wrote long letters to her friends daily, which now took the place of more immediate face-to-face interaction. So long as she had this outlet she would not allow herself to be lonely or bored.

'Explain something to me, Arjun,' said Tara. 'It seems to me that the basic problems of our society, and even their solutions are known to the people who are ruling in Delhi. Then why is it that things don't get done?'

Arjun looked at her thoughtfully.

'Shall I tell you why?'

Arjun nodded.

'Because doing the right thing goes against the interest of the rulers. When you ask them, both the politicians and the bureaucrats come up with reasonable and convincing answers. You know what I call this? I call it tender-mindedness. And there was no one more tender-minded than Nehru. We Indians are tender-minded as a nation. Whenever we are faced with a tough choice, we have a tender excuse for not taking it.'

'If problems and solutions are known and still nothing gets done, it shows an extremely unhealthy state of affairs, doesn't it, mother?'

'Of course. Now go inside and have a shower. You are filthy after the train journey. The geyser is on and there is hot water in plenty.' She winked at him as she made the last statement, for it was a private thing between mother and son: that she had brought her gadgets and worldly goods along with her and she meant to be comfortable here.

He walked back into the house. In his room the walls were covered with family pictures, many of which she had inherited from Bauji. These were now the prized memories of a life gone by, and jealously guarded because they were all that Tara had to live for till she died or decided to adopt a different outlook more in keeping with life at the ashram.

In the shower Arjun's mind was distracted from his own mission as he thought of his mother's life at the ashram. Despite the brave front she put up she was lonely. His father was clearly absorbed in his work and his spiritual life. If she had accepted the guru and been initiated in the path, she might have had an outlet; it might have also opened up the possibility of richer companionship with her husband, based on a shared interest. But she had remained a sceptic, like a true daughter of a worldly, free-thinking father. Now, here she was, removed from the glitter of the life that she so dearly loved, trying to overcome loneliness by growing flowers in her garden and writing interminable letters.

The next morning Arjun was woken up at four, when the ashram gong went off. From his childhood he remembered that the day at the hermitage started early. While he used to be allowed to sleep, the others would have to wake up, bathe with cold water and begin meditation. Today he felt the same sense of guilt as he did as a child as he lazed in bed. While the ashram meditated Arjun thought about the objections which Tara would raise to his marriage. The previous day he had been content to hear the family news and engage in small talk about life at the ashram. He did not have the courage to bring up the subject of his mission.

Tara would object to Priti's age: she had once said that a bride ought to be ideally nine years younger than the groom, 'because a woman ages faster'. That she herself was only a couple of years younger to Seva Ram, she had once argued, was part of the reason for their problems. But Priti was a year older and that just would not do.

More than age, Tara would be uncomfortable with Priti's past. Ever since the scandal with Karan, Priti had been dubbed 'a fast girl' by her sympathizers and plain immoral by the rest of society.

'Haven't you learned your lesson once?' he could hear Tara saying. It would be difficult to argue with his mother, who would naturally be concerned about her son getting hurt for the second time.

That Priti's family were now in a bad way financially, and the lack of a dowry would also bother Tara. But Arjun hoped that he could overcome her objections by appealing to his mother's ideal-istic side. Still it wouldn't be easy, for in matters which affected her, she was known to jealously guard the family interest. Despite her liberal education, the prospect of a dowry-less bride would hurt her deeply. She would reason like a typical Indian mother that she had invested in her son, who had done well in life, and therefore she was naturally due a return on her investment. Besides in the eyes of her friends, the extent of the dowry was a measure of her son's worth.

It was now dawn, and Arjun could hear the house stirring with activity. For the past fifteen minutes he had sat on the bed covered with a quilt, his legs drawn up under him and his chin in his hand, wondering how he would impart the news of his marriage. He quickly dressed and came out in time for a walk with his father. In such a mood every promise of distraction offered relief. And Seva Ram seemed delighted to have his son's company.

'I suppose in Bombay you don't go to bed until late.'

'No, as a matter of fact, I am usually asleep by eleven.'

His father smiled shyly, and with an embarrassed laugh he said, 'Well, we go to bed here by nine.'

'But you also wake up at four,' said Arjun.

They arrived by the river. Arjun saw a bluish fog rising from the water. The air was crisp, not quite frosty. The sun was ascending behind the ashram. Sevan Ram led the way, and they walked along the bank, slowly making a circuit of the holy colony. Seva Ram discussed the progress of the land reclamation. Arjun noted the total absence of machinery, but he quickly remembered that all work at the ashram was done by hand—a labour of love for the guru. He could picture an endless procession of devotees carrying baskets of mud on their heads. Father and son walked on in silence. Between the arable land and the river there was a vast and desolate wasteland where the river had changed course. Only giant reeds and bulrushes grew here or an occasional thorn bush. They walked among towering rushes whose stems were bleached by the sun. At last they were at the railway bridge and they paused and breathed in the pure draughts of river air. They looked down the river and into the horizon and the early sky filled with silence and majesty. Arjun was overcome with memories of his childhood, when he had walked along here and even camped several times under a sky drenched with stars.

On the way back they came across a small party of devotees. They greeted Seva Ram, and immediately plunged into a metaphysical discussion on a point raised by the guru in the previous day's discourse. Arjun waited, feeling suddenly like a city-bred outsider, with his western clothes and manners, and unspiritual mind. The discussion carried with it all the feeling of a tight, inbred world.

Left to himself, Arjun again looked down the river and tried to imagine how it flowed into the mighty Indus. He thought about how the earliest Hindus had occupied these lands, and recorded their primordial experience in man's first book, the *Rig Veda*. From this river bed in the Punjab, Hindu civilization had flowed over into the valley of the Ganges, and as it was spread by Brahmins over the rest of India it had suffered many changes, but it kept intact its old Vedic ideas, born on these banks. This realization had a powerful effect on Arjun.

Arjun felt the pull of the old culture, but yet he could not resist the seductive charm of the other, more virile one of the West. Given that he had succumbed to the latter's temptations, leaving far behind the warm, traditional world of the kindly man who stood beside him, he felt guilty as if he were being disloyal. He wondered if his father too had faced this dilemma, as he had gone about his job of building canals and bridges, using the vigorous engineer's mind and tools of the modern West. Seva Ram seemed relaxed in both worlds, seemingly existing in separate compartments, oblivious to feelings of ambivalence or uprootedness. Arjun felt this was because the Hindu had a peculiar ability to flit from one compartment to another. What might be contradictory to someone else, seemed perfectly natural to the Hindu because of a peculiar detachment in his temperament.

Arjun's feelings of disloyalty were considerably diminished as he realized that the civilization of the West had long become the dominant culture of the world. He stood back and marvelled at the amazing phenomenon of the surging Western adventure in science and civilization as the mellow glow of European Enlightenment spread over the world. As a reaction to the West, thinking Indians, like the guru had tried to reform Hinduism by synthesizing the new ideas with the old, philosophical views of the Upanishads. These Hindus had tried to purge Hinduism of Brahmins, superstitions, and rituals. In this manner they had prevented the conversion of Hindus to Christianity and withstood the pressure of the Western missionaries. Their efforts had resulted in a revival in faith amongst the people, and had given educated Indians like Seva Ram a pride in their own.

A quarter-of-a-hour later father and son were walking home at ease, watching the sun come up in a silence broken only by the distant singing of the Himalayan cuckoo. Quite suddenly Arjun felt the barrier lifted, and he said, 'I'm going to be married. I want you to tell mother for me. I don't know why, but I feel shy about it.'

If Seva Ram was surprised, he did not show it. After a few minutes of walking he gently asked, 'To whom Arjun?'

'To Priti. Priti Mehta,' replied Arjun with controlled precision.

They walked on in silence. Arjun asked, 'What do you think?' not because he wished for an opinion but simply to bridge the wide silence, which seemed to grow wider. Seva Ram's face lit up with a smile, as it always did, and he said, 'I am happy, Arjun. You will be happy and have children.'

Overcome with shyness, Arjun talked to Seva Ram about how he had come to his decision. It felt strange to be talking to his father, with whom he had never in his life shared any confidence. It was always to Tara that he had gone.

'What do you think about mother? She's not going to like it.'

'No, she is not. She had other plans.'

'You will tell her. Please, father.'

'Yes.'

'After I've gone this evening.'

'Yes.'

With the release of this tension and Seva Ram's ready compliance, Arjun suddenly felt a load lifted from his heart. He felt light-footed and wanted to hug his father. Briskly they walked back, but before they entered the house, Seva Ram said, 'Why don't you meet the guru, Arjun? Tell him about your plans. It's an important step after all. He'll give you strength.'

'Do I have to?' said Arjun shyly.

'No.'

'Then I'd rather not.'

'You're not a believer, I know, but he's a good guide. On a human level I mean.'

'I know. But I don't want to talk to anyone about it.'

'Anyway, I hope you will bring her to us soon—to your mother. I think she will appreciate it.'

For two days after Arjun's departure, Seva Ram did not say anything. Tara was conscious that there was something on his mind, but she bided her time patiently. On the third day Seva Ram broke the news and Tara was plunged into the depths of gloom. For days she was unable to think or act. She knew her son, and realized that it was futile to change his mind. Nevertheless, after several weeks she wrote to him; among other things she said:

Marriage, my son, is a serious business, and has to be entered into soberly and irrevocably. I don't want to suggest that it need be gloomy. But the emotions and upsets of courtship which character-ize marriage in the West are not a part of our tradition in India. . . . The main reason we marry is that we shall not be lonely in old age. So we should ask ourselves if we shall be able to converse well with this person into old age. They say that a man should choose a wife by his ear than by his eye. . . . You have the good sense to realize that beauty is only skin deep, and there are more important considera-tions. . . . It is your decision entirely, but do also look into her age, her past, her character, and the financial condition of her family. . . . When a match has equal partners, then there is nothing to fear. Ask yourself: is she your equal? Are you her equal? . . . . Finally, my son, beware of the love of a woman, beware of ecstasy: both are a slow poison. . . .

Arjun's reply came promptly, and it was most unsatisfactory. He was firmly set in his decision. Tara asked Seva Ram whether it would be worthwhile for her to go to Bombay and to try to dissaude him. He emphatically replied, 'No.' She realized the futility of discussing it further and she concluded that putting pressure on him might only alienate him from her. She continued to feel hurt, however. She had had so many plans for him. Over the years she had suggested a number of girls from fine families. But each time he had refused, saying that he was not ready. In her heart she had secretly hoped that he would make 'a great match' with someone from the highest society, but it was not to be. Priti too would have been fine if it had not been for the scandal in her past and the changed circumstances of her family. But perhaps this is how it was destined to be, she thought with resignation.

As the days went by, Tara became more philosophical about Arjun's marriage. She thought it ridiculous the manner in which the human species paired. Animals in comparison seemed more sensible. The inordinate energy and emotion that humans ex-pended on this matter seemed quite unnecessary. Did it really matter whom one married in order to procreate the species? Would it not be better if one's partner were pre-ordained just as one's time and place of birth and death. The important thing was to take choice out of human control for humans were not good at exercising choice. Seva Ram of course disagreed with her as to the existence of choice at all.

8

Tara eventually gave her consent and Arjun and Priti were married.
Tara was also denied a grand wedding because both the young
people insisted on a simple ceremony. They moved into a larger
apartment in Colaba and Priti spent the first few weeks furnishing
the new flat. She had the walls white-washed, bought new hand-
woven curtains and chick blinds for the windows, and equipped
their new house with cane and rattan furniture since they could not
afford teak. She bought some crotons, ferns and umbrella palms
from the nursery near the Sachivalya. A leather chair for Arjun was
the only expensive thing she acquired. She also stopped working
because she wanted, as she put it, 'fulfilment as a wife and a
mother.'

Arjun was happy, without a care in the world. He plunged into
his work with a new vigour. The sight of her in the window waiting
for him as he returned home, and a walk together on Cuffe Parade,
followed by a simple dinner, and many such small things in which
he had never thought he would find pleasure, now made up much
of his happiness. Every morning he would wake up with surprise
to find her beside him on the pillow. He would watch the early
sunlight falling on her cheeks, and then observe her eyes at close
range, looking larger than ever especially when she blinked them
several times in quick succession on waking. Dark brown in the
filtered light of the blinds, they seemed to contain layers of colour,
dark at the depths and growing brighter towards the surface. He
saw himself reflected in her eyes, and he would lose himself in
them.

Leaning on the window sill, her magnificent head slanted to one
side, and her dressing gown wrapped carelessly around her, she
would wave to him as she saw him off. As he set off to work, with
the sun on his back and his nostrils filled with the morning air of the
sea, he thought himself one of the luckiest men alive.

When had life been so good to him, he wondered? Certainly not in his childhood in Simla, when he was alone among boys who were cleverer and had more money in their pockets. Nor as an adolescent, when he could only remember how he had made a fool of himself in the Green Room, and had suffered such anguish on Priti's account. And then for years he had lived loveless and alone in Bombay. But now this beautiful woman, who he had desired since he was nineteen, was his for life! He could not bear to be away from her for long. Each day he would hurry back from work, and mount the stairs to their flat with excitement in his heart.

They would sometimes sit together in the evening and look at old photographs, which he kept in a shoe box. One picture struck her particularly. It was printed in sepia ink and was quite unlike any other. The picture had been composed with an eye for detail. It showed a man standing in the foreground, with several English soldiers lounging about in front of a barrack-like structure. In the background a broad plain stretched into the hazy distance, merging on the left with a row of trees on the dusty horizon. A yellowish sky complemented the harmony of the landscape.

'Your grandfather?' she asked.

'Yes, that's Bauji,' he replied.

'Where was it taken?'

'Lyallpur.'

'When?'

'1919. The year that Gandhi entered Indian politics.'

The photographer had captured a sense of mischief and triumph on Bauji's face. But underneath it, as one looked into the eyes, there was also another tangible emotion: a deep sadness. Either it was the figures of the foreign soldiers in the back, or the distant expanse of the desolate plain and the horizon bathed in a strange half-light, which seemed to add to the feeling of tragic grandeur. Both the age of the picture and the sepia ink contributed to the poignance of the scene.

Arjun got up and moved away from Priti and he said, 'It was taken soon after the massacre at Jallianwalla Bagh, during the dark days of the Rowlatt Act, when Indians had to alight from a carriage and salaam every passing Englishman. Being a proud man, Bauji stopped going out at all. But once he had to meet his Muslim friend, Mian Afzal Hussain, the Principal of the Agricultural College at the station. As their tonga was passing the barracks, which you see in the back, they were stopped by two English tommies. They were asked to get off and made to walk. And they were abused and called "dirty niggers" by the soldiers. Bauji ignored them, but when the soldier struck his coachman with a whip, Bauji shouted back "Soldier, the DC's order does not permit you to strike anyone. Your countrymen have established a rule of law which protects this coachman as much as it protects you."

"'Don't you know, black man, I am a cousin to King George V," the soldier had jeered.

'After dropping his friend, Bauji went to the DC's office and lodged an official complaint. A few weeks later he stood up in the District Magistrate's court and gave evidence. The verdict of the DM went against the soldier. That the punishment, a small fine, was meagre compared to his own deep feeling of humiliation did not matter (as it seemed to, to some of his friends). It vindicated Bauji's faith in the English Raj: an Englishman had arrested one of his own, and had punished him.'

'But why the sadness, Arjun?' asked Priti.

After a pause he replied, 'Because, I suppose, he was aware that despite everything, we were still a subject race.'

'And how did the picture come to be taken?' she asked.

'A few months later,' Arjun said, 'when things were back to normal, some friends of Bauji persuaded him to return to the scene of the incident, and they had a picture taken.'

'That's you, isn't it, in this picture? said Priti, turning to another photograph.

'Yes, it's family picture taken in the garden of our house in Simla.'

'Of course it's Simla! I can almost smell the air and the pine trees in the back.' And she took a deep breath. 'Look at you in the corner in your shabby school shirt and your small boy's brown eyes, shiny kneecaps, and your queer smile with dimples. That's your mother, of course. And your father, looking stern. I don't remember his being stern. But who's that dandy fellow in the corner?'

'That's Big Uncle. In fact he once came to your house.'

'Looks like he has to go to the lavatory, the way he has crossed his legs.'

Arjun laughed.

'What does he have in his pockets?'

'Sweets. He always carried sweets which he distributed to children on the road. He was funny and all the children loved him. He almost didn't make it in time for the picture because he had gone to the Upper Mall for a haircut. He wanted to look his best. You remember that saloon near the post office. It was the most expensive barber in Simla—I forget the name. Big Uncle used to go into raptures as he described the barber's technique. "It's a whole art, you know—all a question of the angle of the razor," he used to say seriously. After the haircut he would always get a head massage, which he called "electric friction". When the ritual was over, he would examine his reflection in the mirror with self-satisfaction. "Yes" he would say in a clipped way giving a short authoritative nod, "it'll do".'

She laughed. 'And who took this picture?'

'Karan,' he replied.

At first Priti enjoyed managing the house. When they had first met at Bombay Gym, she was cynical and disillusioned with nothing more to learn and nothing new to feel. She had merely wanted peace and quiet in her life. Arjun had entered at the right moment, and had created a stir in her, and brought her that quiet stability. She too believed that finally this was happiness. But after some time she slowly tired of the domestic routine and longed for something new. She began to wonder whether this peaceful stable life was the happiness that she had always wanted.

Before the wedding, she had fully thought herself in love. But now she started to question the nature of love between a man and a woman and wondered if there was something higher and more permanent. Not that she cared for Arjun any less; she was merely groping for a new kind of excitement.

Although he was sensitive, Arjun could not have easily guessed what was going on in her mind. As their domestic intimacy grew familiar and into a pattern, she began to observe their life with a kind of detachment, to hold herself more aloof from the routine and to contemplate the meaning of 'family life'. Sometimes Arjun came home late from work, at eight or even nine o'clock. He would be hungry, and as soon as he had showered and changed, they would sit down to eat. Wanting to ease his mind from the day's activities, he would eat silently and in comfort. She would want him to talk about the business world and the excitement of the day, but he found it an effort. Thus they would exchange few words, mostly small talk, and being tired he would go off to bed and immediately fall asleep. His earlier ardour tended to fade and their sexual life threatened to lapse into a routine; his embraces began to lack freshness and vigour.

And yet, occasionally, it seemed to her that this was the finest time of her life. To savour it fully, she felt that their circumstances could perhaps have been different. But what they ought to have been she was not sure. She would have liked to talk to someone about her feelings. But none of her friends, like Neena and Rao Sahib's family, or admirers like Nawab Sahib or Arjun's few bachelor friends seemed appropriate. How could she describe an intangible feeling of discontent that changed from day to day? To the outside world, she appeared to be infinitely blessed, having married a 'rich catch'.

Arjun had learnt to be thrifty from his mother, but Priti found some of his habits downright stingy. This sometimes created a problem between them. But it assumed serious proportions when Tara came to visit them. She found Priti 'spoiled and prodigal'. Priti complained that her mother-in-law was prejudiced against her. Tara, who had carefully budgeted her own household expenses all her life and managed to run her house on Seva Ram's modest salary, was appalled that Priti did not care about the butter, the sugar, and the gas that was used up in a month. She neatly stacked the sheets and towels in the bathroom closet and taught Priti to lock the pantry when she went out. Priti accepted her advice quietly because she did not think it worth arguing over; besides she was basically more detached about her possessions. All day long Tara went around the house worrying about which shopkeeper was cheating them, and she found Priti's cavalier manner irritating. To this was added the humiliation of seeing her son dote so completely on her daughter-in-law that he seemed to forget his own mother. She sometimes felt left out. Tara couldn't help but envy Priti because she couldn't remember having experienced this constant and demonstrative devotion from her own husband. In Arjun's love for Priti she saw a defection from her own love, as if Priti was encroaching on something that was hers. In such moments she observed Arjun's happiness in gloomy silence. Once she even reminded Arjun that it was unbecoming for a man to give into every whim of his wife. She recalled her own past, and she counselled him that 'manly men kept their wives in place' from the beginning and made it known who had the upper hand in a house; it was not proper in a man to worship his wife.

Arjun was caught in a novel dilemma, and did not know what to say. He respected his mother but he utterly adored Priti. He felt

Tara had good judgement and Priti could benefit from it, yet he could not bring himself to openly criticize his wife. Arjun gently tried to pass on some of Tara's suggestions, but Priti responded in such a remote and abstracted manner, that Arjun was soon silenced.

All the time deep inside her, Priti waited for something to happen. She was quite clear in her mind that it was not another man that she desired. But what was it that she wanted? She did not know. Every morning she would wake up and hope to find it there. She looked out of the window, listened to every new sound, but nothing would happen. At sunset, she would grow sad and wait for the next day.

9

One day Arjun came home early. He looked flushed and excited.
Both Priti and Tara were at first concerned, but they quickly
realized that nothing was wrong with him. He had brought news
of a major national event which would in time envelop them and
totally change their lives.

'The Supreme Court has confirmed that she is guilty. It came on
our wire this afternoon,' he informed them.

'Oh no!' gasped Priti.

'How can the Court do it? It is like removing the Prime Minister
for speeding in traffic,' said Tara outraged.

At three forty-five that afternoon the Supreme Court had confirmed that Prime Minister Indira Gandhi was guilty 'of corrupt
election practices'.

'Strange are the workings of the law,' said Arjun.

'She won by over a lakh votes, for pity's sake,' said Tara. 'Can
anyone believe that using a few government people for putting up
some rostrums and mikes could have affected the outcome. It was
a minor impropriety, not an offence.'

'The law is blind, mother. And no one is above it, thank god!'

'You seem almost happy!' said Tara.

'I hope she won't do anything reckless now,' said Priti.

'If she is smart, she will resign,' said Arjun.

'Everyone knows the offences are minor. She will get a lot of
sympathy. In eight months she can return to power at the next
general election.'

'Her father would have resigned. I don't know about her,' said
Priti.

'I too am afraid,' said Arjun.

Their worst fears were realized. On 26 June 1975 the Prime
Minister declared an Emergency. Before dawn police parties acting
under her orders woke up political opponents and locked them up.
In those thirty-six hours Arjun felt that India had changed from a

democracy to a dictatorship. Arjun, Tara and Priti were all numb
with shock.

'She won't get away with it,' he said. 'A democracy can't become
a dictatorship just like that.'

'"Democracy" and "dictatorship" are big words,' said Priti.
'Every five years people go to the polls and vote for whom they are
told to vote. There's no real opposition, there's only the Nehru
family. Is that really a democracy?'

'Come, come, Arjun,' said Tara. 'To talk of dictatorship is a bit
extreme, isn't it? Besides we do need some discipline in our national
life.'

'I bet he's behind it,' said Arjun.

'Who?' asked Tara.

'Sanjay. She only listens to him these days.'

Arjun and his family were not excessively political. Their reac-
tions to these events were not very different to the rest of the
country. What they said reflected what was being talked about in
millions of homes. Many were initially angry, especially the educated. But they got used to the Emergency and were soon absorbed
in their daily lives and their work. Arjun was no different.

Arjun had always enjoyed his work and done it well. A year
earlier he had again been promoted, this time to Sales Director. He
was one of the youngest ever to occupy this position and he was
rightly proud. Inside the office it was generally believed that he had
earned his elevation. He had eventually succeeded in convincing
the company to market the companion product, Bombay Colds
Balm, and it too had been a huge success. In the head office in
Bombay, of course, there were some managers who complained
that he had been promoted too quickly. But they were moved by
envy. As a matter of fact Arjun's new flat had come as a result of his
promotion rather than the compulsions of marriage. Happily the
two events had almost coincided. The company had a limited
number of flats and these were assigned on the basis of seniority.
On his salary Arjun could never have been able to afford a larger
flat, rents being what they were on the island of Bombay.

One of the main issues that Arjun had to tackle in his new
position was a growing militancy in the trade. There was a threat
looming in the east. Over the past few years, the retailers who sold
his products had banded together to fight for higher margins from
the companies. Typically, collectivizing began around a local leader,
who went around from shop to shop convincing the shopkeepers

that it was in their interest to unite. Where there was no strong leader, the market remained passive and dealers were fragmented.

The most successful leader was Ram Kishen Guha, who had united the chemists, wholesalers and the general merchants in central Calcutta. He had recently been successful in forcing the smaller companies to raise their retail margin from ten to seventeen per cent, and wholesaler margin from four to seven.

Having tasted success with the smaller firms, Guha was ready to take on the bigger ones. He hit upon a plan to select one large company as a target and convince retailers to refuse to stock its products until it agreed to a higher margin. Once it 'fell', he would select a second and a third, and soon they would all follow suit. It was certainly a clever strategy. The first company he thus honoured was Arjun's.

One morning Arjun walked into his office to discover that he was boycotted in the large Calcutta market. The traders in the neighbouring markets of Bengal, Bihar and Orissa had also struck 'in sympathy'. Arjun thus found that a quarter of his sales target was in jeopardy. Unless he acted fast the movement might spread.

Arjun flew to Calcutta. He talked to a lot of people and confirmed that the situation was serious. Not a single dealer was prepared to sell his products. Guha's success must have surprised even him. He wanted to meet Guha, but the latter refused. Arjun returned to Bombay and briefed the Board. Billimoria considered giving in to the pressure, because the daily loss in sales was far greater than the value of the increased margin. The Finance Director agreed saying they could accede and immediately recover the loss by raising prices to the consumer. Others in the management also felt the same. Arjun found himself isolated. He strongly believed in holding firm and fighting. He argued that higher consumer prices would reduce the volume of sales, especially of the lower priced sizes. The poor classes would just not be able to pay the extra ten per cent, and would stop buying them.

Arjun argued with the Board that giving in to the trade would be the beginning of appeasement. The traders would merely escalate their demands in the next round. He likened the boycott to a strike by a militant union, and urged them to respond maturely by negotiation.

'But they will not negotiate,' said one Board member.

'We must keep trying,' said Arjun.

'Every day of lost sales is a permanent loss.'

'We just have to accept the short-term loss for a much larger long term gain.'

With some difficulty Arjun succeeded in getting fifteen days from the Board in which to negotiate and reach agreement. He flew back to Calcutta, and settled down in the Grand Hotel for a long siege. Redeploying his best men from other territories, he and his managers set up a field headquarters, and executed a two-pronged strategy: while Arjun attempted to open negotiations with Guha, his men dispersed and set out to win key dealers to their point of view. Using a cogently developed brief, his men pointed out to the dealers the risks of the boycott—it was a 'restrictive trade practice' which might invite action from the government; it meant loss of goodwill from their customers who could not easily substitute some of the company's products, especially the lower-priced packs—and they reaffirmed the company's desire to negotiate the margins with the trade leadership. A week later Arjun took the issue directly to the public in a series of advertisements in the local newspapers. As a result of these moves, a few old loyal stockists and wholesalers started to break ranks and much to Arjun's surprise the boycott began to weaken. Arjun escalated the pressure by announcing in the press the names of dealers where consumers could directly buy the company's products. The boycott now seemed on the verge of breaking and Guha succumbed to the pressure and agreed to negotiate. But the negotiations did not get anywhere because the gap between what Arjun offered and the demand of the association was too great. Before the negotiations broke, Guha threatened Arjun with 'serious consequences' if he persisted in his efforts to break the boycott.

Arjun flew the next day to Delhi. There he met a firm of lawyers, developed a legal brief and filed a complaint with the Monopolies and Restrictive Trade Practices Commission. He also met officials in the Industries Ministry and tried to solicit their aid. One of the Joint Secretaries agreed to help by issuing a letter 'deploring the boycott'. Arjun had the letter promptly published in the Calcutta press. He returned to Bombay and appealed to the industry association to consider a joint action against the trade: he asked for a month's boycott by the larger companies of the trade in Calcutta.

Even though he did not succeed in mobilizing the industry, his moves were deliberately leaked, and when he returned to Calcutta there was fear in the trade and Guha was angry. Guha's next move was totally unexpected. He hired thugs who systematically beat up

Arjun's salesmen and managers; two godowns of the loyal stockists were burnt down within twenty-four hours; the company van in Hooghly was looted; and the brakes of Arjun's car suddenly failed as he was on his way to offer his sympathies to the stockists whose shops had been burned. Arjun went to the police where he discovered that he was up against a different kind of enemy. The police officer 'advised' Arjun to leave Calcutta immediately since his life was in danger. That evening Priti phoned from Bombay to say that she had received a threat to her life. Having discovered that Guha had 'police protection', Arjun's confidence was shaken. His men were totally demoralized. The boycott in the market was also complete again.

That night there was a knock on Arjun's door at the hotel. A man brought a message that Guha wanted to see him at his home. Arjun was afraid, but he seemed to have no choice, because the man looked 'persuasive'. They drove for an hour to Salt Lake, a new suburb of the new rich of Calcutta. Arjun had discovered that Guha was not a trader himself, but a small-time politician who had hit upon a good racket in 'trade unity'. Being a new and distant suburb, Salt Lake was dark and Arjun was even more afraid. Soon they arrived at a brand new, brightly lit bungalow. As soon as he was led into the drawing room Arjun realized that he had totally misjudged his man. On one wall was a huge photograph of Sanjay Gandhi and on another a smaller one of Mrs Gandhi. Far from being 'small time', Guha seemed to have political connections at the highest level.

Guha was alone in the room drinking whisky. He got up with a smile, shook Arjun's hand, and politely offered him a drink. Arjun looked around and realized that everything in the house was new—from the briefcase on the table, the furniture, the refrigerator, to the owner's clothes and shoes. Guha came quickly to the point. He offered Arjun a deal. He wanted to be paid twenty lakhs, and the boycott would be called off almost on Arjun's terms. He requested an extra half per cent to retailers over Arjun's last offer, in order to 'save the face' of the trade association. In order to keep the company's books clean, the payment could be recorded as 'a donation towards the building fund of the trade association'. Arjun would also have to withdraw the complaint in Delhi. Guha had thought of everything. He finally emphasized that this would be much cheaper for the company than a protracted boycott.

'And if I refuse?' said Arjun.

'Then the boycott will be escalated and you will have to personally pay for your refusal.'

Arjun did not dare ask what that meant.

'Why don't you think about it tonight? Talk to your people and call me tomorrow. No one must know about the payment, except your boss and your accountant.'

Arjun stayed awake that night thinking not about whether to pay up but about the consequences. He was clear in his mind that there was no question about paying. He wondered how the company could cut its losses if the boycott continued. The next day he spoke to Billimoria, informed him about what was happening, and advised against the payment. He spoke to Priti, and reassured her that he was all right, and told her not to worry. He booked a ticket to return to Bombay the same evening. Then he called Guha and told him that the payment would not be possible, but he would return to Calcutta with a counter-proposal after reviewing the situation with his people.

'Was it they who refused the money?' Guha asked.

'No. I don't think it can be done.'

Half-an-hour before his departure for the airport two plain-clothesmen came to Arjun's room and told him that he was under arrest.

'On what grounds?' he asked.

'Under MISA.' He was shown a warrant signed by the Deputy Commissioner of Calcutta, dated 1 October 1975. It stated that Arjun was to be detained under the Maintenance of Internal Security Act (MISA). Under the emergency MISA allowed the government to detain a person indefinitely without trial, or without producing charges before a court of law.

'This is Sanjay Gandhi's Raj, eh?' Arjun said bitterly. He realized that he had become a victim of the Emergency.

10

At the Lalbazar police station, officers were waiting, drinking tea and biscuits. In the back room, armed men of the Central Reserve Police lounged around leering at a young female prisoner. Arjun sat stiffly on a bench. Numerous officers and civilians came and went, each repeating the same question and each noting his replies in his little book. Nobody seemed to take much interest in his answers; they were mainly interested in completing the formalities. Through the open door Arjun could see a boy sitting on the floor, his wrists handcuffed, waist roped, one eye purple and swollen, blood trickling down his cheek. There was an iron trestle nearby. The boy was only wearing shorts and shivering with fever. As Arjun was led to his cell, he saw a policeman hit the boy with a rifle butt. Arjun looked quizzically at his guard.

'Naxalite,' spat out the guard. 'Very dangerous! They don't confess easily.'

Arjun wondered how a middle class Bengali youth could be dangerous, even if he were fighting for the rights of the rural poor. The guard flung Arjun inside his cell with such violence that he slipped on the floor, and struck the back of his head. The blow dazed him. He dragged himself to the wall. He huddled there, his back to the wall, his legs stretched out on the floor. Later that evening, the same boy half-dead was brought into a cell next to his. As Arjun lay down to sleep, the boy began to shiver violently. Arjun asked the guard to give him a shirt. The guard sneered in reply. About half-an-hour later, unable to sleep, Arjun took off his own shirt and gave it to the grateful boy.

After a few days, Arjun was shifted to Gaya Central Jail in Bihar. During those first few days, he was numb and barely conscious of being in prison. He had a vague hope throughout that something would turn up, some agreeable surprise. He wondered why no one had come to see him. The answer came soon in Priti's first letter telling him that they would not allow her to visit him. She said that a team of lawyers, engaged by his company, had been working day and night. 'We were all in Calcutta (including Billimoria) the day after your arrest, but it was futile. Everyone says these are different times (referring to the Emergency). I'm sick to death that we haven't been able to help you so far. They won't even let me see you, because you are detained under MISA—they use this word so ominously, as if you had committed some terrible crime.'

From that moment Arjun realized that his cell would be his home for a long time. Gaya Central Jail was a long, low, yellow-ochre dormitory, surrounded by red earth, bushes, and a vegetable garden. Arjun was put in a cell by himself; it was thirty-five feet square and completely bare except for a small earthen pitcher and several coarse grey blankets containing the dirt and grease of his predecessors. He folded the blankets to make a bed on the stone floor. His cell looked out to a yard. The walls were white-washed and pitted with nail holes. In one corner was the toilet, a hole in the wall, with a raised floor on which was cut an oblong slit. The open drain from all the toilets ran past the outer wall of his cell, filling the hot nights with a stench that made him retch. This smell was sometimes intermingled with jasmine because a 'poetically inclined' Superintendent some years ago had planted jasmine bushes along the compound wall.

Not knowing what to expect in prison, Arjun was initially afraid. When he heard the sound of people in the corridor outside his cell, his first thought was that the beating was about to start. He stopped in the middle of the cell, listened, his chin pushed forward. The steps outside came to a halt. He heard a low command, the keys jingled, and there was silence. He stood stiffly between the bed and the toilet, held his breath, and waited for the first scream. But the scream did not come. Then he heard a faint clanging, a voice murmured something, a cell door slammed. The footsteps moved on. Arjun went to the spy-hole and looked into the corridor. The men stopped nearby opposite his cell. They were two orderlies, dragging a bucket of tea, followed by an armed guard. There was to be no beating. They were serving breakfast.

The physical discomfort bothered Arjun less than the isolation. He had not the slightest idea what happened outside his cell; he did not know how many persons were there or who was in the adjoining cells. The only people he saw were those who sloshed out his food from two dirty buckets and cleared the latrine. The Head Warden would come around twice a day to check the lock. Occasionally the Superintendent (in dark glasses) came to inspect, accompanied by armed guards. Shut up for days with nothing to do, idleness was a torment.

The silence almost broke his nerves. At first it did not seem harmful; on the contrary it helped him to think more clearly. But soon he realized that the silence actually made him think less. His brain seemed to stagnate with no one to talk to. At times he played with the illusion that he was dreaming. He tried to make himself believe that the whole thing was unreal. If I succeed in believing that I am dreaming, then it will really be a dream, he thought.

Arjun almost welcomed his interrogators even though they were rude to him and abused him. It was a chance to speak to someone. The plainclothes officers brought a bit of the outside world into his lonely life. He would try to prolong his interrogation through long-winded answers. But eventually his interrogators would leave and he would return to his solitary world, thirty-five square feet. Arjun would walk up and down in the cell, from the door to the window and back, between the bed and the toilet, seven-and-a-half steps there, and seven-and-a-half steps back. It was a natural habit which all prisoners got into; if you did not change direction at the turn, you quickly became dizzy.

One day, angry at the disgusting food and the isolation, Arjun threw his plate back at the guard. The next day he was taken out of his cell. It was eleven o'clock in the morning when they came to fetch him. By the Warden's solemn expression, Arjun guessed that it was serious. He followed the Warden. They crossed several corridors and a courtyard. They passed a staircase leading underground. He wondered what was down there. He did not like the look of the staircase. Then they crossed a narrow, windowless room; it was a blind shaft, rather dark, but over it hung the open sky. They turned into a small room and there he saw the same kind of iron trestle he had seen in the police station in Calcutta. But it was a cane about four feet long and half-an-inch thick. He was told to strip. When he was standing naked, someone knocked at the door, and the Superintendent walked in. Arjun felt humiliated to have to stand there unclothed before strangers. They bent him over the trestle and tied his wrists and ankles. He found it difficult to breathe in this position. At a signal from the Superintendent, the guard came forward and gave Arjun several strokes. He screamed. They put a wet cloth on his buttocks and completed the rest of his 'sentence'. They had put the wet cloth over him so that the skin would not cut too badly and leave permanent marks. Nevertheless, there was blood all over his buttocks. The pain was awful and he felt faint.

Time passed slowly. He tried to devise ways to make it pass quicker: he would count the moments remaining for his daily walk in the compound in the evening; he would count the stars at night; he would count how long it took the cloud overhead to drift out of sight. He tried to remember his past as minutely as possible and he learned to exercise his memory. He would think about his child-hood in Simla. Starting with his bedroom, he would try to make a complete inventory of every piece of furniture, right down to the stains, and each article upon it, and try to visualize every detail of each piece. From the bedroom he would move on to the drawing room, and the kitchen, the garden, the classrooms and so on. Each room would trigger off memories of people and incidents, and before he realized it hours had gone by. His memory grew sharper and he became more and more comfortable living in the past.

The winter evenings were more difficult. He had a thin shirt to protect him from the harsh winds and often he spent the night shivering under ragged blankets. The cement floor was icy cold. To keep from freezing, he would interrupt his sleep, rise and start walking up and down. But after a while his legs would grow stiff, and he would stretch out again on the floor or sit with his back to the wall. His teeth would chatter as he waited for the sun to rise. The sun would bring warmth; he would grow more impatient waiting for the warmth than for the food. He was cold, miserable, and lonely. His whole life revolved around trying to stay warm and hoping that they would give him enough gruel at the next meal so that he would not be hungry.

Thus the months went by. He did not receive any letters, except the first one from Priti. Just as he had given up all hope, the Head Warden himself came one day to fetch him. 'Visitors,' he an-nounced. 'Your family has come. You can meet them at the office.'

The office was littered with files and papers, and crowded not only with clerks but also with other prisoners' relatives. Everyone was shouting or talking loudly. Seva Ram and Tara were seated in one corner with Priti standing beside them; they presented a picture of calm and dignity amidst the confusion. They were wedged between a small peasant woman from Bihar and a fat

Punjabi matron in salwar-kameez, who was talking shrilly and gesticulating all the time. Some of the lower caste prisoners and their relatives were squatting on the floor opposite each other. They did not raise their voices, and despite the din, managed to converse in whispers. Arjun noticed a prison official at each door. He stood in front of his parents and Priti. Seeing him thus, emaciated and ragged, Tara began to cry. He looked at Priti; she gazed at him with a dark sombre brow, trying hard to smile. He thought she looked very pretty, but somehow he could not bring himself to say so in front of his parents in the prison office. As he glimpsed her sad, quick smile, he had a great desire to put his arms around her and hold her to him. Instead he merely smiled back silently.

'How long has it been?' he asked. He had lost track of the time.

'Four months,' said Seva Ram. Arjun was surprised; he thought it must be much longer.

They were silent for some time. He kept looking at Priti. Although she could not bring herself to say anything, her eyes seemed to ask if they were treating him well, if he was all right, if he needed anything. At the same time, he detected a strange, distant look in her eyes, the kind that his father sometimes had. He wanted to know 'how much longer', but he figured they would tell him if they knew.

The fat woman was bawling at the prisoner beside him; he was her husband presumably, a tall and dignified Punjabi peasant.

'Are you all right?' said the peasant gently.

The fat woman laughed loudly. 'What do you think? I'm a picture of health. You're the one in jail,' she said.

Meanwhile the prisoner from Bihar on his right hardly said a word. His eyes were fixed on the peasant woman opposite him, and she returned his look with a sort of hungry passion.

'You mustn't lose hope,' Tara said.

Arjun nodded and looked again at Priti. Her sari heightened her curves. He had a great longing to squeeze her breasts and her buttocks through the thin material.

'Don't worry about her,' said Tara following his gaze. 'She's staying at the ashram with us. She is going to give you a baby.'

Arjun did not know what to say. He was pleased but the fat woman was now yelling louder than ever, telling her husband that she had brought a basket, and describing its contents with the prices. She reminded him to be sure to check because the prison staff were thieves. The younger peasant on his side was still gazing mournfully at the woman opposite him. The strident voice of the fat woman jarred in Arjun's ears. There was no let-up.

One by one the prisoners were slowly led away. Gradually it became quiet. A warden tapped the Punjabi peasant's shoulder and he turned to leave. The fat woman shouted at him—she didn't seem to realize it was no longer necessary to shout. 'Mind yourself, now. We are all waiting for you.'

Soon it was Arjun's turn. He looked back as he walked away. 'But we haven't even talked about the case!' said Tara in tears. Priti had not moved. Her head tilted, she looked at him with the same affectionate smile. As he walked back to his cell, he felt bothered by that calm, unvarying look on her face. He did not understand what it meant. It was a weary, distant look.

The next day he received clothes, home-made sweets, soap and toiletries, and some books and writing paper. As he paced the compound in the evening he was angry with himself for having forgotten to say all the things he had been wanting to for months. The one thing that he particularly wanted to tell them was to ask the prison to get him out of 'solitary'. He desperately wanted to talk to someone. The visit had been an unsettling experience forcing him to remember life outside, the people he loved, and things that he missed. For the first few days he felt an insane desire for a woman; this was natural enough, considering his age. He mostly thought of Priti, and the memories of their love-making surrounded him, hurting him. He could not believe that she was pregnant. He had forgotten to ask when the baby was due. He also thought of other women he had known, in his office, at the Gym, cousins, friends, anyone. His cell seemed to become crowded with faces, bodies, and his lustful frenzy grew.

No longer did he think about the circumstances of his arrest. This was a change from his early days in prison when he could think of nothing else. In those days he would constantly imagine alternative endings: What if he had given in? What if he had left the decision to his boss? Would they have jailed Billimoria instead? He had a lingering suspicion that Billimoria would have paid Guha if his own neck had been on the line. He would try to go further back. What if Mrs Gandhi had not declared the Emergency? Slowly he would realize the futility of thinking about the 'what ifs' of the past. And he would grow sad.

During the early interrogations he had not yet lost hope. He would plead with his interrogators. He would defend his action. He would ask about his rights. But each time he would be told, sometimes politely but usually callously, that under the dreaded MISA he had no rights: he could be detained indefinitely without a trial.

A few days later, quite out of the blue, he was shifted to another cell, which was cleaner and bigger and more comfortable, and most importantly he had a cellmate. Now he was also allowed newspapers, the use of the prison library. He was overjoyed and grateful. His cellmate was a labour leader from North Bihar named Dhiren Jha, who had worked the past few years in the rural areas, but insisted that he was not a Naxalite or a Communist. He had worked in Jayaprakash Narayan's movement and he had been arrested soon after JP himself and the declaration of the Emergency. He too had been in solitary confinement for a long time. Both Arjun and he had been hungry for conversation and they tried to make up for it in the first few days.

The coming of the monsoon brought the news that Priti had given birth to a baby girl. 'Mother and daughter getting along well' said the telegram. But the monsoons also brought physical discomfort. It rained every afternoon. The sky would become black and a tropical storm would pour down with howling winds. Arjun's cell was flooded after each storm. Blankets became sodden. During the rains Arjun and Jha would crouch in a corner with nowhere dry to sleep. Their feet would be wet and cold. Despite this they welcomed the rain. None of the officers came out in the downpours and sometimes they could spend several hours walking around the compound in the evenings in uninterrupted conversation. The warden thought they were crazy to walk in the rain, but after being in solitary confinement for months, they were eager for every opportunity to be outdoors.

One day, during his evening walk, Arjun was attracted by a stone in a quiet corner of the jail compound. Each day the stone was freshly decorated with red powder and flowers. He recognized it as the same auspicious powder which women commonly wore on their foreheads. A few days later he discovered that it was the work of a Bihari weaver, who occupied the cell next to his. He asked him about the stone. At first the weaver was upset and afraid. But gradually Arjun won his confidence.

'It is god,' said the weaver.

'And you worship it?'

'Yes.'

A week later the stone was not there. Thinking his neighbour would be grieved, Arjun asked him, 'What happened to your god?'

'The jail authorities removed it,' the weaver said nonchalantly.

'Well?'

'It doesn't matter. I have already found another stone and anointed it.'

Arjun was shocked. Slowly he realized that any piece of stone which his neighbour anointed became god for him. What mattered was the faith, not the stone. Gradually he began to understand how the weaver's mythical imagination directed his inner life. In his simplicity the weaver had kept alive the ancient way of perceiving the world, which was similar to the sages of the Vedas at the dawn of civilization.

Arjun was fascinated and disturbed. One part of him dismissed the weaver's world as superstitious; it was precisely this kind of obscurantism, he felt, which kept the country backward and perpetuated an unjust caste order. Another part of him was attracted to the weaver's daring subjective world, which enabled him to see organic connections between the animal and the human worlds and all of nature surrounding him.

11

Priti was sitting quietly by the riverbank one evening at the ancient ashram. It was the end of autumn, when the dark night is scratched by the lines of falling stars. With Arjun in jail, she had finally accepted Seva Ram's invitation to visit them. At first she had hesitated, but slowly the idea grew on her. She was lonely and unhappy in Bombay. She had to overcome her feelings for Tara, but Seva Ram's invitation was so warm and affectionate that she was eventually persuaded.

When Arjun first went to jail, she used to be busy all the time, working with his company's lawyers, meeting politicians and bureaucrats, trying to find some way to get him out of jail. She even contacted the Nawab and Dumpy. Billimoria and the others genuinely tried but their efforts were to no avail. The Nawab confessed one day his inability to help because he had found out from a high source that Arjun had insulted Sanjay at the time of his arrest. She cried when she heard this, and from then on she reconciled herself to a long, hard wait.

As she watched the sky expectantly, she remembered that as a young girl in Simla she had whispered a single word, 'love', deep from her heart at the very moment that she had seen a falling star. As the years passed, she had forgotten about her wish. Now she had become a mature woman, having gone through a full range of worldly experience; she had seen good and bad times; she had loved, she had been loved; she had rejected and she had been rejected. Thinking it would bring her happiness, she had eventually married and experienced the routine of married life. Now she had a baby as well. But each experience had left something to be desired. There had always remained a gap. She longed for an experience that would be permanent and bring her fullness. Much as she admired Arjun, much as she was fond of him and missed him, she also knew that he was not what she had wished for as a girl in Simla. A quiet voice inside her always whispered to her, 'It's not this; it's not this.' At the same time she was certain that it was there somewhere.

The turbulence in Priti's heart contrasted with the calm prevailing at the ashram. Earlier in the day she had experienced an utterly different feeling of peace while sitting at the feet of the venerable master. The shadows of her old attachments and experiences had passed before her eyes and had vanished. Her former efforts at excitement and love seemed ridiculous to her. For a brief moment she understood the meaning of her adolescent wish before the falling star, and she actually felt that it might be fulfilled.

The ancient guru had a strange power to awaken strong feelings towards himself, and she found herself gradually coming under his spell. In a simple yet powerful way, he taught her that the first duty of human beings is to seek the truth.

'Truth is known,' the guru told her, 'by the practice of contemplation in degrees of increasing intensity, rising to mystical ecstasy. In so doing one leaves behind the isolated, fearful, self-centred individual that one is, and becomes one with the universal and absolute reality. What the world thinks of as life is really death; our task is to escape from it to that which is truly life—the kind of life that man is intrinsically capable of and for which he is divinely intended.'

Priti was powerfully impressed with the idea that she could free herself from her own ego and from the control of her selfish longings which seemed to bind her to the needs of her body and to other transitory concerns.

Priti had not been particularly receptive in the beginning. Seva Ram had asked her if she would like to meet the sage and she had declined. But after a few days she felt inquisitive and she went to the morning assembly on her own. She was shy and therefore she sat at the back of the large hall. There were a number of people sitting on the floor in rows, the women on one side, the men on the other. The guru lifted up his head and looked directly into her eyes. She felt as if he were inviting her to come nearer. She was struck by the soft beauty of his eyes, so simple and direct. His attitude was natural and she no longer felt shy and began to attend meetings and to visit him.

'The essence of the truth,' said the guru, 'is basically the same in all the religions. It is that there is only one God and it is within each of us. We can find God through the practice of meditation under the direction of a living guru.'

The guru was over ninety years old now, but he was still extremely alert and confident. He stood tall but he had grown thinner; his skin was the colour of old ivory; his hair was white but it did not flow quite as it used to; his movements were easy and calm. He always sat cross-legged, his head slightly bent. His physical frame was weak and he used to get tired after some time and go inside to rest.

Watching the autumn sky one day and thinking of her life, Priti felt ashamed and foolish for having pursued the wrong people and the wrong things. It pricked her pride and made her feel foolish and sordid to realize that the people she had most respected as a youngster were the ones she most despised today. She grew angry at her own inertia. Slowly she became more agitated. Her distress was related to her doubts, her lack of will and her feeling of helplessness. She decided to go home. As she was rushing back she heard the guru's voice. She stopped and looked around. There was no one. She started to walk, and again she heard the same voice. She stopped again. She wondered if she was losing her mind. She could not make out what the voice said, but she clearly felt that the guru had spoken to her. She was attracted to the voice and wanted to pursue it. But it stopped. She waited and waited, but it was gone. When she reached home she wanted to tell Seva Ram about it, but she felt embarrassed. Secretly, she regarded the voice as a positive sign, and she was happy. Thinking of the guru, she felt her doubts dissolve and she felt free.

But Priti's tempestuous spirit could not bear to wait for long. The next day, sitting in the garden with Seva Ram, she told him everything: about her strangely powerful feelings for the guru, about the voice, about her doubts, even about her childhood wish before the falling star. Seva Ram listened intently. Eventually he spoke, 'When the student is ready the master appears.' Gently he described the life of the spirit, of the guru's love and of the soul's journey towards God. She felt lifted by what he said. As they talked, she felt extremely happy. She forgot her former unhappy moments, and no longer felt ashamed of her sensual past. She felt she could one day reach the highest state of mysticism, which was bare of everything except the infinite love of God. She told Seva Ram, 'The best thing about Bombay is the sea. And then you come here, and you feel that the sky is grander. And then you meet the guru, and you know that the inside of the human soul is the grandest of all.'

It was reassuring to learn from Seva Ram about the mystery of the love between the guru and the disciple. The living teacher was at the very heart of the matter, he explained, and she must not feel ashamed of her strong feelings for him. The guru would guide her soul through its difficult spiritual journey. He would teach her to meditate properly so that she could shake off the bonds of her mind and her body. Love was the only real basis of the relationship; she must never stop loving him.

Priti's behaviour underwent a change. She would wait patiently at the guru's door, for long hours of the day and night, just for a glimpse of his face. She did not mind the crowds, the jostling, and the heat. During the morning discourse, she would listen to him in rapt attention, her eyes scarcely moving from his face. While her hands remained closed in adoration, occasionally tears would flow down her cheeks. Anywhere else this behaviour would have been considered odd, but at the ashram it was regarded normal for initiates. Only Tara seemed to mind, and she reminded her daughter-in-law to conduct herself with more dignity.

'Priti,' said Tara one morning. 'Where is your diamond ring? I haven't seen it for days.'

Priti blushed and turned very red. 'It's ah. . . it's ah lost,' she said in a fluster.

'Lost! What do you mean, child? Nothing gets lost at the ashram.'

'I must have misplaced it then.'

'The servants couldn't have stolen it, but I don't know about the woman who comes to wash the clothes. She's new.'

'I'm sure she didn't steal it.'

'Well, what could have happened to it?'

'I. . . I don't know.'

'Priti, what is it? Why don't you come clean.'

'Well, I can't tell you.'

'It's up to you, my dear. It's a valuable ring. I got the diamond as part of my dowry. And Bhabo got it in marriage from her father.'

Priti remained upset the whole day. She did not come out at lunch, nor did she go to sit by the river in the evening. When Seva Ram returned home at night, she went up to him and burst into tears. He put his arms around her and tried to quiet her. Through her tears she explained that she had left her ring in the guru's pocket.

'He has given me so much and I have given him nothing in return. He's given me his love. I feel so ungrateful. Well, the other day I offered him my ring. He wouldn't accept it. I insisted that he take it as a token of my love. He still didn't take it. He merely smiled in his usual way. I tried to argue with him, but it was no use. So when he went out of the room I quickly hid the ring in the pocket of his coat—the one he never wears.'

'But why did you do it, Priti? What would he do with a ring?'

'Well, he could wear it. I have noticed his fingers are not very different from mine.'

'You know he won't.'

'He lives so simply. I mean he seems poor. I just couldn't bear it that I live so well. When it gets cold, he doesn't even have enough warm clothes. I thought that if he felt cold he could sell the ring and buy himself warm clothes.'

Priti spoke so naively and innocently, that Seva Ram had tears in his eyes. He hugged her. He was moved by her childlike affection for the guru. He went to his room and brought her ring and he said, 'Priti, a true guru doesn't take anything from a disciple. In accepting anything he would take on the burden of the disciple's karma, which he doesn't want to. The other day when you left the ring, he sent for me. He gave the ring back, and he said, "This jewel belonged to Bhabo and to Tara, I can't take it—too much there. But tell Priti that I love her very much. I also know that she loves me."'

During the Diwali holidays, the guru left for his annual tour to deliver discourses in the major cities of India. In his absence Priti felt forlorn. She would sit alone on the banks of the river. The weather was dreary. Winter clouds hung over the sky and chilly winds had started to blow from the Himalayas. In the absence of the guru there was no cheer in Diwali: no gaiety, no sweets nor even delight in her own daughter. But Tara and Seva Ram loved the baby with a passion and so there was always someone to look after her. Sometimes they spoke sadly of Arjun. Priti discovered that she had grown so detached from her former life that she seemed to listen to talk about Arjun as if she were an observer. Tara would get tears in her eyes when she spoke about her son, and Priti would console her. Priti realized that she still cared about Arjun, but it was a different feeling from Tara's. She began to think of Arjun's life in jail as a necessary outcome of his karma, something that he was destined to go through. Since she now believed that the real world was the inner one deep inside her, the outer world of Arjun and Bombay seemed faded and bland in comparison. Even the baby did not feel quite real or something that was her own.

12

The evening chanting of the *sandhya* was over. For a quarter-of-an-hour Arjun had watched from his flat the magnificent pink light turn into dusk over the sea; for a quarter-of-an-hour voices of Seva Ram, Tara, Priti and his two daughters and their girl friends had interwoven a rhythmic chant in Sanskrit. During the melodic strain the whole atmosphere in the white stucco drawing room seemed to change. Even Rajah, their princely Indian hound, given to the girls by their grandmother, looked penitent and abashed.

Now, as the voices fell silent and the lights were switched on in the apartment, everything dropped back into its usual disorder. Golden-haired Rajah jumped up and ran about barking. The women rose quickly to their feet, their silk saris rustling as they left the room. The girls fussed with their dresses and their hair, exchanged quick glances and snatches of boarding school slang. For over three weeks his daughters had been home from their school in the Himalayas. It was their summer break, and they were happy to be back with the family. The grandparents were also visiting Bombay, glad to escape the northern heat. Restlessly, Priti glanced around at her noisy children and her quiet husband, and walked out towards the kitchen to oversee the dinner arrangements. A large number of people would be dining with them tonight. Apart from the family, numerous friends were expected (including friends of friends of the girls) to celebrate Arjun's fortieth birthday.

Meanwhile, Arjun too rose to his feet. He had filled out and looked prosperous and substantial, a man ready to enter middle age. With a quick eye and a glint of pride, he took in his family assembled around him. But the lofty feeling was tinged with sadness. For despite his worldly success, all was not well in his world. He has been out of Gaya Central Jail for six years now, but its memory continued to impinge on his present life. Priti had been initiated by the guru for the same amount of time and she had changed even more.

Arjun's release had come with as little warning as his arrest. After fifteen months in prison he was suddenly discharged on a sunny morning in January. As he was going through the formalities of departure at the jail office he happened to glance at a newspaper on the clerk's desk. The headline announced that Mrs Gandhi had called an election. She had relaxed the Emergency and political opponents were being released so that they could contest the elections. 'In a democratic system the government must face the people periodically and reaffirm the power of the people,' the paper quoted Mrs Gandhi. Even a tyrant, Arjun had thought with amusement, needs the people's consent.

After an emotional meeting with Priti, the baby, and his parents at the ashram, Arjun went to Bombay where he was accorded a hero's welcome at his office. He learned that his strategy on the margins issue had been vindicated and the trade boycott had rapidly fizzled out. Not having succeeded in raising quick money, Guha had lost interest and moved on to more lucrative ventures. With the Emergency over, Arjun's company now retained a high-powered criminal lawyer to press charges against Guha, the Calcutta police officer who had signed his FIR and the deputy commissioner of Calcutta, under whose signature the MISA warrant for his arrest had been effected.

Arjun was not bitter about his fifteen months in jail largely because of his positive outlook on life. Much like Bauji after the partition, he had pulled himself together and gone back to doing what he did best. He felt it could have happened to anyone. But he was no longer innocent of suffering and cruelty; he had certainly become acutely sensitive to the value of liberty. He did not gloat over Mrs Gandhi's defeat at the polls; nor did he believe that the Emergency was more than a temporary insanity.

'I sometimes wonder,' Tara told Arjun, 'if our democracy isn't just a matter of the blind leading the blind.'

'The taste of democracy becomes bitter, mother, when the fullness of democracy is denied; when the weak do not have the same opportunity as the strong.'

Although Arjun had now reached the dangerous age, he had not grown fat; he looked strong and significant, as successful men have a way of appearing. He had never been big; in fact he was shorter than most men, but his broad shoulders made him seem large. He had also been elevated to the board of his company, which continued to be a blue chip on the Bombay Stock Exchange. He was one of the youngest in the corporate world to have won that privilege, and he continued to successfully steer the company to growth and profitability through difficult times. Everyone expected him one day to become chairman of the company. Outside, he was admired for excelling at his work and his views were solicited by both industry and government. Thus Arjun had more than fulfilled Bauji's prophecy.

Scattered around him were the material symbols of his worldly achievement: rich Persian rugs and carved chests from Chor Bazaar with gilt ornamentation, hooked clasps, and inlaid polished brass; his spacious penthouse flat was furnished with controlled simplicity, which is the best sort of elegance; on the white stucco walls several old-fashioned windows offered awesome views of the sea.

The fast fading rays of the setting sun over the Arabian Sea lit up Arjun's honey-coloured skin; they emphasized his northern profile and Punjab lineage, the influence of Tara's side being stronger than Seva Ram's. His hands, like Bauji's, were broad and strong, unlike his father's delicate, long ones. There was more than a hint of passion on his face unlike Seva Ram's cool and distant look. His face also suggested perseverance, which according to his colleagues, was the quality that best explained his success. However, he had inherited his father's naive smile. Its casual simplicity suggested that despite his success, Arjun had neither become self-contented, nor cynical; on the contrary, he appeared to still want to fulfil some lofty goal over and above his everyday life. What exactly this goal was he was not quite sure. And because he could not seem to do anything about it, he felt a hopeless gap between aspiration and reality. It was this gap which partially accounted for his perpetual regret, and prevented him from becoming capricious and arrogant, like many senior Indian managers and officials.

Filled with humiliation at his own inability to act, Arjun would sometimes blame his father. He was resentful with Seva Ram at having ill-prepared him for a life of public affairs. He felt that Seva Ram had been too preoccupied with his own spiritual quest to have bothered with his son. The only goal that he had offered his son was the unpalatable one of worldly withdrawal.

Seeing the frown on his face one day, Tara took him by the arm, 'Son, what is it? Why are you unhappy? You have everything a man could ask for: health, happy children, you're a success in your job, a wife who respects you, parents who dote on you, and this magnificent flat. What more do you want?'

Arjun sighed, 'You won't understand, mother.'

Between the pride and the drive of his mother and the detachment and spirituality of his father, Arjun thus lived in a state of discontent. He watched Priti become steadily more distant from him as her involvement with religion deepened. He felt frustrated at not being able to do anything to save the situation. During his days in prison, he had become convinced that an excess of religion was partly to blame for the country's problems: it supported an unjust social structure; it made people obscurantist and fanatical; it allowed them to accept injustices; it turned their minds to their personal salvation and the other world, and prevented them from acting to improve this world. It would never have entered his head to dispute Seva Ram's religious convictions, but to watch Priti change before his very eyes was depressing.

The hour between the *sandhya* and dinner was a good time to escape and savour the evening alone. When he mentioned to Priti that he was taking the dog downstairs, she frowned and reminded him to return soon as he had to shower and dress; people would be coming early. With a wildly excited Rajah bounding ahead of him, shaking his thick tail, Arjun went down the lift into the garden of their apartment building. Enclosed between three walls and the sea its seclusion gave the garden an unreal air. Palms, laburnum, and casuarina trees filled the reddish earth. On each side rested faded green wrought iron benches surrounded by bushes of musanda and wisteria. Tropical greens—crotons, monstera and rubber plants—grew in thick but orderly fashion; the hibiscus hedge seemed to prevent movement rather than guide it. The gardener had made a heroic but unsuccessful effort to grow cannas, asters, zinnias and other plants. The gleaming purple bougainvillaea bush in the western corner provided the only real note of colour and gaiety.

Arjun would have preferred a less orderly garden, something that looked more like a tropical jungle. He had suggested it to the gardener but he had been vetoed by the formidable Sindhi lady on the third floor, who was secretary of the flat owners' society. His preference for disorderly vegetation was in contrast to his structured business life, but in keeping with his present emotional state. He sat on the bench, watching with embarassment as Rajah leaped about among the plants, and he debated the merits of the third floor lady getting cleanly run over by a BEST double-decker bus. Having put her to rest, he looked on without guilt at the devastation wrought by the irrepressible Rajah, who returned periodically to his master with large innocent eyes seeking praise for a job well done. The garden might still turn into a jungle.

13

Three weeks later the summer dissolved in the monsoon. The pavements of Bombay were continuously wet from the rain. The city's air was heavy with moisture, and it reflected the mood of the tired inhabitants. Walking slowly past the Parsi statue on Veer Nariman Road, Priti brushed against Arjun's arm. He turned around and she looked into his eyes with a sad expression.

'I'm thinking of going away to the ashram,' she said in a quiet voice. 'Something is happening to me.' Suddenly tears came into her eyes and she added. 'I am afraid for the first time, but I don't know why.'

This year's monsoon was worse than Arjun had ever known it before. Before dawn the skies would turn dark grey and then slowly darken further, and the clouds would swell before exploding over the commuters who gushed out in a black tunnel of umbrellas from VT and Churchgate. The city had, as always, shuttered itself tightly against the gales from the southwest. But this year it wasn't enough. The dark and bitter rain weakened the light of the sky for weeks together. In the darkness of the shuttered, ill-lit offices, water invaded everything, appearing magically among files, books, paper clips, and pictures, even inside the locks of doors and under fingernails. The air caused people to cough and sneeze, while the sea swelled and churned in anger. The wet wind let up from time to time, giving the trees, the buildings, the monuments and the people some respite, but then the rain took over, so that one had the illusion of being permanently trapped in a whirlpool. As a result, the usually energetic people of Bombay were seized by a listlessness of spirit which made them impatient and reckless.

As if to match the city's mood, the relationship between Arjun and Priti was equally weighed down. Indeed, even the act of making love had become exhausting and perverse and not life-giving as it had once been.

Looking at the bathroom mirror, Arjun reminded himself that he had turned forty and already there was a white hair or two at his temples. He thought about his daughters. Although he had a hard time imagining himself a 'family man', he was desperately fond of the girls. They lit up the grey monsoon days. They adored him, and they were proud of him. He thought of Priti, and he frowned. When he had returned from prison five years ago, she had told him everything that had happened to her at the ashram. But she had spoken in such an ordinary, nonchalant way that he had not taken her seriously. Besides, so occupied had he been with himself and the changes that jail life had brought upon him that her life seemed insignificant in comparison. Moreover, the enduring after-effects of their emotional reunion after he came home from prison had helped to disguise the truth of their gradual alienation from each other. Fortunately her strong sexual nature was not affected by her growing spiritual preoccupations. (The guru had impressed upon her that she must live like a complete woman in marriage even as she pursued the life of the spirit.) But in recent months, her 'secret side' had begun to disquiet him.

Priti had begun to spend more and more time by herself. Even in the gloomy monsoon evenings, she would go out alone and look at the angry waves climb the sea wall at Nariman Point. She would watch the spray glowing in the fluorescence of the streetlamps, and the water invading the broad walk along Marine Drive, wildly lashing at the cars returning home to the suburbs. She would walk alone, her dark face full of troubled reserve. Arjun found this wounding. He could not fathom what she was looking for. He began to have doubts about himself, and wondered for the first time whether he had ever really had her confidence. The thought that she might be unfaithful to him occurred to him more than once, and each time it left him feeling sick. The silence of his huge flat became unbearable. But in his clearer moments, gathering his whole mind around the fact that there was no proof of her unfaithfulness, he was convinced that it was only an attempt on her part to free herself and make her own life. His heart seemed to be satisfied with this explanation, and he maintained a tactful silence.

Her behaviour, too, was inconsistent, for suddenly she would respond to him with a new warmth, ardour, and gratitude. Early that morning he had woken up to find her sleeping in his arms, her hair blown by the monsoon wind across her smiling mouth. Soon he could taste the bright pleasure, the warm sensual pressure of her tongue upon his, her hand touching his body. He was overwhelmed by the vastness of his happiness.

'No, no, no.' she said in a whisper, but drawing herself closer, she pressed her body still further to him. The smell of her mouth, brought back long-sought-after memories of years ago.

Later, as she sat before the mirror naked, combing her hair, Arjun asked, 'Priti, what is happening? Why are you so far away?' She tilted her beautiful head and shrugged her shoulders. He kept looking at her smooth brown skin and wondered where her true self lay. In the mirror her dark eyes shone as the comb travelled through her fine, long, black hair. Suddenly, fugitive memories of Simla returned to Arjun, and he grew sad. Slowly, he began to recognize that she too was wounded.

'Arjun, I can't bear to be away from him,' said Priti.

'From whom?' he asked.

'From the guru. I think of him constantly. I feel like a disturbed, lovesick girl in those silly romantic stories who can't bear to be parted from her lover.'

'What about me?' he said.

Arjun felt ashamed of his growing resentment. His shame was of those who love but are not equally loved in return. He was sobered by the thought that her quest was bigger than himself, bigger than his world. But he was also troubled, because he himself did not believe in anything beyond the here and now. She was heading towards a dangerous precipice, he thought, and he felt powerless to save her. He started to alternate between bursts of self-confidence and depression, and could not understand nor analyze these new feelings within himself. The high periods were followed by low ones in which the agony of his exclusion from Priti's world became unbearable. He thought more and more often of his childhood, of those sunny days in Pine Villa, when he used to catch butterflies in Tara's garden, of rhododendrons and English flowers, of flying a kite on the grassy slopes of Chota Simla; and how Tara took him to buy a sweater from the Mall, and how they encountered a smiling Seva Ram waiting for them. He thought of the comforting shade of his father and mother in those days before Priti entered his life.

One evening during an unexpected lull in the monsoon, Arjun and

Priti sat on the terrace of their flat looking at the grey sea. Tara and Seva Ram had long since returned to the ashram; the girls were away visiting friends. Behind them lay the city, which maintained its tenuous grasp on their affections through deep and rich memories of their life there together, of their children, of incidents long past. Soon the evening turned into night. They sat in silence looking out at the water, neither wanting to coerce the other, nor wishing to think of life in terms of resolutions and promises.

Priti was the first to speak. 'The difference between the wise and us is that we flit around the world, absorbed by all the silly, distracting happenings around us. While the wise turn inwards; we turn outwards.'

'What do you mean "inwards"?' Arjun asked.

'Reality is inside us,' she said.

'What is reality?'

'The Absolute. God,' she said baldly.

'What is god?' he asked with sincerity in his voice.

'Pure consciousness,' she said. 'It is so pure that its knowledge of itself cannot be conscious knowledge—for that would imply two things, the knower and the known: the one which is aware and that which it is aware of.' There was an uncomfortable pause. 'This unity must be internalized,' she continued. 'I must know it not merely as an intellectual proposition, but I must meditate upon it till it fills my being. I must dissolve my soul into it. Then I shall realize god.'

'But what is god?' he persisted.

'It isn't this and it isn't that. It is what is left over after all the things which exist have been denied, and after all thought has been denied.'

'It's too abstract for me, Priti,' he said with frustration. He thought to himself that she had been properly brainwashed by the guru.

'Don't dismiss it like that, Arjun. I can tell from your look you're not even making an effort to understand.'

'I don't understand, that's all,' he said, getting impatient.

'Because you have a closed mind.'

'No. You are asking me to have faith in something I can't feel or touch. I'm only certain about my ordinary world of stones and trees. And even of that I'm sometimes not so sure.'

'Precisely, because it is not real. The only reality is God, and to merge ourselves with it is the only legitimate aim in life. To do so, you must turn away from your world of stones and trees. And to do that you have to subdue your ego and your mind. The mind is the real villain, because it constantly brings us back into the world. You have to control it. The guru says that the mind is an "unruly monkey prancing among branches of a tree".'

'How can you talk like that Priti? The mind is capable of beautiful ideas, and extraordinary imaginings. Come on, you've read poetry. And look at what science has achieved! It is all due to our minds. Our minds can be so creative.'

'Only God is creative.'

'Your way of thinking dwarfs me, Priti. It makes me puny and powerless.'

'No, it exalts you, Arjun. Because in you lies the Absolute. It raises you to the level of the Absolute itself.'

'Priti, what you are exalting is an abstraction, which you call my 'soul' and you equate it to another abstraction, which you call 'god'. Both of these I have no way of knowing.'

'Yes, you do have a way of knowing it through meditation. Have faith and meditate and you *will* know it.'

'By hypnotizing myself.'

'That's not fair. How can you say that before you have even tried?'

'And meanwhile, I must give up my joyful world of trees and birds and flowers and children as a delusion of the mind. I love this world.'

'Your world is ultimately sorrow, Arjun, not joy.'

'Look at you. You have a beautiful body, Priti. You ask me to deny that as an illusion.'

'Desire is so short-lived, Arjun.'

'Life is short-lived.'

'Precisely. What is the point of attaching yourself to something so transitory? When you can attach yourself to the eternal—eternally beautiful, true, and loving.' There was a pause. 'Arjun, you and I are not what we appear to be in the everyday world. We are not our bodies, not our senses, nor even our minds. Only our soul is real. And our soul is a bit of the Absolute.'

Arjun fell silent, and Priti felt embarrassed. Both were uneasy in the huge silence. They were thinking about different things. She wondered why he had become so stubborn. Was it the experience of prison that had so completely closed his mind to religion? Before the Emergency she remembered him as an open-minded person, who did not have strong convictions. He found it unspeakably strange to sit beside this woman who had been transformed beyond recognition. He studied her keenly but she avoided his eye and now confined her conversation to laboured commonplaces. The only reprieve, he felt, was that every now and again, behind her new identity stirred a hint of her old sensual self. He consoled himself with the thought that women of her age often turned to gurus and religion in India.

To divert his mind from these thoughts Arjun turned to look at the ocean. The sea looked tranquil. Somewhere out there, beyond the silver horizon, lay Arabia. He conjured up a rag-bag of romantic images: of Shahrazad in a veil and purple silk pants, bedouins on camels watching from sandy dunes, and oil-rich sheikhs, shaking the banks of New York with petrodollars. As it became dark, the evening sky was filled with summer stars. The lights of the ships awaiting berths at the dock dotted the horizon. To the right was the deep silhouette of Malabar Hill, crowned by apartment towers that rose out of the silence of the Parsi burial. Still further to the right was the city resting from the day's baking under the hot sun, the tired inhabitants of Bombay clutching at the Arabian breeze. As Arjun's eyes went east to west the landscape tones changed from silvery grey of the sea-horizon to the dark metallic rust of the bruised city.

14

'Of course you won't go,' Priti said when Arjun suggested that he wanted to accompany her to the ashram. 'Don't. I have to be alone.' She spoke sharply, and her gaze followed his, as if wanting to make sure that his eyes did not escape her. She stood over him in the misty early morning light. 'You are not to. Answer me.' And as if to make sure, she slipped off her sari and petticoat and fell softly in bed beside him. Her warm hair and mouth and the soft movements of her nervous body folded around him like a healing balm. He surrendered himself to this therapy. He became small in her arms. Softly he touched the warm slope of her legs, caressing them, stroking them unhurriedly. His hand moved patiently past her loins, down between the round softness of her buttocks. She shivered. As she felt his desire, she let herself go to him. With silent force he now took over. She yielded, her arms open, and her body helpless and expectant.

Later, as she lay beside him, he kissed her again softly. She turned to him. He held her arm but said nothing. She crept nearer. He was utterly still. Slowly he opened his eyes and he saw a grave expression on her face. She was staring at him with her wonderfully expressive eyes. Her silence was difficult to penetrate.

'You do love me, don't you?' he asked.

She kissed him softly.

'Speak to me,' he said.

She nodded and put her arm on his.

'Tell me, yourself,' he looked pleased.

'Don't you feel it?' she said clinging to him.

She smiled and turned her back to him. She lay quietly on the bed, and he stared at her curved naked back, and he had no idea what she was thinking. He bent down and kissed her soft flank and rubbed his cheek against it. She stretched back and stroked his face.

'Do you believe that this is how things were meant to be?' he asked sadly.

'Arjun, what do you believe in, if you don't believe in god?'

She rose, opened the curtains wider, and began to put on her clothes. She stood there, above him, fastening the drawstring of her petticoat and looking down at him with wide eyes, her face a little flushed and her hair mussed but still beautiful in the misty morning light. It made him want to hold her, for there was a sleepy remoteness in her beauty. She kissed him between his dark eyes, and she left.

After she was gone, Arjun's happiness slowly began to fade. She was sympathetic even warm-hearted to him, but she did not permit him to possess her. She did not depend on him. This, he realized with regret, was the hold that she had over him. As a normal, possessive man, he found the thought painful. He remembered Seva Ram once saying, 'After the pleasure must come pain.' The more detached she became the more he wanted to possess her.

In the evening Priti joined Arjun on the terrace. The air was still. The darkness, the silence, were broken by the uneven lapping of waves below. The sea was tame after the monsoon. The cicadas in the garden were also quiet.

'What are you thinking?' he asked.

'Of you,' she sighed. 'Of how I can get you to think my way. I can't get you to love the guru. So I must appeal to your reason. Truth is so simple.'

'Is it?'

'Look at that pot of clay. The reality is clay, the pot is only a verbal distinction, a name. In the same way the only reality is pure consciousness, the rest are verbal distinctions.'

'Not true, my love. Because a pot can hold water and clay alone cannot. Your guru even dismisses my joys and sorrows as verbal distinctions.'

'What is so great about our emotions? As a child I was afraid of people; as an adolescent I was tormented by lust and men; as an adult I am afflicted by worries of my children; when I am old there will be the fear of death. What kind of life is that?'

'What about love and beauty. I love you, Priti.'

'Love is a transitory illusion, like life itself.'

Arjun sat silently, smelling the heavy tone of her body's scent; soon he was lost in the memory of his most solitary moments—those of coitus with her. He could get no nearer to the truth. After a long pause he said, 'Don't you feel outrage, Priti, at the circumstances that crush our people?'

Priti looked up defensively; she wondered what sort of mental trap he was preparing.

'By offering dreams of god, religions have been distracting people for a thousand years from the immediate wrong-doings, especially of the upper castes. Since god's moral law governs the world, every injustice is explained away. They want the oppressed to change their perception because they dare not change their circumstances. In this manner every village tyrant gets his way, and the weak merely say, "It's god's will, Sir."'

Priti continued to listen attentively. Arjun looked at her, but he could not make out what she was thinking. Outwardly there were no signs of any struggle. He was caught between his argument and his passionate concentration of watching his wife's face in the dark.

'The only thing that matters to me, Priti, is to have compassion for human suffering. God has no place in it. I feel sympathy for the vulnerable and I try to avoid causing further pain. I remind myself every day to do something, even the tiniest action will do, to improve the prospects of the worst off.'

Priti was surprised to hear Arjun speak with such conviction. Listening to him she was convinced that the months in prison had left a deep impression. She could not have imagined him talking like this earlier. After a pause she said, 'The Gita says the same, Arjun. Although to be one with god is our great goal, there are many paths. One such path is that of action, provided we act without thinking of the rewards of what we do. The realized soul inevitably transcends selfishness and devotes himself to the welfare of others.'

'The Gita is certainly a big step ahead,' said Arjun. 'But it's an exception. Usually, I am urged to withdraw. I am not expected to be concerned with right and wrong behaviour, but with my own spirit, which is not affected by worldly pain and suffering. Then, where is the spur to action, to alleviate suffering? And since god is the source of what exists in the world, why should I, a humble non-entity, tamper with His design? If anyone is in pain or if he is hungry and poor, he deserves to be, for it is His justice.'

'Arjun, you are wrong. You forget that each soul is equal to another and all of us are reflections of god. As we are all one, we must treat each other alike.'

'There you go again, equating abstractions and deriving how people should behave from it. I am expected to suppress my pain and make it an intellectual thing. Look at our thousands of holy men! Their search for god usually ends in self-attachment and callousness.'

'At least our holy men are tolerant of others. The holy men of other religions convert at the point of a sword.'

'Tolerance is not always a virtue, Priti. To tolerate an unjust social structure such as ours is to condemn millions to misery.'

'All holy men are not the same, Arjun. What about Gandhi?'

'Gandhi was not a holy man. He used religion as a spur to action. You know, Priti, I used to have a wrong impression of Gandhi. Like Bauji and others I didn't like his fads and his religious fancies. I never saw what a revolutionary he actually was. Nor did I realize how much he was detested by the orthodox Hindus. His attitude to holy men and scriptures was that of an explorer after truth. And he regarded the Hindu texts as guides left behind by earlier explorers, not to be held in superstitious reverence, but to be subjected to the test of his own conscience and experience. He refused to believe that man's spiritual quest could coexist with his living in degrading circumstances like untouchability and privation. So he fought British imperialism, battles for the poor and the casteless.'

There was a long pause. Having said what he had to, Arjun began to experience a sense of relief as if he had shaken off an old illness. He was filled with self-confidence. Looking at her, he knew that he had not converted her to his views. But he had dissented, which would have been difficult earlier. The experience of Gaya Central Jail had toughened him.

15

'You are unhappy because you have too many preconceived ideas of what you want in return for marriage. Look at that child!' Priti pointed to an urchin as they rode to Bombay Central. 'He lives in a totally spontaneous way.' They reached the station and were swallowed up by the noise of crowds, and the clanking wheels of luggage carts. They passed pavements covered with slime, and yellow pools of sodium light. As the wheels of the train began to move, he hugged her to himself. She said she was going away for two weeks to the ashram, but in a panic he feared that she might never come back. She touched his face gently, and tilting her head she looked at him with bright eyes. He was filled with unease. They looked at each other. 'Priti,' he called out to her but the cacophony of Gujarati farewells blotted out his words. Suddenly the dark platform was empty. Beside him a tall, shadowy Sikh trudged back from the station platform.

Driving slowly home through the dark bazaars of Lamington Road, he smelled the brackish aroma of the alleys. Arjun remembered Priti saying harshly as she lay in bed, 'We hurt those whom we love the most.' He looked up into the dimly-lit rooms in buildings he passed. Their uncurtained windows revealed the peeling walls on which were hung rows of calendars depicting colourful gods and film stars. Between the walls strings were drawn, on which clothes were hung, in the absence of closets. Occasionally a petty businessman carrying a black moulded briefcase would come down a dingy stairwell from his ramshackle office in an upper storey, where fleas jumped out of the rotten woodwork of old fashioned desks. 'Bombay!' he muttered. Here was a city dedicated to making money. You could almost smell it in the bazaars. Soon he was before a row of garishly lit cinema hoardings which provided a ghastly splendour to the otherwise drab Opera House crossing.

He wondered where Priti's obsession had actually originated. After all they had been through similar schools, and if anything, she had been the more sceptical. He had never argued with his father, but he had always felt that mysticism appealed to the weaker side of man: to his feelings of incompleteness, to his fear of the unknown. Since the guru's was an abstract god, here was a challenge, which evidently appealed to her. How is one to judge others, he thought. At what point do questions of personal happiness intrude into the judgement? He recalled her unexpectedly boyish laughter.

He turned into Marine Drive. With her gone Bombay seemed to take on an unexpected strangeness. The same streets, the same crossings had a bland quality. Whenever he passed a familiar landmark she was there quickly, brightly, her head tilted familiarly. Old memories and conversations returned, things she had said in Juhu, Khandala. Near the Princess Street flyover he remembered how she had stopped one evening to adjust the strap of her sandal; she had looked so desirable in a white cotton sari.

On a sudden whim he decided to turn back and visit the Nawab. On Altamount Road he noticed that the Nawab's study window was open. He rung the bell. The door opened and Arjun stepped into the silence of the palatial apartment. It had a strange feeling during the evening; Arjun had known it only late at night when the house was always filled with guests and gaiety. Feeling intimidated, he wondered if he had made a mistake. He was about to turn around and leave when the Nawab walked in. He greeted Arjun warmly and putting his arm around his guest, led him to the study. He was wearing a Chinese silk dressing gown above his pajamas, although it was late evening. A copy of Proust's *Recherche* lay face down on the table beside a gold cigarette lighter and an ash tray. Arjun was grateful for the calm. They had coffee on a hundred-year-old silver service and Arjun spoke nostalgically of his love. The Nawab knew that she had left today, as he seemed to know everything else that happened in the city. With his eyes closed he listened for a long time. It seemed to cost him a great effort, and at one point a tear fell on his cheek.

'I loved her very much, Arjun, but she preferred you. But I never ceased to care. I cared for both of you.'

Together they sat thus, talking of Priti, while the evening shadows lengthened. Arjun was calm now with a moving resignation that was eloquent. He was grateful to the Nawab, for his sympathy was both dignified and genuine.

A week later there was a freak storm in the city. Alone in his apartment Arjun savoured the strong breeze from the sea. He pictured Priti wrapped in a light cotton sheet, asleep on his bed. Then he thought of the different places in the apartment where they had made love. The sad thing about love, he said to himself, is that one of the two must always love more.

Suddenly he thought of his father. The fact was that it was Seva Ram who had invited her to the ashram; it was he who had introduced her to the guru. True, it was she who had responded to the old holy man; but he had encouraged her to get initiated. The evidence was clear that his own father was behind his wife's alienation from him. 'I feel close to your father,' she had once admitted to him, as she had breezed out of the house in a smart white chiffon sari.

One day Arjun sat up panting slightly in bed. He felt the sweat begin to start down his forehead. He looked into the mirror and felt relieved that nothing of his inner struggle was visible on his face. He stayed thus for a long time, emotionally spellbound with no further thoughts shaping themselves in his mind. He was on the point of feeling sorry for himself, when he jumped out of bed. He dressed quickly and stepped out into the night air of Cuffe Parade. He was sufficiently alarmed to seek the healing contact with other human beings. What terrified him was the unfamiliar sensation of utter loneliness. Later, out in the open where he found himself beginning to think clearly again, he felt it strange that Priti could feel close to Seva Ram when he himself had never been able to feel that way.

Arjun walked rapidly among the human shadows. The damp street exhaled the smells of the Koli fishermen, their stale quarter forgotten by the fevered city. He walked briskly into the narrow alley, soft now from the rain. He noticed a dimly lit tea stall in the distance. The garishly painted booth advertised an orange drink. At its urine-smelling door sat a dark child, her hands gathered in her lap. The child shivered as the wind from the sea blew past. Arjun turned towards Colaba bazaar. The child continued to sit raptly like a yogi.

In the bazaar Arjun went and sat down in an empty Irani cafe and ordered tea from the sleepy waiter. While he sipped the heavily sweetened tea, he thought of his life in Bombay, starting from the day he arrived in the water-soaked city. 'Don't spit,' said a sign on the wall. His soul he felt had become absorbed by the city and he could not conceive of himself without it. The idea lifted his spirits momentarily as he recrossed the bazaars towards his lonely flat. He walked past flesh and excrement, through a maze of narrow intersecting alleys. He met a tattered little one-man circus, a teenaged boy carrying a monkey on his shoulder; he was a familiar sight and Arjun tossed a coin at him.

He walked past the sweetmaker, who adulterated milk and short-weighted the halwah. Arjun watched his fleshy face concentrating in the harsh multi-coloured lights. The wall behind him was covered in slogans from the last election of the Congress candidate. The election slogans had been overwritten with obscene abuses. He passed a flower girl selling strings of marigold to propitiate Krishna. An old money-lender-cum-jeweller lay sprawled on dirty cushions, half asleep, while rats whisked in the gutter in front of his shop. Ever so often the jeweller would flinch and raise his head, as he did now, at the screeching song of a leper couple. Arjun tossed another coin to the beggars, a shiny rupee, which the woman caught in the folds of her dung-coloured sari. She recognized Arjun and prostrated herself at his feet, while her husband seated in a wooden cart, folded his hands in gratitude. Arjun escaped from their deafening screams and the soiled smells of the open gutters choked with piss and excrement. He moved rapidly through crooked lanes, filled with bare feet, droppings and the many languages of India and had soon left the bazaar behind.

Arjun was glad to have slipped out of the suffocating bazaar to the wide, ordered streets of the British-built cantonment at the southern tip of the island. He took a deep breath of fresh air in a tree-lined avenue, and went towards Afghan Church, which was dedicated to British soldiers killed in the Afghan campaigns of 1832–42. He was attracted to the colonial style houses, which were now occupied by high Indian naval and army officers. It amused him that the lives of the new occupants were a faded copy of their English predecessors, as they sat sipping whisky on their spacious lawns in the company of their brown memsahibs.

16

Priti had been gone almost nine months. Although Arjun continued to miss her, he was now more and more absorbed by his job.

Priti had been gone almost nine months. Although Arjun continued to miss her, he was now more and more absorbed by his job. Without her to distract him he realized what pleasure he could get from his work. Billimoria was getting old and he had delegated most of the operations to him. Arjun had begun to model the company's future according to his own ideas and he derived great delight in developing the organization, especially the careers of young and bright managers.

Gradually, some of his earlier feelings of discontent began to diminish. The turning point came with the success of a new project involving medicinal herbs, which were hand-picked by thousands of tribal women in the forest. The naturally growing herbs went into a new remedy for asthma which his company had developed. At Arjun's urging the company set up hundreds of collection centres in central India, where the tribals sold the herbs at a pre-established price. As the product gained a market share, the demand for the herbs grew, and more and more tribal women got employment. Arjun estimated that at certain times of the year as many as twenty thousand women were collecting the herbs on behalf of the company.

Arjun was so gratified with this project that he was already planning two others on similar lines. For the first time, he began to derive great emotional satisfaction from his job, and became convinced that business in fact could provide scope for positive and socially useful activity. The gap between aspiration and reality had begun to narrow. He concluded that providing work, for example through picking and selling of herbs, was a far better form of social service than giving charity to the poor. Earning one's living, he thought, led to self-esteem and confidence, which in turn resulted in self-reliance. Arjun felt so enthusiastic with his discovery about the social benefits of the market economy that he no longer felt the need to be defensive about business.

Priti returned to Bombay on a fine, ringing morning with low mists hanging over the outlines of the great sea. Arjun waited on the platform while his chauffeur and car stood outside under the palm trees at Bombay Central station. Priti took one wild look around her, as she stepped onto the platform in the same chiffon sari that she had left in almost a year earlier. Arjun walked across the grey width of platform number two, and swung her into his arms. They embraced as the untroubled, incurious city looked on. She had come after a year, even though she had decided to go for two weeks.

As they rounded Babulnath and turned on to Chowpatty, Arjun sank back in the spacious, airconditioned car with a sense of sureness, almost of beatitude. With his dark-browed, queenly companion at his side, he felt his relations with the world enhanced and calmed. He could feel her appraising eyes upon him, lighted with compassionate curiosity mixed with admiration. Priti looked out at the water, smiling and eager as if she were on a holiday. She giggled at the dancing and winking waves, as they swept along Marine Drive. Then she turned away to watch children's kites glisten against the morning light above Hindu Gymkhana. At Cuffe Parade she excitedly pointed to the coloured sails of fishing boats in the back bay amidst the white waves.

He looked at her closely as she got out of the car. She had put on a little weight on her face. Her hips and her features seemed to have broadened. But her glistening eyes and her quick, incisive way of breathing were still there; so was the characteristic tilt of her head. She had written to him regularly from the ashram, but her letters had merely described the eventless, mundane toil of the place. He looked at her again and equal he noted that she had changed. For one thing, her self-destructive, feverish look was gone; so was the insolent, unbalanced air.

Inside the house, they were shy with each other. Priti claimed to be happy and spoke with uncharacteristic humility. She described the austere life of the ashram simply and unimaginatively. Arjun noticed that her once finely-tended hands were calloused and rough. The physical labour at the ashram must be tough, he thought. He felt ashamed because he himself was immaculately clean, reflecting good city food and leisurely baths. Watching her now and remembering the touching and tormented person of a year ago, he found it hard to comprehend her transformation into this rounded, peasant-like person with coarse hands.

Priti showered, then came out in the living room and sat de-

murely beside him. She covered her head with the end of her sari
as women did at the ashram. When it slipped she put it back hastily.
Although meant to be a sign of modesty, this repeated gesture had
the opposite effect of emphasizing her femininity.

'What?', said Arjun.

'What did you say?' she said.

'I said "what"?'

'So?'

'So what.'

They burst out laughing and they embraced.

'The girls will be down next week,' he said.

'Yes, they wrote to me from school.'

'Their winter break is always the nicest.'

Later that night a whim seized him to drive her to Hanging
Gardens in the late moonlight. They sat in the car for a long time in
silence, gazing out at the moonlit city, the winding curve of the
Queen's Necklace gleaming below them against the gentle waves
of the bay. It was during this silence that he perceived the truth
about her. She had not really changed inside. She had merely
adopted a new mask. A saint and a sinner's mask, he realized could
be interchanged. Priti had been seeking temptation, and saintliness
was also a temptation. She had always been passionate, and of
course it was easier to make a mystic out of a passionate person than
out of a prig.

Never had the city looked so entrancing as it did that night in the
soft sea air. He felt the light breeze from the water on his cheek. She
put her hand on his, and spoke softly of older days. He did not take
in all that she said, so glad was he to have her back, and so drunk
on the beauty of the city which was now a part of him.

Bombay gave dignity to people, he thought. Even though it
might mean living in a crowded shanty or on the pavement, this city
gave a job and an escape from the tyranny and the debasement of
a rigid caste system in the village. It represented liberty to hundreds
of immigrants who came daily from the villages of India. This was
a great deal and this was the city's real beauty. He had once asked
the low caste woman, who cleaned the floors at his office, 'Why did
you leave your home and family and come so far away from your
village in Bihar?' She had replied, 'Arjun Sahib, ever since puberty
I had been free game for the upper caste landlords of my village; I
used to be scared and I had learned to walk with my head lowered
and my arms over my breasts. Here, in Bombay, I feel free again. I

don't depend on anyone and I walk with my head high up.'

Arjun did not speak of the ashram, except to ask guarded questions about Tara and Seva Ram. Priti, too, stayed clear of the subject which was on both their minds. The two of them had certainly had enough time to think about it. He, for his part, had pondered it for months, and having thought through the matter, he was now more than ever convinced that spirituality, no matter how attractive, was an evasion of moral commitment to the here and now. It was an escape from having to face the misery of the deprived and the vulnerable. To ameliorate the tragic conditions in which most Indians were condemned to live was what really mattered. As always, Gandhi had said it best, 'If god were to appear in India he would have to take the form of a loaf of bread.' Service to man was more important than devotion to god! The two were not necessarily incompatible, but even Mother Teresa had made her choice, as had Gandhi. God in each case was reduced to a facade. It couldn't be helped because both man and god required a single-minded commitment to the virtual exclusion of the other. The most satisfying attitude, Arjun had come to believe, was one of self-giving compassion, flowing freely towards all men. Indeed this was also the way to personal happiness. Unhappiness, he believed, was caused by a selfish preoccupation with oneself. By subduing one's ego and identifying with others, especially with their sorrow, led to enduring peace and joy. There did not appear to be any room for god or immortality in his earthly way of thinking.

Where did one go from here, he wondered? There was little hope from the rulers who were in power. So one had to rely on oneself. It required courage to reach out to the poor and the defenceless. But that was where hope lay. Hope lay in the private individual, who was liberal and educated, reaching out to the silent and the suffering, and showing through his example how the liberal institutions could work. 'Each one, teach one,' Mahatma Gandhi had said and he had reached out and identified with the weak with all his being—wearing their clothes, eating their food, living their life. We can't all be like the Mahatma, thought Arjun. But each of us in his small world could reach out and help just a little bit to root the institutions in the people, so that they were just a little bit less like dream castles built out of middle class aspirations. Arjun had no use for the spiritual till human dignity was established through an unsentimental concern for others.

Arjun had vowed never to question Priti's beliefs, nor to resent

Seva Ram's choice in favour of the other world. As for himself, he would be content to give of himself when Priti needed him and sympathize with her joys and sorrows. He was no longer tormented by his own lack of action in the social area. The herbal project had shown the way as far as he was concerned. And he no longer felt the need to pursue a lofty goal beyond his everyday life in the company and his family.

The best that could be said about the bigger picture was that democracy in some form had taken root on the Indian soil. Up until this point in his life the Indian voter had twice peacefully driven the ruling party out of power. Mrs Gandhi had lost the election because of the sins of her Emergency, but she had returned laughing a few years later when the same people got sick and disgusted with her quarrelling successors. As for the Emergency, Arjun believed that it had been an aberration, but the ease with which liberty was snuffed out on 26 June 1975 occasionally sent a shiver down his spine, and made him appreciate the delicate jewel that democracy was.

A week later the girls came down from boarding school for the winter break. They came by train, accompanied by their grandparents, who too thought it was time for a holiday. Arjun entered the drawing room when everyone was on a second cup of tea. Seva Ram was reading the newspaper. Priti was stitching a fall on her sari. A considerably mellowed Rajah sat beside her, watching her with polite interest. Tara was teaching embroidery to the older girl. The younger girl, whose cheeks glowed red from the fresh Himalayan air, was absorbed in trying on bangles on the divan. As soon as she saw Arjun, she ran up to embrace him. She held up her wrists. 'Do you think I am wearing too many bangles?' she asked.

'Certainly not,' he said. 'You must put on more.' She giggled and ran back to the divan.

A fine family, thought Arjun.

MORE ABOUT PENGUINS

For further information about books available from Penguins in India write to Penguin Books (India) Ltd, B4/246, Safdarjung Enclave, New Delhi 110 029.

In the UK: For a complete list of books available from Penguins in the United Kingdom write to Dept. EP, Penguin Books Ltd, Harmondsworth, Middlesex UB7 0DA.

In the U.S.A.: For a complete list of books available from Penguins in the United States write to Dept. DG, Penguin Books, 299 Murray Hill Parkway, East Rutherford, New Jersey 07073.

In Canada: For a complete list of books available from Penguins in Canada write to Penguin Books Canada Ltd, 2801 John Street, Markham, Ontario L3R 1B4.

In Australia: For a complete list of books available from Penguins in Australia write to the Marketing Department, Penguin Books Australia Ltd, P.O. Box 257, Ringwood, Victoria 3134.

In New Zealand: For a complete list of books available from Penguins in New Zealand write to the Marketing Department, Penguin Books (N.Z.) Ltd, Private Bag, Takapuna, Auckland 9.

FOWL-FILCHER

Ranga Rao

While the British still rule India, a son is born to a hunter who works for a minor maharaja. From the time of his birth, the boy, who is known only by his nickname Fowl-filcher (which has its origins in a crime of which he is wrongly accused), gets into a series of increasingly hazardous and hilarious scrapes with, among others, tigers, dogs, nymphomaniacs, ghosts and mundane municipal councillors. Eventually this wildly comic romp turns sombre as *Fowl-filcher* gets involved with a crooked politician and comes to grief.

Apart from being a wonderfully funny first novel, *Fowl-filcher* paints a fascinating picture of India after the Raj.

A SITUATION IN NEW DELHI
Nayantara Sahgal

Michael Calvert, an English writer, arrives in New Delhi to find the capital in chaos. Shivraj, India's charismatic leader, is dead. And with his passing, the country he had ruled so brilliantly, for over a decade, has begun to fall apart. Devi, Shivraj's sister, is unhappy as Education Minister, as is her friend, Usman Ali, Vice-Chancellor of Delhi University. Both are aware that Shivraj's successors are destroying what he built and betraying his values. Michael, once in Shivraj's circle of intimate friends, renews his relationship with Devi, only to be caught up in her anxieties and beliefs...

"She is herself a leading example of India's emergent writers, blending the Hindu with the Christian outlook, possessed equally of a cool analytical brain and broadly human sympathies."
—*The Times*

STORM IN CHANDIGARH
Nayantara Sahgal

Two new states, Haryana and Punjab, have been carved out of the single region known as the Punjab. Chandigarh, the common capital, is claimed by each new government for its own; to further complicate matters, Gyan Singh, Punjab's Chief Minister, threatens to cripple both regions by launching a strike. To avoid catastrophe, Delhi sends Vishal Dubey, its best troubleshooter, to Chandigarh to calm things down. Vishal finds much to admire in Punjab's Chief Minister but he also realizes he is a formidable enemy... While the tension builds in the capital, Vishal finds himself drawn into the lives of two young couples—Jit and Mara and Inder and Saroj—and the small dramas and casual betrayals that are a universal feature of human relationships...

The theme of Nayantara Sahgal's novel is violence, not necessarily an obvious physical thing, but the more subtle infliction of one person's will on another.

"Deep and delicate... Sahgal's voice is original."—*Cosmopolitan*